Nicole Helm grew up with her dream of one day becoming a writer. Luckily, after a few failed career choices, she gets to follow that dream—writing down-to-earth contemporary romance and romantic suspense. From farmers to cowboys, Midwest to *the* West, Nicole writes stories about people finding themselves and finding love in the process. She lives in Missouri with her husband and two sons, and dreams of someday owning a barn.

Carla Cassidy is an award-winning, *New York Times* bestselling author who has written over 170 books, including 150 for Mills & Boon. She has won the Centennial Award from Romance Writers of America. Most recently she won the 2019 Write Touch Readers' Award for her Mills & Boon title *Desperate Strangers*. Carla believes the only thing better than curling up with a good book is sitting down at the computer with a good story to write.

Also by Nicole Helm

Hudson Sibling Solutions
Cold Case Kidnapping
Cold Case Identity
Cold Case Investigation
Cold Case Scandal
Cold Case Protection
Cold Case Discovery
Cold Case Murder Mystery

Covert Cowboy Soldiers
Clandestine Baby

Also by Carla Cassidy

Marsh Mysteries
Stalked Through the Mist
Swamp Shadows

The Scarecrow Murders
Killer in the Heartland
Guarding a Forbidden Love
The Cowboy Next Door
Stalker in the Storm

Cowboys of Holiday Ranch
Sheltered by the Cowboy

Discover more at millsandboon.co.uk

VANISHING POINT

NICOLE HELM

HUNTED IN THE REEDS

CARLA CASSIDY

MILLS & BOON

All rights reserved including the right of reproduction in whole or in part in any form. This edition is published by arrangement with Harlequin Enterprises ULC.

This is a work of fiction. Names, characters, places, locations and incidents are purely fictional and bear no relationship to any real life individuals, living or dead, or to any actual places, business establishments, locations, events or incidents. Any resemblance is entirely coincidental.

Without limiting the author's and publisher's exclusive rights, any unauthorised use of this publication to train generative artificial intelligence (AI) technologies is expressly prohibited. HarperCollins also exercise their rights under Article 4(3) of the Digital Single Market Directive 2019/790 and expressly reserve this publication from the text and data mining exception.

® and ™ are trademarks owned and used by the trademark owner and/or its licensee. Trademarks marked with ® are registered with the United Kingdom Patent Office and/or the Office for Harmonisation in the Internal Market and in other countries.

First Published in Great Britain 2025
by Mills & Boon, an imprint of HarperCollins*Publishers* Ltd
1 London Bridge Street, London, SE1 9GF

www.harpercollins.co.uk

HarperCollins*Publishers*
Macken House, 39/40 Mayor Street Upper,
Dublin 1, D01 C9W8, Ireland

Vanishing Point © 2025 Nicole Helm
Hunted in the Reeds © 2025 Carla Bracale

ISBN: 978-0-263-39718-5

0725

This book contains FSC™ certified paper and other controlled sources to ensure responsible forest management.

For more information visit: www.harpercollins.co.uk/green

Printed and Bound in the UK using 100% Renewable Electricity at
CPI Group (UK) Ltd, Croydon, CR0 4YY

VANISHING POINT

NICOLE HELM

For the good ones.

Chapter One

Detective Thomas Hart was exhausted, and the last thing he wanted to do was go to a child's birthday party.

But he'd promised. And maybe the fun and innocence of a birthday party could wash the gross feeling of the case he'd worked today off him. He was *sure* Allen Scott had killed his wife, but so far the evidence was minimal. If he didn't drum up something soon, they were going to rule the death a suicide.

Thomas shook it off, or tried, as he pulled to a stop in front of the Delaney-Carson house out by the Delaney Ranch outside of the Bent city limits. The party was clearly already in full swing.

Years ago when his dad had gotten transferred to Arizona, his parents had wanted him to move with them. There were police jobs in Arizona, and he'd been young and unencumbered. Why not try something new, somewhere where the population didn't skew old and rancher?

But he'd liked working at Bent County. He just hadn't been able to fathom leaving. Sometimes home was just home, no matter who was around.

So, when his parents had left, he'd stayed. In the early days, he'd been a little lonely. For a variety of reasons. But these days, he had more friends that were basically family clamoring at him than he knew what to do with. He felt like he was *always* on the hook for a party. Birthdays, christenings, holidays. A never-ending onslaught.

Some he could weasel his way out of, but not this one.

Sunny Delaney-Carson was his goddaughter.

He grabbed the gift bag out of his back seat and then got out and walked up the drive. He was greeted at the door by a very skeptical seven-year-old in a sparkly blue dress, and it was somehow his life that he knew which Disney princess it correlated with.

"What is it?" she demanded, pointing at the gift bag.

Thomas held it up a little higher, because knowing Avery, she'd just shove her hand in there and yank it out. "I think the birthday girl is supposed to open it and find out."

Avery gave him a look, the kind of look he'd seen often enough from her mother. Disparaging disapproval. "She's *two*."

"And when you were *two*, you loved pulling all the paper out of the bag."

A dark-haired girl, Fern Carson-Delaney, Avery's cousin who was only a few months older than Avery herself, skittered over. She whispered in Avery's ear, then the two disappeared. No doubt to do some mischief, though Thomas never understood how Vanessa Carson and Dylan Delaney had created a child so shy.

But the world was a strange place, especially in Bent, Wyoming.

After weaving through more kids, exchanging greetings with more Delaney-Carsons and Carson-Delaneys, he finally made his way to the girl of the hour.

Sunny had Laurel's blond hair, an ability to exude as

much mischief as her father, and unflagging energy at just about all times. Thomas still couldn't imagine what had possessed Laurel to have another one.

On sight, Sunny flung herself at him, so he lifted her and gave her the twirl he knew she was hoping for. She gave a squeal of delight.

"Here you go, Sunny bunny. Happy birthday."

She settled down with the gift bag, and just like her sister had a few years back, got more enjoyment out of playing with the tissue paper than finding out what was at the bottom.

"If it's a musical instrument, or anything that makes noise, I'm kicking you out," Laurel said in greeting.

"I take it that's been a theme?"

She scowled around the room. "Traitors. All of them." Then she looked at him, the scowl turning into more of a worried frown. "You look tired."

He knew she was weaseling for work information, not actually commenting on his appearance. But he pretended like he didn't know that. "I won't comment on how you look then."

She rolled her eyes. "Tough case?"

"You're on maternity leave. No police talk, remember?"

The scowl returned. "Come on. I'm getting you some food." She led him around kids and toys and all sorts of things strewn about the packed house. In the kitchen was a spread of sandwiches and chips and salads. He loaded up a plate, because Laurel would fuss otherwise, then sat down at the kitchen table and chatted casually with Laurel and her husband, Grady, who was holding their sleeping newest addition, Cary.

Thomas put in a good hour before he started to think

about making his excuse to leave. A few couples with younger kids had already made their escape. But Laurel gave him the perfect out.

"You know, Thomas, I have this friend. She lives over in Fairmont. She's just so funny and—"

Thomas drained his plastic cup of the grape soda he didn't particularly like and stood. "Well, that's my cue to leave."

Laurel scowled at him. "She's nice."

"I'm sure she's great. I don't want you setting me up, Laurel."

"Why not?"

"Because you're a nosy boundary-pusher?" Grady offered lazily, Cary still asleep in the crook of his arm. He grinned at his wife.

Laurel turned the scowl on her husband, but then back to Thomas again. "You'll never find someone if you don't put yourself out there."

"Maybe I don't want to find someone."

Laurel gave him a look—much like the disdainful one her daughter had aimed at him when he'd first arrived. It made him smile. But not so much he also didn't make a break for it.

But Laurel followed. "Tell me about the case."

"No."

She groaned. "I know they gave Beckett my spot. If you're working late, it's a doozy."

"It's fine." He made it to the door.

"Is it because Beckett's a lousy detective?"

It was Thomas's turn to give her a disparaging look, though he recognized what this was *really* about. "You worried he's going to keep it when you come back?"

She smiled sweetly, but he'd seen her give that smile to

enough criminals for Thomas to know it wasn't *kind*. "He can try."

Thomas laughed. "Take it easy, Laurel. Enjoy that last month."

She grumbled something, but he made it outside. Fresh air. Blessed quiet. Now he could go home and sleep. And he'd been right, all in all. All that family, those kids, birthday cake and happiness had washed some of the ugliness the case they were working on had left on him.

He drove off the Delaney-Carson property and headed home. He'd lived above the post office for years, but last year had finally sucked it up and bought a house. It was small, fit for a single guy who wasn't a spring chicken anymore. And it helped to not live over a business when he was trying to sleep off a night shift.

But it meant driving back through town, to get over to the residential area he lived in. He drove down Main, but slowed as he spotted a woman standing outside the general store, peering into the windows.

The store was closed, and the area around it was dark. He doubted she was trying to steal anything but it was hard to know for sure. He parked his car, then got out. He heard a baby crying, and realized the woman was holding a bundle.

He approached, thoughts of burglary turning into concern.

The woman turned as though she'd heard or sensed someone approach, the squalling baby in her arms. He saw the fear in her expression, so he stopped his forward movement and didn't step any closer.

He didn't recognize her, and as a lifelong resident of Bent, and a police officer in Bent County for over a decade, he knew most of the locals.

He held up one hand in a kind of surrender, used the other to pull his badge out of his pocket. "I'm a local police officer, ma'am. Can I help you with something?"

None of the fear left her face. In fact, she looked even more tense. But there was something...familiar underneath all that anxiety. He squinted, stepped a little closer without meaning to—but the light was better the closer he got.

"Vi?" He didn't mean to say it out loud, because he was certain he must be...making things up. It had been something like fifteen years since he'd seen Vi Reynolds. And maybe she'd occupied most of his growing-up years, and still that soft first-love place in his heart, but there'd be no reason for grown-up Vi to be here now.

She'd left Bent a long time ago, and she didn't have any family left nearby that he remembered. Maybe some cousins or something, but not *in* Bent, and no one she was close to. Or had been.

But...

"Thomas," she said after several quiet moments ticked by. "You... You look different."

"God, I hope so. I think I weighed a buck ten soaking wet the last time I saw you."

She laughed at that, shifted the baby onto her other hip. But that tension didn't leave her. Not fully. Maybe because the baby was still whimpering. But she didn't say anything else.

"Uh, so, are you visiting?" he prompted.

"Um." She looked back at a car parallel parked—poorly—a few yards away. It had Wyoming plates. "I moved back a little while ago. I... I'm living out closer to Sunrise. My cousins have a ranch."

Thomas nodded, not sure what to do with this very

strange trip down memory lane. But her baby was crying, and she was standing outside the closed general store. "Can I help you with something?"

"I just… Mags is running a bit of a fever, and I ran out of Tylenol. I thought the general store was open until six." She gestured helplessly at the store.

"Not anymore. Closes at four on Sundays."

"I should have checked." She smiled thinly. "That's what I get for thinking I know things. I guess I'll drive up to Fairmont. Surely something there is open?" she asked, a little desperately.

The baby was inconsolable, and Vi looked like she wanted to melt into the concrete. Thomas glanced around. "Yeah, you'll have a few options, but hey, just wait here one second, okay? Just one minute."

She frowned but nodded. Reluctantly, he could admit. Still, she nodded. So he jogged around the back of the store. His friends Zach and Lucy were staying in the apartment above with their two-year-old while their house out in Hope Town was getting a new addition for *their* upcoming new addition. Surely they'd have something on hand.

VI REYNOLDS FIGURED as far as rock bottoms went, she'd already reached hers. So running into her ex-boyfriend while she looked like a bedraggled sea witch and Magnolia screamed her adorable little head off wasn't going any deeper in the rock bottom department.

It was just icing on the garbage cake of her life.

And still, this was all better than what she'd managed to drag herself out of. She reminded herself of that, almost every single day.

Magnolia wriggled and did that awful head swinging

thing that usually ended with them *both* crying when head smacked into head.

"Come on, baby. I know you're miserable, but now I am too, if it helps any." She tried to hum a lullaby as she bounced Magnolia, who was as exhausted as she was cranky from the fever. Vi tried to offer Mags quiet reassurances, but her throat was getting too tight. She should just get in her car and drive. What could Thomas possibly manage to do?

Thomas Hart.

God, she'd loved that skinny little goofball. He wasn't skinny anymore. No, he looked very…sturdy. And that baby face had aged. Same blue eyes, but the face had that…rugged Western look about it. Broad shoulders that had once housed a skinny frame now looked more filled out. His hair was cut short, so the color was some indistinguishable light brown, and his eyes…

Well, they were the exact same. It sent a pang of longing through her—for a simpler time, for a time before she'd made so many mistakes.

Why did he have to be *hot* now? Instead of just cute and sweet?

Well, he probably wasn't sweet anymore. He was a cop. He'd pulled out a badge. Just the thought made her tense. She knew how that went, didn't she?

She squeezed Magnolia tighter. "Let's run, Mags," she muttered. She even took a step back to turn and go, but Thomas reappeared before she could even get her keys out of her purse.

He was holding a box of children's Tylenol. He held it out to her. It was opened.

Why would he have access to children's Tylenol? Opened at that? Did he have kids? Oh, God, he probably had a parcel of them with some beautiful, skinny, smart, perfect mother who didn't run out of medicine.

He took the bottle out of the box, pulled one of the little syringes they gave out at pharmacies for oral medication for babies. He unwrapped it. "How much?" he asked, like he did this all the time.

She found herself absolutely speechless at the idea of him married with kids, which was ludicrous since she'd been married for a time. And had a child.

He smiled at her gently. "I'm friends with a ton of people with babies." He didn't ask, but she could *feel* the question in the air.

Is she yours?

Vi hugged Mags a little tighter.

"My friends live upstairs," he said. "They've got a kid, so I know how it all works. How much?"

She told him the correct dosage for Magnolia's weight. She watched him expertly fill the syringe with the right dosage, then hold it out to her. But she had both hands supporting Mags, so then he offered it to the baby.

Mags leaned forward a little and took the medicine. She'd always been a good medicine taker, probably because she'd been so sickly those first few months. But she was healthy now.

They were *both* healthy and safe. And no matter her failures, that was all that could matter.

Except in this moment, Vi's high school sweetheart was feeding her baby medicine. On a dark street in the middle of their hometown.

Vi wished she could travel back in time. For a blinding, painful moment. She'd take their breakup moment over this one, and that had been...

Awful. Gut-wrenching. Because no amount of being foolish and eighteen and desperately in love with each other had allowed their dreams for a future to match.

What would her life have been like if she'd compromised?

The question nearly took her out at the knees. She'd crumble under the weight of all those what-ifs if she gave this any more time. "Thank you. Thank your friends for me. I really have to go."

He handed the now-empty syringe and box to her. "They insisted."

She swallowed at the lump in her throat. "Thanks."

"Any time."

He stepped back. Once. Twice. "Hope I see you around, Vi." Then he turned and walked away.

She did not return the sentiment but noted he didn't drive away until she did.

Chapter Two

Thomas didn't consider himself a stick-in-the-mud. He'd learned in his years as a deputy and then a detective that, sometimes, a few rules had to be bent.

But if he looked Vi Reynolds up in the county's computer system, he definitely wasn't bending rules for the right reasons. Just to satisfy his curiosity. Which wasn't right.

But he hadn't been able to get the other night out of his head.

He knew fifteen years changed a person. Hell, he was hardly the guy he'd been at eighteen. Being a cop had changed him, hardened him in some ways, matured him in others. No doubt Vi had gone through her fair share of growing up and maturing in fifteen years.

But she'd seemed sad. Beat down. More than just because of a screaming baby. Like life had been considerably unkind.

Which shouldn't matter to him. They hadn't kept in touch. He didn't know her anymore. Hell, she had a kid and probably a husband.

But the interaction had settled inside of him, like yet another regret when it came to her.

Now she was back, or near Sunrise anyway, where she'd always claimed she didn't want to be.

He hadn't been able to leave back then—in high school he'd worked hard to complete a program to go to community college for free. He'd had a plan to move straight into the police academy once he turned twenty-one. He hadn't been able to afford to go anywhere else.

Vi'd had big dreams and a full ride to Clemson. Premed. Get out of small-town Wyoming. Get away from her parents' constant fighting. Build her own big, beautiful, amazing life.

He had loved her, wanted her to have all those things, but he knew he didn't fit in her plans. The end had been hard, but he'd always been pretty certain it was the right thing for both of them, no matter how hard.

Over the years, when none of his relationships had worked out, he'd always wondered what might have been different if he'd been able to find a way. Move almost across the country with nothing in his pocket, make something work.

But mostly, he felt he'd ended up right where he should, so how could he regret the choices that had led him there?

"Going to stare at that screen any longer?"

Thomas looked up from his laptop to his current partner, standing in the doorway of their shared office.

Copeland Beckett was a rare out-of-state transfer. Most Bent County deputies were homegrown, or at least from Wyoming, and that meant those in charge tended to be Bent County natives and tended to promote from within their community.

But when Laurel had gone out on maternity leave *again*, Sheriff Buckley had decided Copeland—what with his big-city experience in Denver—should take her place in the detective bureau.

Bent County was growing, and with growth came more complicated cases. Thomas wouldn't be surprised if by the time Laurel got back, they'd have to be a three-person department.

Thomas liked Copeland well enough, though he was a bit...unpredictable. There was definitely what Thomas could only describe as big-city energy pumping off the guy. He wanted action. He wanted results.

Thomas didn't have the first clue how he'd wound up in Bent County, but Copeland wasn't one to spill about his private life, unless it was about his superficial, social one.

Thomas wasn't sure how Copeland and Laurel would get along. But that was a problem for later.

For now, he dealt with Copeland just fine, and he had indeed been staring too long at an empty search screen.

"Did you get the coroner report yet?" Thomas asked, ignoring Copeland's question.

"No."

Damn it. "Regardless of if the report is ready or not, let's see if Gracie will take a meeting with us tomorrow."

"I can give her office a call right now."

Thomas waved him away. "She's Laurel's cousin. I'll do it."

"Is Laurel related to everyone?"

Thomas might have found the disgust in Copeland's tone funny if he could find any humor in this case. Before he could pull out his phone to call Gracie, Vicky, currently working the desk, poked her head into their office.

"Rosalie Young here to see you, Hart. Want to see her or have her come back some other time?"

It wasn't unusual for a private investigator to want to talk to him. He'd had meetings with Rosalie over the years since she'd been working for Fools Gold Investigations out of Wilde, and any other PIs who worked there. Usually Rosalie scheduled them in advance, but answering questions for a PI sounded a hell of a lot better than dealing with his current predicament. "You can send her in."

Vicky nodded and left.

"I'll call Gracie. If it needs the Bent native touch, I'll let you know." Then Copeland followed Vicky out. Not five seconds later, Rosalie entered.

And seeing Rosalie Young in person made it all click. Maybe it was the red hair, maybe it was just bound to be a memory that popped back eventually.

The Young family were those cousins of Vi's who lived in the area. Rosalie and Vi hadn't been close. They weren't the same age. He *knew* they hadn't been close because he'd known Vi's life in and out, back then.

But Rosalie had an older sister. Thomas couldn't remember her name for the life of him. He still didn't think Vi had been close with her either, but it was possible he didn't remember *everything* from fifteen years ago.

Besides, Rosalie did indeed live out by Sunrise, on a ranch with her sister. Which sounded a lot like what Vi had said the other night.

"Vi mentioned she ran into you the other night," Rosalie said, making herself at home in his office as she so often did. Quinn Peterson, the head of Fools Gold, tended to hire women like her. Brash, unafraid, and tough as nails.

"I didn't realize…" He didn't often find himself completely speechless these days. He'd been through a hell of a lot. But he really had no idea how to deal with this situation. "I guess I forgot there was a connection."

Rosalie smiled thinly, but she didn't say anything to that,

which wasn't like her. Usually she said whatever the hell she wanted.

"We've got a little issue out at the ranch. Vi's…a little uncomfortable with cops. I've been trying to get her to let us bring in some help, but I didn't know you two…knew each other. Until she mentioned it. I think she'd trust you. Anyway, can you come out to the ranch tonight? I know it's a drive, but…"

"Somebody in trouble?"

"*I* think so."

"Vi?"

Rosalie popped right back to her feet. She never did sit still long. "Just come on out, huh? Audra will make a cake or some cookies or something. She's a hell of a baker."

Right. *Audra* was the older sister's name. He didn't think Vi and Audra had been close, but maybe he just didn't remember. Didn't really matter. "If someone's in trouble, you don't have to bribe me with cake, Rosalie. I'm an officer of the law."

She studied him for a second, then smiled a little. But she definitely wasn't herself. "You're a good guy, Hart. We're gonna need one of those."

VI FELT ALMOST human again. Magnolia's congestion was finally starting to clear up and she was sleeping better, so Vi was too. She'd even gotten a shower with Magnolia down for the night. And now that she was clean and Mags was sleeping, Vi could actually go downstairs and eat dinner with everyone.

She didn't know what she would have done without her second cousins. It had been a crazy, last-ditch effort to call them up out of the blue last year—people she'd only seen at funerals and family get-togethers even when she'd still lived in Wyoming.

And they'd taken her in, very few questions asked. They'd given her not just a home, but a place first to hide, then to heal, and finally to bring her baby home to. They'd kept her going through Mags's stint in the NICU, and when they'd finally brought Magnolia home, they—along with their fourth roommate, Rosalie and Audra's cousin on their mom's side—had fed her, taken turns with nighttime feedings, ensured that not only Magnolia thrived, but Vi did too.

They'd become her best friends in the world, her family, her support.

The other night had been the first time in months she'd felt overwhelmed, and that was only because Franny had been away on her book tour, Audra had been at some women-in-agriculture meeting, and Rosalie had been off on a case.

Vi didn't let herself get self-recriminatory about not being able to handle it all on her own. The old Vi would have blamed herself, called herself every terrible name in the book, and known she was an utter failure as a person and mother.

But new Vi—the woman who was going to be strong for her baby girl and find a *life* after the horrible things she'd been through—had accepted that everyone, especially mothers, had bad nights when their babies were sick.

Maybe they didn't *all* run into their hotter-than-they-were-in-high-school ex-boyfriends when that happened, but…

She paused on her way down to the dining room, as she had multiple times over the past few days when Thomas had popped into her mind.

It was so strange. She didn't trust cops. She'd made that mistake in so many blinding colors, and had vowed to never, *ever* let herself fall into that trap again.

But this was *Thomas*. It was hard to imagine him as a cop, as a detective, even though that had always been his plan. He'd been one of the sweetest guys she'd ever known, and that was a direct contrast with the police officers she'd had dealings with over the past few years.

Well, she supposed she could have a fun little fantasy where he was that hot, *not* a cop, and she was anywhere near capable of rekindling some old high school flame. Because it was only ever going to be a *fantasy*.

She shook her head, started heading for the dining room again. The doorbell rang almost at the same time she was about to pass the front door.

"I'll get it," Vi called out. She hated answering the door still, which was ridiculous. In the almost two years since she'd finally left him, Eric had never once tried to come here. Sure, he still left her threatening messages sometimes—no matter how many times she changed her phone number—same with emails and the like, but he wasn't going to expend any energy to come all the way from Richmond to *nowhere* Wyoming.

He'd have done that by now if he wanted to, she was sure of it.

Had to believe it.

"No, I will!" Rosalie shouted from deeper in the house. She came barreling out of the kitchen like a wild woman, which was not *unlike* her younger cousin.

"Hey, thought you were showering," Rosalie said, sliding to a stop in front of Vi like she was going to jump between her and the door.

Which was a bit much, even for the energetic Rosalie.

Vi pointed at her wet hair. "Yeah, I was."

"You know, you've had a rough week. Why don't you head back upstairs and I'll bring dinner up to you?"

"No, I'd like some company. I'd like to feel like a normal human being."

Rosalie opened her mouth, but no words came out. She looked like she was scrambling for some other excuse. Which made no sense.

Vi pointed at the door. "Are you going to open the door?"

"Oh, it's probably some salesman."

"Rosalie, no salesman is coming all the way out here in the middle of nowhere. What is going on?"

"Nothing! *Nothing.* Was that Mags? I thought I heard a cry."

Vi pointed to the baby monitor hooked to her waistband. Then went ahead and moved past Rosalie and twisted the doorknob open.

"Vi—"

But if she mounted any other excuse, Vi didn't hear it. Because there on the porch stood Thomas Hart. He was dressed much as he had been the other night. Slacks. A sort of business casual polo shirt underneath an unzipped jacket.

Everything kind of stopped for a second. "Thomas." She didn't know how he did it. Looked so completely like the boy she remembered, and yet so much…well, *better.*

Men. They had all the luck.

He smiled. Kindly. But she recognized that type of kind. It was saved for victims.

Vi turned to look at Rosalie. Shock and betrayal stung deep. She'd done this. She'd…*told* him. "Why did you do this?"

Rosalie got that stubborn look about her, dark blue eyes flashing. "Because I wanted someone's professional opinion."

"It's not yours to want a professional opinion on," Vi said through gritted teeth. She turned to Thomas, trying to smile. "She shouldn't have brought you all the way out here."

He looked completed unfazed by any of this. He shrugged. "I don't mind."

"Surely whoever you go home to minds."

"Not going home to anyone these days."

He said that without breaking eye contact, with that same, easy forthrightness he'd always had. And she blushed in spite of herself, because that had sounded like fishing.

Because it was. Even though it shouldn't be and she hadn't really *meant* to fish. "I... I didn't mean it like that."

His smile was still kind, but a little...something else. Not pitying, she knew that, because it made her heart do all those old flippy things it used to.

"I know."

Rosalie cleared her throat. Right. Vi was *furious*, and not talking to Thomas Hart about *anything*.

"I don't know why Rosalie has overstepped like this, but I can assure you, everything is fine."

"Have him listen to the voicemail and we'll see if he thinks it's fine."

Vi glared at Rosalie. "It's nothing," she said through gritted teeth again, trying to send Rosalie a million warning glares.

Rosalie took none of them. She crossed her arms over her chest, looking even more stubborn. "It's not nothing." She turned to Thomas. "He keeps leaving her threatening voicemails."

"Who is he?" Thomas asked, still standing on the porch like he dealt with this kind of thing all the time.

Because he's a cop. "No one," Vi said bitterly. "Now, you can go—" She was trying to edge Rosalie out of the way, close the door on Thomas as nicely as she could, but Rosalie reached out a hand and stopped the door's forward movement.

"Her ex-husband. His name is—"

Vi felt as though the blood just…rushed out of her head. Tears threatened so fast, she didn't know how to stop them. She had worked so hard to feel in control, to get her *life* back.

Rosalie was *ruining it*. "How dare you," she managed.

"I am worried about your safety, Vi. I don't understand why you won't take this seriously."

"Seriously? Seriously? I got out. I got divorced. I *left*."

"He's still harassing you."

"I tried to stop him. I *tried*. And he very nearly had me committed. So I left. I ran away. I *stay* away because there's no beating him. He wants to poke at me, what do I care? As long as he stays most of a country away, *I* don't care. I'm not risking Magnolia to try to beat him."

"What about stopping him?" Rosalie demanded.

"There is no stopping him. There never will be." She looked from Rosalie to Thomas, embarrassment swamping her. She could not stand here and do this. She just *couldn't*. She'd said her piece. "If you'll excuse me, I have to check on my daughter." Then she turned away from both of them and stormed upstairs.

She wasn't hungry anymore.

Chapter Three

"I thought that would go better," Rosalie said with a scowl.

"I'm not sure why you did," Thomas replied. "Don't you help investigate things for women who've..." He wanted to choose his words carefully. Both for Rosalie's sake, and because he didn't like the idea of using any reckless words on Vi. "Been through it? You should understand how little a victim likes being treated like a child."

"I wasn't treating her like a child."

"You called a cop behind her back and against her will. And clearly gave her no warning after inviting me here."

"If I gave her warning, she wouldn't have *been* here."

"It doesn't seem like her being here worked out."

"I want you to listen to the voicemail," Rosalie said, clearly undeterred.

"No." God, he wanted to. He wanted to sweep in and immediately fix this for Vi. Whatever it was. But she'd looked absolutely...betrayed by Rosalie.

He couldn't add to it. What was more, he knew that in cases like this—whatever the details might be—if the victim didn't want help, there wasn't much he could do about it.

"Hart."

"If she wants my take, she'll bring it to me. Otherwise, you need to let this lie."

"And if it escalates?"

He didn't have a quick and easy answer for that. Because he wanted details. Names. And it wasn't *just* because he'd been in love with Vi a million years ago. He dealt with too many victims of harassment, abuse. He'd seen too many men get away with it.

He was currently in the midst of a case where someone was getting away with it.

He wanted any man that small and vicious to pay.

But it wasn't up to him. "You're licensed to carry a gun, and I know you've got plenty. Didn't Audra win some sharpshooting contest not that long ago?"

Rosalie sighed. "We might be tough as nails, Hart, and I know you probably can't understand this because men are so predictable, but being able to defend yourself doesn't mean you'll have the opportunity to."

He thought of every case he'd failed to solve, every call he'd been able to do *jack shit* in time to stop something terrible from happening. "Pretty well-versed in that, actually, Rosalie."

Rosalie looked at him, pleading in her eyes instead of frustration. "Can't you try to get through to her?"

She was clearly changing tactics. It was beyond obvious. Unfortunately, Thomas was not immune to obvious. "I know you're worried, but—"

"You don't have to change her mind," Rosalie said quickly. "Just…talk to her from like a police perspective, but also like a guy she knows."

"We don't know each other, Rosalie. Not really. High school was a long time ago."

"But you're the best shot we have of her actually listening to someone. You know as well as I do that burying your head in the sand of a problem asshole doesn't make the asshole disappear."

Which was more true than he liked to acknowledge. It wasn't like his job allowed him a *ton* of faith in humanity, but he tried to maintain some.

And that was how he found himself going up the stairs, and then knocking on the last door on the right, per Rosalie's instructions.

"Rosalie, you need to give me some space," the voice on the other side of the door said.

"It's Thomas."

A long pause. Maybe she wouldn't open the door, but he waited.

Eventually the knob turned.

She opened the door but stood in the doorway clearly not wanting to talk to him, clearly not wanting him to have a glimpse inside.

"She had no right to call you," she said firmly.

"No, she didn't."

Vi let out a sigh, but she said nothing else. He supposed she didn't look *exactly* the same as she had in high school, but she was just as pretty as she'd been back then. Even with her deep auburn hair wet and her dark blue eyes full of sadness. He'd once had that little pattern of freckles across her nose memorized.

He kept thinking this *ache* around his heart would ease, what with the passage of fifteen years, but it seemed to only twist. But the past—*their* past—wasn't why he was here.

"I don't want to get in between anything going on with your family," Thomas said, choosing his words carefully.

Or trying to. "I certainly don't… Hell, Vi, I might feel like I know you because of high school, but I know people change a hell of a lot from eighteen to thirty-three. We're practically strangers. I don't expect you to just…believe I'm the same guy I was. Or trust me with something like this. I didn't come up here to change your mind about anything."

"Then why did you come up here?" she asked skeptically.

"To tell you that I believe in helping people. I always have, and I *always* will. No matter how often that's been an incredibly complicated thing. I don't expect you to want my help. I just want to make it clear. You can trust me, and I will help in whatever ways I can. Whenever and however that happens." He held out his business card to her.

She looked at it, clearly not about to take it.

"You never have to use it if you don't want to. What's the harm in just having it?"

He could see her relenting, but she still didn't take it from him.

So he tried to lighten the mood a little. "And you don't have to use it for professional reasons."

She frowned at him, but he saw a little spark of humor in her eyes, as he'd hoped.

"Are you flirting with me?"

"Sure. Why not?"

"I'm a single mother with a terrible ex-husband and tons of baggage, and I certainly don't look like I did when I was eighteen."

Maybe not. But the impact of her hadn't changed, even if she had. "You look just fine to me."

She shook her head, but her mouth had curved ever so slightly. "You always were a sweet-talker."

"Lots of things change, but not everything."

"Thomas."

"Just take it, Vi." And when she finally did, he considered that a win for the day. He knew when to retreat. He stepped back. "Hopefully I'll see you around." Then he turned and left.

And was *slightly* gratified that he didn't hear her door close until he was halfway down the stairs.

Vi REALLY WANTED to stay in her room and pout and sulk, but she was hungry. And, weirdly, Thomas had taken away *some* of that cloud of embarrassment and shame. He'd made her smile, just a little bit.

Just like always.

But of course they'd changed. God, she wasn't sure she'd even recognize eighteen-year-old Vi. So sure she'd become a doctor and conquer the world.

Now she was everything she'd told Thomas she was— a divorced single mom with a ton of baggage. A *victim*.

You look just fine to me.

He was probably just saying that to be nice. Trying to cajole her into…whatever it was Rosalie was trying to make happen. She was going to have to convince herself there'd been no actual flirting.

She didn't know him anymore. He was a cop. No doubt he looked at her and saw a pitiful victim.

But he hadn't treated her like one, and the way he'd smiled at her had reminded her of all those years ago when he'd first done it and asked her to go to the homecoming dance with him in ninth grade.

It was a million years ago, but he made it seem like not *so* much time had passed. At least for a few minutes.

But time had indeed passed. A lot of time. And not just time, but an entire lifetime of mistakes on her part.

Besides, she'd been back in Bent County for almost a full year and had managed to avoid running into him or anyone else she knew by spending most of her time on the ranch. And she liked it that way. She liked the life she was building out here where it felt like no one could reach her.

She had family—not just Mags, but actual family. And it was because they'd become her family in heart as well as blood, Vi didn't stay in her room sulking.

Well, and because she was starving after all.

When she got to the dining room, Rosalie and Audra were already at the table, eating and chatting. Franny was still off on her book tour for another two days. Since Vi didn't have a job, she usually handled the household duties—like cleaning and making dinner—but since Mags had been sick everyone had insisted she take the week off.

So someone else had made dinner. Vi was determined she would at least clean up after it. She had to earn her keep *some* way.

Both sisters looked up when she entered the dining room. Audra smiled. Rosalie looked sheepish. Which was how Vi knew that Rosalie hadn't told Audra about this.

"Your sister had Thomas Hart come out here, without telling me."

"Rosalie," Audra said, clearly pained and, as ever, despairing of her sister.

"You listened to the same voicemail I did," Rosalie said, scowling. "The threats are escalating."

"I'm not going to have you listen to any of them after this," Vi returned, sitting down at the table. She didn't know what possessed her to let Rosalie listen in the first place.

"She isn't...wrong about that, Vi," Audra said, clearly concerned. "This did sound more...violent."

Vi refused to accept it, even if it was true. "He wants me to live in fear. I won't do it. I'm certainly not going to ask for help from a cop." Maybe she had a hard time believing Thomas would be like Eric, but it hadn't just been Eric that she'd had to deal with back in Richmond. It had been his whole squad.

Every last one of them either so taken in by Eric they couldn't see the truth, or just...didn't care about the truth. Too many of them had figured it was her fault that Eric liked to knock her around.

She took a seat next to Audra and accepted the passed casserole dish.

"Thomas isn't just *any* cop. You know him. Like biblically."

Vi spared Rosalie a scolding look. "That was fifteen years ago."

"So?"

"I knew my ex-husband *biblically* too. Enough to have a child. Should I ask for his help?"

Rosalie grunted in frustration.

"I know you're worried. If you want me to leave—"

Audra put her hand over Vi's. "Don't do that," she said in her soft way. Even though Audra was tough on the outside, with her ranching and sharpshooting, and her ability to handle the rough-and-tumble life out here in the middle of nowhere, she was such a gentle softie underneath it all. "We're not worried because it's trouble, we're worried about *you*."

Which made Vi want to cry. She didn't know why her two second cousins she'd barely known growing up had taken such a risk to get involved with her life. How they were so good at pulling her into the fold, accepting her and Magnolia as family. How this had begun to feel like a real, good life instead of the nightmare she'd escaped.

She filled her plate, gave herself a second to get her emotions under control. And then she worked on letting anger and resentment go.

Because it didn't get them anywhere.

"I understand why you did it, Rosalie. And if I ever…" She had a hard time saying the words, because she had to believe it would never, ever happen. "If there's ever a real threat, where he might actually come here, I'll call Thomas. I promise."

And she prayed like hell that would never be the case.

Chapter Four

"The prosecutor isn't going for it."

Thomas didn't look up at Copeland. He knew he'd see his own frustrations and powerlessness reflected back at him. "So what now?"

"I wish I knew." Too many dead ends in the case, and Thomas knew he couldn't blame the lawyers. They needed evidence, a case. They couldn't go on his word and his gut.

But Thomas *knew* that guy had killed his wife and staged it as a suicide. There was too much history of assault there. Too many inconsistencies in how the body had been found.

And there just wasn't anything he could do, unless they found some real damning evidence somewhere along the line.

It was time to take off for the day, and he had to get over to Wilde for yet another party. Copeland walked outside with him, neither of them saying anything.

But once outside, with radios and cameras turned off and put away in their cars, Thomas and Copeland faced each other.

"I got the name of a bar he frequents over in Fairmont," Copeland said, squinting into the sunset. "Might find myself there tonight."

They couldn't both go. It was too obvious. Still, Thomas found himself conflicted. "I've got an engagement party to go to."

"You've sure got a lot of parties to attend for a single guy."

"You try never moving out of your hometown. Look, we can't take risks here. The prosecutor is already being too careful. One wrong move, and he won't look at *anything* we find."

"I'm just going out for a drink, Hart," Copeland said with a grin. "What could possibly go wrong?"

But Thomas knew. Copeland could push too far and screw the case. Still, for all his big-city brashness, Copeland wasn't the type to botch a case. So Thomas just rolled his eyes. They parted ways, and Thomas got into his car.

The drive over to Wilde wasn't too long. And he'd just make a quick appearance. Say hi to his cousins, his friends. Congratulate Dunne and Quinn. Then he'd go home and…

What? Wallow?

No. He'd just…go over the case again. So what if it'd be the hundredth time? That was the job. Tedious going over things until you found the one thing that led you to the next thing and so on.

He wasn't giving up on this, not yet. Even if the prosecutor wouldn't take it, that didn't mean he had to stop investigating.

The party was being held out at the Thompson Ranch—a place that had once belonged to his no-good uncle, where his cousins had grown up. Amberleigh had passed away, but Zara and Hazeleigh still lived on the property with their husbands.

Cars littered the yard in front of the ranch house. Even

with the cold temperatures, the front door was open. Thomas stepped inside. Chatter buzzed, people were packed into corners, and a makeshift bar was set up on the kitchen counter.

He could use a drink, he decided. Just *one* since he was driving home, but before he could greet people, wind his way through the crowd, he stopped short.

Standing there, hiding a bit in the corner, was Vi Reynolds. She was watching Rosalie, who was in the kitchen pouring shots, with a slight smile on her face. Her hair was down around her shoulders. It was dry, so it looked redder than when he'd seen her out at the Young Ranch. It looked like she had on the tiniest bit of makeup, which reminded him of the first time he'd danced with her.

Homecoming. Ninth grade. She'd smelled like strawberries and smiled at him like she had all the answers to every secret in the universe.

"Hey, you made it."

Thomas had to drag his gaze away from Vi and look at his cousin. "Hey, Zara." He chatted with Zara for a minute, then tried to move away with the excuse of going to get a drink.

But he wanted to get to Vi. Old habits and memories from fifteen years ago apparently died very hard.

As he moved for the bar, he didn't see her anymore. He frowned, scanning the room. He ended up having to congratulate Quinn and Dunne, answer Sarabeth's—a teen he'd once saved from a burning building—determined questions for a gruesome story she was writing for school.

Once he got free of people, he surveyed the room again and still didn't see Vi, but Rosalie hadn't left yet, so—

He turned, just as someone was coming in from the hallway where the bathroom was.

And then they simply stood face-to-face.

"Oh," she said on an exhale. "Hi."

Her eyes had always reminded him of those bright cold days in the middle of winter. A piercing kind of blue. And he wanted to laugh. Everything that had happened to him in his fifteen years of being a cop could fade away in that color. He could stand here, an adult man with a hell of a lot of experience under his belt, and still find himself tongue-tied over his high school girlfriend.

"Hi."

She looked away, gestured toward the kitchen. "Rosalie tricked me into coming. Her date fell through, and she said she couldn't bear celebrating love alone. But she couldn't bail on her boss's engagement party, and Audra's a big, mean stick-in-the-mud who hates parties, so I *had* to come and let Audra watch Magnolia." She gestured over to where Rosalie was taking a shot with the bride-to-be. "I think she just wanted a designated driver."

"She's a tricky one."

Vi laughed. "Yeah. I assume you know the bride or groom?"

"Both, kind of. Two of Dunne's brothers are married to my cousins. You remember Zara and Hazeleigh, right?"

"Sure. The triplets."

"Amberleigh passed away, so it's just the two of them now. With my parents in Arizona, and their mom passed, I tend to be folded into the holiday celebrations, so I've gotten to know Dunne and Quinn. Besides, I deal with Quinn and her PIs, like your cousin, at work from time to time."

"No escaping the ties in Bent County, is there?"

He wasn't sure she said that disparagingly or with a kind of wistfulness. He'd never left, so he couldn't really imagine. Maybe it was both. "You said you've been back for a while, and it's taken me this long to run into you."

"And now we've run into each other twice in two weeks."

"Must be fate."

She shook her head and rolled her eyes, but her smile didn't dim. "You don't believe in fate."

"Didn't."

"Oh really? And what changed your mind?"

He thought about the stories he could tell, about people in this room alone. The horrible things they'd seen, but *something* had brought them to the other side. A better, happier side.

But those weren't his stories to tell. Still, he had some of his own. And one even involved her, sort of.

"About eight years ago, when I was still a very young and eager deputy, two armed men stormed the station to free someone we had in holding. They were connected to the mob, on the search for their boss's kid. It was a whole thing."

"Clearly."

"Anyway, seconds before they come in and fire the first shot, I was standing at the front desk talking to someone on the phone. I hung up, and I saw something out of the corner of my eye on the ground. A little flash of silver. I wouldn't have thought anything of it, probably, but it was a dime."

He watched her face, the bolt of recognition that changed her expression from a little uncomfortable, to more invested.

"I remembered how you always said a dime was a sign from your grandfather saying hello. I didn't think any spirits were saying hello to me, but still, because of your story I bent down and picked it up. The first shot—that likely would have got me in the head—missed me." He could still remember the way the sound had exploded around them, just as his fingers had brushed the dime on the floor. "They still shot me—but in the side. It was bad, but I survived it."

"That…wasn't fate," she said but was quiet. Maybe shaken.

In fairness, it was probably too much to bring up at a party when they'd barely seen each other in fifteen years. Because it *had* been bad. The worst he'd ever been hurt, though not the first or last time. Still, he couldn't deny that he always remembered that dime.

"Felt like fate to me."

She blinked, then looked down and away. He should find something more casual to talk about. Something…about the old days or…the weather. "Can I grab you a drink? Maybe we can—"

She held up her phone. "I have to go call Audra and check in on Magnolia."

Ouch. He nodded, and even though the rejection hurt, he kept his smile in place. "Sure."

"It was…nice seeing you again," she said, clearly just trying to be polite and not meaning it *at all*. Then she smiled a little and turned to walk away.

Well, it sucked, but he figured that was that.

But he watched her go, and she looked back over her shoulder. Their eyes meeting. He knew he should keep his big mouth shut, but history was a hell of a thing.

"You know I gave you my number, but I don't have yours," he said, across the few steps she'd taken away.

He watched her hesitate. But hesitation wasn't refusal, and he'd hold on to that, even if she didn't give him her phone number.

Then she stepped back toward him, held out her hand, palm up.

He typed in his phone password, then handed it over to her. She went to Contacts and added her name and number. For a moment, she hesitated again, then looked up at him and gave him the phone back.

"I can't promise I'll answer if you call," she said, very seriously. But that wasn't a *don't call*. She was conflicted. He could be respectful of conflicted.

"Okay, then I'll text."

He watched her try to fight a smile and lose. He felt all of fourteen again, but she nodded once before she turned away and weaved her way through the crowd.

Vi HADN'T *MEANT* to start dating Thomas.

Again.

Over the next few weeks, it just seemed to…happen. He'd started with texting her, like he'd said at the party. Sometimes he'd ask if she remembered something from high school. Sometimes he'd ask if she'd seen a movie or liked some band—usually one she'd never heard of. When he asked if she wanted to go out to see a movie, she'd told him no.

He was a cop. She had sworn off cops. If there were any signs from the universe, it was that his chosen profession was one she couldn't trust or be comfortable with.

She'd changed her mind the very next day. Mostly because Audra, Rosalie and Franny wouldn't let up on it and this would shut them up.

But also because she couldn't get the story of him being *shot* out of her head. Because yes, back in the old days she'd believed in silly things like dimes and seeing 11:11 on the clock were her late grandparents saying hello.

And she wanted to find something to believe in again. Nothing about that felt safe.

Except it was Thomas Hart, and he'd *always* been her safety net. When her parents had been screaming at each other, when the divorce had gotten nasty, when her stepmother had overstepped, or one of mom's boyfriends had gotten…handsy.

Thomas had always been the safest place she could find.

So she went to a movie with him. All these years later, she'd gone on a date with her first boyfriend. And when he'd kissed her cheek before dropping her off, she had wanted so *badly* to have this kind of normal again. She didn't know who else she'd be able to have it with, because the thing about Thomas was she'd known him for *years*.

She'd loved him, hard and long. He'd been her first. They'd had their fights, disagreements and dramas, but he'd never been mean to her. He'd never hurt her. A foundation existed there.

He took her and Magnolia on a picnic on a particularly nice day. He even came to a dinner at the ranch, dealt with Franny, Audra and *especially* Rosalie asking him the most ridiculous questions. But he handled them all good-naturedly.

And when she'd walked him out to his car that night, he'd kissed her. *Really* kissed her and told her that he was sorry for everything that had happened to her, but he was damn glad she was back in Bent County.

On Valentine's Day, he'd had to work, but he'd sent her flowers and Magnolia a teddy bear. The next day, he took her out to a fancy restaurant in Fairmont.

When she'd let him sweet-talk her into going back to his house for a while, she wondered if maybe fate just got lost sometimes. Or to balance some karmic table, you had to go through the unthinkable to get…this.

But every time she saw his badge, or his gun, or someone called him detective, she got that cold feeling of dread and told herself she was going to break it off.

She didn't. Weeks went by and she didn't. She told herself there'd be a sign, that was when she'd know it was time to go.

But he never bad-talked Rosalie or Audra or Franny, never resented the time she spent with them or Magnolia. He wasn't perfect. He was terrible with time management, almost always late to pick her up on their dates. Sometimes if work called during a date, he got distracted. Or if a case was particularly frustrating, she might not hear from him except for very rote texts for a day or two.

But the thing was, he was never mean. Never cruel. Not to her or anyone around them.

Because while Eric had kept a lot of his horrible traits under wraps until they were married, there had been signs she hadn't recognized when they'd been dating. Separating her from her family, making it clear he didn't like them. Making sure his criticisms were carefully wrapped up in pretending to care about her. Pulling the silent treatment, then love-bombing her into oblivion.

He hadn't physically hurt her until after the *I dos* had been said, when she'd felt trapped into trying to make it work for far too long.

So Vi kept vigilant. She waited. For the commentary or criticism to start. For it to feel familiar. For her apprehensions about what being a cop did to a guy to be true in Thomas.

They weren't.

She didn't know what to do with falling in love with him all over again, with watching him be amazing with Magnolia. And every time she told herself to stop this ridiculousness, she wondered why.

Why shouldn't she have a great boyfriend who was so good with her daughter? Why shouldn't Magnolia have that kind of positive male influence in her life? Magnolia deserved the *world*, and Vi had already made so many mistakes that might negatively impact her, how could she not want everything for her baby?

Besides, if it didn't work out, if the cop thing became a problem, Magnolia wouldn't even remember.

Vi convinced herself of that.

And still, months went by. Thomas never showed any "true colors," and Vi fell more and more in love with him by the day. He became part of her life again, and part of Magnolia's, and the one thing she kept waiting for—him to push her to talk about her marriage—didn't come.

One night, curled up together on the porch swing after a family dinner and putting Magnolia down together, she wasn't that shocked to hear him say the words, *I love you, Vi*.

For a second, it felt like they could erase fifteen years.

But they couldn't.

"You've held off saying that because you want to know about my marriage."

There was a pause. "Ouch," he said, with a self-deprecating laugh. "Didn't know I was that transparent."

He wasn't. Not really. But she *knew* him.

"You don't have to tell me," he said.

She knew he meant it. He wanted to know, but he wasn't going to manipulate it out of her. It just wasn't *him*, and as much as she still doubted herself sometimes, she could never find the well of distrust within her to not trust Thomas.

So she took a deep breath, and did the unthinkable. She went back to where it all began.

"He never hit me before we got married."

Thomas was very still. He didn't say anything. Just watched her with those patient eyes. Kind eyes.

Because didn't it mean Eric won *again* if she didn't believe any man could be kind, just because she'd had rotten taste in the man she'd agreed to marry?

"I always feel like I have to start with that."

"You don't have to defend yourself to me, Vi. I've seen… plenty," he said after considering that last word. "I know it's not simple."

She nodded a little, grateful for that. An open-mindedness, even if it reminded her that not everyone who responded to domestic calls had that kind of empathy or ability to see a gray area.

"And he was good at…charming *some* people. My mom loved him. My dad didn't, but you know my dad."

"He's not going to like anyone who touches you."

She snorted a laugh. There was this strange, stabilizing comfort in the fact that he'd known her *before*. That maybe, just maybe, he saw her as the Vi she'd been back then. And she wasn't that girl anymore, but she liked to think she was getting back some of that old confidence and strength.

"Yeah. In fairness, my stepmom didn't like him either. But my friends were split. And it's not like he's the reason I dropped out of premed. I couldn't pass those stupid chemistry classes. Sometimes I think, that's really where it started. I'd felt smart and successful and important my whole life, and I couldn't make it through my freshman year requirements and keep my scholarship."

It still burned. Even after all these years. What a failure she'd made of her chance at something…great.

"I dropped out of Clemson. We couldn't afford it without the scholarship. My dad and stepmom wanted me to get into a nursing program, so I did. But I felt…like a failure. And that made it more of a struggle than it needed to be. Especially when it came to taking the licensing tests. I just…" It still hurt. The way one failure had started a domino effect of self-doubt and no self-esteem. "I was too scared to take them."

"You'd make a great nurse, Vi."

He said that like she still had some kind of chance at something like that. And the craziest part was believing him. Maybe…maybe she could go back to school. Maybe she *could* be a nurse. Wouldn't that be a great thing for Mags to grow up and see?

"Maybe," she said, because she didn't want to get excited about it until she figured out the logistics. She wasn't *young* anymore. She was a mother. And she still had to tell this awful story.

"I coasted for a long while. Waitressing and just, honestly? Getting more and more depressed. I isolated myself from my friends, from my family, because I felt like such a failure. And then I met Eric. He seemed like a great guy. Funny and fun. And really into me. I felt like I needed that. Someone who didn't look at me and seem disappointed."

He didn't have to say anything to know he wouldn't have been disappointed in her. Then or now. But he hadn't been there, and she'd felt surrounded by people who thought she'd failed.

"He really pursued me, and it made me feel…special. Which I hadn't felt in years. I look back and I think…he knew just who to target. Someone who needed an ego boost. Someone who'd be grateful for any positives."

"That is generally how it goes," Thomas said quietly. Not passing judgment. Just agreeing with her. And still, with her curled up against him, his arm tight around her, like none of this changed anything.

God, she hoped it wouldn't.

"He was like this up-and-coming SWAT team guy, and he didn't need a successful girlfriend. He needed a wife who would support him. So, when he asked me to marry him, I figured I'd throw myself into that. His schedule was crazy. His work demanding and stressful. He used that excuse a lot. Once we were married. Once he started hitting me. I knew it was wrong, but I felt like if I gave up, it was another failure."

Thomas's palm rubbed up and down her arm, and for the first time while going over this she didn't feel shoved back into that place. Of helplessness. Of failure. She could actually look back on it as a past version of herself. A victim, yes.

But now she was a survivor.

"So what changed?" he asked gently.

"Magnolia. The day I found out I was pregnant, I had a black eye and a bruised rib. Eric didn't want kids, but I didn't know what I was more scared of. His reaction if I told him, or his reaction if I decided what to do about it on my own."

She could still feel echoes of that old fear. That complete powerlessness. Knowing she wanted her child and knowing she didn't have any real say. It had been a breaking point.

"Even if he'd let me keep a baby, I just... I remembered how awful it was to be a kid whose parents screamed at each other. I couldn't imagine how much worse it would have been if my dad had ever physically hurt my mom. I didn't want that for any child of mine, and I wanted her. So badly I wanted...to be a mother. To love someone."

He held her tighter against him. "You said, back when Rosalie first had me come out, you said he tried to have you committed."

"I called in a report that day. At first, the officers who responded took me very seriously. But as the days went on, I heard more about how I'd waited. How the prosecutor wouldn't take on a case like mine. I knew Eric was making sure everyone thought I was lying."

Thomas's expression was mostly blank, but she saw in the way he held his jaw, tight and hard, he wasn't just *absorbing* this information. It bothered him. She supposed she couldn't be hurt by that.

"The next time he hit me, I called the police right away. He didn't even stop me. I thought... I don't know, I really thought that would be it. But he just laughed and told me he'd always win. I didn't know how at the time, but then the cops showed up. They knew him, of course. And when he said I'd hurt myself, that I was a danger to him and myself, that I should be involuntarily committed and he'd be *sure* I got the help I needed, I realized there was no real end. He had all the power."

"He doesn't," Thomas said firmly. Then he relaxed a little, as if he was trying to make himself. "But you figured that out. You left."

"It was my word against theirs, and there was no proof, so they couldn't involuntarily commit me. But I knew if he got another chance, he'd make it happen. They made us separate for the night. And I just took that as my opportunity to run. I went to my dad. I was afraid... Well, I thought maybe he wouldn't help, but it was my only chance."

"I know your dad wasn't perfect, but he did love you."

Vi nodded, trying to blink back tears. "Yeah. Him and Suze saved me. They got me a divorce lawyer. At first, I thought it would be enough." She shook her head, swallowing at the lump in her throat. "Stuff started happening at Dad's house. Tires slashed. Mailboxes knocked over. Little petty things, and no way of proving it was Eric."

"But of course it was Eric."

"Yeah. Luckily, they served him the divorce papers at work. Apparently it was embarrassing enough for him that he got his own lawyer. They somehow made it look like he'd wanted the divorce first. Tried to make it out like I was unstable and a danger to *him*. I didn't even care at that point. Whatever got me out, especially if he never knew I was pregnant. But it left me flat broke, and too close. I couldn't stand the idea of Dad and Suze getting hurt just for helping me, so I was going to leave."

She inhaled, just as her therapist told her. Breathe in and let it all out. Feel your body. Know you're safe.

"Dad insisted on helping me, and I didn't have a choice. I had no money. No...anything. So first, they got me on a flight to Suze's sister in Chicago. Then my aunt and uncle in Phoenix. My aunt and uncle drove me up to Denver, and Audra and Rosalie picked me up there. We thought he wouldn't find me."

"How long did it take?"

"It was almost six months before he called my new number. Every time I'd change it, he'd find it sooner. But it was just…messages about how I was nothing. How much better his life was without me. How he'd won. It's all kind of a blur. Magnolia was born two months early, and I was more focused on that than what messages he left."

"Has he ever threatened Magnolia?"

"I never told him I was pregnant. I didn't go to the doctor until I got out. He doesn't know she exists."

Thomas was clearly confused by this. "If he's gone through the trouble of phone numbers and email addresses, don't you think he knows you had a kid?"

She hesitated for the first time since she'd started. Because the next bit was…well, illegal. "Let's just say…it wasn't exactly… I didn't perhaps give the hospital the full truth."

He frowned at her. "You can tell me, Vi. I'm not going to arrest you."

He seemed irritated enough by the idea, so she figured he deserved the full truth. "Audra… She had me use all her information. Name. Social. Insurance. If anyone looks at Magnolia's birth certificate, they'd think Audra was her mother."

He inhaled slowly, let it out. She couldn't really decide what he thought about any of that, but she'd told him. It was all out there. Whatever happened from here on out was with the whole true story between them.

If he balked now, that was on *him*. She really tried to convince herself it would be on him.

"And that's the whole story?" he asked.

"Pretty much every terrible detail. He calls and leaves a message from time to time or writes an all-caps email from some fake email address. He's usually drunk when he does it. And maybe they sometimes have gotten a little threatening, but he's never left Richmond. Never come looking for me. It's just…him convincing himself he can still mess up my life. He can't."

"No, he can't." Thomas reached out, tucked a strand of hair behind her ear. "I need you to tell me when it happens. Even if it's not a threat. Even if we then pretend it never happened. I need to know."

She didn't like that but was trying to let this relationship be the real deal. Which meant listening to her therapist, not *reacting*, but dealing. Not retreating but putting herself in another person's shoes.

And Thomas dealt with this kind of thing. The crushing regularity of a man who terrorized his significant other. So how could she keep something like that from him?

As much as she wanted to. "If it makes you feel any better, I promised Rosalie and Audra too. Back on that night you came over. I know it's hard to believe, but I… As much shame as I'm still working through, I *am* working through it. I know it's not my fault, what happened to me is not my own failure to hide. Or I'm working on knowing it."

"Vi. That's a lot of important words, but none of them are *I promise*."

She studied his face. The faint hint of whiskers from a long day. The lines around his mouth and eyes now. But those eyes were exactly the same. Blue and earnest and in love with *her*.

She cupped his face with her hands, pressed her mouth to his. "I promise," she managed to say, through a too tight throat.

"I love you, Vi. Call it old, call it new. I don't really care. It's all there."

She hadn't expected *that*, but maybe she should have.

"I'm not sure I'm ever going to be okay with you being a cop."

He sucked in a breath, pained. Like she'd stabbed him clean through. Still, he didn't yell. He didn't withdraw or get cold. He just nodded.

Because he *wasn't* Eric. No matter how she kept waiting for her judgment to be wrong, but this wasn't just any guy.

It was Thomas Hart. The first boy she'd loved, and she still recognized that boy, but he was settled in a strong, mature man who'd seen his fair share of bad.

"But I do love you, Thomas."

He studied her face a long time. "I just want you to be happy, Vi."

She thought about her life. Living out here on the ranch and taking care of the ranch. Watching Magnolia grow. Falling in love with her sweet high school boyfriend who maybe had a job that terrified her but was still the same good person she'd loved as a boy.

Two years ago, she'd had no hope she'd ever experience happiness again, and these days she felt it more than all the other things.

"I am happy, Thomas. Very happy."

Chapter Five

He was late, and Thomas *hated* running late for work. Or he had, before Vi. Spending the night out on the Young Ranch tended to override that worry over it. Still, this morning he rushed into the station, offered half-hearted greetings before making it to his office.

God, he needed some coffee. Maybe five minutes to get his thoughts in order. Did he have strained carrots on his pants from feeding Mags this morning?

Laurel was sitting at the desk they had to share. She had been back from maternity leave for a while now, and as Thomas had predicted, the sheriff had expanded the detective department rather than send Copeland back to the road. They had the caseload for it these days.

Laurel looked up at him, then the clock on the wall. "I want to meet her."

She'd hinted, suggested, tried to trick him, but he still hadn't introduced her to Vi. Laurel was five years older than them, so while Vi might have known *of* Laurel Delaney since the Delaneys were a big deal in Bent, Laurel didn't remember Vi.

"Hell no."

"Why not?"

Thomas grinned at her, hanging his bag up on the hook behind the door. "Because it's driving you crazy." And because he tried to keep all the *cop* parts of his life away from Vi. Even if it was hard. Even if it hurt.

But love was a hell of a thing. He'd keep a million things out of her way if it meant waking up with her every morning. Putting Mags to bed at night together. He'd sacrifice a million things for those quiet, perfect moments.

"I've never seen you this happy," Laurel said, a bit like an accusation.

Thomas didn't know what to say to that, since it was true. So he just grunted.

When Copeland walked into the detective office, blissfully later than Thomas himself, Laurel jabbed a finger at him. "Has *he* met her?"

"No."

"Well, that's something." Laurel and Copeland had learned how to deal with each other, but Thomas wouldn't call it an *easy* relationship. Neither one of them quite trusted the other yet, but Thomas figured it would come with time. They were both too good professionally to let oil and water personalities get in the way for long.

"Look, she's a homebody and she's got a one-year-old." Thomas shrugged. "We just don't get out much."

Laurel pointed a finger at him. "Play date."

"No."

"My kids are desperate to meet new kids."

"Your kids have three million cousins their age to play with. Besides, Mags is just starting to walk. She doesn't need your brood running her over."

"Mags?"

"It's short for Magnolia," he muttered. "Now can I have my desk? I've got that report to finalize."

"*Our* desk, buddy." But she got up.

It was indeed *their* desk, because littered across it were pictures of the Delaney-Carsons. For a moment, Thomas was distracted not by the old, vague sense of envy, but a new one of how that *could* be his future.

Future being the operative word. Because it had only been a few months. Even if fifteen years before, it had been four years. But they'd been different then. Everything had been different.

When he caught Laurel staring at him, probably because he'd been staring at her pictures, he ignored it and got to work.

Later when they ate their lunches in the office, discussing Copeland's current robbery case, Vicky stuck her head in the door.

"This was delivered to the front desk for you, Hart," Vicky said. She tossed a slim envelope onto his desk.

He set his sub sandwich aside and lifted the envelope. The return address was a police department in Texas. "We had any dealing with someone in Plano?" he asked offhandedly, breaking the seal.

"Not that I recall," Laurel replied.

Inside the envelope was a stack of pictures. He frowned at the first one. It was kind of grainy, the lighting not very good, but he recognized that wavy red hair.

Everything inside him went utterly still at the trickle of blood running down her nose.

With a slight tremor in his hands, he flipped to the next picture. A close-up this time, still grainy. A black eye, dark and big.

Every single one featured Vi. With a bruise or injury somewhere on her body. And with each picture, his blood ran more and more cold. He reached the end of the stack, expecting some kind of note, some kind of *something*.

But there was nothing but the pictures. Thomas was on his feet, the chair clattering behind him, without a thought to Copeland or Laurel asking him what was wrong. Nothing mattered but getting to Vi.

But there she was. In the doorway. No bruises. No visible injuries. But she was pale.

And clutching an envelope to her chest that looked just like the one on his desk.

THREE SETS OF eyes were on her, but Vi only noticed Thomas's. Worry and anger. She saw the envelope on his desk that looked just like the one that had been in the mail this afternoon.

Eric had sent Thomas pictures too.

Oh, *God*. For a second, she thought her knees might buckle. She shouldn't have come to his work. She shouldn't have come. She shouldn't have.

He skirted the desk so quickly, she didn't even have time to flinch when he grabbed her. But it wasn't a *grab*, or at least not the kind her body was preparing for. He hugged her. Tight and close.

She felt her knees sag. Fear had propelled her from the ranch all the way to the Bent County Police Station, but Thomas's strong arms around her was like a wake-up call.

"Thomas, I have to…" Run. Just *run*.

"Let me see the envelope," he said, carefully loosening his grip but only just, so enough space remained between them to take it out of her hands. When he held it out, the woman who'd been in the office with him—no doubt Laurel the detective he occasionally talked about—had a bag open and he dropped the envelope in.

"Copeland?" he said.

The man was another detective Vi knew just from putting little clues together, because Thomas didn't talk about his job much. Purposefully. He had taken her *I'm not sure I'm ever going to be okay with you being a cop* to heart and did everything he could to keep that life separate from theirs.

For a moment, that felt like another pain, just to go along with all the others. Another failure in the never-ending cascade of them.

She closed her eyes, took a deep breath. Those knee-jerk meltdowns would probably never go away, but she wouldn't let them sabotage the life she was building.

Copeland took the bag with her envelope in it, while holding another bag with an identical envelope in it.

"I'll get them processed and printed." He nodded at her, intense and direct. The female detective—short, blond, pretty, no doubt Laurel—was watching Thomas.

Thomas kept his arm around Vi, but moved so they were more hip to hip. "Copeland will see if we can get a print, more information on where they came from," he said. He pointed to the woman. "This is my other partner, Laurel Delaney-Carson."

Vi nodded, beyond uncomfortable his coworkers were witnessing this…awful, awful thing. She didn't want them seeing the pictures. She didn't want Laurel, this person she *knew* Thomas looked up to, seeing…all her failures.

Not failures, Vi. Don't let him win this.

"I'll give you two some privacy," Laurel said with a

kind smile. "You let me know if I can be of any help." Then she left.

Thomas rubbed his hand up and down her arm. "Did you drive out here? Where's Mags?"

"Franny's got her. I didn't want to… I was going to call you, but I didn't want you coming to the ranch, bringing all this ugliness out there more than it already is. I couldn't…" She wouldn't cry. She just wouldn't allow herself to do that here. Maybe once she was back in her car alone. Definitely tonight in bed. Alone.

Because how could she keep doing this thing with Thomas with this hanging over her head?

Eric had sent him those pictures too. A new bolt of fear struck her at her core. Eric had never involved anyone else once she'd left her father's house. All his threats were to *her* and her alone.

But if he knew she was dating Thomas… If he was threatening *him* by sending these pictures…

She turned to face Thomas again, grabbed on to him. He was real, he was strong. But… "If he sent them to you, this is more. It's… He can't come here. He can't know about Magnolia. He can't—"

Thomas took her hands in his. Squeezed. "So he won't."

His gaze was so direct. So sure.

She wished she could believe his certainty. But she'd once been certain. She'd once believed all it would take was going to the police to save her from Eric.

She'd been so wrong. "Thomas. I have to leave. I have to run. If he comes here…"

"You will be protected."

"I don't think you understand," she said, trying to maintain her calm, her composure. She had to be composed or he'd look at her and see everything those other cops had seen.

Hysteria. Overreaction.

"It's not like I just ran. That was a last resort. I tried to tell people. I tried to get help. But his entire precinct believed him, supported him. He was *this* close to having me involuntarily committed. If I hadn't run away, he would have made it happen."

Or maybe he would have killed me. She knew how possible it was. How likely he would have been to get away with it.

"This is Bent County. He doesn't control us."

"But you could control them if you wanted to." She hated the words the *second* they were out her mouth. She squeezed her eyes shut. "I'm sorry. I know you don't deserve that."

"No, I suppose I don't." Then his arms were around her, pulling her close. Gently this time. "But you didn't deserve what happened to you. Life isn't fair. We know that."

Chapter Six

Thomas had been shot. He'd been injured a number of times in the line of duty. Hell, he'd lived through Vi breaking his heart once before. It wasn't like he couldn't live through her saying stuff like that.

He knew it wasn't about *him*. It was about the hell she'd lived through. Survived. Escaped. But it was never going to be past tense as long as her ex-husband had the means to reach her like this.

He pulled her back by the shoulders, ignored the hurt on his heart, and looked her dead in the eye. "You were right to run the first time, because he'd isolated you and you didn't have a choice. But you ran to your dad because you knew he would help. Now you ran to me, because you know I'll help. Who else is there to run to, Vi? Who else has a better chance of keeping you safe?"

He could see the push and pull in her expression. She wanted him to protect her. But she couldn't quite let herself believe he would, or could.

But this was not about their relationship, his ego, or anything about them on a personal level. It was about a threat.

"Thomas, I don't want you stepping in the middle and getting hurt."

"Why the hell not?" he demanded, with enough heat that she winced and he hated himself.

He took a deep breath, gentled his tone. "Vi, I took an oath when I put on that badge. And it involves laying my life down for the law, for the citizens of this county. If I'd do that for a stranger, I'm sure as hell going to do it for the people I love."

She was shaking her head, but the hell with that.

"It doesn't matter whether I love you or not, Vi. That's how I'd feel. You could be a stranger bringing me a case, and I'd damn well be getting to the bottom of it, regardless of the danger. That's my job. That's an oath I took. That's who I am."

And that was hard to say. Not because it wasn't true, but because if she couldn't accept that, he didn't know how to move forward. He could overlook a lot, compartmentalize almost everything. But not this.

"So there's no point in arguing this," he said, trying not to sound as destroyed as he felt. He dropped her shoulders, settled a hip back on his desk. "Walk me through getting that envelope. Start at the beginning."

She looked at him, too many heartbreaks to name in those dark blue eyes. But he couldn't let that sway him. If he was going to promise her he'd do this for anyone, then he had to do this like he'd do it for anyone.

She was quiet for so long, he thought she might not say anything. He thought…maybe, this was a wall he couldn't get through. And then what? How did he proceed knowing she was in danger? Knowing she didn't want his help?

"Audra came in for lunch and brought the mail like she always does," she finally said, her voice rough.

A weaker man might have collapsed to the floor at the

sheer weight lifted from his entire being, but Thomas held himself firm.

"That envelope was in with the other mail. She asked me if I knew anyone in Texas. I don't. So we opened it together. I made it through…two or three pictures before I stopped looking. I don't know how many Audra looked at."

"Then what?"

"I knew I had to bring them to you. I didn't want you coming out to the ranch. Maybe I should have. Maybe they're in danger. Maybe…"

He reached out and took her hand, couldn't stop himself from offering some physical comfort. "Let's not deal in maybes, sweetheart. Let's focus on what you did. You had Franny watch Mags and you got in your car and drove straight out here?"

She nodded.

"No stops? Just right here?"

She nodded again. He supposed it soothed something inside of him that her first instinct, even if she'd since questioned it, was to come to him.

"Before this, how long has it been since you'd heard from him? Phone. Email. Whatever. I know there was the phone call a few months back when Rosalie first told me about all this. Anything between then and now?"

She blinked, got a slightly confused expression on her face. "No, of course not. I would have told you."

Relief was wrong to feel right now, with so many unknowns around them, but it *was* a relief. If she could trust him enough to tell him, to be confused he might even think she wouldn't, they could get through this. He was sure of it.

He was going to be sure of it.

"I want to listen to those voicemails. Read those emails. From the beginning."

"I deleted them," she said, with a bit of a wince again. Like she expected him to explode. "I think Rosalie made copies, though."

"I'm going to drive you back to the ranch. We're going to tell everyone there what happened. I'm going to take a statement from Audra. I'm going to see what Rosalie has on the past threats—no doubt her own case file."

"But..." She looked around his office. "You're working."

"Yes, I am working. This is my case now."

"Thomas, you can't—"

"I can. I'm going to." On that, he wouldn't take no for an answer. "I'm going to need to bring in Laurel or Copeland. Do you have a preference? Some women prefer to work with Laurel."

"Can't it just be you? I..." She looked at the door that Laurel had closed behind her when she left. "I don't know these people. I can't..."

"For a lot of reasons, I need more hands and eyes than mine." He stood behind her, wrapped his arms around her and held on. Because he needed to, and when she leaned into him, relaxed her shoulders a bit, he knew she needed it too. "But the main reason is I want someone else's opinion. I want to make sure I'm not missing anything."

"I guess, whichever one you trust the most then."

"I trust them both, Vi. I need you to know that. I won't put your case in anyone's hands I don't trust with my own life."

She'd stiffened a little but didn't pull away. She just nodded. He gave her one last squeeze, released her. "Give me a few minutes, then we'll head back to the ranch."

"Okay."

He left her in his office, but he closed the door so she could feel like she had some privacy. He found Laurel alone in an interrogation room, going over some paperwork. She looked up when he came in, and he saw sympathy in her gaze.

"You looked at the pictures."

"Yeah. I assume she knows the asshole who did that to her?"

"Ex-husband. Some SWAT guy in Virginia who basically had his whole precinct eating out of his hand and not believing her. I have a bad feeling we're not going to be able to find proof he sent those pictures, but it's a starting point to end this for her. I'm going to the Young Ranch to get official statements from Audra Young. I'm also going to talk to all the other residents. I want your help on this, but more on the periphery. She doesn't trust cops, and who could blame her?"

Laurel nodded. "Okay, I'll let you know when we get the results on the envelope and pictures. Any other cases you want to hand off to me or Copeland, just say the word. Focus on this one for right now."

There'd been no doubt Laurel would understand, that she'd have his back and give him what he needed. And still, he was just…relieved. At anything that went right, he was going to be grateful.

"Keep me updated, and let us know if you need anything else," she said.

"Yeah. Thanks."

"We'll get to the bottom of it," Laurel said, reassuringly. "We've always got your back, Hart."

He knew they did, particularly Laurel who'd been his first training officer. She was the one who'd recommended him to take over as detective when she'd been on her first maternity leave. She'd been a mentor from day one, and she'd become as close as a sister to him.

But with Vi and Magnolia's safety on the line, her words didn't reassure.

No one's could.

THOMAS DROVE VI back to the ranch in her car. When she asked how he'd get back to Bent, he told her he'd handle it.

She believed he would and could, even with fear and nerves and embarrassment and a hundred other terrible feelings battling it out inside of her. She knew that Thomas was more than capable of handling all this.

It was strange. So strange it almost felt *wrong*. Because she'd spent her whole life being the one who figured out how to handle it. While her parents had been acting like spoiled children when she was a kid—using her like some kind of bargaining chip in a failing marriage. When she'd gone off to Clemson thinking she knew how the world worked and how her future would pan out. Even when she'd been married to Eric, who'd been controlling in a way that at first had almost made her feel safe and protected and not the one who had to *do* everything, eventually she'd started to feel like the only one who could hold it all together. Like the fate of her life rested on every single minute decision she made.

Her cousins, Franny, they had all been amazing since she'd made it out here. They'd helped so much, especially when Mags had been in the NICU, but even then, Vi had insisted on handling as much as she could on her own. Only in the past few months had she really started to relent. To Audra and Rosalie, to Franny, to Thomas.

Her therapist said it was healthy, but now it seemed dangerous. Like every step forward was drawing more people into the hell she'd escaped. If this was just about her, she probably would have bolted. Even now, she considered it.

Audra had every legal right to raise Magnolia. If Vi just disappeared...

"I need you to promise me one thing in all of this, Vi."

Vi blinked out of her whirling thoughts, looked at Thomas. His expression was grim as he drove. "What's that?"

"You'll be honest with me, no matter what. With anything that happens, with what you're feeling. Any contact that feels off. If you're considering running. Just tell me."

Could he read her mind? Was she that transparent? Or did he just understand, because he dealt with *victims* like her, all the time? And there was something about that awful thought—that she was just like the people he helped—that had her saying the truth.

"I'll probably consider running every day."

He glanced at her once, oh-so-serious. "It would break my heart if you did."

A quick, painful stab went right in her own heart. "That's not fair."

His mouth quirked up on the side as he looked back at the road. "I know. That's why I said it. I'm not above being unfair to keep you safe."

"I just don't want anyone else paying for a mistake I made."

"So, let me handle this for you, Vi. And there won't be mistakes."

She wondered if the confidence was natural, something born from all the work he'd done, or something he was putting on to settle her, but it worked.

When they got to the ranch and went inside, Thomas talked to everyone and Vi got Magnolia down for her nap. She knew she should go see what Thomas was saying to everyone, but instead she just watched her daughter sleep.

For over a year, she'd been running. Hiding. For over a year, she'd spent time healing herself, but there'd always been this little part of her—the *victimized* part, she could accept now—that was waiting.

Waiting to be hurt again.

Waiting to run.

She'd known this moment was coming.

Thomas slid into the room. He came to stand next to her, wrapped his arm around her. He looked down at Mags, fast asleep in her crib. And Vi saw one of the things she'd first allowed herself to recognize about Thomas.

He loved her daughter.

"I want you to come stay in town with me for a little bit," he whispered, tearing his gaze from Mags to her. "The ranch is too big. My house is small. I've got great neighbors who know who should be coming and going and are just busybodies enough to let me know. I've got some security, and a friend who can bulk it up."

"What about Audra, Rosalie and Franny?"

"I talked to them. Audra said she's going to talk to the neighbors, ask that anyone who sees something off to let them know. Rosalie's going to put up some cameras she uses for work. She also informed me they are 'armed to the teeth,' which I can't say made me feel great. I'll have whatever manpower I can manage check in throughout the day, drive by at night."

Vi tried not to feel like she'd ruined everyone's life. Made everything ten times more difficult on the people who'd helped her through the worst.

"Everyone is happy to rally around you, Vi. You and Mags. Because they—because *we* want what you want. This life you've built. For you. For Magnolia. We want you to have it, and we want to be a part of your life."

Vi looked down at her sleeping daughter, felt the easy strength of Thomas next to her. Thought about this life—and he was right, she'd *built* it. Out of the wreckage of her old one, with the help of her loved ones, *for* her daughter.

Her daughter, who called Thomas *Tata*. Magnolia loved him. And her honorary aunts. Audra was Aw. Rosalie, Ee. Franny, for some inexplicable reason, was Geen. She'd taken her first steps in this ranch house and was thriving. After all the NICU business, she was *thriving*.

So Vi met Thomas's gaze and nodded. Yes, this was the life she wanted for her daughter.

"So, we'll fight for it. Together."

For the first time since she'd gotten those pictures, Vi thought…maybe they could.

Chapter Seven

After Mags woke up from her nap, they packed up a few things and Thomas drove Vi and Magnolia back to his house.

Zach's truck was still out front when they got there. "Do you mind meeting some friends of mine?"

Vi grimaced, but she nodded. "Oh. Well. Okay."

They got out of the car, just as Zach was coming out of the front door. He was grappling with his very energetic three-year-old, Cooper.

"Hart. Ma'am."

"Zach, this is Vi Reynolds. Vi, this is Zach Simmons. A friend of mine, and he has a security business with Cam Delaney, Laurel's brother."

"Hi," Vi offered.

"Nice to meet you, Vi. I'd shake your hand, but if I let him go, he's going to bolt."

"I'm a dinosaur!" Cooper shouted. Then gave an impressive roar. Magnolia stared down at him dubiously and clutched onto Vi tighter.

"I checked out the security system," Zach said, while Cooper grumbled and tried to escape the hold Zach had on him. "Should be able to get everything upgraded by tomorrow. Mostly done through my computer, but Cam or I might need to stop by tomorrow to do some on-site stuff."

"Thanks, man."

"Any time." He wrangled his wriggly toddler. "Lucy's inside. She wanted to make everything look nice." Zach rolled his eyes. But as if on cue, Lucy came out the front door and walked up to them.

Vi's eyes got real wide. It was kind of funny, Lucy had been a fixture around Bent for enough years now that Thomas forgot to a lot of people, she was someone else. Before anyone could make introductions, Vi spoke.

"You… Daisy Delaney," Vi said, clear awe in her tone.

Lucy clearly wasn't surprised by it. She no doubt got that just about everywhere she went outside of Bent. "I just go by Lucy around here."

"You… I listen to your…music. All the time."

"Good to hear," Lucy said. She stood next to Zach, gave the wriggling toddler one quelling look and Cooper stopped trying to escape his dad's hold. "And who's this?" she asked, reaching out and giving Magnolia's hand a little shake.

Vi looked down at the daughter on her hip. "Magnolia. I… I named her after your song."

Lucy's smile widened. "Isn't that something?" She studied Magnolia in Vi's arms. "I miss this age. If you can't tell, our three-year-old is like a human wrecking ball."

"And just moved to a toddler bed. So they're letting us borrow some things while you're staying here," Thomas said. "Crib. High chair. We should be all set."

"Oh, well, thank you. I… That's so nice."

"No worries." Lucy patted her tiny baby bump. "We'll need them back in a few months, but for now, they're all yours. We've had them in storage anyway while we're redoing our house."

"We'll leave you to it, but if you need anything else, let us know," Zach said. He started moving for his truck, but Lucy didn't. She pointed at Thomas.

"You're coming to Cam and Hilly's baby shower, right?"

Thomas tried not to sigh. "Yeah, if I can swing it."

"Bring the whole gang," she said, smiling at Vi and Mags. "The more the merrier. Hope to see you there, Vi." She had to speak louder with every sentence over Cooper's roaring.

Magnolia reached out for Thomas, so he took her. She snuggled in. "Not sure Mags was a fan of Cooper," he said, holding her close. "Come on, sweets," he walked up to his front door, ushered Vi in.

"I don't need to go," Vi said. "To the baby shower," she added, when it was clear he'd lost the thread.

"Oh, if I'm going, you're going," Thomas said. He'd forgotten about the co-ed baby shower. His least favorite kind of forced party. Weddings and adult bridal showers at least usually had some alcoholic social lubricant, and kids' birthday parties were easy to hide in, what with all the screeching and sugar.

"But I don't even know these people," Vi continued.

"Good. Then you won't leave my side and I can have an excuse not to play one of those horrible baby shower games."

"Thomas."

He didn't quite know why she'd not want to come, except maybe she thought it was a cop thing. "Cam and Hilly aren't cops. Zach was FBI, but he just does security now. Laurel will be there, but I think that's about it on the cop front. Cam's her brother, so she'll be too sappy to bring up any shop talk."

"That's not what I'm worried about."

He studied her then. The frustrated look on her face, which poked at his temper when it shouldn't.

It *shouldn't*.

"Then what is?"

She looked up at him, but she didn't answer his question. "I just don't think I should go."

He supposed the fact she wouldn't give him a real answer made him say what he shouldn't. "They're my friends, Vi. And you're my...for lack of a more adult word, girlfriend. I love you. Why wouldn't you want to be part of my life?" And he should not be laying that at her feet after the day she'd had. Before she could say anything, he kept right on, hoping to dig himself out of the hole.

"Look, today's been a lot. It's not the day to have this conversation. Let's have some dinner." He tried to shake his frustration, and holding on to Magnolia helped. "I don't have much. Soup?"

Vi was still standing by the door when he looked back at her, but she'd closed it. She didn't say anything for the longest time. When she finally did, it wasn't at all what he expected.

"You know Daisy Delaney."

"Yeah." She was letting it go. So he smiled at her. "Did I not mention it?"

She scowled at him. "No, you did not."

"I've got all sorts of surprises up my sleeve, Vi."

She grunted, then came over to him. "I'll handle dinner since you've handled just about everything else."

He would have argued, but it seemed like she needed it. And he understood. The desire to *do* something when feeling helpless. He entertained Mags while Vi made them dinner. Then they sat down and ate together.

Which wasn't the first time. They'd been doing this a lot. But out at the ranch. Out in *her* space, with *her* family. This was *his* home and it made it feel like...

They were a family. Which was too soon, he knew. Vi had a lot to work through, and he could be patient.

But it still wound through him like pain, how much he wanted this to be his life. They bathed Mags, put her to bed. Since Magnolia's crib was set up in his bedroom, they made out on the couch in the living room watching a movie like they were teenagers again. There was something kind of fun about that. About forgetting the ugliness she'd been through and just being their old selves for a tiny sliver of time.

When they went to bed, Vi snuggled in next to him like she belonged there. In this life he'd built for himself over the past fifteen years. He wanted that to be the only thing he thought about.

He watched her sleep for a while, trying to see this—the beautiful woman she was, who loved him enough and trusted him enough to let him protect her.

But instead, all he dreamed about were those pictures.

Vi WOKE UP in a foreign bed, late morning sunlight streaming through the curtains. She sat bolt upright in bed, *Thomas's* bed. The crib in the corner was empty, and she looked at the clock.

"Ten?" she screeched. She practically raced out of the bedroom, then skidded to a halt at the sight that greeted her.

Thomas was in the kitchen. He had his work khakis on, but no shirt. One of his county polos was draped over the back of a chair.

He had Magnolia on his hip, bouncing her while she smiled and babbled. The highchair was a mess, so Mags had clearly eaten.

"I did not learn my lesson," he offered to her over his shoulder. "My shirt got peach smushed. Coffee's up."

It was like...all those things she'd imagined married life would be. It was all those things she'd wanted, so much so she'd ignored her intuition over and over again when it came to Eric.

And here it was, in her high school boyfriend. In all the simple things she probably would have scoffed at fifteen years ago. Letting her sleep in. Coffee made. Baby taken care of.

And she wasn't eighteen, or even twenty-four anymore. She was a mother in her thirties. She'd been through hell. And hell wasn't over yet.

But she had to be the one to end it. Once and for all. So she could enjoy all this glorious simple.

She crossed to him, wrapped her arms around him. Enjoyed the strength she found there—physical and otherwise. "I love you very much."

He wound his arm around her, kissed her head. "Well, I love you too."

"And if there's anything I need to do. Answer questions. Get those police reports from Richmond." She swallowed hard at the way her throat closed up at the next suggestion. "Go through each and every one of those pictures with you. Whatever I can do to end this, I will do it. I'm ready to do it."

He studied her a long time, then ran his free hand over her hair. "I'm glad to hear it. Right now, you're just going to sit tight and let me do my job. Okay?"

She nodded, leaned into him. "Okay."

"I'm going to go into the precinct, check up on those prints. The return address. A few other things. Franny is already on her way to hang with you today. I want you to stay close, but don't feel like a prisoner. I'll show you both how to work the security system before I leave. And I'm only a phone call away."

He handed Magnolia off, who wasn't happy with the transfer at all. "Tata!"

"Gotta clean up the mess you made out of me, sweets." Then he gave her a loud kiss on her cheek and disappeared into his bedroom.

For a moment, Vi let herself believe this could be her life. If she could be strong. If she could keep the promises she was making to Thomas.

This could be everything.

The doorbell rang, and Vi opened it up to Franny. Mags squealed in delight and Franny grabbed her enthusiastically. They babbled nonsense at each other, their favorite greeting, and when Thomas came out of the room, he was dressed for work.

He walked Franny and her through his security system, then gave her and Mags a kiss and was off. Vi stood in the doorway watching him go.

When he was out of earshot, she said what the little voice in her head kept insisting. "Am I stupid for trusting him, Franny?"

"You'd be stupid not to, Vi. He's great. He loves you and Mags. And he's going to do everything to protect you. What more could you ask for?"

"What if it's all too good to be true?"

"Seems like if anyone has earned a little too good to be

true, it's you. Besides, your ex-husband is harassing you. That's not good."

"No." She closed the door, turned to the living room, Franny by her side. "I'm sorry you're getting dragged into this. You have work to do, I know."

"Are you kidding?" Franny rubbed her hands together. "This is great research. I'm going to poke around his house and see how a real detective lives."

"You can't snoop."

"Why not?"

"Because..." Vi was sure there were a lot of good reasons why not, but she couldn't think of one.

"Like, what does a detective keep in his fridge? Am I going to find a Glock hidden in the freezer?"

"I hope not," Vi muttered, watching as Franny went right over to the fridge and looked through its contents.

Vi got out her phone. Opened a text to Thomas. She didn't want him coming home tonight and angry about someone touching and moving his things.

Franny is snooping around your house for research.

His response was almost immediate. That's okay. Nothing to hide. Except in my underwear drawer.

Something inside of her eased, and she realized she sometimes—without realizing it—still expected him to react like Eric would. Which wasn't fair, and she hated that it still snuck up on her.

She typed her response firmly, wanting to focus on Thomas and Thomas alone. And what's in your underwear drawer?

Guess you'll have to snoop and find out.

She didn't. She wasn't going to. She trailed after Franny while Franny went through his kitchen drawers, bathroom cabinets. While she complained about how *normal* his stuff was.

And then, when Franny had settled herself in Thomas's office, Vi quietly left the room and went to Thomas's bedroom with Magnolia on her hip.

"He basically told me to," she said to Mags. She carefully opened the top drawer of his dresser. Maybe it was a joke. Maybe...

But there in the far corner was a little prayer book, of all things. When she opened it up, she saw the inscription. *To Thomas, From Grandma.* His Grandma Hart had been very religious. She'd passed away their senior year, and Thomas had been devastated. Vi remembered going to the funeral.

It was one of the few times she'd thought staying in Bent wouldn't be so bad. To be part of a community that rallied around, that grieved together. Then she'd gone home that night to her mom, who was passed out drunk while one of her boyfriends rifled through her purse.

She'd only thought about getting out from there after that.

Magnolia reached out and swatted the book. "Gentle," Vi said quietly.

She didn't think this was what he'd been talking about in his text. Not when she flipped through the pages and a picture fell out.

Their senior prom picture. Her terrible eyeliner, his baby face. But so ridiculously in love. So happy.

"Ma," Magnolia said, bouncing happily.

Tears filled Vi's eyes, but she blinked them back. "Yes, that's Mama. And Tata."

Because Franny was right.

They all deserved a little too good to be true.

Chapter Eight

Maybe Thomas shouldn't have come into the department today. Even after adjusting his hours for the late morning, he wanted to snap just about everyone's head off.

The prints weren't ready. There was no information from the Texas police precinct. No one had any answers, and no one seemed that keen on getting them.

Which he knew was not a fair characterization. Police work was slow, methodical, and rushing things didn't help solve any cases.

But damn, he wanted to rush. He didn't like this hanging over their heads for a lot of reasons, but doing slow, methodical *waiting* while Vi and Magnolia were back at his house, even with Franny, really grated.

Her ex-husband sending those pictures was an escalation. Likely there'd be a few more before he escalated far enough to actually threaten Vi's physical well-being, but there was a lot of psychological well-being to threaten in the meantime.

Rosalie swanned into his office, clearly not having gone through the front desk. He might have scowled at her, but she dropped a folder on his desk in front of him. "All the emails, and a transcription of all the voicemails she gave me access to. I can email you the file too, but I thought this might be...safer."

Thomas nodded and immediately flipped the folder open. While his email was on the county police server, with lots of security, he didn't know about Rosalie's. "Do you think there are ones she didn't show you?"

Rosalie paused. He wasn't sure if she was deciding on her answer, or on whether to *tell* him her answer, but in the end, she shrugged. "I don't know why she'd let me see some, and not others. Maybe if she didn't have Mags I'd think she was hiding the worst of it from me, but she's going to protect Magnolia at all costs."

Luckily, that lined up with what he thought, but he wanted to hear it from someone who'd been around Vi this past year. "Good."

"I'm glad she's staying with you, because the ranch *is* too big to protect. But it's hardly a long-term solution to have her and Mags at your place."

He looked up, into Rosalie's worried blue eyes. "Why not?"

"We don't know how long this is going to take. That ex-husband has been pretty careful, and this still isn't an actual threat. This could be an ongoing issue. She's been here over a year. Who knows how long it continues. Are you just going to have them permanently move in with you?"

He looked at her evenly and tried not to let it show how much he wanted exactly that. Just not with Vi's ex-husband's threats hanging over their head. "Again," he said, very calmly, "why not?"

She grinned at him. "Just testing you, Hart. She's been through hell. She doesn't need some stupid guy with good intentions stomping on her heart because he's careless. I guess you're not."

"I've never been careless, Rosalie."

"Good." She got to her feet. "I'm doing my own investigation, obviously, but keep me in the loop."

"I guess it would be a waste of breath to tell you to leave it to the police department?"

"It would indeed."

He sighed. "All right. I'll keep you in the loop, if you do the same."

She nodded, then exited the way she'd come. Not a few minutes later, Laurel entered the office, a woman behind her. Mid-to late thirties, dressed professionally in a blazer and a skirt and sensible heels. Not a cop. Maybe a lawyer?

Hell, he did not want to deal with any lawyers today.

"Thomas, this is Postal Inspector Dianne Kay."

Thomas stood, held out his hand and shook hers. After he did, she held out a badge. "I'm out of the Fort Worth, Texas, office. I need to ask you a few questions about an envelope you received in the mail yesterday."

Texas. Envelope.

Suddenly, he was a little more interested in dealing with a postal inspector. "Have a seat," he said, taking his behind the desk. Laurel took a chair toward the side. "You work quick to be up here already."

"We try, but we've been following this for a while now. We're investigating a series of fraudulent uses of the mail. All stemming from the police department in Plano, Texas. I was in Denver yesterday when we got word that another set of envelopes had been flagged by postal employees here in Bent County."

"I did receive an envelope yesterday with a return address of the Plano Police Department."

Inspector Kay nodded. "As far as our investigation is concerned, no one who works at the Plano Police Department is behind these letters. We're trying to find out who is."

"What were in the other letters?"

She smiled at him. "I think you know I can't tell you that."

Irritation simmered, because she *could* tell him that, if she wanted. She didn't have to play things like that *perfectly* by the book. But if he put up a stink about it, he knew what people would say. That he was too close to the case, and he'd start putting himself in danger of getting taken off it.

He trusted Laurel and Copeland, but that didn't mean he'd be able to handle not being involved.

"Did you keep the envelope and its contents?" she asked.

"They were somewhat threatening in nature, so we're doing some analysis. Once I have the answers, you can take a look at whatever you need to."

"I'm sorry. You can finish your tests, I suppose. But it'll be a little bit more than taking a look. Those objects are now evidence in a *federal* investigation. I'll have to take them."

She said it apologetically, and not like some of the federal agents he dealt with—with a kind of smug superiority. Still, it grated. The last thing he wanted to do was hand it over to someone who had to deal with federal red tape.

"It was addressed to me. The return address had no name. No identifying information. Just the return address of the Plano Police Department."

"I'm going to need the envelope." When Thomas opened his mouth to protest, she kept talking. "I don't need to take it just yet, as I'm planning to stay in Bent a few days, but I do need to see the address now so I can verify."

"Will a photograph work?"

She nodded. He motioned her to come around to his side of the desk, and he brought up the pictures he'd taken of the envelope.

"Cute. Those your kids?" she asked, pointing at all the picture frames on the desk.

"Oh, no. They're Detective Delaney-Carson's," he said, nodding at Laurel. "We share a desk."

He should put a picture of Vi and Magnolia up too. But for now, he focused on the computer screen. "Here's the return address. The address here, with my name as the addressee."

She had a notebook and was taking notes.

"And the contents?" she asked.

"Pictures."

"Of?"

He didn't want to tell her, but that was silly. Maybe their investigations would line up and this could be over all that much sooner. "A friend of mine. We're working under the theory that they came from her ex-husband."

"I'm going to need the names of both," she said. "Spell them out for me. Any other information you have about either one of them. I'd also like you to email me these," she said, pointing at the computer screen.

With a sick, heavy feeling in his gut, Thomas told her Vi's name, and Eric's. When it came to Eric, Thomas gave her the information Vi had given him yesterday. When it came to Vi...

"Can I get an address?"

He couldn't exactly tell this federal agent the person was

living *with* him. Was his *girlfriend*. She wouldn't understand. "It's a ranch out by Sunrise. A ways away. I can give you her phone number."

"That'll work."

He rattled off the number.

The woman pulled a card out of her bag, then scribbled something on the back. "You can email me the photos of the envelope at the email on the front. And there's my cell on the back if you need it."

"Sure. Thanks."

"I'll be back probably around midday tomorrow to collect the evidence. Hopefully I'll have a few more questions for you once I've talked to the names you gave me." She stuffed everything back in her bag. "I don't suppose you know a good place to get dinner around here?"

There was something about the way she said it, smiled with her head cocked so that was just enough warning to tread lightly. That and Laurel's eyebrow raise aimed at him.

Lucky for him, Copeland walked by in the nick of time.

"Hey, Copeland. You know any places the postal inspector could get a decent meal in Fairmont?"

Copeland smiled at Dianne. "Sure. I live out that way. I can give you a few suggestions."

"Detective Beckett is part of our department too," Thomas explained. "Inspector Kay here came up from Texas by way of Denver to investigate some mail fraud with that envelope we got yesterday. Copeland used to be a detective in Denver."

Inspector Kay offered Copeland a bland kind of smile. "Not quite a promotion coming out this way, is it?"

Copeland didn't take any offense to that. He grinned. "Well, I'd love to tell you all about it. There's a pretty decent Italian place. If you're looking for some company, I'm about to clock out. Be happy to take you."

"Oh." She looked back at Thomas, then straightened her shoulders. "Well, thanks, but I think I'll just do some takeout. It's been a long day." She turned back to Thomas, aimed that megawatt smile at him. "I'll be back tomorrow, Detective Hart."

"Sure. I'll be here."

Then the inspector left, leaving the three of them in the detective's office.

"Did you just strike out?" Laurel demanded of Copeland, clearly delighted at the prospect.

"I wasn't batting," Copeland grumbled.

"Like hell you weren't," Laurel said with a laugh. "You asked her out. She said no. Then gave Hart some big eyes."

"Yeah, Hart's a real popular guy these days."

"He finally grew into that baby face," Laurel said, pinching his cheek before Thomas could sidestep her. "You know when he started at the county, he only weighed one-fifty."

"It was more than that," Thomas said, glaring at Laurel. "Maybe we could focus on our case instead of everyone's romantic life?"

"What romantic life?" Copeland demanded. "She's saddled with four kids, and you're hog-tied and babysitting."

"Trust me, Beckett. My husband could make a life with *ten* kids romantic. You should be so lucky." She gave him a little nudge so she could move around him. "I'm clocked out. See you tomorrow, boys."

"You clocking out too?" Copeland asked Thomas, too used to Laurel giving him a hard time to get worked up about it.

Thomas stared at the computer, scowling. He wanted to

get home to Vi, but he just didn't like the idea of the postal inspector poking around at all, plus he had two hours to make up for. "She said she's going to have to take the evidence for her case. I don't like it."

"Well, she gave us time to do our tests, right?"

"Yeah."

"Relax then."

He knew he should.

But he couldn't.

Vi WAS HUMMING when Thomas got home. She'd made a perhaps more elaborate than necessary dinner. It was the least she could do. Just like out at the ranch. If she could cook and clean up some, she didn't feel so bad for essentially sponging off people.

"Tata!" Mags squealed, getting up off the floor where she'd been happily playing with some magazines Vi had found in Thomas's office. They'd been in a recycling bin, so Vi didn't feel bad about letting Mags rip them apart.

She toddled over to Thomas, who picked her up on a big, dramatic swoop that made Magnolia squeal.

"I saw Franny outside. She told me to let you know she's heading home. At least I think that's what all those grunts meant."

Vi laughed. "Snooping around your house really got her creative juices flowing, and I don't think Mags's impressive concert of squeals was conducive for getting any of it written down."

He didn't look especially frustrated or tense, but he wasn't particularly happy either. Still, he came over, gave her a kiss, peered down at what she was making. "You didn't have to, but this looks amazing."

"I like to cook."

"Good, because I do not." He stood there, his arm around her while she stood over the stove. Mags sat on his hip, plucking at the chain around his neck that held his badge.

She waited for that to settle in her like a jolt. Fear. Worry. PTSD. Call it what you will. But he was holding her daughter, holding her. Everything he'd done for her, everything he'd been to her. It trumped that symbol of her old life. Her old mistakes.

She leaned into him, giving the pasta another stir. "What are you procrastinating telling me?"

He sighed, then kissed her hair. "That obvious, huh?"

"I'm learning to read the signs."

"A postal inspector came in today and had some questions about the envelope I received with the pictures. Something to do with mail fraud. She can't tell me how it connects quite yet, but I'm hoping to get more out of her tomorrow. She's probably going to give you a call. I imagine if she's staying here a few days, she'll want a face to face and to ask you questions."

"Can you be there?"

"She's very by the book, so I'm not sure she's going to go for that. That okay?"

She wanted to balk at that. At *all* of this. But she'd promised him. That she was ready. Ready to fight for herself and for Magnolia and a future with Thomas.

"Of course," she said firmly. "Whatever gets us to the end of this."

He settled Mags into her highchair, then said he wanted to take a quick shower. So she set the table and got Magnolia her dinner and let it cool a bit before Thomas came out and joined them.

They ate dinner and talked about different things. She knew he was carefully avoiding the topic of those pictures, and she let him. He patiently picked up Magnolia's sippy cup every time she gleefully tossed it to the ground.

"Where did you learn to be so good with kids?"

"I don't think I have any childless friends left. Except my Hart cousins, but that won't last forever and there's still kids running all over the place out at the ranch anyway. It's just…go to parties, see people, end up holding a baby or entertaining a toddler or feeding somebody, or be alone."

"You never did like to be alone."

"Not my forte. Though with as much work and social engagements I have these days, I don't mind a night home alone every once in a while. Well, as long as you're there." He grinned at her across the table.

And this domestic moment, that grin, his patience with her daughter maybe finally gave her the courage to ask a question that had been in the back of her mind since she'd seen him again.

"So, why didn't you ever get married?"

He shrugged. "Nothing stuck."

"Why? And *don't* say me. You haven't been pining after me for fifteen years."

"I guess not pining. You were always in the back of my mind, but you're right, it wasn't like I was expecting you to come back."

He didn't offer anything else. And maybe she should have let it go, but she…couldn't. "So?"

"I don't know. Nothing ever got serious."

"You are getting all the terrible nitty-gritty about my terrible relationship. The least you can do is tell me about your failures."

His mouth quirked at that. "I've got a demanding job, which isn't conducive to dating. If I ever got past the first few last-minute date cancellations, it is not my experience that women are particularly comfortable with me having a female partner, particularly one I think so highly of. That's mellowed out the past few years, what with Laurel's heap of kids and all and being out on maternity leave half the time. But it's been a sticking point."

Vi thought of the woman she'd met in his office yesterday. Pretty. Confident. In the same profession, so lots to talk about and lots of time spent together. "Was it ever fair to be a sticking point?"

His gaze went down to his plate. Then he took a very *large* bite of pasta. "This is delicious."

"Thomas."

"What? It *is* delicious." When she gave him a *look*, he sighed again. "Nothing ever happened with Laurel. Even before she got married what seems like a million years ago. And it never will. She's like a sister to me now."

"That is *not* what I asked."

"What did you ask?" he asked innocently. *Too* innocently.

"Thomas."

"It was nothing."

"Oh. My. God." But she found herself laughing in spite of it, and that in itself was kind of amazing. Because she just... knew he loved her. In the here and now. He never made her question it, never used it like a weapon or an excuse. How could she sit here and pick that apart?

"It was a very brief crush when I first started at county," he said.

Of course, believing he loved *her* didn't mean she wasn't curious. "How brief?"

"I don't know. It was a long time ago. She met Grady not long after that, and then they just became…like my family. The whole lot of Carsons and Delaneys. Well, after Jen and I stopped dating anyway. Kinda swore off any Delaneys after that."

"Who's Jen?"

He reached down to pick up Magnolia's sippy cup. "Laurel's sister."

"You had a crush on Laurel and then dated her *sister*?"

"Very, very briefly. A long, *long* time ago." He got up, took his empty plate to the sink. Then grabbed a washcloth and used it to clean up Magnolia while Vi watched him and finished her dinner.

Once Mags was clean, he took her now empty plate to the sink. Vi got up to put the leftovers away, trying to picture the Thomas she'd known. Skinny and baby-faced, becoming a cop, dating other women. Living a life, just like she had done.

And somehow they'd both ended up back here in Bent, in each other's lives. She didn't believe in fate anymore—no matter what he'd said at that party months ago about picking a dime up off the floor because of her.

Fate would have meant she'd been in an abusive marriage for years because it was meant to be.

No, there was no *fate*. There was only the choices you made.

She'd made some bad ones. Now she was making good ones.

"Are we done investigating my romantic history?" he asked, handing her a Tupperware so she could pack up the leftover pasta.

"I don't know. Maybe." She took it but faced him and

trailed her fingers through his hair. "I snooped in your underwear drawer. Did you keep it the whole time? The picture."

"Not exactly, no. When my parents moved, they gave me a bunch of my high school stuff. I got rid of a lot of it. But I couldn't bring myself to get rid of that. I figured… No matter how it ended, it'd been a good four years. I learned a lot. Why not keep a memento?"

"Got any other mementos from other women who haven't stuck?"

He wrapped an arm around her, drew her close. "Not a one." Then they both looked at Mags who'd pulled herself up on his pant leg and was tugging on his pants.

"She really loves you."

"Good, because I really love the both of you." He dropped a kiss on her mouth, then picked up Mags and pressed a kiss to her forehead.

They cleaned up the kitchen together. Put Mags to bed together. They fooled around on the couch, and for the first time in a very long time Vi really let herself relax. Enjoy.

Believe. That she was on the other side of *awful*.

So when the postal inspector called in the morning, she made an appointment to answer her questions at Thomas's house. Thomas insisted, since he had a doorbell camera and other security measures. They didn't have to tell the inspector Vi was living there just because they were meeting there.

Since Thomas had court, and so did Laurel, he'd offered Copeland to come over and sit with her, but Vi decided she'd rather do it alone.

She wanted to stand on her own two feet. For herself, as much as for Thomas.

When Thomas suggested he run Magnolia out to Audra

at the ranch before work, so she could have full concentration to answer the inspector's questions and then have her tele-therapy appointment this afternoon without having to worry about Mags, she agreed.

"Use the security system. Mr. Marigold next door is always home and usually being nosy, so he'll let you know if anything is funny. Call me if you need anything. When Inspector Kay gets here, wait for me to text that it's really her at the doorbell camera, okay?"

Vi nodded, gave him a kiss, and then watched as he expertly wrangled Mags into her car seat. And she stood there, watching the car go, trying to fight that feeling this was all just too good to be true.

"I won't let it be," she muttered, turning back inside. She locked the front door and then took her time getting ready. Brushing her hair, putting on light makeup. Actually putting on jeans and a top instead of living in sweats and yoga pants.

When the knock sounded on the door, she waited for Thomas's text.

It's the postal inspector.

So she opened the door and smiled.

The woman held out a badge. "Hi, I'm Inspector Dianne Kay. Are you Vi Reynolds?"

Vi nodded. "Yes. Come on in."

The woman was pretty, polished. But she had that *cop* way of looking around, cataloging everything, and making Vi feel like she was a series of failures for them to judge.

Why didn't it feel like that when Thomas did the same thing, she wondered? Probably just knowing him.

They sat down at the kitchen table, and Inspector Kay

took the offered coffee. "I just have a few questions about the envelope you received two days ago, and then I'll get out of your hair."

"Of course."

"You received an envelope, addressed to your name, at a ranch out in unincorporated Bent County?"

"Yes. That's where I've been living."

"And what were the contents of this envelope?"

"Don't you have the envelope?"

The inspector looked up from the notes she was taking. "I will once the Bent County detective bureau releases them to me. But I want to hear it, in your words. That will help my case."

"They were the same pictures that were in Detective Hart's envelope."

"Okay." The woman tapped her pen against the paper, studying Vi. "And you're the subject of the pictures that both you and Detective Hart received?"

"Yes."

"And in the pictures you received, you're injured as well?"

"Yes." She knew the woman wanted more information, but Vi knew enough about dealing with cops at this point. Postal inspector. Detective. SWAT. It didn't matter.

She wasn't giving up information she wasn't specifically asked for.

"Can you tell me the circumstances of those injuries?" Inspector Kay asked.

"How does that connect to mail fraud?"

"I don't know yet, and it might not." The inspector smiled kindly. "But I can't determine that if I don't know."

Vi inhaled and nodded. It made sense, even if she didn't like it. Still, she wasn't quite strong enough to meet the inspector's gaze. She looked down at her hands. "My ex-husband used to beat me."

"So, were these police report photos?" the inspector asked. She was being incredibly patient, but it didn't make Vi feel any better.

She clenched her hands into fists under the table and kept her voice even and calm. "No."

"Then…"

"A few of them I took myself, to document what he was doing to me." For as much as that had mattered. "He used to confiscate my phone all the time, so it's no surprise he has access to them. As for the ones I didn't take I wasn't aware he took those."

"And these pictures are from an incident how long ago?"

"I'm not sure. The ones I took were from about two years ago. The ones he took… I'd have to take some time and try to remember. We were married for almost five years."

"So, you…let him do this to you? For years? That's what you're saying."

Let him. Twin emotions assaulted her at that turn of phrase. A guilt and shame she was so familiar with, she almost sank into that. But there was a new feeling in there.

Outrage. Because her therapist, her cousins, her friends, Thomas, no one let her talk about herself that way.

So she wasn't about to let anyone else. "I was a victim of systematic physical, emotional and financial abuse, Inspector Kay."

The woman reached across the table, rested her hand over Vi's. "Of course you were. I wasn't trying to say otherwise. I'm just trying to get the facts."

"Those are the facts."

She nodded, but it gave Vi the same feeling as the cops she'd dealt with at Eric's precinct.

Like they just thought she was crazy. Or overdramatic.

"So, you think the sender was your ex-husband?" She flipped through her notebook. "Eric Carter?"

"Yes. I don't know who else would have access to those photographs."

"And do you have any idea of what connection your husband might have to the Plano Police Department return address he used?"

"Ex-husband."

"I'm sorry." And she sounded it. Her expression was even a little chagrined. "Does your ex-husband have a connection to Plano that you know about?"

Vi had to stop being so touchy. "No. He was from Virginia. We lived in Richmond the entire time we were married. As far as I know, almost all of his family are in Virginia or Georgia. I suppose he could have a friend or a former coworker who moved to Texas, but I don't know of any specifically."

"Okay. That should be all the questions I have for now. If you get any more suspicious mail—from Texas or anywhere—would you contact me?" She pushed a business card across the table. "Or if you think of any connection Eric Carter might have or have had with Texas?"

Vi nodded, relieved this was over. The inspector stood and Vi led her back to the front door, opened it for her.

The inspector paused, looked her over once, that cop calculation not well hidden. But then she smiled. "Don't worry, ma'am. We're going to get to the bottom of this. I promise."

Vi wished it made her feel better.

Chapter Nine

"Well, that was a waste of time," Laurel grumbled as they stepped out of the courthouse together.

So often trips to court were. It seemed more often than not the defendant wasn't too keen on showing up to their own trial. Or their lawyer got things stalled out for another month.

He'd pulled his phone out of his pocket the minute they were released. He had a text from Vi.

She just left. Run-of-the mill questions. Hope court went well.

"Everything good?" Laurel asked, sliding into the passenger seat since he'd driven them over.

"Vi said the questions were pretty run-of-the-mill."

"You're going to have to surrender those envelopes and pictures today."

"I know." He blew out a long breath. "Want to take a long, *long* lunch?"

"It won't change anything."

"No, it won't," Thomas muttered. They hadn't gotten any prints off the envelope. Nothing that could give them proof on who'd sent it. Still, it grated. He didn't want to surrender evidence that had been sent to him to some federal agency.

"So, what's your theory? Coincidence, or this Eric guy is up to more bad than just terrorizing his ex-wife?"

He knew what Laurel was doing. She was posing it as a question, but she was reminding him there was more to this case then just those pictures. Because of course it wasn't coincidence. The postal inspector's case was bigger than whatever Vi's ex was up to.

Even if to *him*, and to Vi, the biggest thing was Eric causing her harm.

"I bet that postal inspector would let you in on more of her case if you took her out to dinner."

He eyed Laurel out of the corner of his eye as he drove. "And if you were to take out a male postal inspector to get more details on a case, how would Grady react?"

Laurel laughed. And then she laughed harder. "Touché." They reached the parking lot of the station and got out.

"You bringing her to Cam and Hilly's baby shower this weekend?" Laurel asked as they grabbed their bags out of the back.

"Trying to convince her. She acted a little squirrelly about it."

"Guess she's got a reason."

Thomas frowned, because he didn't know what that reason would be.

Laurel nudged him as they walked through the parking lot. "Now who's acting squirrelly?"

"Not squirrelly. I just don't…get it. But I haven't had time to think about it. I have to know they're safe before I can worry about little dumb stuff." Dumb stuff like why she didn't want to be in his life outside of the small worlds they'd created.

So maybe that was the answer. Laurel's *guess she's got a reason*.

Vi still didn't trust those worlds outside the ones she'd built. And could he really blame her after what she'd endured?

"You know, I hope this one sticks," Laurel said as he gestured her to go inside ahead of him.

"Yeah, me too. Why?"

"You deserve a nice family, Hart."

He liked to think so, but he also knew… For the past fifteen years, maybe nothing romantic had worked out, but that didn't mean he'd been alone. "Got one, don't I?"

She smiled at him. "Yeah, you do. But more doesn't hurt."

When they walked into their office, the postal inspector was already there. She was sitting in a chair and looking at her phone and took her time addressing them.

"Got a few minutes for me, Detective Hart?"

"Sure thing."

She paused, as if waiting for Laurel to give them privacy. Laurel, bless her, pretended like she didn't notice and went over to their desk and settled herself into the chair, then busied herself with the computer.

Thomas had to fight back a smile.

"I talked to Eric Carter this morning. He says he doesn't know anything about any envelopes or Texas."

"Naturally."

"I also spoke with a few of the people he works with, including his captain. No one knew of any connections he might have to Texas. He hasn't missed a scheduled day of work in months *and* hasn't taken any time off."

"Are you going to investigate that further? Someone can get from Richmond to Texas on a weekend off."

She lifted a shoulder. "Look, I can't rule him out, but I can't concentrate on him without more of a lead. There's no evidence he's left Virginia, and the postal stamp *is* from Texas. It's feeling a little bit more like a dead end than a lead."

"So how do you explain the fact he's the only one who would have had those photos?"

The inspector sighed. "I don't know, Detective Hart. I'd like to. Part of that will be continuing my investigation by focusing on the evidence we *do* have. I'd like the envelopes and their contents." She smiled, but there was no confusing that smile for anything but politeness over a demand. "Now."

Laurel stood. "Why don't I go get them for you?" she offered.

Thomas nodded, even though he hated it. He wasn't getting around a federal agency on this. Besides, he had copies. It wasn't a total loss. Laurel gave his arm a reassuring squeeze before she left the office.

Once Laurel was gone, the inspector spoke again. "Can I ask why I questioned someone at a house that you own, Detective Hart?"

Whatever accusations Inspector Kay was offering were veiled under a smile and a friendly enough delivery. Thomas tried to match it instead of getting defensive. He hadn't expected her to check on the owner of the house.

"Like I said yesterday, she's a friend." Thomas kept himself as relaxed as possible. "She lives with family and she didn't want them worried, so I let her use my place. Is that a problem?"

"No, I just want to make sure I know all the details of the case."

"It's a small town, ma'am. We watch out for each other around here. You've got all the details."

"I'm heading back to Denver this afternoon, but it's possible I'll be back." She stood up from the chair. Just a *shade* too close. But he pretended not to notice.

"You've got my number. Feel free to call me if something changes."

He smiled thinly. "I will. I hope you'll do the courtesy of letting me know when you wrap up this case."

"Of course."

She stayed there a beat, and then Laurel came in. She slid a sealed evidence envelope between what little space Inspector Kay had left between her and him.

"Here you go," she said cheerfully.

The inspector took them. "I'm not your enemy, guys. I hope you realize that." Then she scooted past him, *against* him, and out the door.

"She's right," Thomas muttered in frustration, irritation. He might not like her on a personal level, but it wasn't like they were on opposite sides. They were both looking for the truth. He just had a vested personal connection. "We're all on the same side. I've got to stop acting like I'm the only one who can protect Vi."

Laurel patted him on the back. "You're doing all right, Hart. We'll get there."

He wished he believed it.

Vi THOUGHT HER therapy session went well enough. She talked about the postal inspector's questions, and the comment about *letting* Eric happen.

She worked through her feelings on that, why she might be touchy about word choice, and how some people projected their own issues onto others. Whatever the inspector thought didn't have anything to do with Vi.

So she had to let it go.

Easier said than done, but at least she had an action plan. When Thomas got home, Mags in tow, her heart filled.

Who else's opinion could matter when she had these two?

But that joy quickly petered out when they sat down to dinner, and Thomas started talking about *socializing*.

"The baby shower is Saturday at noon. Kids welcome. It's basically just a barbecue and we're all bringing baby gifts. You know, Hilly is a nurse. Just started last year. She could give you information if you were still looking in that direction."

"Thomas, I don't know that Mags and I should go."

He didn't say anything at first. There was a kind of heavy silence that might have reminded her of her past if it wasn't *Thomas* sitting there.

"Okay." He took the last bite of food from his plate, put it in his mouth, then got up and moved to the sink. Without anything else.

Vi looked helplessly at Mags, who'd made a mess of herself as usual. And like he often did, Thomas came over with a washcloth and wiped her up.

But he didn't say anything, and he didn't smile. And it made her feel…small. Like her stomach was tied in a million knots. She couldn't finish her meal.

"Thomas. Talk to me."

"About what?" He went over to the sink, dropped the washcloth in it. Turned on the sink.

She got up, frustration and some other emotion she didn't

quite understand brewing deep inside her. "You can't be afraid to tell me what you want just because I have this... trauma sitting there. This won't work if you treat me with kid gloves."

"I did tell you what I wanted. You said no, and I said okay."

"And now you're mad."

He shook his head, and to his credit, he didn't actually seem *mad*. He turned off the sink, turned to her. "I'm not mad. I'm...confused and disappointed."

"But you said okay."

"What am I supposed to say?"

"That you're confused and disappointed."

"I'm not going to manipulate you into going to this with me. If you don't want to, that's your choice. And I'll live with it. The end."

"It's not the end, because it's not...*manipulating* to explain to me how you feel about something I've done."

He crossed his arms over his chest. There *was* some anger, but it was carefully guarded. "What about *your* feelings? What about *your* decision? You want me to unload, but you won't even tell me why you won't go."

"I just..." Maybe it was because she'd had her therapy session this afternoon that she found the courage to say it. "I hate the idea anyone I meet has to eventually know the truth about me. They'll know what happened to me and it colors who I am."

He didn't say anything to that, didn't drop his arms, but that carefully guarded anger turned into something else. Something too close to pity for her liking.

"It doesn't color who you are to me."

"I know. But that postal inspector..."

Thomas stiffened. "What about her?"

Vi shrugged. She didn't have the words for it. "I don't know. I don't like the way she talked to me. The questions she had to ask. I know that's not fair, but it just... I'm tired of having to dredge it all back up. When I was living at the ranch, I only talked to Audra, Rosalie and Franny. I barely left. I felt...safe."

He inhaled. "Do you feel safe here, Vi?"

She didn't even have to think about the answer. "I do."

"All right then."

Mags chose that moment to throw her sippy cup halfway across the room, knocking over Vi's half-full glass of milk. They all jumped to action to clean everything up, and then comfort Mags when she started crying.

They put Mags to bed. They didn't make out on the couch. Maybe they'd both had a rough enough day. But when they crawled into bed, he pulled her against him and held her close and tight.

"I love you, Vi."

"I love you too." And she fell asleep fast enough, or must have, because the next thing she knew a trilling phone woke her up. Panic immediately slammed through her.

Eric was calling.

Eric...

"Hello," Thomas's deep voice said into the quiet room.

For a moment, addled by sleep, she thought he'd answered her phone. But her hand was on her phone on the nightstand. And the screen was black. No call coming through.

It had been *his* phone ringing.

"And it can't wait until morning?" he said in low tones as Mags made some whimpering noises.

He grunted some kind of assent, then put his phone down

on the nightstand again. "I've got to get down to the station," he whispered. "A break on an old case we can't wait on." He pushed out of the bed. He was only a shadow in the dark. Then he cursed. "Hell, Vi. I can't leave you here alone."

"It's okay," she said, her mind whirling a bit. Still hung up on Eric. Weird threatening calls from robotic voices were usually the only phone calls that woke her up in the middle of the night.

He slid out of the room, and she could see the light come on under the crack of the door. Mags had fussed, but had quieted back down, so Vi snuck out of the room, letting in the least amount of light.

He'd brought his clothes out here and was putting them on. "I'm sorry." And he looked genuinely worried, genuinely conflicted as he pulled on his county polo. "I don't usually get called in in the middle of the night, but I should have thought this possibility through when I had you guys come stay here."

"We'll be all right. You said it yourself, the postal inspector talked to Eric at work today. In Virginia. He's just trying to scare me. Not hurt me. You can't watch me 24/7, Thomas. It's just not possible."

"I'm going to see if I can get a deputy to drive by, maybe park outside for a bit." He strode over to the closet. She usually didn't watch him do this part, because she hated knowing there was a gun in the house.

But tonight, she did. Watched him reach up to the gun safe on the top shelf in the closet, unlock it with the key on his keychain, and then pull out the gun and shove it into the holster attached to his belt.

As their marriage had gone on, seeing Eric in his uniform, with his guns, had made her more and more nervous. Always wondering when he'd turn it on her.

But tonight, she worried about what Thomas might have to face that would force him to pull his gun. Because that was the only way she knew he'd use it.

He crossed back to her, pressed a kiss to her mouth. "All the back doors are locked. Just make sure the security is all set up once I lock the front door behind me. Okay?"

"I'll be okay. We'll be okay. I promise." She managed a smile.

He definitely didn't smile back. He was going off to do dangerous work in the middle of the night. That was his job. A job she was very familiar with, because Eric had done the same.

Of course, even in the beginning of their relationship, before he'd started hitting her, she'd never minded. It had always been nice to get a little time alone. And he usually came back from an actual emergency call in a good mood.

Work made him feel important, powerful. It was when he felt weak, small and useless that he took to using his fists to make her feel the same.

Thomas stepped out the door and closed it behind him. She heard him lock it with his key. Then she made sure the security system was on.

She didn't think she'd be going back to sleep, so she settled herself on the couch and turned on the TV. She must have dozed off eventually, though, because she was jerked awake by the text message notification on her phone.

She looked at the screen, thinking the text would be from Thomas. But it was from an unknown number instead.

Count your days.

Chapter Ten

Thomas arrived at the station and found Copeland in their office. His expression was grim, but there was a light in his eyes. Because after months of nothing, and just having to *accept* that they couldn't prove Allen Scott had killed his wife, they had a glimmer of hope.

A woman was accusing Scott of battery.

It wasn't his poor dead wife, whose death had been ruled a suicide, but it was something. A chance to dig deeper once again. And Scott behind bars, as long as their victim didn't bolt.

"Deputy Clarion's with the victim at the hospital. Scott's in holding. Which one you want?"

Thomas considered either option. It all felt a little too... *close* now. Like he'd see Vi in the victim, and her ex-husband in the assaulter. He didn't like either eventuality, but he knew which one would allow him to be at least somewhat in control. "Probably best if I handle the victim."

Copeland nodded, and then got him up to speed on the police report from the deputies. They had a quick discussion about strategy, about what questions they wanted asked of both parties, and what steps they'd take after questioning.

"You going to be okay with this?" Copeland asked, eyeing Thomas like he didn't quite trust him, right before they split up.

"It's not the case." Or at least it wasn't *only* the case. "I don't like leaving Vi alone with all her stuff going on. I've got the night shift driving by the house every once in a while, but with Clarion at the hospital, they're short-staffed."

"But this can't wait," Copeland said.

"No, it can't. Which is why I'm here."

Copeland nodded as if that was good enough for him, and then they split up. Thomas drove to the hospital armed with the police report the deputies had taken, additional information from Copeland, and the usual mix of dread and anticipation.

He would not like the answers he got tonight, but answers would lead to justice. Justice for a woman like Vi, and a woman who hadn't been lucky enough to survive an awful man.

Deputy Clarion stood outside the victim's hospital room. They exchanged greetings.

"Was it your call?" Thomas asked.

Clarion nodded. "Neighbor called it in. Scott was gone by the time we got there, and she was in rough shape, but she named Scott. Gave us his address and everything."

"Good." There was more he wanted to say, like *Let's get this SOB*, but with Clarion's body cam no doubt rolling, Thomas kept it to himself.

When he entered the hospital room, after he knocked and the victim gave him the go-ahead, Christine Smith looked at him through a swollen eye. She sat in a hospital bed, her face an array of stitches, bandages and loud bruises. She had one arm in a cast, and thanks to the doctor's report, he knew she had three cracked ribs, a bruised kidney and a fractured ankle.

"Ma'am. My name is Detective Thomas Hart, and I'd like to ask you a few questions about what happened tonight, if you're up for it." She'd told the doctor and the deputy she was, but Thomas wanted to make sure.

"I've answered a lot of questions already," she said. But she clasped her hands in her lap and didn't send him away.

"I know, and I know how frustrating that can be."

"What about traumatizing?" she demanded with a snap.

"That too," he agreed, and tried not to think of what Vi would have gone through. Answering these questions, only to have the interviewer not believe her. Only to have every *right* step thwarted, all because her ex had worn a badge.

"But you still have to ask them," the woman said on a long sigh.

"I'm afraid so. And I'd like to record your answers, if you're okay with that."

She looked away from him, at the window. The curtains were closed, so it wasn't like there was anything to see beyond, but she still stared. He gave her time. Time to breathe. Time to think.

Eventually, and gingerly, she nodded. "Yeah. Whatever will end this."

He set up the recorder, then asked her about the evening, and she answered questions in surprising detail. There was a kind of determined detachment as she described how the man she'd been dating had started to beat her in a furious rage.

She didn't shed any tears, until she got to the last part.

"All I did was ask about his wife. And he just…lost it. He wanted to kill me. And I still don't know *why*."

Thomas's heart beat triple time, but he kept his voice even. His eyes steady. "Does Scott have a wife?"

"She died. And he'd mentioned it, played up the grieving widower thing." Christine swallowed. "So a few times I've asked what happened, thinking that's kind of what he wanted. To talk about it, you know?"

Thomas nodded.

"But tonight, the story didn't match what he'd told me a few dates ago. I pointed that out. I haven't had much luck with guys, so maybe I was kind of a bitch about it."

"Doesn't mean he gets to hit you, Ms. Smith."

She inhaled sharply, then winced a little. "No, it doesn't. Anyway, I was getting on him for lying to me and he just… snapped. Said he was going to kill me."

"He said that to you? In those words?"

She looked Thomas dead in the eye. Tears glimmered there, but she didn't blink, didn't look away. "He told me in those words. He told me he was going to kill me, just like he killed his wife."

For a moment, Thomas didn't say anything. He had to fight his reaction. It wasn't enough to charge Allen with murder, but it was a step toward this being a lot more than just a domestic assault case.

"Are you willing to say all this in front of a jury?"

Her jaw worked for a second, and she was clearly in pain, even if she was on some pain medication, but when she spoke, it was with conviction.

"I'm willing to scream it from the rooftops," she said

firmly, her expression grim, despite the bruises, bandages and swelling. "I want him to rot in hell."

So do I.

VI HAD THOUGHT about waiting. She'd thought about trying to wave down the cop Thomas had driving by the house intermittently.

But in the end, she'd called Laurel Delaney-Carson. If only because Rosalie was too far away. It felt safer, smarter, to call someone she knew lived close by. Someone Thomas trusted more than anyone else. Someone he'd told her to call if there was trouble.

She was considering it a leap of faith. A gesture to Thomas that...she was here to stay and fight for their lives together, even if sometimes she wanted to stay hidden away forever.

God, she hoped it was the right choice.

She opened the front door, because Laurel had called and told her she was there. The woman stepped inside, closed and locked the door behind her in quick, efficient *cop* moves. She was dressed in the same kind of drab uniform Thomas usually wore—khakis, a Bent County Sheriff's Department polo. Her hair was pulled back in a tight ponytail, and even though it was the middle of the night, she looked ready to handle anything that came her way.

Vi had to swallow down the battalion of nerves duking it out in her throat. She was in pajamas. Her hair was probably insane right now. She should have thought about her appearance, but she hadn't wanted to wake up Magnolia and...

This wasn't a *social* call. Vi breathed out. It didn't matter how she looked. It mattered that she'd received a threatening text message in the middle of the night, after Thomas had been called in to work.

When she'd called Laurel, Laurel had assured her that Thomas was fine. At the local hospital questioning a victim. So, it hadn't been some fake call. Thomas was okay.

And Vi was okay too. Maybe the text was more threatening than the usual screeds about how useless and terrible she was, and even more threatening than the voicemail he'd left a few months ago saying he couldn't wait until she was a rotting corpse. Because that had been disturbing, but vague enough.

Count your days wasn't vague. It was a countdown.

Vi let out a slow breath to steady herself. She'd done the right thing. This woman was Thomas's friend, his mentor. Even if Laurel didn't believe *Vi*, she'd at least do her due diligence for Thomas.

Unless she convinces him you're just as crazy as Eric always said.

The fear of that, no matter how hard she tried to push it away, made her stutter when she spoke. "Thank you for coming. I shouldn't have bothered you in the middle of the night. I know you've got kids and…"

"It's part of the job," Laurel said gently. "If it wasn't, Thomas would be here and handling this himself, right?"

Vi nodded. She was almost glad he wasn't. She wasn't sure what he would have done if *that* had been the message that had woken them up. She was half-afraid he would have flown to Virginia himself.

It seemed better, or at least *almost* better, to deal with someone who might not believe her.

"Besides," Laurel continued. "My husband is used to middle-of-the-night phone calls and me being called away. He's superdad at that. We've been doing this for a long time. So, don't worry about anything. You did the exact right thing. Now, can I see the text message?"

Vi nodded and pulled her phone out of her pocket. She'd had to unlock her phone to call Laurel, but she'd left the text message unread. After a short hesitation, she forced herself to open the message and hold the phone out to Laurel.

Laurel took the phone, read the screen. Her expression didn't change, except maybe her mouth got a little tighter. "Not particularly clever."

"No, not his strong suit."

She looked up at Vi. "You're sure it's your ex-husband, then?"

Vi wanted to look away. To shrug and say who really knew anything. But if Laurel told Thomas she acted that way... "I don't know who else it could be but proving it is the problem."

Laurel nodded. "No, it's not going to be easy to prove, but that doesn't mean we won't give it our best shot. We'll try to get some information on the number, to start. I want you to screenshot that message, text it to me. I'll forward it to Thomas after he's done with his current case, or you can. I know he's got a file of these from when we first got those pictures."

Vi nodded, but she didn't act right away. Maybe Thomas hadn't told Laurel everything. Maybe Laurel didn't fully understand. Even if she used *we* like they were all in this together.

She forced herself to screenshot it, forward it to Laurel's number. She'd forward it to Rosalie in the morning too.

"I'll have Thomas call the postal inspector. Maybe something about this can connect everything."

Vi tried not to pull a face. She just *hated* all this being passed around, but it had to be. It *had* to be.

Laurel didn't ask too many questions. At first Vi was relieved, but she got more and more tense about it as she started to realize it was because there was already a file. All about her and her ex-husband. Because of the pictures. Because of the postal inspector. Because of...

She stopped the negative thought spiral. Any *becauses* were due to *Eric*. And she had to remember that.

But Eric was still the crux of the problem.

"The thing is, even if you connect it to Eric, it doesn't matter. He has his whole precinct under his thumb. He's so great, so brave, his ex-wife must just be crazy. He even got his lawyer to somehow make it look like *he* filed for divorce and *I* contested it."

Laurel was quiet for a moment, nodding slowly. "All of that may be true, but if he's mixed up in this federal case about mail fraud, he's crossing lines no amount of influence can fix for him."

"Are you sure about that?" Vi asked, not certain how that question sounded to Laurel. Because to *her* ears it felt as derisive and scoffing as she felt. Which wasn't the right attitude, she knew.

But it had been *years*. Why should she believe something could change?

Because you're here. Alive and happy. In love with a great guy who's protecting you.

As it so often did, that truth and hope felt too dangerous to believe in.

Laurel studied her, like she didn't quite understand the question. "I know justice doesn't always work out, but—"

"There's no buts to that. Sometimes, no amount of doing

the right thing gets anyone justice. I did everything you're supposed to. Maybe not right away. Maybe I didn't get out when I should have, but when the abuse got to a certain point, I called the cops. I wanted to press charges. He made me out to be the villain, and *nothing* ever stuck to him. I know what cops can do."

Laurel didn't say anything right away. She didn't even look mad or pitying. There was a kind of resigned sadness to her sigh. "Fair enough. Are you worried that Thomas would do the same thing?"

For a moment, just a moment, it seemed her whole world tilted. The idea of Thomas shaping everyone's thoughts and feelings about her. That all this would just disappear, and everyone would think of her as Eric had portrayed her.

But even as the picture took shape in her imagination, she couldn't imagine Thomas doing any of it. It was still just Eric, poisoning her life here.

Because she knew better than to believe in someone wholeheartedly. She knew better than to think happily-ever-afters were real or easy. But she also knew Thomas Hart.

"No. I know he wouldn't. I just…"

"Good. I'm glad to hear it," Laurel said firmly. "Now, I don't expect you to trust the rest of us point-blank, but Thomas has been a friend of mine for well over a decade. He's my daughter Sunny's godfather. He's a great cop and a greater guy."

Vi knew all this.

"I have *never* seen him so happy as he's been the past few months. Or so protective of…anyone, and he's a pretty protective guy. He talks about your daughter like she hung the moon."

And even though Vi *knew* that last little bit, it still had tears welling in her eyes.

"I can't pretend to know what it's like to be victimized by your own husband, but…there are people in my life who I loved, who turned out to be the opposite of what I thought they were, and I know what that does. It makes it hard to trust people."

"I trust Thomas."

"Good. And I hope somewhere along the line, you learn you can trust the rest of us too. Anyone who's got Thomas's back, has yours. I can promise you that. He'll call me a busybody, but oh well. Maybe I'll just accept I am one. If you let all of us get to know you, the way Thomas would like us to, then we'd all have your backs because of *you*, not just Thomas. It's just what we do."

Vi realized this wasn't about the case so much anymore. "He told you I don't want to come to the baby shower."

"It's my brother's baby shower," Laurel said, a bit ruefully. "So, it's not like he was spilling state secrets. It was more an RSVP conversation thing. And, because I'm an *excellent* detective, I deduced that wasn't exactly his preference."

"No. It wasn't. But it's…a private matter."

Laurel's rueful smile didn't change. She didn't get offended, or at least she didn't show it if she did. She looked down at her phone. "Thomas is almost here, so I'll get out of your hair and let you guys talk. You're probably exhausted."

Which was when Vi realized Laurel hadn't brought that up just because she'd seen the opportunity. Or at least, not only. Laurel had brought it up to spend more time here. Time until Thomas got back.

Something about that had Vi saying something more vulnerable than she liked to get with veritable strangers. But, she supposed, if she loved Thomas she had to stop letting everyone he cared about be a stranger.

"It's hard. To…let people get to know you when you're still learning not to hate yourself."

Laurel took a deep, careful breath. Her smile was kind, but a little sad. "Fair enough, Vi. Fair enough."

Chapter Eleven

"It's okay."

Vi said that before Thomas had even managed to get his arms around her. But he hugged her close anyway. Tight, just to assure himself she was here, good, in one piece.

Laurel's voicemail had explained the situation and assured him everything was fine, but that didn't mean he'd been fully able to believe it.

"I don't like the timing, Vi," he muttered into her hair. Finally able to breathe again. Maybe because he'd spent his night talking to a woman who'd been beaten so badly, he just…wasn't okay.

"No, I don't either," she said, patting his back. "But it's not like he could have set up you getting called away. I think it's just a coincidence."

Thomas nodded. He finally released her, at least a little. Looked back at Laurel. "Thanks for coming."

"No thanks needed. You know that. I've got the text. I'll add it to our file, write the report. I was thinking we should pass it along to the postal inspector too, just in case it might connect to something."

Thomas nodded. "Yeah, good idea."

"I'm going to head into the station, do all that. You get some rest. We'll talk more later."

Thomas nodded. He couldn't bear to let Vi go, and he knew Laurel would give him a hard time if he said thanks again. "I'll be back in around noon. Copeland and I have a meeting with the prosecutor."

"Get some sleep in the meantime, huh?" Laurel said, then let herself out.

Thomas hugged Vi close again. He wasn't sure he'd taken a full breath from the time he listened to Laurel's voicemail until now. "I want to see the message."

He felt Vi stiffen. "Okay, but…"

He pulled back so he could read her expression. And too easily he could see those pictures. See the woman in the hospital bed as her instead of his current victim. "But what?"

She studied his face. "I just don't want you to… Well, I guess it's stupid to say I don't want you to worry."

"Maybe not stupid, but pointless."

She sighed, then nodded. She pulled her phone out, hit a few buttons and handed it to him. He read the screen.

Count your days.

He didn't lose it. God, he wanted to, but there was a sleeping baby and victimized woman in his house. "That's far more of a concrete threat than the others have been."

Vi nodded. "I know."

Before he could think of anything else to say, he heard Mags start to make noises from his room. Vi moved first, but Thomas stopped her.

"I got her."

"You've been up all night."

"So have you."

"Yes, but just sitting around. You've been working. Is everything…okay?"

Thomas almost nodded, but it wasn't really *okay*. "A woman came in, badly beaten. She ID'd the guy who did it to her, as a man Copeland and I investigated a few months ago for murder. We couldn't find enough evidence, and the death was ruled a suicide. So, this has two parts to it. We've got him on the assault, now we want to try to get him on that murder."

"Who did he kill?" she asked, like she knew.

Thomas didn't have to tell her. He could lie. He could do a lot of things, but he held her gaze. "His wife."

Vi nodded once, sharply. "Well, then I'm glad he's in jail."

"We're going to do everything we can to make sure it stays that way." He stepped into the room where Mags was fussing. She'd pulled herself up on the rail of the crib. But when she saw him, she stopped whimpering and grinned.

It eased so much of what had felt like barbed wire wrapped around his lungs. This sweet little baby, who loved him easily and without reservation, just because he'd shown up in her life.

All because Vi had been strong enough to escape an impossible situation, and she'd had enough family to help see her through. It wasn't lost on him how lucky they all were, even in the midst of what felt like a decided lack of luck.

He picked up Mags, who sleepily snuggled into his shoulder. She'd be running around like a screeching banshee in about fifteen minutes, but the first time when she woke up, she was sweet and sleepy and cuddly.

Thomas let that soothe him. Or he tried to.

Eric Carter was going to come after Vi. He had no doubts

about that. And with the text message, Thomas knew that was coming sooner rather than later.

So, he'd have to do everything to protect her and Mags. But not just physically. After tonight at the hospital, he needed Vi to understand. Not just because he was here, but because he said the words.

"I need you to know, I see this a lot. Before you came. I'm sure I'll see it more. And I may not be in that victim's seat, but I know just how much strength and courage it takes to stand up against someone who could do that to you. I know that everyone thinks it's easy because you're hurt and angry. And I know they're wrong, because anyone who would physically hurt someone is taking something away from them. Nothing about surviving this is easy, and even if I've never experienced that, I do understand it."

She kept very still. Her expression was almost startled. Before she blew out a breath.

"Then I need you to know that I called Laurel because I knew it was what you wanted. And no matter what happens because of Eric, I don't want to hurt you, Thomas."

He held out his arm, and she stepped into him. One arm holding Mags against him, one arm curled around Vi's shoulder. A trio.

A family.

He kissed her hair. "I love you, Vi."

"I love you too. And I'll...go to the baby shower."

He tried to follow her. For a moment, he didn't even know what baby shower she meant. "Oh. Well, we don't have to talk about that right now, sweetheart. I just..."

"No, I want to go. I want you to know that I want to go." She swallowed, tears swimming in her blue eyes. She swallowed audibly. "I *want* to be part of your life, Thomas."

Thomas had to go into the station for a few hours the morning of the baby shower, so Vi drove with Mags out to the ranch to catch up with everyone, and to see if Audra had any clothes suitable for a baby shower she could borrow.

Thomas had been a little…overprotective the past few days. Rightfully so, she knew. And maybe it could be frustrating not to be able to go do what she wanted, whenever she wanted. But she also didn't want to do anything that would put her or Mags in danger.

So every day was carefully planned. Monitored. When she reached the ranch, she texted Thomas that she'd arrived. Then she tried to put the worry aside and focus on an outfit for a baby shower.

Audra took her through her closet since she was the closest in size to Vi, and it was a blessed slice of normal. To try on outfits, have a trio of women weigh in on which one was the best.

In the end, she picked a cute floral skirt and her own plain T-shirt, with some of Franny's jewelry. She felt cute and casual and…well, *nervous*.

She didn't regret saying she'd go. She couldn't. It was a symbol. It was giving Thomas something when he'd already given her *so much*. It was important, and she supposed that was why she was so nervous.

This wasn't just a baby shower. It was a gesture, and she desperately wanted it to go well. She was studying herself in the mirror, Mags playing with Franny and Rosalie on Franny's bedroom floor when her phone rang.

She grabbed it, looked at the caller and tried not to blanch.

Franny must have seen it, because she got to her feet. "Vi—"

"It's the postal inspector's number." Vi tried to smile,

because hey, it wasn't *Eric*. But it was probably about him. She answered the phone, stepped out of the room, knowing everyone would look after Mags.

"Hello?"

"Hi, Ms. Reynolds. This is Postal Inspector Kay. How are you?"

"I'm…fine."

"And no doubt stressed that I called you," she replied, good-naturedly. "But I have good news. I'm really close to being able to put out a warrant for Eric Carter's arrest. But I have a few follow-up questions I'd like to ask you. Are you home?"

Vi thought her knees might have dissolved. She had to lean against the wall to stay upright. "Arrest?"

"Yes. Tampering with mail is a federal offense, hence my involvement with all this. As long as my case is airtight, he's going to do some time. So, are you home?"

"Uh, no," Vi said, her mind whirling. Federal offense. Arrest. Eric. Was this *real*? "Well, yes." Because the inspector didn't know she actually lived with Thomas. "Not where we talked initially. I'm at my cousin's ranch out by Sunrise. It's a ways from Bent," she tacked on, remembering the inspector wasn't from around here.

"I'm not too far from there. There's a coffee place just off the highway, isn't there?"

"Yes. Coffee Klatsch."

"Okay, can I meet you there in fifteen minutes or so? I just have a few questions. Won't take more than a half hour."

Vi thought about the timing. She still had two hours before the baby shower. She could do this, get it over with, and maybe know more about the actual potential of Eric being arrested. "Okay, I can do that."

"Great. See you soon."

They hung up and Vi returned to the room. Everyone looked up at her with questions in their eyes. Vi wasn't sure she had any answers. Her brain couldn't really function beyond *arrest*.

But the inspector needed some answers first. "Can you guys watch Mags while I run an errand?"

"What kind of errand?" Rosalie demanded.

"I just have to meet with the postal inspector. Answer a few more questions. Real quick at Coffee Klatsch."

"Let me come with you," Rosalie said, getting to her feet. "I have some questions for *her*."

Vi considered it. She knew Rosalie was running her own investigation. She also knew Rosalie didn't always know when to be…polite.

"I think it's best if I do this alone. She said it'll only take a half hour at most. Guys, she said she's *this* close to putting out an arrest warrant for Eric."

Rosalie and Franny exchanged a look.

"I don't want to get my hopes up, but this is huge. It's just a few questions, then I'll be back by noon to pick up Mags and head out to the baby shower. And I'll text Thomas where I'm going too."

She went over to Mags, kissed her head. "I'll be back before you guys know it." Then she hurried out before Rosalie could decide she needed to come anywhere. On her way to her car, she wrote out the text to Thomas.

Meeting the postal inspector at Coffee Klatsch to answer some questions.

Thought she'd headed back to Denver.

Apparently not.

Take Rosalie with you.

I'd like to stay in the inspector's good graces. It's just a short drive there and back to the ranch. I'll keep updating.

Okay. Love you.

She texted back her own Love you, then drove out to the coffee house. The postal inspector was already there, leaning against the trunk of her rental car.

Vi pulled into the parking space right next to her, then steeled herself to face the intimidating postal inspector.

Who thought Eric had committed a *federal offense*. That was enough to get Vi out of the car.

"Don't you look pretty." Inspector Kay said in greeting. She shaded her eyes against the sun.

Vi managed a smile, doing the same. "Oh, well, thanks. I'm going to a baby shower."

She frowned for a split second, but then smiled kindly. "Why didn't you say so? These questions can wait. I don't want to make you late."

"No, you said it'd be quick. Let's just get it over with."

The inspector seemed to think this over. "All right. Well, let's skip coffee then," she said, waving at the building. "When you received the envelope, the address was your cousin's ranch."

Which wasn't a new question at *all*. "Yes."

"I talked to the mail carrier, and he said he didn't think he'd seen an envelope that fit the description that day.

delivering mail to the Young Ranch for years."

"Well, it was in the mailbox with the rest of the mail. Thomas asked Audra about it, and that's what she said."

"Yes, that's all in the report. It's just strange, because the mailman who delivered the envelope to the police station remembered dropping it off there *and* is on security footage doing so. He's also been with the USPS for a few years, so unlikely involved."

This all felt like the very *opposite* of leads that would end in Eric being arrested.

"Does your ex-husband have any connection to Bent County? And listen, I know you've probably already thought of that, but I just want to make sure there's no tiny stone you've left unturned."

The thought absolutely *petrified* her. But she tried to think through that. Tried to focus on what the inspector was asking. "I thought long and hard before I came here last year," Vi said carefully. "If I'd thought he had even a tiny connection to Bent County, I wouldn't have ended up here."

"What about to the post office in some way? A friend who was a mailman? A case maybe he talked about with postal inspection?"

"There was a case where he worked with a postal inspector," Vi said. She only remembered because before that she hadn't even known postal inspectors were a thing. And Eric talked about what a joke of a job it was, and how useless he'd thought the guy working with him on the case was. "I don't remember details, but I know it was a long time ago. Early on in our marriage."

The inspector nodded and typed something into her

phone. "That's good. Maybe I can get a subpoena for that information. It's something to go on, anyway."

"Really?"

She nodded. "Really. We're so close. We just need one little break. One little connection, and the dominoes will start to fall. I'm sure of it."

Vi stood there, the wind blowing around them. She was dressed for a baby shower, going to meet a bunch of her boyfriend's friends and be folded into yet another area of his life.

And this might be over.

"I might have a few more for you once I get a chance to question him myself," Inspector Kay said. "I'm hoping to do that Monday afternoon. Will you be around Tuesday morning? At Detective Hart's house this time?"

It wasn't an accusation, so Vi didn't know why it felt like one. "Yes."

"Great. I'll meet you there. We'll plan for nine, but I'll call if it needs to change."

"Sure."

The inspector reached out, gave Vi's shoulder a squeeze. "We're getting to the end, Ms. Reynolds."

Vi swallowed. Hope seemed too dangerous a thing, but it was there. Flapping its wings in her chest. "I hope so."

Chapter Twelve

Thomas headed home from the station. He was running a little late, but he didn't mind showing up at these kinds of Carson and Delaney chaos get-togethers a little late. He was surprised to find Vi pulling up to his house about the same time as him. He hoped that meant her meeting went well.

"You sure look pretty," he said in greeting.

"Is it okay?" she asked, doing a little twirl.

"Of course."

"No, I mean, will it fit in?"

"Sure."

"Ugh. Men." She rolled her eyes. "Mags is asleep. I can just sit with her in the car if you want to go get ready and grab the present."

"Sure, but how'd the meeting with the inspector go?"

She scrunched up her nose. "I don't know that I really had any answers that helped, but she said she's questioning Eric Monday. She seems to think it's all leading to his arrest."

"You don't seem relieved by that?"

"I want to be, but I guess I've seen him get out of too many things to fully believe it until he's behind bars."

"That's fair."

"She wants to meet me at your house at nine on Tuesday to ask me a few more questions, but she seems to think she'll have a warrant by then."

Thomas scowled at that. "I've got court again." And it was incredibly important this time. Allen Scott's initial assault and battery trial, which could lead to reopening his wife's "suicide" case.

"That's okay. I can handle it." And she sounded like she could. Like she wanted to. Every day she seemed more...determined to see everything through. To live in spite of it. Really live, not just hide out at the ranch, or even in his house.

It would have never lasted. She wanted too much for her daughter. So he knew her growth there didn't have anything to do with him. He didn't need it to, as long as she understood that it was really something that she'd managed.

"I'm proud of you, Vi. I hope you know that."

Her mouth curved. "Well, that's sweet, but talking to some postal inspector is hardly much of anything."

"It's everything." He pulled her close, kissed her temple. "I'll be right back." He went to change and grab the present. If Mags woke up, she'd be fussy in the car and want out of her car seat, so he tried to hurry.

In under fifteen minutes, he was driving them out to Cam and Hilly's house. Thomas tried to prepare Vi for the onslaught of people—some she'd know of, some she might even recognize from high school, but mostly it was a whole horde of people who all knew who *she* was, and she didn't really know.

Cam Delaney had built a house just outside of town, and the driveway and road in front of it were filled with cars. Balloons and streamers decorated the outside of the house, and a big arrow sign directed people into the huge backyard, enclosed on all sides by pine trees and then mountains.

Thomas looked in the back seat at Magnolia, who was blinking her eyes open and yawning.

"We're here, sweets. At the party."

"Party," she repeated, smiling and kicking her legs a little.

Thomas got out of the car and moved to get Mags out of her car seat before Vi could. He unbuckled her, then pulled her out and settled her on his hip. She dropped her sleepy head to his shoulder, warm and somewhat sweaty, but it was weird how when it was a little kid, who somehow held your entire heart in her tiny, pudgy hands, that feeling was nice instead of vaguely gross.

He could hear the commotion of the party from here, so he wound his free arm around Vi's waist and led her into the back and the *fray*.

Thomas dropped off the present with Hilly, introduced her and Cam to Vi and Magnolia. He saw Laurel and Grady and their crew with Zach and Lucy and theirs, and started making his way over. They had to stop, make multiple introductions along the way.

Including to Ty and Jen Carson. Which wouldn't have been weird, because he'd literally gone on *maybe* a handful of dates with Jen almost *ten* years ago. But, as they walked away, he *felt* Vi studying him.

"Jen and Laurel look a *lot* alike," Vi said once Jen was out of earshot.

He gave her a sideways glance. "I guess."

She laughed and shook her head. "I bet you were *so* transparent."

"Hey, *she* went on the dates," he replied, leading Vi over to Laurel.

It was kind of funny, because he was just always with the same people all the time, so he forgot things that had once been surprising. Like Daisy Delaney walking among them not using her stage name here. Like the Carson and Delaney feud that used to be the talk of Bent, like how mismatched Laurel and Grady *appeared*, even though he knew they were perfect for each other.

He introduced Vi to Grady, tried not to laugh when she kept surreptitiously looking at Grady's sleeve of tattoos, and then Laurel's sunny ponytail and trim and tidy outfit, as if trying to figure out a complex math equation.

Mags was awake and alert now and demanded to be put down. She watched another group of kids from between Thomas's legs with avid eyes.

Laurel's oldest raced over, her cousin-shadow Fern not far behind.

"What's her name?" Avery demanded of Thomas, pointing at Mags. Then making a funny face at her and making Mags giggle.

"Magnolia."

"She can come play with us," she said to Thomas, then looked at Vi with assessing eyes. "I'm the *best* with babies," Avery said with all the confidence of an oldest girl. "And Fern is second best."

Thomas looked at Vi. She was studying the makeshift playground the kids were playing on. Most of the little ones were being herded by older ones.

Vi offered Avery a smile. "Well, as long as I've got the first and second best to watch after her, I guess it's okay."

Avery held out her hand, and Magnolia took it without much shyness. Then Fern offered her hand and Mags took it with her free one. Then they walked her over to the other kids.

"She's very into the whole babysitting thing right now,"

Laurel told Vi. "Which she's discovered is basically a way she can boss everyone around."

"Which is not something Avery ever tires of. I don't know where she gets it," Grady drawled, earning him a sharp look from Laurel. But it softened, because little baby Cary was tucked into his arm.

They chatted for a bit, mostly about the kids. Thomas got Vi a plate of food, then maneuvered it so Hilly started talking about nursing school to Vi. He kept an eye on the girls watching Mags and the other kids. The older girls would do a good job, but still he found himself looking over at her just as much if not more than Vi during her conversation with Hilly.

Thomas helped himself to some food, and once he'd gotten his plate full, he saw Laurel approaching him.

"Hide me so I can eat in peace," she said, standing behind him. She grabbed a plate and started to fill it. "Sunny is in a mama-only phase, and it's going to end me."

"That's what you said when Ward was doing the same thing and you survived. And then went on to have two more."

"Some friend you are," she said, taking a big bite of her hot dog.

But Thomas dutifully hid her. He glanced at Mags who was happily watching Fern with big, admiring eyes. Then he glanced at Vi, deep in conversation with Hilly, sunlight dappling her hair burnished copper.

He just couldn't take his eyes off her. Couldn't concentrate on anything else except how much he wanted this. This right here. Every day. Forever.

"Hey, what day do you have free after work this week?" he said to Laurel.

"Why?" she asked, through a mouthful of potato salad.
"I need some help."
"With what?"
"Buying a ring."
She made a noise perilously close to a squeal that had Grady looking over at her, but she waved him off and grabbed Thomas's arm. Shook it.
"Chill out," he muttered.
"Chill out? You're going to ask her to *marry* you."
"Firstly, *shh*. Secondly, maybe. It's too soon. I know it's too soon. I just… But if I had a ring, then… Well, I could be ready. Whenever. Soon. Not soon. I don't know."
"Monday Grady's helping out at the saloon so I've got the kids once I'm off work. But Tuesday I could manage it."
"Okay. Tuesday it is."

VI CONSIDERED THE whole baby shower thing a success, if only because Thomas had been in a great mood ever since. And okay, it had been a success because Mags had gotten to play with other kids. Vi had gotten to talk to Hilly about nursing and…

And maybe there was a future there. In her old plans. No, she didn't want to be a doctor anymore, but there were a million other healthcare options, and she could hardly spend the rest of her life cowering in other people's houses, hoping cooking and cleaning offered enough to offset her existence.

Maybe thirty-three was a little old to be starting completely over, but she already *had*. What was one more thing?

Monday afternoon, the postal inspector had called her and confirmed their meeting the following morning. She'd been unwilling or unable to give any updates over the phone, and it left Vi with a mix of dread and anxiety. She tried not to let any of that show, but Thomas seemed to see right through her.

He was dressed in a suit for his day in court, and studied her with concern in his eyes. "Maybe I should be here."

Vi straightened his tie for him. "Don't be ridiculous. You weren't here last time, and I handled it. Besides, if you don't go to court, doesn't that hurt the case?"

He didn't say anything to that, and she knew how important this case was to him. He hadn't given her a lot of specifics, but she knew it was the woman who'd been assaulted the night Eric had last texted her. She knew Thomas thought this was an important step toward proving the man also killed his wife.

"I'll text you right when we're done with all the details. Franny's going to take Mags out for breakfast, then maybe to the park if the weather cooperates. I'll meet them there after the meeting with the inspector. I might head out to the ranch, but I'll let you know if I do."

"Right. Well, that would be good. Going to the ranch, I mean." He smiled, but there was something *odd* about it. "I might be a little late tonight."

She stared at him, something strange and foreign in her gut. At least foreign when it came to Thomas.

She was pretty sure he was lying.

But why would he lie to her about being late? Something with the case? Maybe he just was keeping details of it away from her since it was a domestic assault.

"I have to go. Make sure it's Franny and the postal inspector at the door before you open it, okay?"

Vi nodded. He leaned in, gave her the usual kiss goodbye. Then scooped up Mags until she squealed in delight.

Usual. Because this was usual and their life and she needed to stop being paranoid. Thomas didn't *lie.* Not to her.

He put Magnolia back down, grabbed his bag, and then was off, reminding her to lock the door behind him.

Franny arrived on time as promised. Mags was babbling a mile a minute as they left. Then Vi was left in Thomas's house alone. Everything was quiet.

Too quiet. Too much space for her thoughts to whirl. Worry that Eric wriggled out of whatever he almost had pinned on him. Worry that Thomas was lying about something weird.

So, she threw herself into deep-cleaning the kitchen until her alarm went off, giving her a five-minute warning before the inspector was to arrive. She cleaned herself up a little bit, and the doorbell rang, two minutes before nine.

Vi dutifully checked her phone—where Thomas had added the security app so she could see the door camera as well. Standing on the stoop was the postal inspector, just as she was supposed to be.

Vi opened the door, greeted the inspector and managed a smile as she invited her in. But as Inspector Kay passed, Vi couldn't help but stare.

The inspector had a black eye. Oh, it was covered up with makeup, but Vi knew the telltale signs.

Inspector Kay smiled ruefully, gestured at her eye. "Occupational hazard."

Which means it had happened at work, and she *had* said she was questioning Eric. To Vi, the only logical leap was: "Did Eric do that?"

For a moment, the inspector stood totally still, looking at her with wide eyes. "What?" she said, sounding strange…guilty.

Well, the inspector *had* said that thing about *letting* Eric hit her. Maybe this was her first time suffering from a physical assault. Maybe she had the same shame coursing through her that Vi had once had.

"When you questioned him?" Vi offered, trying to sound soft and kind and understanding. All the things she wished she'd been brave enough to ask for. "Did he hit you?"

"Oh." Dianne lifted a hand to her eye, let out a weird, breathy laugh. "No. He tried to, though. In the scuffle, I got an accidental elbow to the eye from someone trying to restrain him." She shrugged it away. "It happens. But you'll be happy to know, Mr. Carter is under arrest."

"Arrest." The breath simply whooshed out of her and she thought her knees might buckle.

The inspector nodded, heading for the table where they'd had their first meeting. Vi trailed after her, trying to absorb those words.

Arrested. *Arrested.* "In Virginia?"

The inspector put a bag on the table. "I just have a few questions for you, Ms. Reynolds, and then you maybe never have to see me again." She smiled brightly at Vi, but Vi couldn't quite take her gaze off the puffiness around the woman's eye.

"But what did you arrest him for?" Vi asked, walking over to the table, but unable to get herself to sit. "How long will he be in jail? Will there be a trial? I have so many questions."

"Of course you do." The inspector gestured at the chair across from her.

Finally, Vi forced herself to sit. Breathe. Even if she didn't have all the details, it was good. It was… "Are you certain? That he's been arrested? That he's in jail?"

Inspector Kay studied her intently. "Let's focus on the questions *I* need answered first. Does the name Elgie Doyle mean anything to you?"

Vi didn't know how she was supposed to focus when the inspector wouldn't answer a very basic question, but she searched the recesses of her brain for any way that name sounded familiar. She came up empty. "No. Should it?"

The inspector tapped something on her watch, then her gaze turned to Vi. Something about it made Vi...want to run.

Don't be ridiculous and paranoid.

"Not necessarily," Inspector Kay said. "What about the name Burton Slade?"

Now *that* one... It rang some vague bells. "A friend of Eric's, right? But he moved to..." Vi trailed off. Texas. She remembered going to the little farewell party the precinct had thrown him.

For a moment, Vi couldn't catch her breath.

"It's very good of you to want to be so cooperative. It's a shame you recognize the name," the inspector said. Kind tone and smile still in place.

"A shame?"

"Yes, because now we'll have to do this the hard way." Still with that kind smile in place, Inspector Kay pulled a gun out of her bag.

And pointed it right at Vi.

Chapter Thirteen

Thomas hated defense attorneys on a *good* day, and the day Allen Scott tried to weasel out of a clear-cut domestic battery case was *not* a good day. "I hate that guy," Thomas muttered as he walked out of the courthouse for a lunch break.

"He's just doing his job," Laurel offered. The prosecutor wanted her on the stand over a previous case she'd been involved with that tied Scott to the victim.

"You won't be saying that this afternoon when you're up there and he's trying to trip you up on what can be *proven* on body cam footage."

"I sure won't," she agreed with a smile. "You know we could take a lunch and stop by the jewelry store now," Laurel said.

It was a good idea, but Thomas was distracted. His phone screen had no alerts. He didn't have any texts or messages from Vi, and considering how long he'd been in the courtroom, he should.

"Vi didn't text me what happened with the postal inspector."

"Maybe she forgot."

"Maybe, but that's not like her."

"Maybe it's bad news she doesn't want to text you. She wants to tell you in person."

"Yeah, maybe." But it still didn't feel right. He called her. The phone went to voicemail. Then he clicked the location finder. She'd been fine with him tracking her phone, as long as she got to track his. The problem was, if the phone was off or in use, no location came up.

And that was exactly what happened. "I don't like this," he grumbled. He checked the time. "I'm going to swing by my house. I'll just grab a sandwich there."

"Sure," Laurel agreed easily. "We don't have time to split, so I'll just come with if you're worried."

"Yeah. I'm going to call Franny. She was supposed to meet Vi for lu—" Before he even managed to go into his contacts, his phone rang. Sadly, it wasn't Vi.

But it *was* Franny. Maybe Vi's phone wasn't working.

"Franny?" he answered.

"Hey, Thomas. Sorry to bother you. Have you heard from Vi? She was supposed to meet me at the park at noon, and she isn't answering her phone. I could go by your house, but if she's still meeting with the postal inspector, I didn't want to barge in. She's only ten minutes late, so…"

His whole body went ice-cold. If she missed meeting up with Franny and Mags, and wasn't answering her phone, something was *wrong*. Even if it was only ten minutes.

He got in the patrol car, motioned for Laurel to do the same . "I need you to do me a favor, Franny. Just…stay put or head back to the ranch. I'll catch you up once I get to the bottom of things."

"Is something wrong?"

He wanted to lie, but there was no good lie for it. "I'm not sure. Look, I'm on it now. Can you just take Mags to the ranch and focus on taking care of her? I'll focus on finding Vi."

There was a brief pause, but he didn't have time for it. "Please, Franny. I've got to go." He hung up, prayed like hell Franny would listen, then pulled up the doorbell camera app on his phone.

He watched the footage in double time. "The inspector leaves." He checked the time stamp. "Nine fifteen. Adds up. But then there's nothing. Vi doesn't leave."

"Then she's at home," Laurel said. "We'll drive out. In the meantime, who's close by that's home that could stop in?"

"I'll call Zach and Cam." He started the engine, pulled out of the parking lot. "Their office isn't even a ten-minute drive from my place."

"If they're there and not out on a job. I'll text them. You call... Lucy. Her and Zach are still above the general store, right?"

"Yeah, but she'll have Cooper to wrangle."

"You know what? I'll send out a full Carson-Delaney family text. *Someone* will be free to go pop by and see if everything's okay."

"It could be dangerous."

"She didn't leave the house or it would have shown up on your doorbell camera. And no one besides the inspector went *in* the house, so... It's just... Maybe something happened to her phone."

And maybe something happened to her. But Laurel was right. There was no clear sign of anything...

"You know what? While I text, you call the postal inspector. Maybe see if she'll tell you about the meeting."

"Good idea." He flipped on the lights and sirens, which

would make a phone call impossible. "But we're going to get to my house first."

He drove like hell from the courthouse, and toward his house. When his phone sounded—a sign that someone was at his front door on the doorbell camera—Laurel picked up his phone.

"It's just Lucy and Cooper, ringing the bell." Laurel watched the screen and Thomas focused on the road, since he was running code. They were maybe fifteen minutes out still.

"She didn't answer," Laurel said. She kept her voice perfectly calm, but Thomas knew her well enough to know she wasn't as breezy about this whole thing as she had been.

Ten minutes speeding up to and then through Bent felt like *hours* with this worry making his muscles so tight they *ached*.

He pulled up to the house with a screech. Lucy was playing with Cooper in the yard, Mr. Marigold was standing on his side of the fence, clearly chatting with her. "Call the postal inspector," he told Laurel, already out the door and jogging up the walk to his front door.

"Thanks for trying, Lucy," he offered somewhat halfheartedly. He had his keys out and unlocked the door in record time. "You guys should go home," he called.

Maybe it was a mistake, maybe it wasn't dangerous, but it was no place for a kid.

"Vi?" he called out. Too many thoughts assaulted him. Calls he'd answered as a deputy—falls, accidental deaths, natural deaths. Always a family member who'd just… stopped responding.

But she didn't answer, and as he moved through the house, it was clear she wasn't in it. She wasn't *here*.

He forced himself to stop. Breathe. Look around. Was anything out of place?

Not really. It looked exactly like he'd left it. The kitchen was sparkling clean, but she'd no doubt stress-cleaned before the postal inspector had arrived. She'd even put the highchair away so that it looked like a kid didn't live here.

"Damn it, Vi. Where are you?" he muttered. He went through one more search, ending up right back at the front door.

Which was when he realized Vi's purse was still on the hook by the door, and when he opened the purse, her phone was in there.

Laurel came to stand in the front door. "I sent Lucy and Cooper home."

"Good."

"She didn't see anything out of the ordinary. I talked to your neighbor, and he didn't see anything either. Postal inspector's phone was off, but I left a message."

Thomas nodded. "Vi's stuff is still here," he said, pointing at the purse.

Laurel eyed it. "Well, maybe—"

"Her phone is still in it."

Laurel cursed again. "Okay. Let's look through the house. Not just big things, even the tiniest things. Kitchen's as clean as I've ever seen it."

"She cleans when she's stressed," Thomas muttered. He didn't want to go through the house again. He wanted to go around in a rage, screaming for her from the rooftops. But Laurel was right. The smart thing to do was to go over the house one more time.

"She must have cleaned before the inspector got here. Everything out here looks pristine." He took the hallway, pointed into the bathroom. He studied the sink, the shower, the towel hanging on the rack—where he'd put it this morning. "Her stuff is where it usually is. So is mine, and Magnolia's." He moved down to the bedroom. Flipped on the light. "Bed's made—that's all her. Closet is closed, just like she usually closes it." He paused, then heard something odd. And saw the curtain flutter.

"Wait." He strode over to the curtains, jerked them back. The window was open. "I didn't leave this window open." He peered out, realized it wasn't just an open window, the screen had been popped out. And carefully leaned against the side of the house.

He and Laurel swore in unison.

Thomas was about to jump out the window himself, but Laurel grabbed him. "We'll call in Copeland. Have him bring out the fingerprint kit. So go around the front. We don't want to contaminate the scene."

She had her phone out and was dialing already. "Breathe, Thomas. Breathe," she said, and then Copeland must have answered, because Laurel started barking orders. She reached out to him, squeezed his arm.

"Any idea what she's wearing?"

"No. She would have changed for the meeting with the inspector."

Laurel put her mouth back toward the receiver. "No purse. No phone. We're going to canvass the neighborhood. You get what you need to print the house, then get out here. Call the postal inspector on your way. As far as we know, she would have been the last one to see Vi."

Copeland must have agreed, because Laurel ended the phone call, then turned to Thomas. She was calm. She was in control, and it helped him remember he needed to find that calm and cool too.

Maybe it was Vi. Maybe he was terrified, but it was a case like any other.

He had to think of it that way.

VI LAY IN the back seat of the postal inspector's rental car in stillness and tried to see what she could out of the window as the inspector drove. Mostly, she just saw sky, but if she could catch a glimpse of the tops of mountains, she at least would know what direction they were driving in.

She was pretty sure they'd headed south-ish out of town. She could be wrong, because really there wasn't much south of Bent. Ranches and small towns. Sunrise, eventually.

Her wrists and ankles were zip-tied, so she knew there was no getting out of the bonds, but if she could have some idea of where she was, then she still had a chance.

Except, small towns and ranches meant plenty of places to hide.

Plenty of places to dump a body.

She blew out a breath. *We're not going to think like that*, she told herself sternly. A trick she'd learned in therapy when her thoughts spiraled to blaming herself for Eric's abuse. Usually she said it out loud, but with the postal inspector right there in the driver's seat, Vi kept all words internal.

Maybe she should have fought her. Maybe she should have taken the chance. But the inspector had given her a choice—leave with her out the bedroom window, or they could sit there and wait for Thomas to come home and she would shoot him in the head when he walked in the door.

Maybe it had been a bluff. Maybe Vi should have called it.

But she thought about his story with the dime, how he'd already narrowly escaped a gunshot wound to the head once. She just hadn't been able to take that kind of chance.

So, she'd let the zip ties be put on her wrists. The only thing Vi had bothered to ask was if the woman was really a postal inspector. Dianne had just laughed and tightened the zip ties.

Vi didn't know what that meant, really. She supposed it didn't matter.

She'd let the lady pull her through the house, into the bedroom, then the woman had opened the window and pushed her out.

Vi's ankle had rolled on impact and it ached even now, but she was well-versed in aches you had to just live through.

She was going to find a way to live through this. She had a daughter. She had a man who loved her. She had *family*, and even if she'd made a mistake in being allowed to be taken to a second location, she would fight.

Because wherever the inspector was taking her was hopefully away from Thomas and anyone else who might get caught in the crossfire.

Maybe she didn't know what the inspector wanted, or why Vi was the target, but she'd fight her like hell…as long as no one else could possibly get hurt.

She tried to keep track of time or miles or *anything* about the car ride, but in the end, she had no idea how long they drove. How far. Even when the inspector pulled the car to a stop, opened the back seat door, and then pulled Vi up and out of the car, Vi didn't know where they were.

Deep in a wooded cove. Mountains seemingly all around them, blocking out the sky. There was a dilapidated-looking cabin a few yards away.

"I don't know why you bothered to bring me all the way out here just to kill me. Thomas is going to find you." Vi was going to believe that was true. She'd been purposefully rude to his neighbor who had stopped her and Dianne, because she knew Mrs...well, whatever her name was, was a bit of a busybody and always bothering Thomas with silly neighborhood disputes.

If the neighbor didn't go running to tell him about the car and the woman with her, Vi would eat her hat. She'd only wished the inspector had put the zip ties on her ankles at that point, but the inspector had made sure it looked like she was walking around of her own volition.

The inspector didn't really say anything as she pulled Vi out of the car. She just pointed at the cabin, gave Vi a careful nudge—because too hard of one would send her toppling. "Let's go."

The inspector had her elbow and was trying to move her forward at the snail's pace required of having her ankles tied together.

Vi eyed the cabin. It looked like it had been abandoned *decades* ago.

"I'm not going in there."

"Yes, you are," the inspector said, pulling her by the elbow.

But Vi had a one-year-old. She knew all about dead weight. So she simply dropped to the ground. When the inspector just grabbed her by the wrists and began to painfully drag her across the ground, Vi bucked and wriggled and did everything she could to get the inspector off her.

The woman just grunted and fought right back, and since she had free hands and apparently impressive strength, she kept making progress toward the cabin.

Vi tried not to feel defeated, but by the time they reached the one stair up to the porch, and the inspector used two hands to painfully jerk her over it and onto the porch, Vi didn't know what she was going to accomplish trying to fight anyone, all tied up the way she was.

"On your feet." The inspector jerked her up. Vi considered just flopping back on the ground, but what did that do? Maybe if she was upright there'd be some way to kind of throw herself into the inspector. Push her in some way.

The inspector shoved the cabin door open and pulled Vi inside behind her. Immediately, Vi heard someone else. Someone already in the cabin. When her eyes adjusted to the darkness, she saw a figure sitting at the table.

"Hello, Vi."

Vi didn't say anything in response. She immediately turned and tried to escape.

Chapter Fourteen

Thomas figured the cold, empty feeling inside of him was good. It meant he wasn't freaking out. If he was tethered to his body, he might start tearing his house apart piece by damn piece. Until he found a clue.

Right now, he stood in the side yard next to Laurel, studying his open window. Copeland hadn't shown up yet, but Thomas had to believe it would be soon.

Had to.

"Look," Laurel said. "We talked to your other neighbors, watched your doorbell cam footage from front and back doors, but we didn't talk to anyone in the back. If no one facing the street saw them, if none of the cameras caught them, they had to go somewhere outside those things." Laurel pointed behind him, where his backyard backed up to neighbor's backyards.

"If she came out the side window, she could go that way, and the camera wouldn't pick it up."

Thomas was halfway across the yard before Laurel was even done talking. He talked to all his neighbors as a matter of course. A lot of the older ones had sought *him* out, with their variety of "complaints" about the neighborhood and what he could do to solve them in a law enforcement capacity.

His backyard catty-corner neighbor was one of the people who loved to complain the most. If Vi had gone through her yard in any capacity, Mrs. Harolds would know.

He was at her front door in seconds flat and had to remind himself not to bang on the door like a man determined to break it down. Just three sharp knocks.

He counted in his head, trying to keep from kicking the door open. When it finally did, Mrs. Harolds stood on the other side of her storm door.

"Oh, hello, Thomas. Well, aren't you dressed up nice? You know, I'm glad you stopped by."

"Mrs. Harolds—"

But she kept talking, opening the storm door and stepping out onto the porch as Laurel came up behind him.

"That girlfriend of yours was *very* rude to me."

Thomas thought his knees might give out. "Today? You saw Vi this morning?"

"Yes." She pointed out toward her perfectly manicured lawn and beautiful gardens. "There was a car parked in front of my mailbox when I went out to check on my roses. Then her and her friend started to get in. Well, I told them not to park in front of my mailbox, because the mailman always gets a bit prickly about it and won't deliver my mail, and I'm expecting a very important package."

Thomas nodded, trying to absorb this information. A car parked in front of Mrs. Harolds's house. There was no reason for that, except sneaking around.

"She didn't even apologize. She told me to mind my own business. Can you believe it?"

"What kind of car? Can you describe the friend?"

Mrs. Harolds frowned. "It was *very* rude."

"Yes, Mrs. Harolds," Laurel said, before Thomas could explode on the older woman. "What kind of car?"

"I took a picture of it. I know you told me that the police can't help me just because someone parks in front of my mailbox, but *I* was going to report it anyway. Hold on."

She disappeared inside and Thomas had to clench his hands into fists to keep from barging in after her.

Laurel put her hand on his shoulder. "It's a lead. It's a start. Any idea who the friend might be?"

"None. She was supposed to be meeting Franny and Mags at the park."

Mrs. Harolds reappeared with her phone and held it out to him. "Her friend was driving. So, I suppose it was her friend's car, but still. She could have said sorry. *She* knows me. The other woman doesn't. And isn't from around here, far as I can tell."

Laurel peered over his shoulder at the photo of a navy blue sedan. He couldn't make out anything going on inside the car.

"Rental car," Laurel said, pointing to the sticker on the back that indicated it was from the rental company. "I'll text the plate to Copeland. Someone can get in touch with the rental company."

Thomas nodded. "Can you describe her friend?" he asked Mrs. Harolds.

"She was dressed much nicer than Vi. You know, I don't know why young women wear those jeans. In my generation, we got dressed up if we were going anywhere. We cared about our appearance."

Thomas wanted to scream, but he kept his cool. It was the only way to get the information. "And the friend did? Was she wearing a dress?"

"No, she looked very professional. Like Laurel here," Mrs. Harolds said, pointing to Laurel's court outfit. A blazer, button-up, and modest skirt. "Dark hair, pulled back. Dark sunglasses. I thought maybe she was a cop, though I didn't recognize her."

"Okay." There were no other female cops in the department who'd be out of uniform. Could it have been one of the municipalities in Bent County? Except why would they come this way, and why wouldn't Vi *call* him?

"Thank you. You've got my number right, Mrs. Harolds? If you think of anything else, if you see that car again, can you call me? Right away."

"Well, of course. I'd like to see them punished for blocking a mailbox."

He narrowly resisted telling her he didn't give a shit about her mailbox. Probably because Laurel was pulling him away. Back through Mrs. Harolds's backyard and then his own. Copeland was just pulling up with a deputy in a county van.

"I'll show Bridgers where to get the prints from," Laurel said. She motioned for the deputy to follow her inside once he had his toolbox.

"I've got Clarion working on dealing with the rental company," Copeland said to him. "Once we know who rented it out, it'll go over the radio."

"She's with a woman. Dark hair. Blazer, skirt. No idea height or weight. No idea anything beyond that car."

"Then we'll get to the bottom of that car. Hey." Copeland studied him. "Listen, I know you want to be a part of this—"

"You aren't about to suggest I sit this out?"

"Sit out the case involving your live-in girlfriend? Me? No. Why would I do that?"

Thomas scowled at him. "I'm letting you and Laurel take

the lead as best I can. But I have to be here. I have to be part of this."

"Look. I'm going to ask this, because it has to be asked. Because Laurel's got too soft a spot for you to do it, but someone's got to. Is it possible she left of her own accord?"

Thomas wanted to be offended. He *was* offended. But he was also still numb enough to know Copeland was just doing his job.

"Even if I take myself out of this, she wouldn't leave her daughter, her cousins without a word. She just wouldn't." Speaking of cousins... "I'm going to call Rosalie while you guys process the house."

"You sure you want to bring a bunch of reckless PIs into this?"

He already had pushed in Rosalie's number and was listening to the phone ring in his ear. "Yeah, I'm sure."

Vi hadn't gotten more than one step before she fell. All on her own. Like an idiot. But panic had shot through her with such a violent surge of shock, she hadn't thought. She'd only acted.

Eric was here. Working with the inspector? How? *Why?*

"Dianne," he said, in that terrible, patient way of his. The kind she knew meant terrible things were coming. "Get her on her feet."

The inspector yanked Vi up again. "Where do you think you're going tied up like that?" She laughed, the sound full of menace, not humor.

Vi looked up at the woman, wondering how this had happened. "You said he was arrested."

"I lied." *Dianne* shrugged. "Like you should have." She shoved Vi forward, and then into a chair. Facing Eric. Who just sat there, looking calm and still as he so often did. If there was anything *off* about him, it was the faint hint of a beard growing and the fact his hair was a little long. In all their time together, he'd preferred to stay clean-shaven with a short buzz cut.

He looked at her, nothing but smug satisfaction in his expression. Just like when she'd tried to go to the police the first time, and nothing had come of it.

It lit something within her. An anger that she'd had to push down deep when she'd been with him for fear that everything would spiral out of control. An anger she'd avoided out of fear for so long.

But these past two years, she'd climbed out of fear. So anger and temper snapped inside of her like a storm.

"Well, Eric, this might be the stupidest thing you've ever done."

Some of that smug melted off his face. "What did you say?"

"You heard me."

"And I want you to repeat it. Word for word." He stood, using his height and his overmuscled, compact body to create a threat. Looming over her, the table between them.

Two responses warred within her. The old one where she said nothing, kept her eyes downcast, and prayed he stopped. *Prayed* he would just stop caring anything about her and leave her to her survival.

Then a new one, where she held his gaze, said all the reckless things cluttering up her mind, and took whatever he dished out.

"This is the stupidest—"

He lifted the table and hurled it so that it crashed into the wall, one of the legs knocking against her knee on its way.

She swallowed down the yelp of pain and she did *not* look down. "—thing you've ever done."

"You know I hate that word, Vi." Because *his* father had called him stupid. *His* father had beaten him, and she'd let that sympathy keep her for far too long in a terrible, dangerous situation. She thought she could break the cycle of abuse.

He made *sure* she thought she could, she realized in retrospect. He'd known how to use the sob story of his childhood to keep her tricked and trapped.

"I do know," Vi said. "That's why I used it." Then she squeezed her eyes shut and braced herself for the backhand. The stomach punch. Whatever horrible blow was coming.

When nothing happened, she opened her eyes. Eric was still hovering above her. *Smirking.* His hand was in a fist, reared back and ready to do damage. But for the time being, he was just watching her.

He got off on the fear. On the cowering. And she'd given him that, year after year. Always convincing herself it was self-protection.

Maybe it had been. Maybe if she'd stood up to him then, she'd be dead, and Magnolia would have never been born, and Thomas…

It was an alternate reality worse than this one. This one where he'd somehow gotten the postal inspector to *kidnap* her. She looked at Dianne. "Why are you doing this?"

Eric looked over at the woman. "You know, Dianne here is a perfect example of what a woman *should* be to the man who loves her. Loyal. Willing to go above and beyond to make her man happy." Eric reached out, ran a hand over Dianne's hair.

Like they were intimate. Like he cared. She might have even believed it if she believed he was capable.

"Once you're out of the way, we're going to get married," Dianne said, wrapping her arm around Eric's waist. She looked down at Vi like that was some kind of great injury. "If you hadn't come up with that connection to Texas, we might have let you go. But..." Dianne shrugged as if this was all Vi's fault.

The fact she'd let him make her feel at fault for so long burned like acid in her gut. "You have a new wife lined up, then. Congratulations. Enjoy hell, Dianne." She glared at Eric. "So why aren't you killing me and getting it over with?"

Eric leaned in close, some horrible mix of sneer and grin on his face. He smelled like beer and sweat and it made her want to retch.

"Do you know how long I can draw this out?" he said. "How much I can make you hurt and suffer for *weeks*? And no one. *No one* will find you. *No one* will stop me. I never would have killed you, Vi. I would have loved you and taken care of you forever, but then you left. You brought this upon yourself."

The fact he could even *pretend* he had loved her baffled her. "Do you really believe that?"

"If you'd learned how to be a better wife, I wouldn't have had to hurt you the way I did. If you'd kept it to yourself, not tried to drag my entire precinct into it, everything would have been *fine*. If you'd stayed, we could have worked things out. But you ran. So now you have to pay."

But he'd had all this time. All this space. And still, she was sitting here breathing.

"I'm going to torture you, Vi," he said, seeming to get immense physical pleasure just from saying those words. "As long as I can draw it out. We're in the middle of nowhere—thanks for the idea, by the way. I couldn't have found anywhere as isolated as Bent County if I tried."

She knew he meant it as a threat, but it sent a bolt of hope through her. She was still in Bent County. That meant she still had a chance. A hope.

Because Thomas would find a way. She knew he'd find a way. Maybe he'd be too late, and that would be horrible... He'd blame himself. He'd...

No, she had to do everything in her power to stay alive. To survive whatever Eric did. If she gave Thomas enough time... She would not be the corpse he found. She *wouldn't*.

"No one's saving you from me, Vi." Eric grabbed her by the neck, squeezed until she was struggling to suck in a breath. *"No one."*

Thomas will, she told herself. And she held on to that belief as hard as she could.

Chapter Fifteen

Thomas hung up with Rosalie. She was going to try some not strictly legal methods of determining Eric Carter's whereabouts and report back to him. He was glad to have more eyes on this, but mostly felt a sick tangle of guilt over worrying Rosalie. Over all the ways he'd failed this.

Failed.

Where the hell was she? Who was this friend? The only thing that kept him from going absolutely ballistic was that Mrs. Harolds had said the friend, the driver of the car, was a woman.

Not that women couldn't hurt people, but it wasn't Vi's ex-husband. If Rosalie came back with absolute proof Eric Carter was in Virginia and had no connection to this, maybe... Maybe it was all a misunderstanding.

He wanted to believe that more than he wanted to take his next breath.

He tried to stay out of the way of everyone processing the house. He let Laurel and Copeland make the phone calls. He focused on his notebook, writing down a list of everything he could think of that would need to be done. Then he'd go through each piece, one by one, until she was found.

She was going to be found.

Thomas wasn't sure how many hours passed of seeming *nothingness*, but eventually Copeland and Laurel came to where he'd situated himself at his kitchen table. Notepad and phone in front of him.

He kept checking it to make sure he hadn't missed a message from her.

"A few updates," Laurel said. And it was her cop-to-victim voice, so he knew it was only bad news.

"We got the identity of the person who rented the car," Copeland said. "Dianne Kay. Postal Inspector Dianne Kay."

The postal inspector was the friend? He supposed the description Mrs. Harolds gave matched, but it didn't make any sense. Why had she come back after questioning Vi? Why wouldn't she have gone to the front door? Why would she park on the opposite street? Why would Vi leave out a window to get to her?

He wanted to feel relief, but dread was the winning emotion.

"At least, she *was* a postal inspector," Laurel said. "I called her office, but I was forwarded to a different inspector who told me Dianne Kay put in her two weeks last week. Then didn't show up to work yesterday."

"But…she was working by questioning Vi this morning."

"Apparently not officially," Laurel said. "I talked to her supervisor, trying to get some information on the case she was working on and what it might have to do with leaving with Vi. He wasn't very forthcoming. We'll need warrants and to wade through all kinds of federal red tape."

"We don't have that kind of time."

"We've got an APB out on the car. They put out an emergency ping on the postal inspector's phone, but it's been turned off. I put Vicky on starting to get whatever paperwork we need to get a hold of her case information, and we'll be getting a search warrant to get the inspector's phone location history. Hopefully we find Vi before that matters, but it's good to have it rolling."

"All the deputies have a description of both Vi and Kay, and anyone not on a call is going to be on the lookout for either woman or the car. Day and night shift. It's early to call it a missing person, early to assume this is nefarious, but…"

"But we all damn well know it's nefarious." Thomas pushed out of his seat. He went to stand by the front window. The sun was setting. Most of the police officers had dissipated. Some would be running tests on what they'd found. Some would be going home.

And somewhere out there, Vi was… God, he needed her to be okay.

So he turned back to the table, his list. And as he went over it, he realized there was something they were leaving out. "What about Eric Carter?"

Laurel and Copeland exchanged a look.

"What about him?" Copeland asked.

"Where is he?" Thomas demanded.

"We're still figuring it out," Laurel said calmly. She held up her hand when he all but exploded. "We called his precinct and it's his scheduled day off. We asked them to verify his residence, but the person we talked to refused. So, we're working on getting another agency out to his residence. One we can trust. I've got Zach pulling some FBI strings."

Thomas let out a long, slow breath. FBI strings were good. And it was better this way, because Laurel was right. After everything they'd heard from Vi, they couldn't trust the precinct Eric worked for.

"If he's not there, I want his credit card records pulled immediately. And his cell phone pinged."

"We've got everything set up to do that immediately once we get word."

It was something and it was *nothing*, because it didn't find Vi. And the wheels of justice moved far too slow when people were in danger. He walked away from the table again, needing to move. Just…move. He narrowly missed stepping on a mangled little stuffed animal.

His heart just cracked in two. He picked it up off the floor. "Mags can't sleep without it," he muttered. Franny had taken Magnolia back to the ranch, and they had plenty of stuff out there to get Mags through the night. But…

Laurel held out a hand to take the stuffed animal. "I can drive it out to—"

But Thomas didn't relinquish the lamb. "No, I'll do it."

"You're going to exhaust yourself, Thomas."

He knew Laurel was worried about him. "I have to do it. I have to see… I just have to."

Laurel swallowed. He could see the emotions in her eyes, and he *hated* it. They'd worked too many cases together where the people in trouble were people they loved.

They'd never failed before. He wouldn't fail now. "I'll head out now. Keep me updated."

"Thomas…" But Laurel didn't say anything, and Thomas didn't wait around to hear what she had to say.

There was nothing *to* say. He'd overlooked something. He hadn't been observant or diligent enough, and who suffered? Not him. Vi. *Again*.

He could try to believe she'd left of her own accord. He could try to fool himself into thinking he'd deliver the lamb stuffed animal, and Vi would just be at the ranch. He wished with all his might that she was just tired of him, his overprotectiveness, and…anything. *Anything* that could make this about leaving him and not about being hurt or in danger.

He could suffer through anything else as long as she was okay. He told that to himself, to God, to whatever deities wanted to listen, as he took the long, lonely drive out to the Young Ranch.

But when he pulled up, he hadn't convinced himself of anything. He knew something was deeply wrong, Vi was in danger, and he didn't know how to *fix* it.

So what good was he?

With lead limbs, he got out of the car and trudged up to the front door, lamb in hand. The door flew open before he was even up the porch stairs.

"Is there any news?" Franny demanded.

"I'm sorry, no," Thomas managed, though his voice sounded mangled even to his own ears. "I just wanted Mags to have this tonight." He held out the lamb.

"Tata!" She squealed happily from where she'd been playing with blocks on a rug in the living room. She pulled up on the couch onto her feet and then toddled over to him. He stepped inside so she didn't try to come out. She reached up for him, for her lamb, and he handed her the stuffed animal, picked her up in one fell swoop.

It was worse than being shot.

Worse than anything he'd ever experienced. Her excitement at seeing him, the way she leaned into him, held on, happily babbled to him. When he'd failed her mother, failed *her*.

Still, he closed his eyes, held on and squeezed tight. "I'm sorry, sweets," he whispered. "But I won't stop until she's home."

Vi's throat burned from where Eric had choked her. It made every breath in and out painful.

He was good at that. Always had been. And he'd used it—those hurts and pains no one else could see, that were minor enough to suffer through, as a reminder.

No one crossed Eric Carter.

But she *had* crossed him. Maybe she hadn't been able to put him behind bars, but her *trying* had been enough that it had forced him to agree to the divorce or risk getting out who he was.

She had lived almost two years without him. She'd had a child, and since he hadn't brought Magnolia up, she was almost certain Eric didn't know about her.

That, and Thomas, and her cousins and her friends— new and old, all worked inside her to remind her that she would not fall back into the trap of thinking Eric controlled the world.

She wouldn't go down cowering. She wouldn't go down at all. She would swing and swing and swing, until Thomas found her.

And she shoved aside a niggling fear he wouldn't get here soon enough. She sat in her chair, breathed as easily as she could with the burn in her throat.

On the terrible off chance she didn't escape this, at least everyone would know she'd gone down fighting. This time, she wasn't running away.

She looked from Eric to Dianne and decided that, if nothing else, she was damn well going to get some answers.

"I still don't understand how you two connect."

"We met at a law enforcement conference in Fort Worth," Dianne said with a little smirk. "Four years ago."

Four years. Vi could only stare at Dianne for a moment, and really the smirk made it clear what she meant by four years.

She wanted to laugh, and then thought…what the hell? She let it fly, earning arrested glares from Eric *and* Dianne.

"So, you were cheating on me?" She laughed again. All his talk about love and devotion and… Wow. Just *wow.*

"Maybe if you weren't such a frail little sad sack I wouldn't have had to," Eric shot back.

"Burton introduced us. Eric and I bonded over law enforcement, because I wasn't too stupid to finish school," Dianne said.

But the barb didn't land for a number of reasons, mainly because suddenly Eric's attention was on Dianne. And it was *not* good.

"Shut the hell up," Eric said, giving her a hard shove. She stumbled back a little but caught herself on the wall. Eric followed, hulking above her while she pressed herself against the wall. "What the hell is wrong with you? Are you *stupid*? You don't give the hostage *information*, you useless waste of space."

"I'm sorry," Dianne whispered. Not so smug and happy with herself now.

But he stood there for ticking minutes, menace and violence shimmering in the air around them. Dianne looked at the ground, looked like she was trying to melt into the wall.

Finally, Eric relented. He turned away from her, grabbed a gun that had been propped up in the corner.

"I'm going to go see what I can hunt up for dinner." He dramatically waved around his giant gun. He aimed at Dianne for a moment, cocked his head.

Vi held her breath, and if she wasn't mistaken, Dianne did too.

"You better shut your mouth, Dianne. I don't want to have to hurt you again, but you've made a lot of big mistakes the past few days."

"I'm sorry, Eric."

He grunted, lowered the gun slowly. Then shrugged. "I should be able to get some deer or elk. You better be ready to butcher and cook when I get back."

"I am. I will. I've been practicing."

"You see, Vi," Eric said, turning to her. "A man provides for the woman he loves, and she makes his dinner. He provides. She supports. Why could you never learn that?"

Vi thought of all the dinners she'd made. Reheated. The lunches she'd packed. The breakfasts she'd gotten up early to make from scratch, so he didn't get mad. So he didn't hurt her.

Only now that she was out of it, with the help of Mags and therapy and Thomas and her cousins did she fully understand...

It would have never been enough. She could have been perfect in every way, and he would have found fault. Because *she* was not the problem.

He was.

Once Eric was gone, Vi studied Dianne. Could she get through to her now that Eric was openly threatening her?

Based on Dianne's frantic scrubbing of the kitchen counters, Vi didn't think so. But maybe Vi could show her the truth.

"He gave you that black eye."

Dianne ignored her, but her only chance of actual escape, at least before the police managed to track her down, was to get through to Dianne. "Do you think you can do everything right and he'll stop? Because he won't. This will be you." Vi pointed to herself with both hands, since her wrists were zip-tied together.

Dianne looked down at her haughtily. "I don't believe that. *I* know how to learn a lesson. See? I made a mistake and he didn't hit me, did he? He gave me a warning. Because he knows I can get better."

"He shoved you and held a gun pointed *at* you."

Dianne didn't say anything. Just went back to furious scrubbing.

"There's no lesson to learn. No perfection to claim. He will beat the will to live out of you, and then you'll be wishing he'd just kill you and get it over with."

Dianne whipped a furious gaze at Vi. "You're the one who's going to wind up dead."

"Maybe, but you'll only be next."

"He won't kill me. He *loves* me. And it took a lot for him to trust me after what *you'd* done to him."

"You mean, when I was busy scrubbing his counters terrified he'd come home and beat me again, and you two were apparently having an affair?"

"You don't know what you're talking about."

But Vi absolutely knew exactly what she was talking about. Now she just had to think of what she could say that might get through to Dianne. Was there anything? Was there anything anyone could have said to her to get it through her head that she didn't deserve what Eric was doing to her?

"He'll never come back, you know. That man you first met. Who charmed you. Who *you* thought was building you up, making you forget whatever failure you were mired in."

She could see it clearly now, but in the moment she'd only seen someone giving her attention.

Not someone who made sure she knew how little she deserved it. Not someone who knew just what wounds to press on. She'd spent a good amount of years thinking maybe she deserved the abuse if she could be so blind, but to see him do the same thing to someone else, to make a victim out of someone else to the point this woman was willing to hurt other people…

No, she wasn't stupid. No, it wasn't her fault. And if she got out of this, she certainly wasn't going to be worried about anyone thinking that anymore.

Chapter Sixteen

By the time Thomas had left Mags with Franny and Audra and headed back to Bent it was late. He didn't go to his house, for a lot of reasons, but the main one was being there without Vi and Magnolia might just break him. He was barely hanging on as it was.

He went to the station instead. Copeland and Laurel weren't there, but they had been texting him updates, and he knew they were hard at work. Unfortunately, most of the updates were boring, pointless and unhelpful.

They were running the prints. Talking to the hotel where the postal inspector had stayed. Waiting to hear the results of pinging the postal inspector's phone.

So Thomas spent the entire evening leaving messages, sending emails, spreading as wide a net as possible. He asked anyone he knew of with even the tiniest connections to law enforcement to see what they could do. Zach's FBI connections. Jack Hudson, the sheriff of Sunrise, who Thomas had worked with at Bent County when they'd both started out as cops and then again over the past year, when Jack's family had been in some trouble. He was friends with Zeke Daniels, who was pretty tight-lipped about his past, but Thomas knew he had something to do with some secret gang-busting group, so he messaged him too. He even reached out to his cousin's husbands who were former military, to see if they had any ideas.

He thought about driving around with some half-cocked idea that he would just *sense* where Vi was, but it was dark and he was exhausted, and while sleep would be impossible, driving around wasn't smart.

He wasn't going to magically find her like that. It required work, and investigation, and being *smart*. Everyone was working overnight on this. Everyone he trusted. The best detectives he knew.

But he had never been on *this* side of things, not like this. And suddenly he had a lot of empathy for the people in his past who hadn't followed his, at times, black-and-white view of the law and helping people.

Was this his punishment?

He shook that thought away because this wasn't about *him*. It was about Vi. Who had driven off with the postal inspector for some unknown reason. He held on to the tiniest sliver of hope that it might have been of her own volition, for a good reason that would become clear as soon as possible.

Thomas went back to his computer, focusing on Dianne Kay. But there was nothing to indicate a woman who was anything other than what she'd presented herself as. A postal inspector from Texas. And wasn't that good? That Vi was with someone who appeared to be on the up-and-up?

Except for the whole quitting her job thing and questioning Vi when she technically wasn't *on the job.*

He clicked off the monitor with more force than necessary. He needed more coffee, and probably some food. Though he didn't think he could stomach either, but he'd try.

Before he could leave his office, and still far too early for anyone to be awake, Rosalie stormed into his office. "I got some intel for you." She slapped a grainy black-and-white still from a surveillance video to his chest. "That son of a bitch isn't in Virginia."

Thomas took the picture away, stared at it, resisting the urge to crumple it. He could surmise who the *SOB* was just by the violence in Rosalie's tone. "Where was this?"

"Convenience store in Fairmont. *Friday.*"

Thomas swore. Fairmont. *Friday.* Eric Carter was in Wyoming. In Bent County. In the same town the postal inspector had stayed.

He couldn't hear much else beside the hammering beat of his heart echoing in his ears.

Vi's ex-husband was *here*. Close enough to *do* something. Maybe... Maybe the postal inspector had known that. Maybe she was helping Vi.

But Thomas couldn't find a way for that to make sense and ease this slam of terror and fury that the man who'd abused her for years was in his own county.

"Did you find out where he was staying?" Thomas demanded, skirting his desk.

"No. I tracked him to this convenience store using his alias, but as far as I've been able to tell, he hasn't used his credit cards or his alias since that gas and food purchase on Friday. I've got Quinn on it, though, and she'll call me if she finds anything else or anything new comes across."

Thomas had no doubt the way she was going about getting access to credit cards was illegal, but he didn't ask for details.

He grabbed his keys. "Let's go then."

But Rosalie stopped him, arms crossed over her chest, blue eyes wary and assessing.

"Probably best if you stay out of this one, Hart. You've got all those pesky laws to follow."

"I'd break any damn law to find her, Rosalie." Any of them. "If we take my patrol car, we can ride code all the way to Fairmont."

Rosalie paused for only a second. "All right. Let's go."

ERIC CAME BACK in a foul mood. He hadn't managed to shoot anything, which was hardly a surprise since he didn't know what the hell he was doing. Maybe he was a good shot in the realm of police work, but he'd never hunted anything a day in his life.

Oh to have the unearned confidence of a man.

Vi sat on the chair, wondering if there was anything sharp in this cabin that she could use to cut through the zip ties. She moved her hands this way and that, testing if she had the dexterity to do it. Maybe not the ones on her wrists, but she could do the ones on her ankles.

And then she could run.

Maybe it all *felt* hopeless, but she was determined to trick her brain into only seeing possibilities. *Positive thinking* in the most negative of situations. That was kind of what her therapist had taught her—though for mental spirals, not actual danger.

"Well? Why aren't you making anything for me to eat?" Eric demanded of Dianne. Who jumped up and scurried into the kitchen area.

"I can make you a sandwich."

"A *sandwich*? After the day I've had?" He advanced on her, and she pressed herself against the old, grimy countertop that he had her blocked into.

"I'm sorry," she said desperately. "I just don't know much about cooking. I can bake. I can—"

"If you take these zip ties off me, I can make dinner," Vi interrupted. Because she just…couldn't stand it. It felt like watching a movie of her old life. The fear, the desperation, but so deep in it there was no seeing the abuse and intimidation caused by a warped man—not by her own failures.

Eric turned slowly. He'd always known how to use slow in the most menacing ways. His dark, empty gaze bored into her. But he wasn't turning Dianne into an old scene out of her life anymore, so she relaxed.

For a minute.

Then he started moving toward her. With every step he took, Vi's body reacted. Freezing. Heart tripling its beat. Hands getting clammy. Fear gripping her throat and making it hard to breathe. So that she was no longer *watching* old scenes from her life. She was *feeling* them.

He moved over to her, each step a loud, violent *threat*, and she knew *something* was coming. Even if he didn't hit her right away. He liked to draw it out, to see how afraid he could make her before he snapped.

But she'd just watched him do that to Dianne. She'd just spent two years crawling out of that. So she held his gaze, and tried to hide the physical fear reactions of her body under a cold, unperturbed mask.

He leaned his face in close to hers. He smelled like cheap soap and beer. His face was twisted in fury, an expression she still saw in her nightmares. She was shaking now, no matter how hard she tried to hold herself still.

"Do you think I'm stupid?" he asked in that deceptively mild tone he'd once employed so well. The last line of control before he lost all control. She'd been on this precipice so many times—and there'd been *years* she'd thought she controlled the outcome. That if she did the right thing, he wouldn't fall over the edge and take her with him.

She'd been so very wrong.

Physically, she recoiled. Everything inside her trembled because her body knew. What would come. That there was nothing she could do about it.

But her mind also knew a thing or two she'd learned over the course of these past two years. She fought the old self-preservation instinct to look down, cower away.

She would never cower to this man again.

"Stupid?" she asked lightly, and even though her hands shook, her voice was clear and strong. "I'm banking on it."

The blow was swift, vicious. Hard in her stomach, under her rib cage. Right where it would do a considerable amount of damage. The pain shouldn't be shocking. She'd spent so many years suffering under this man's blows.

And still, she hadn't braced herself in quite the right way. The force of the blow had the chair she was sitting in toppling backward and splintering into pieces. She fell to the ground and pain shot through her shoulder blade as chair hit floor, and shoulder hit the edge of the chair back. Then the back of her skull erupted in pain as the force of impact made her head snap back onto the floor.

Then he was standing over her, a foot on either side of her hip. He kicked a part of the chair out of the way, and she couldn't stop herself from flinching. He sneered down at her. He was wavering a little bit—the blow to her head hard enough to make her vision feel off.

"I wish I could let them find your body, Vi. Because every inch of it will be bruised and bloodied once I'm done. It's a shame you're just going to disappear forever."

She didn't say anything else. She might have if so much pain wasn't throbbing through her body. The knock to her head made her dizzy and nauseous. She couldn't really concentrate on him standing over her.

She should have. She should have remembered.

He grabbed her by the hair, laughed when she howled in pain as he jerked her by the hair out of the chair and off the floor and onto her knees.

"That's better," he said.

He released her hair and she fell forward, managing to catch herself by her palms even with her wrists zip-tied.

She struggled to inhale, holding herself up on all fours. Struggled to calm herself. Struggled to blink back the tears that wanted to spill over.

He wanted her screams and her tears and her pain. He wanted her to beg him to stop. He wanted to know he had all the control, and she was nothing.

She had to find some way to not give it to him. She sucked in a breath, squeezed her eyes shut. Two tears fell onto the ground beneath her. If they fell, maybe he wouldn't see them when he looked at her face again.

She stared at the two drops of moisture, willing them to be all. And that was when she really looked at the floor, the splintered chair, and the little glimpse of something shiny.

A piece of metal lying in between a gap in the floorboards. A dime. She almost sobbed right then and there. She'd stopped believing in signs from the universe, from people she'd lost a long, long time ago.

But seeing a dime had saved Thomas. Or at least, he claimed it had. He'd told her that story about not getting shot in the head, and in this moment... She wanted to believe. Believe *everything*.

It was her own sign. She would make it through this. Someone was watching after her.

And when she looked just a few inches beyond the dime stuck in the floorboard gap, her breath caught.

There was a nail. It wasn't very big and kind of rusty. The chances of it actually cutting through the zip ties were slim to none, and it was too short to be much of a weapon.

But it was sharp, and it was something.

Chapter Seventeen

Thomas drove to Fairmont at illegal speeds, sirens screeching. But once he reached the city limits, he slowed and turned off the sirens. He didn't want to scare off anyone who might work at the convenience store, and he had a few questions for Rosalie he didn't want to have to scream over the sirens to ask.

"I don't need the illegal details, but how did you manage to track down an alias? We've been trying to get information out of his friends and family and workplace since we got those photos."

"And what did every single person you guys tried to talk to have in common? They're all *men*. Dad, brothers, SWAT team. Dude doesn't have one woman in his inner circle, and I figured there's a damn good reason for it. So I searched the precinct's employee list for a woman. I called an administrative assistant, a road officer and a woman in their crime scene squad—the only three women in their entire precinct, which is *huge* by the way. Red-flag city."

It was ingenious. The men had closed ranks around one of their own, but when there was one female victim, why wouldn't there be others?

"The road officer was no help. Guess she drank the Kool-

Aid," Rosalie continued as he pulled into the convenience store parking lot. "And the crime scene lady didn't get back to me, but the administrative assistant had a *lot* to say."

"When we find Vi, we'll send her flowers."

"Damn right," Rosalie said firmly, probably needing to hear that *when* as much as Thomas needed to say it. "The big breakthrough was she mentioned that one time Eric had submitted receipts for reimbursement after some SWAT trip, and she'd had to give one of them back and refuse repayment because the name on the receipt hadn't been his. He'd tried to claim it was an undercover name, but since the department hadn't approved an undercover name credit card, they refused to pay him back. He raised a big stink about it. Big enough that she remembered the other name."

Thomas pulled into a parking spot next to the store.

"I spent all night...very *legally* researching the alias." She flashed Thomas a smile that was half-hearted in its rebelliousness. "I got a credit card and *magically* got into his recent purchase history. I saw it was used here, and then... *very much* obtained security footage through the letter of the law, and here we are."

"Here we are. Thank God we've got someone who's not a cop on our side." He pushed the door open, but his phone trilling stopped him. It was a call from Copeland.

"What's the update?" Thomas answered by way of greeting.

"The ping of the postal inspector's phone is a dead end. She turned it off before she left Bent city limits. They'll keep trying. If she turns it back on, we'll have her."

He wasn't surprised, but he was disappointed. It was a big if. Clearly, she didn't want to be found.

"We did get some information this morning from poking

around Fairmont. Dianne Kay had a meeting with a Realtor Monday. Laurel's on her way over to meet with the woman and talk to her and see what she can find out."

"A Realtor?" Was the postal inspector just...planning on moving here? Was this a dead end, a great happenstance coincidence?

"I'm in Fairmont. Rosalie got me a lead I want to follow up on." He relayed everything Rosalie had told him in the office. "We're going to interview the convenience store employees. I need you to go to the postal inspector's hotel. See if Eric Carter was staying here. I'll forward you the security cam still and his alias."

"That's promising. I'll show it around. If we can prove that Eric Carter and the postal inspector are working together, we should be able to get a search warrant to ping his phone."

He'd probably have it turned off like the inspector, but it was something. A chance. Thomas was going to believe in every chance he could.

"Keep me posted," he said to Copeland, then hung up. Rosalie had gone ahead of him into the store when he'd have preferred it if she would have waited. Frowning, he moved for the door, but Rosalie was jogging out.

"The guy who was here apparently just got off shift. Parked around back." She was already jogging around the side of the building and Thomas followed.

There indeed was a guy getting into his car. "Al Jones," Rosalie shouted.

The man stopped, half in the car and half out. He looked at them both with lots of suspicion, but slowly got back out of the car. "Who's asking?"

"Thomas Hart. Bent County Sheriff's Department. I have a few questions I need to ask you."

Al studied him. "You aren't dressed like a cop."

Thomas pulled his badge out of his pocket. "I'm a detective. We have information that a man going by the name Jim Errin bought some stuff from the store Friday night."

He shrugged. "Lots of people do."

Rosalie held out the picture she had. "This guy."

To his credit, Al studied the picture with a furrowed brow. "Yeah, I remember him." He handed the picture back and said nothing else.

Thomas only resisted growling because Rosalie did it for him.

"Can you tell us what you remember? When he came in? What he did?" Thomas asked.

Al sighed. "Yeah, I guess. It was kinda early in the night. I start at nine and it was before ten for sure. He bought gas. Some food and a twelve-pack. I only remember because he complained about the price of beer. Told him if he didn't like it, go to a grocery store. Thought I was going to have to call the cops the way he looked at me. But then he just left."

It wasn't much, but it was something. "He have a woman with him? In the store or maybe waiting in the car?"

Al shook his head. "He was alone, but he bought enough snacks for two people or a long time."

"Anything else?" Rosalie demanded.

"He was definitely carrying, but that's about it. Made his little complaint, then left."

Carrying. Great.

"Which way did he go?"

"Hell if I know, lady."

Since Rosalie looked like she was about to start punching, Thomas intervened.

"Thanks for your cooperation." Thomas took a card out of his pocket. "You think of anything else, even if it seems small, give me a call."

Al took the card, eyed it. Then pocketed it. "Sure."

Thomas doubted anything would come of it, but every little lead got them something else. Maybe he couldn't prove Eric was with Dianne from this, but it was a step.

They walked back to his car, and he considered driving over to the hotel and see where Copeland was in interviewing people. He'd have to talk to the front desk and the housekeeping crew. Other residents. It was a big job, and he could help make it go faster.

But before he could even pull out of the parking lot, his phone rang again. The readout was Jack Hudson, the sheriff of Sunrise. His family also ran a cold case investigation business.

For a moment, Thomas was frozen with the gripping, terrible fear that if they didn't find something soon, Vi could become a cold case herself.

"Well, are you going to answer it?" Rosalie demanded.

Thomas managed to snap himself out of it, cleared his throat. "Hart," he answered, telling himself it would be good news. Good news only. Great news.

"Hart, Jack Hudson here. I got your email. I don't know if I have a lead for you, but I talked to one of my deputies this morning and I think I might. We had a run-in with a rental car out here this weekend."

Thomas tried not to get excited. He knew the postal inspector had been in Sunrise Saturday morning, because Vi had met with her at Coffee Klatsch.

Rosalie cleared her throat and gave him a pointed look. So he put the phone on speaker so they could both listen. "What kind of run-in?"

"We don't get a lot of visitors out this way, so it's notable to see a rental car at all. But we had one speeding around Saturday morning. One of my deputies pulled the driver over. She claimed not to know the speed limit. My deputy ended up letting her off with a warning. No big deal."

"And I'm guessing this was Postal Inspector Dianne Kay?"

"That's what her license said. Honestly, even with the information you sent me, I wouldn't have thought anything of it, but later that afternoon he got a call out at Fish 'N' Ammo. Some guy was arguing over ammo prices, and you know Vern. He'd die poor and out of spite rather than take someone's money he thought was disrespecting him. He refused to sell to the guy after that. The guy put up a stink. Vern called us. The same deputy who pulled over the inspector answered the call, but by that time, the guy had already left. When Vern gave a description of the car and a partial plate, though, it was the same car from the speeding woman."

Which connected Eric Carter and Dianne Kay. "Do me a favor, Jack, forward all reports and any information you've got on both calls to me, Laurel and Vicky in admin at Bent County."

"Sure thing. I'll get right on it, and I'll let you know if we see the car again, or any of the people in your email."

"Thanks, Jack. Appreciate it." Thomas hit End on the phone, everything inside of him humming with possibility. This wasn't going to be a cold case. They had a lead.

Laurel and Vicky would work on the search warrant for

Eric's phone. But it was clear, if Eric and Dianne were sharing a rental car they had *both* been in Sunrise on Saturday. Which led him to believe, Eric wasn't in Fairmont anymore. Or at least, he had somewhere to hide near Sunrise.

Thomas turned to Rosalie. "I think we should go to Sunrise."

"Get up," Eric yelled.

Vi inched forward, pretending she was trying to push up, but what she was really doing was inching her hand closer to the gap, to the nail. Once she was close enough, she pushed back onto her feet, then in a quick move, blocked by her body, swept her hand over the crack and managed to pick up the nail and palm it before standing.

It felt like nothing considering the pain she was in, but *positive thinking*. It *could* be something, in the right moment.

Once on her feet, she carefully did a shuffle turn to face Eric. Her entire head throbbed. Her shoulder was a dull ache. Her throat still hurt from where he'd choked her.

Part of her wanted to say something snarky. To just keep fighting back. But she knew eventually he would snap, and she'd be dead. For every day this dragged out, it was another day Thomas might find her.

Maybe he didn't know Eric was here, but he knew the postal inspector was the last person to see her. He had to know that. Between him and Laurel and Copeland, and Rosalie no doubt, they were going to find her.

So she had to stay alive, but that didn't mean she'd cower. She met Eric's dark, empty eyes, chin up, no matter how everything ached.

"Now that you ruined sitting for yourself, you can just

stand." He turned to Dianne. "Clean that mess up. Then bring me a sandwich." He stalked out of the room, into a hallway that must have led to a bedroom and a bathroom.

Dianne scurried over to pick up the pieces of broken chair. Vi pretended to move out of the way, when what she was really doing was trying to hide a piece of debris that might help her.

She shuffled back, taking a small splinter or two with her, and Dianne was apparently worried enough about making that sandwich that she didn't see them. Once Dianne was in the kitchen, pulling food out of bags and a cooler, Vi just kept shuffling back until she reached the wall. She leaned against it.

She breathed until she had stilled some, until her vision calmed. Everything was going to keep throbbing no doubt, so she ignored the pain.

And focused on the nail in her hand. There was no way to bend her fingers or hands to get the nail to push against the plastic of the zip ties. She did everything she could, even as the plastic bit into her skin. But it was no use.

Okay, so that doesn't work. Doesn't mean it was pointless. She looked down at the two shards of wood, then back up at Dianne. Who now had a full sandwich on a paper plate. She didn't so much as glance Vi's way as she rushed into the hallway.

Murmured voices, a shout, but Vi couldn't pay attention to it. She crouched and picked up the pieces of chair. She examined them. One was flimsy. Any kind of pressure on it and it would snap. But the other had some decent thickness to it, though it was a little sharp.

What the hell did she think she was going to do with these sad items?

Something. I'm going to come up with something.

A crash sounded from the other room. No thuds followed, so Vi assumed Eric had just thrown something, not hit Dianne. She knew the sounds all too well.

Vi straightened, just in time for Dianne to come rushing out. She kept her back to Vi, but Vi could see the woman's shoulders shake, like she was crying. Still, it was a silent cry.

Eric didn't appreciate tears.

She started putting the food away, back to Vi.

"Are you going to knock me around if I sit on the ground?"

Dianne looked over at her with a sneer. Her eye was bloody, along with the tears, and it gave Vi a full body shudder. "I guess you'll have to risk it and see."

Which didn't feel like too big a risk considering the woman was hurt and crying, and no doubt knew she would get worse if she left a mess in the kitchen and Eric reappeared.

So carefully and slowly, Vi lowered herself to the ground, using the wall behind her as a kind of balance. With the zip ties around her ankles, she could only either keep her knees up at her chin or slide them out in front of her. Carefully, so her legs would hide the chair debris, she straightened her legs and leaned against the wall. It wasn't the most comfortable sitting position, but it was better than standing.

Dianne was sniffling in the kitchen, occasionally eating the tiniest bite of food. And Vi just…didn't understand. This woman had been a professional in a law enforcement job. Maybe Vi didn't know what her childhood had been like, but on the outside she seemed like a strong, successful woman.

And she was letting Eric knock her around. Why? Why

did he just get to *do* this? What made a mean, vicious man so powerful?

It didn't make any sense. Maybe she could see why Eric had targeted her, manipulated her, but she'd been vulnerable and desperate to find something *solid*, and he'd pretended to be just that.

But this woman was none of those things. So *how*?

"Don't you want to stop this?" Vi demanded. Undeniably *angry*—not even at Dianne, but at this whole situation and that one mistake years ago had upended her entire life to bring her here. Kidnapped and injured, even after finally clawing her way out.

And now, because he'd found some new woman to manipulate and torture, she was sucked back into this hell.

But *that* woman wasn't tied up.

"You can walk right out that door. You can grab that gun and stop him. Why are you crying and *taking* it when you can get the hell out?"

Dianne stood very still, her back to Vi. And for a moment, Vi felt a surge of hope so big, so deep that tears sprang to her eyes. Maybe she could get through to Dianne. Maybe she could end this right here. Right now.

But Dianne didn't move, didn't speak, so Vi wracked her brain for the right thing to say. What would have gotten through to her if she put herself back there?

It was deflating, because she wasn't sure anything would have. She'd been so certain it was her punishment for the mistakes she'd made. It had only been saving Magnolia that had become bigger than that shame. And only after she'd gotten out did she realize none of it was her fault or her shame.

But that didn't mean she could give up on Dianne.

"I know you can do this," Vi said. "*I* did it. And it took *everything* I am." And a bigger purpose. But if she thought about Mags anymore right now, she'd just lose it. "But you're…you're in such a better position. You can take him down, Dianne. We can stop him from hurting us and other people."

"He has the bullets," she muttered. "And two more guns in there."

Which wasn't a *no*. Vi's heart was beating against her chest, almost like she'd run a marathon. "We can outsmart him," she whispered. "I know we can."

Dianne finally turned to face Vi. Her eye was bloodshot, likely from a blow. A trickle of blood came from the corner of her mouth. But Vi didn't see any kind of *fight* in her eyes.

"He loves me," Dianne said, as if under some kind of spell. "And once this is over, I won't be getting on his nerves anymore. It'll go back to the way things were. And we'll be happy. Once you're out of the way, we'll be happy."

"Is that what he told you?" Vi shook her head, and it was impossible to keep the tears in check right now. "He doesn't. He doesn't love anyone or anything, including himself. He's broken, Dianne. And if someone can save him, it's a trained professional. *Not* us."

"I have saved him, and I will again."

"No. You won't. He won't go back to the fake guy who talked you into loving him. He didn't hit me until I was married to him, did he tell you that? We dated for almost a year, and he never once laid a hand on me. Not because of *me*. Because of *him*."

Dianne rolled her eyes. Some of that fight was coming back, but only against Vi. Not for them.

"Dianne, you do not have to live like this. You are a *postal inspector*. The cops will help us. Everyone will—"

"Just shut up, or I really will knock you around. And I'd be happy to end it all." She looked at the gun in the corner, as if considering it, even though she'd said the bullets weren't in it. "Right here, right now, not drag it out. So I can get on with my real life."

Which was enough of a threat for Vi to keep her mouth shut. And she went back to thinking about her sad little weapons and what she could possibly do with them.

Legs free, she could run. Arms free, she could fight.

Someway. Somehow. Because Dianne might still be a victim of Eric.

But Vi wouldn't be.

Chapter Eighteen

Thomas screeched to a stop in front of Sunrise's Fish 'N' Ammo, little more than a shed off the highway and in the very outskirts of Sunrise proper. He beat Rosalie to the door, but only narrowly.

There was a young man behind the counter, early twenties. Thomas didn't recognize him but supposed he couldn't know *everyone* in Bent County. "Is Vern here?"

The young man looked from Thomas to Rosalie. His eyes lingered on Rosalie. Who smiled wide and bright at the kid.

"Faster the better, sweetheart," she said with a wink.

The guy blushed, then scurried out from behind the counter. "Yeah, sure." He went into the back room and when he came out, Vern, followed.

He was a short, burly man in his late seventies who'd been running this hole-in-the-wall of a shop since Thomas could remember.

"Hart," he offered gruffly. "Ma'am."

Rosalie rolled her eyes, but she didn't say anything.

"I've got a few questions about the incident you had here with a man on Saturday."

"Out-of-towner," Vern said with a sneer. "If it ain't some dumb kid, it's some out-of-towner."

Hart nodded, trying to find some deeper well of patience left inside of him. "Sheriff told me you guys had a little argument."

"That's right. He comes in here, complains to my face, then thinks I'm going to sell to him? Fat chance. He got real agitated and I figured best if I had a deputy nearby. Had Gav here call the cops." He jerked a thumb at the kid.

Gav nodded, still looking a little lovelorn in Rosalie's direction. The Fish 'N' Ammo wasn't exactly a hot spot for young people.

"He left though. He definitely wanted a fight, but something scared him off." Vern shrugged.

"When he drove away, did you see which way he went?"

"Yeah, west into town." Vern pointed out the door. "I talked to Gladys at the diner Saturday night, and she said she saw the car speed past, so I know he went that way."

That was good information. Maybe. But west of Sunrise still wasn't a *location*. Still, he thanked Vern, handed his card to the man with instructions to call if he returned or if Vern thought of anything else.

Before Thomas and Rosalie could leave and decide their next move, a bell tinkled above the door. Jack Hudson strode in. He nodded his head at Vern, approached Thomas and Rosalie. "Hart. Rosalie. Figured this'd be your first stop. When Vern told me Gladys had seen the car too, I decided to go around and talk to the business owners along the highway and see if anyone else had seen the car. We don't get a lot of traffic all the way out here, so I figured we'd get a few mentions. And I was right." He pulled out a small spiral notebook from his front pocket, flipped a few pages.

"I can give you a list of all the people I talked to, all the places that saw him, but the most important sighting was outside the library. Dahlia, our librarian, happened to be locking up to head home. The guy flew by. She said she might not have remembered or paid much mind, even with the speeding, but he made a screeching turn at 124th Street. She was worried because the Underkirchers let their kids ride bikes up and down the road since so few people drive it."

"124th. There's nothing down that road but ranches and more ranches. It doesn't even hook up to any of the main highways, does it?"

Jack shook his head. "It's a lot of space. Some of the ranches might back up to the interstate, but he'd have to drive over their land to get there. Seems unlikely, or at least I would have had a call about property damage by now."

Thomas nodded. "So he could be holed up somewhere out along there?"

"Seems possible. I don't know what other end destination would be out that way. My deputies can start searching and canvassing, but most of the houses are a way off the street, so not a lot of eyes on the road. Not sure we'll get much, unless someone thinks they got a trespasser and, again, I'd have a call by now on that."

"I'd appreciate them asking around anyway."

Jack nodded. "I'm sure you've thought of everything, but what about bringing in the K-9 unit?"

Thomas knew Jack brought it up because his fiancée was on the unit, so it didn't grate that Jack was suggesting something Thomas had already considered. "It's too big of an area, and we don't have enough information yet. This is good, but it's still not enough for the sheriff to approve it."

"You guys follow me out to the ranch, I can hook you up with Cash. Maybe the area's too big, but I'm sure he'd be willing to give it a shot with his dogs." Cash Hudson was Jack's brother who trained dogs for a number of things, including for the sheriff's department and for search and rescue.

Thomas knew it couldn't hurt. "Okay, we'll follow you out that way."

He and Rosalie got into his patrol car and started driving out to the Hudson Ranch.

He hadn't gotten far when Laurel called. He answered the phone on speaker.

"Hart."

"I just got done harassing a real estate agent and everyone in her office. She told me what Kay was looking for—land, out of the way, outbuildings preferable but didn't need to be in good shape. She didn't want to give me specifics, but I finally got a list of the addresses she'd given to Inspector Kay."

"Are any of them out by Sunrise, on 124th Street?"

Laurel was quiet for just a second. "As a matter of fact, nearly all of them. I take it you've got a lead?"

"Yeah, send me the addresses, though. They'll narrow it down." He hoped. "Any word from Copeland?"

"No, think he's still interviewing hotel employees. I'm going to apply for search warrants on these addresses, then I'll head over and give him a hand. If we don't get anything there and nothing else crops up, we'll meet you in Sunrise. Unless you want us to come out now?"

"No. But I want to know why we don't have a search warrant to ping Eric Carter's phone yet. The evidence is there. I want it done."

"On it. Talk soon." The call ended.

No doubt Eric, or his alias, had also turned off his phone,

but if they could get a ping anywhere in the Sunrise vicinity, even if it wasn't a direct hit, maybe they could narrow it down.

"That isn't a coincidence," Rosalie said, leaning forward in her seat. "It *can't* be."

"If you've got service, see if you can look up anything about the addresses she texts me."

Rosalie nodded. He followed Jack out to the Hudson Ranch, passed the main house and up to a big outbuilding that Thomas knew housed Cash's many dogs.

Cash and his wife, Carlyle, were standing outside eyeing both police cars skeptically when Jack and Thomas got out of their cars. Thomas knew all the players, because not only had he worked with all the Hudsons, but Carlyle had essentially saved Laurel's life a while back. She was the newest Delaney-Carson addition's namesake, in fact, though they called her Cary to avoid confusion.

"We've got a missing person case we're hoping you can help us with," Jack said by way of greeting.

Thomas explained the situation, doing his best to leave his personal connection and feelings out of it, but considering all the different connections, he doubted very much that Cash and Carlyle didn't *know* Vi was…his.

Cash considered the information Jack and Thomas gave him.

"I only have two dogs right now trained to do scent-specific tracking. But we can give it a shot. If you've got an idea of where you want to start, we can head out now. But we do have to get property owner approval before we do any searching. Legally, anyway."

"All three properties I want searched are up for sale. I'm working on a search warrant." But… "I don't care about legality right now. I want her found, then we can worry about the rest."

Cash nodded. "Then let's head out."

Vi HAD FIGURED that at some point Dianne and Eric would sleep and she'd be able to work on using her pathetic tools for some kind of escape chance. She was tied up. Wouldn't they think that was good enough?

Apparently not, because Dianne never left the main room. Even as the cabin had gotten pitch-black as night fell, Vi would occasionally hear Dianne do something in the kitchen, or she'd see a flash of light that was Dianne's phone screen.

Vi had used the dark time not to sleep herself—if she even could have in this uncomfortable sitting position. But she'd considered her nail, her shards of chair. She couldn't hold the nail in any way to break her bonds, but if she could somehow get the nail into the floor, sharp point upward, she could use her bodyweight to push plastic against sharp point.

She'd figured out it would take more than one puncture to get herself free of the zip tie, so it would take time. But it was possible. If she could manage to get the nail upright and sturdy.

By the time daylight started illuminating the cabin, Vi had an idea. But it'd have to wait until Dianne wasn't quite so close.

The woman in question was hard at work in the kitchen, clearly trying to put together some kind of breakfast feast for Eric.

Vi almost pointed out the futility. She was sure he would find something wrong with it, and if Dianne wanted to listen, she could predict, with dizzying accuracy, just what he'd say was wrong.

Rubbery eggs. Cold toast. Slimy bacon. It didn't matter if any of those things were true. It wasn't about *truth*. It was about power. It had taken Vi too long, and a lot of space away from Eric, to be able to learn that.

But since she *had* learned it, she went ahead and told Dianne exactly that. Why not? Dianne would have to find the bullets to do anything about it.

Besides, maybe just maybe, one of these times, she could get through to Dianne. Poke enough holes in her theory of *love* and show Dianne how wrong she was. How wrong this *all* was.

"He'll eat his fill, then throw the plate at the wall and tell you all the ways it's trash. Because it doesn't matter if you can cook or not, Dianne. It doesn't matter how hard you slaved away at it. He just wants to make you feel bad."

Dianne pretended not to hear, and marched off down the hallway, plate heaped with food in her hands.

Vi figured she had *maybe* five minutes of being alone. So she got to work. Carefully, meticulously, she balanced the nail on its head next to her on the ground.

Then, she scooted onto her knees. She took the skinniest shard of chair and carefully positioned it over the sharp point of the nail, with the nail in the center. Since the wood wasn't sturdy, it only took pushing down with her bodyweight for the nail to pierce the wood.

It wasn't as stable as she would have liked, the wood splintering a bit on impact, but it was something. If she could stabilize the wood with her knees, she now had a somewhat unmovable sharp point that would allow her to do the same thing with her zip tie that she'd just done with the splinter.

Push the zip tie against the sharp point, using her bodyweight as some kind of lever to pierce. Through the plastic. She just needed to find the right way to arrange her body so that she didn't actually impale her hands *with* the nail.

Luckily, it wasn't a long nail, so whatever damage she ended up doing to herself would likely be minimal. What was some tetanus if she managed to get freedom?

She nudged the wood under her knees, managed to get them close enough together that her own bodyweight held the wood, and thus the nail, still.

She gave one furtive look down the hall. No sound yet. No yelling. She still had time. She placed part of the plastic zip tie on top of the sharp nail, then used her bodyweight to push down.

For a moment, nothing happened, then she fell forward. She looked at the plastic and nearly laughed out loud.

It worked. It *worked*.

It didn't actually get her hands unbound yet, but there was now a tiny hole in the plastic. With enough tiny holes, the plastic would break. And her hands would be free and…

She eyed the gun on the kitchen corner. Well, she'd have to get over there with her feet still tied. She'd have to find bullets.

But it was something. Chances. Opportunities. If she was smart. If she was careful. Everything could…

There was no yelling. No crash. But Vi heard footsteps getting closer so she quickly moved back onto her butt, and hid the nail and chair shard under her legs.

Dianne returned with an empty plate and a smirk. Like she'd won some contest.

Woo-hoo, he didn't hit you this time. Congratulations.

Eric appeared just a few seconds later. His hair was wet, like maybe he'd showered. He was wearing new clothes. He was whistling as he came out of the hallway, but he stopped short when he saw Dianne put the plate in the sink.

Then move away.

Vi closed her eyes. She knew what came next.

"What the hell do you think you're doing?" Eric demanded in a cold, distant voice.

Dianne stopped on a dime, freezing with eyes wide. "I was just going to…to eat my…"

"Eat? You were going to leave this mess and *eat*?" He didn't storm over to her. He moved with a quiet kind of stealth that no doubt made him good at his job. All menacing force in the quietest of moves.

Even Vi found herself holding her breath as he advanced on Dianne, towered over her as she hunched down and looked away.

"I'm so—"

Before she could finish the word, Eric's hands were around her throat. She made terrible noises as he squeezed. She fought him. Kicked and scratched out, her eyes getting wider and wider until Vi had to look away. Squeeze her eyes shut.

"You eat when I tell you to," he said, his voice low and cold. "You clean up when you make a mess or you are *useless* to me. Do you hear me?"

But Dianne obviously said nothing, because he had his hands around her throat still. Vi didn't want to look, but it wasn't *stopping*. So she did.

"Eric, you're going to kill her," Vi said, knowing it was pointless. Knowing there was nothing to be done. He either didn't hear her or just didn't care. He just kept squeezing as Dianne's fight got jerkier and less... Just *less*.

He didn't look away. And when he finally dropped Dianne, she didn't move. She just crumpled onto the floor in a heap.

Vi was shaking, trying to breathe without making noise. But he was coming for her now, and no matter how hard she tried to hold on to her strength, her hope, her determination, fear won.

He rolled back his sleeves, looked down at her with that pleasant smile that was only ever a lie. "Now it's your turn."

Chapter Nineteen

In the end, they split the three addresses between them.

Cash took Rosalie and a dog to the one closest to Sunrise and one of Jack's deputies was going to meet them for a police presence. The online listing Rosalie had found showed that the sale was really more for the property rather than any of the buildings, though there was a barn still in good shape.

Carlyle went with Jack and a dog to the one farthest down 124th. This property had no pictures on its listing and was definitely just about the land. The description listed some "rustic" buildings that could easily be razed by someone with a "creative plan" for the acreage.

Thomas and another Hudson brother, Palmer, went to the address sort of in the middle of the other two. The thought being if the dogs on either end found something, Thomas could get to either of the other properties quickly and involve Bent County if necessary.

The property he was driving to had included a house and pictures in the listing. A little small, a lot old. Definitely not something someone would buy if they were looking to move into it in the near future.

All three listings gave Thomas hope they were on the right track. Why was the postal inspector looking at land for sale with no houses, no signs of life, if she wasn't looking for a place to hide? And if she'd found one, now Thomas would find her.

And Vi. *Please God, let me find Vi.*

Thomas drove his patrol car down the street with Palmer in the passenger seat. They'd brought a dog with them too, sitting happily in the back, but it wasn't trained for scent-specific tracking. Cash had explained the difference, but Thomas hadn't been paying much attention at that point. He'd been looking at the property listings.

In the end, he got the gist. The two with Cash and Carlyle could track Vi's specific scent. This one could only alert him to human presence, not Vi specifically.

The scent-specific dogs would search for Vi thanks to a scrunchie Rosalie had in her purse that Vi had last used, and Thomas's bag because it had been in the same house Vi had last been at.

The dog in his back seat was more search and rescue, on the scent for *any* body. Cash had warned that hits with any of the dogs were a pretty big reach considering the sheer area they had to case, but he'd also seen no reason not to try.

And with the addresses narrowing things down, Thomas hoped there was more of a chance.

"Right there," Palmer said, pointing at an entrance off the highway Thomas probably would have missed. It was covered in over brush, but they could see a green sign with the property number amid the brush. And it wasn't *totally* overgrown. Someone had driven through here recently.

Probably in an attempt to sell the place, take the pictures on the listing, etc. The photographer had certainly avoided certain parts of the property. Like the overgrown entrance, the barely-there gravel on the gravel road that would lead to the house.

He followed the road at a slower pace, watching the world around them. Mountains in the distance, and overgrown, poorly kept ranch land around them. Thomas kept an eye open for *any* thing that pointed to *people*.

But it was all so damn abandoned. He thought something in the distance was maybe the house, but in the end, it had just been a pile of trash. A rusted-out car, old appliances, rusty ranch equipment that had no doubt been left to the elements at least a decade ago, if all the overgrowth obscuring half the trash was anything to go by.

And still the gravel road went on, the house not coming into view until they'd been driving a good ten minutes. It felt like the deadest of dead ends, but Thomas didn't say that. They had to check into every possibility. That was why he was lucky to have so many people helping. All over Bent County, people were working to find Vi.

He tried to have that be the central anchor of faith he held on to. Because he'd worked a lot of hopeless cases and found hope somewhere along the way. He'd done what felt impossible, time and time again, so why shouldn't he believe the same was possible *here*? When it mattered to him most.

He couldn't give up hope on Vi.

He stopped his car in front of the house and got out. Palmer got out on his side, then let the dog out. He gave the dog whatever orders it needed, and the dog got to work.

Though the *work* looked a lot like running around.

Thomas moved for the house, hand on the butt of his gun in its holster on his hip. He did a quick perimeter check, then carefully walked up one of the porches. He tried to look in windows, but most were grimy or covered with curtains.

The knob had one of those Realtor lockboxes on it. He could get the bolt cutters out of his trunk and take care of it. Maybe he would, but... He looked out at the dog, who sniffed the porches, and different trees. But everything seemed heavily deserted, and even the dog didn't alert to *any* sign of human life.

Thomas went to the back door, jiggled the knob there, then listened with his ear on the door. But he heard a whole lot of nothing.

Palmer came to stand at the bottom of the stairs of the porch Thomas stood on. He gestured at the dog, bounding through the tall grass of the side yard.

"He's not coming up with anything," Palmer said. "Except squirrels. I can send him out into the woods, but..."

"Seems like a waste of time," Thomas finished for him.

Palmer nodded. "If someone had been around here in the past few days, even if they hadn't been in the house, the dog should come up with something." He shoved his hands into his pockets. "I can have the dog trail the car back up to the highway, see if he sniffs anything along the road. I doubt he'll come up with anything, but you'll feel better if we cover every base."

Thomas blew out a breath. It was the death of any case. Focusing so much on tiny details you missed the big picture—or being so obsessed with the big picture, you missed the details. You had to find a middle ground, and Palmer's idea was probably it.

"All right."

Palmer called the dog, gave him some more orders as Thomas climbed in the driver's seat.

"You don't have to drive slow enough for him to keep up, just slow enough he can keep us in sight," Palmer said as he took his seat. Thomas nodded and Palmer rolled down the window and Thomas drove.

Impatience bit at him. Hopefully the other two groups were having better luck, but what if they weren't? They were reaching a second night of her being gone. Every minute was a chance something bad could happen to her, and he was driving around damn dead ends.

Not dead ends. Lead after tiny lead. But there was a war inside him. Between a detective who knew what to do, and a man desperate to save the woman he loved.

They were not compatible.

About halfway back up the road, Thomas's phone started pinging, and he realized they'd been out of cell range. He steered with one hand, pulled his phone out of his pocket with the other. He had texts and voice messages coming in. He started with the messages. The first one was from Jack.

"We've got something," Jack said. "We haven't even let the dog out because there's a run-down cabin with a car out front. The rental car."

Thomas didn't even bother to listen to the rest. He just tossed his phone down, slammed on the brakes.

"Get the dog," he ordered Palmer, who was already halfway out the door. When Palmer got back in the car with the dog, Thomas put both hands on the wheel and hit the gas pedal. Hard.

VI'S KEEP-A-STIFF-UPPER-LIP MANTRA was slowly fading. Because she was almost certain Dianne was dead. *Dead.* Eric had just strangled her like she was *nothing*, and it left Vi feeling…alone or less protected. Even though Dianne had been working against her, she'd been a hope. She'd been a distraction to Eric. She'd been *something*.

Now it was just Vi and her ex-husband. Who'd just *killed* someone. Someone he thought he loved. Or had thought loved him. Vi didn't even know anymore. She just knew she had to get out of here.

"I thought you were going to draw this out, not kill me," Vi managed to say, but her voice shook. And Eric grinned. It made her want to throw up.

"I don't think she's dead." He looked back at Dianne's lifeless body. Shrugged. "Or she is. But you're right. I've got plans for you before I kill you." His eyes moved over her whole body, until death seemed a better alternative than what she had a horrible feeling he was thinking about.

He put his hand on his belt, laughed when she followed the move with her eyes, no doubt fear and terror evident on every last inch of her face.

"Oh, come on, Vi. You always liked it."

Vi had to breathe through the terror, the utter panic. How would she fight him off? Kicking and fighting hadn't worked for Dianne, and she'd had all her limbs free.

What was she going to—

The silence in the room was interrupted by something outside. A kind of... A dog was barking outside. Vi held her breath. *Please. Please. Please.*

"What the hell is that?" he muttered. "No one should be around here for miles." He moved back into the kitchen, with absolutely no regard for Dianne's body on the floor. He grabbed his gun, then disappeared into the hallway. Probably getting those bullets Dianne had mentioned were in the bedroom.

He returned, loading the gun as he walked. He didn't even look at Vi. Just went to the front door and disappeared outside.

Vi wanted the dog barking to be some kind of sign, some kind of *help*...well, as long as Eric didn't end up shooting the help. But she also knew it didn't matter what happened out there. On the chance Eric came back and the dog barking meant nothing, she had to be free.

She got her tiny board from under her legs and positioned it under her knees again. She realized she was crying when the tears fell off her cheeks and landed with a *plop* on the wood.

She ignored it all and got to work. Pushing the plastic of the zip tie against the sharp tip of the nail over and over again, as many times as she could, making as many holes as she could.

Maybe he'd come in and catch her. She didn't care. Dianne still hadn't so much as moved or made a sound. God, she had to be dead.

It wasn't going to be Vi. She wouldn't let it be her. She wouldn't let herself be a victim for one more second. She wouldn't abandon her child. She wouldn't lose a future with Thomas. A future for *herself.*

But the door flew open. Vi scrambled to hide her lone hope for escape.

"Someone let their damn dogs run loose," Eric was grumbling. "Stupid country hicks." He kicked the door shut with his leg. He marched back to the kitchen, without even looking at Vi, so she was able to keep subtly moving her board under her legs.

Eric leaned the gun in the corner, then reached down and grabbed Dianne's lifeless body.

He dragged her body over the floor. She was nothing but limp limbs. Vi wanted to look away, but something kept her glued to the morbid sight.

He shoved the body against the door. A human block. "There. Let anyone get past *that*," he said, oh-so-pleased with himself.

But Vi could only stare at Dianne. Was she hallucinating or was there still the faint rise and fall of Dianne's chest?

"Now you. You can't be anywhere near these windows until I know for sure no one's lurking around out there."

Vi tried to think clearly as he came for her. This was better than what he'd been planning just a few minutes ago. She hoped.

He grabbed around the zip tie on her ankles and began to drag her. The plastic dug through her pants and into her skin. She tried to hold back the whimper and the sting of pain, the rough scrape of floor against her back, the bruised shoulder blade from yesterday.

But she *did* whimper, and he laughed and laughed all the way to a door in the kitchen. He opened it with another loud slam. Inside the dim closet was an array of shelves and some random kitchen items. A broom, a mousetrap, some canned goods. It was some kind of pantry.

He'd dragged her as far as he could from her feet, but she still wasn't fully in the pantry. So he started using the boot of his heel to push her body into the pantry. Then he kicked her once, luckily on a more padded part of her leg so it didn't hurt as much as he'd probably like. But she got the hint. She pulled her leg in so that she was completely in the pantry.

"Sit tight. We'll have fun later." Then he slammed the door. The closet was completely and utterly dark. She couldn't see. She couldn't do anything to free her legs. The doorknob jiggled, so he must be doing something to lock her in here.

But she had put a lot of holes in the zip ties around her wrist. If she could find something in the closet to hook around the tie and then use her bodyweight to pull and put enough force on it, it might break where she'd weakened it.

And then her hands would be free. Which wasn't *much*, but if Eric left that gun loaded, and in the kitchen, just a few steps from this pantry door...all she had to do was get out, grab the gun, shoot.

But none of it mattered unless she broke these zip ties, so she set out to do just that.

Chapter Twenty

Thomas arrived at the address Jack and Carlyle had originally taken to search. It was a lot like the one he'd just been at. A kind of overgrown entrance, and Thomas really would have missed this one if not for Jack's patrol car parked out front, half in the ditch since there was no shoulder along the road here. Jack and Carlyle were standing in the ditch.

Thomas pulled up behind him and was already getting out of the car even *as* he pushed it into Park.

Jack wasted no time to explain the situation.

"Like I said in the message, we got here and did a quick canvass. The rental car that my deputy pulled over this weekend was parked behind the… Well, it's kind to call it a house anymore. After I left you that message, we let the dog out, just to see if she'd get a hit for Vi specifically. The dog alerted that she smelled Vi with a bark."

Thomas didn't like that. A bark could alert those inside of police presence, especially someone like Eric who *was* police, and could have experience with K-9s and how they worked.

"We had a visual on the door, but kept out of sight," Jack continued. "A man fitting Eric Carter's description came out. He was carrying a gun—semiautomatic. He didn't see us or the dog, as we'd called her back. He scanned the yard, then went back inside. I don't think he suspects police, but you never know."

Thomas was already itching to move, but Jack was still talking.

"We've called Sunrise and Bent County for backup. Sunrise should be here in ten minutes, tops. Bent might be a few more with the regional SWAT team."

Thomas shook his head. "No SWAT."

"This is, essentially, a hostage situation," Jack said pointedly. Like Thomas might not have the most objective handle on the situation.

And he didn't, but... "Yeah, and I know how to handle a hostage situation."

"But maybe you shouldn't handle it in this case," Jack said.

Thomas looked from Jack, to Palmer, to Carlyle. He'd worked in some capacity with each of them over the past few years. When he and Jack had been deputies at Bent County. Then with Hudson Sibling Solutions, their cold case investigative business, and then over the past year with dangerous situations that had cropped up with their family.

And not *once* had they backed off when people they cared about were in trouble.

So Thomas didn't even bother to tell Jack he was wrong. He just kept talking, like Jack had never voiced an objection. "We have a volatile criminal who is trained SWAT—hence why I don't want them going in there. He knows their moves, the training. It isn't safe," Thomas said. "We have a postal inspector we don't know much about likely in there unless they have a second vehicle. Seems unlikely. She's *also* trained law enforcement, though, and we have to keep that in mind. Likely also inside we have the..." He couldn't use the word *victim*. "...kidnapped subject, Vi Reynolds, who at the very most, knows how to shoot a gun because her cousin taught her how."

Thomas tried to hold on to that thought. Vi had learned how to protect herself some, so there was hope. He had to hold on to hope.

"You need to draw the bad guys out," Carlyle said. She held the dog by the collar, but her gaze was on the entrance with a frown.

"That would be ideal, but we have to make sure they come out of their own accord. And that they leave Vi safely out of range."

"I have an idea," Jack said. "This happened on a case a while back. A car fire was used as a distraction to draw people out. It worked pretty well then. So, what if we set a fire in their car? Maybe they'll come out to try and stop it or get anything out of the car they might have left in there. If they're concerned enough about the property, they might leave Vi in the house."

"Destruction of property? That doesn't sound like you, brother," Palmer said, at almost the same time Carlyle rubbed her hands together and said, "Ooh, I'll do it!"

"*Can* you do it?" Jack asked.

"Of course," Carlyle said with a shrug. "I'll need five minutes. Tops."

"All right," Thomas said. Maybe it wasn't the best plan, but it was a plan. Better than letting SWAT take a crack at it. "Jack, do you know anything about the property?"

"Not really any more than the listing told us."

Thomas nodded. "We'll need to surround the house best

we can before Carlyle starts the distraction. At the very least cover any exit points."

"I can follow this fence on the other side down the property line, past the house a ways, then jump the fence and come in from the rear," Jack said, gesturing at the dilapidated line of wooden fence along that marked the edge of the property.

"Okay, I'll find some cover and try to get eyes on the front…"

A car crested the rise. A Bent County patrol car. And not far behind it, a Sunrise one. Both cars parked behind Thomas's, then got out. Bent County was Laurel and Copeland. Sunrise was a deputy by the name of Clinton.

"We were already on the way when we heard Jack's call go out over the radio," Laurel said as she approached. "What's the situation, the plan?" she asked and looked right at him. She didn't suggest he might not be involved, or someone else might take over.

It gave Thomas the slightest amount of relief that he wasn't doing the wrong thing by refusing to step aside.

Thomas filled them all in. Laid out the plan. They'd all spread out around the house, out of sight as much as possible at first. As more police came, they could fill in gaps. Once they had a good presence, Carlyle would start the distraction.

Ideally, it was that easy. Eric and Dianne emerged to stop the fire and were instead immediately arrested.

When another car came up, Carlyle scooted closer to the entrance. "Uh-oh, that's Cash. I better get in there before he tries to stop me. I'll draw it out. Someone signal me when you're ready for the blaze." Before anyone could agree or argue with her, she jogged off, through the entrance.

Cash pulled up behind the Sunrise patrol car. He got out and walked over with a scowl. Rosalie hurrying up behind him.

"Where exactly is my wife?" Cash demanded, like he already knew.

Palmer and Jack exchanged looks and then rocked back on their heels. "Well…"

"Setting up a distraction," Thomas supplied.

"She's going to be the death of me," Cash muttered.

"You're the one who fell in love with her," Palmer returned.

Cash only grunted. "I'm going to load up the dogs to get them out of the way, unless you think you'll need them?"

Thomas shook his head. "No, I don't think so. Best to handle this from long range."

Cash nodded, then whistled for the dog that had been with Carlyle, and let the one in Thomas's car out. So Thomas focused on the task at hand.

He had a small group of trained law enforcement. They could do this. "We spread out and surround the house. We surround, then approach, hoping the distraction lures Eric Carter and Dianne Kay out. As more cops get here, we add them to the mix. Eric Carter is our number one target. Dianne Kay is an accomplice." Thomas turned to the Sunrise deputy. "Make sure you know who's who."

"I've read the descriptions of everyone."

Thomas nodded. "Rosalie…" She wasn't going to like this. "I need someone to stay here and—"

"Bite me, Hart," she said. "I've got a gun I'm licensed to use, and like hell I'm going to stay here when you've got two civilians who can."

"I'm not exactly a civilian," Palmer said with a frown.

Then sighed when that earned him quite a few sharp looks. "Fine, I'll stay here and coordinate. Make sure any new officers know the players and descriptions, then send them out to plug holes."

Thomas nodded, then looked around. A decent police presence. A lead. More officers on their way.

Vi wasn't spending another night out there.

VI MANAGED TO hook the zip tie around her wrists on the doorknob. She carefully pulled down. She couldn't position the weaker part of the plastic exactly where she wanted it, but there was no other option that she could find here in the dark.

So, she pulled. Then leaned forward so most of her bodyweight was pulling against the plastic. The bonds bit against her skin, but she was so scared and desperate, she barely even noticed the pain.

She heard a creak, like the wood of the door splintered, and she was about to scramble up so she didn't break the damn knob off, but she heard a *snap*.

And her hands fell apart.

Apart. For a singular, shocking moment she just stood stock-still and *breathed*. Then slowly she lifted her hands up, moved her arms apart.

She'd *done* it.

She wanted to crumple to the ground and sob, but this was hardly a war won. This was one tiny battle and there were quite a few to go. She inhaled deeply, let it out and tried to decide what to do now.

Her ankles were still tied, and she didn't know how to change that without something sharp enough to cut the plastic. There might be something that sharp in this pantry, but she'd already felt around on the floor and shelves and hadn't found anything here in the dark.

She could shuffle a little with her ankles tied, but she could hardly attack or run. But if someone was out there... She didn't know where Dianne had brought her except out of town. South out of town. Would dogs really just be running around without owners? Didn't that mean there had to be neighbors or something?

Or someone coming to find her. She sat with that feeling, the horrible, overwhelming tide of hope. But if she let it infiltrate, she'd just wait. Wait for help, wait on hope, and what if it wasn't anybody?

She couldn't hope. She had to fight.

She reached out, slid her hands along the wall in front of her until she found the doorknob again. She tested it. It was locked, of course, but she could maybe fling herself at the door enough times to break it open based on the way the door had splintered when she'd used the knob, but that would make too much noise, draw too much attention.

Unless Eric was outside the cabin searching for people snooping around... Could she take that chance?

She pressed her ear against the door and listened. For a door to open, for footsteps on the porch stairs. For anything.

Just when she was about convinced that he'd left, because the house was just too still and silent, she heard the distinct sound of a shotgun being pumped.

She knew that sound, because he'd once done it a few times in front of her to scare her.

So he was still inside. She was stuck here until she heard him leave. He would leave, wouldn't he? Or was he just going to sit around with a loaded gun and wait?

It didn't matter. She couldn't worry either way. She had

to set herself up for every chance, every possibility of survival. She touched the doorknob, trying to discern what kind of lock held it closed.

She could detect the tiny hole in the middle of the knob, like it was one of those Thomas had in his house where you only had to stick the little key—which was just a straight piece of metal—into the hole and then get it to catch on the mechanism inside, turn and it would unlock.

She put everything out of her mind except moving around the pantry, painstakingly slowly with her little shuffle, running her hands over every shelf. She felt cans, boxes, bags. Her fingers drifted over what were no doubt dead bugs, among other unpleasant things she wouldn't let herself think about.

God only knew how long it took. It could have been minutes or hours—she had no sense of time in the dark. In her focus.

She inhaled sharply as a slice of pain went through her finger. Damn it. She'd given herself a splinter. She couldn't *see* it, but she could feel a little sliver of wood in her finger. Of course that pain had nothing on what Eric could inflict, but it… It gave her an idea.

Could she find a splinter of wood small enough but strong enough to shove it into the keyhole of the door and undo the lock mechanism?

She carefully moved her fingers back over the wood shelf until she thought she was at the place she'd gotten a splinter. She felt around with her nails, trying to find a loose place in the wood that she could peel back and break off a chunk.

She pulled a piece off, shuffled over to the door, realized immediately it was too short and too flimsy to get the job done. So the next time she did it, she broke off multiple pieces, trying to make them thicker, sturdier, longer.

She didn't let herself think beyond that. She ignored the splinters she was getting, the pain, the fatigue. She didn't even listen for Eric. Nothing mattered right now except finding a way to unlock that door.

She was shaking by the time she got to a piece she thought might work. She was dizzy, even in the dark. No doubt because she hadn't eaten or slept, *and* she'd been knocked around. She probably didn't have much left in her if she didn't get out of this soon.

She bit down on her lip, hard, to focus. She worked tediously to get the piece of wood splinter in the keyhole, to find the right place. It took multiple tries, nearly sobbing in frustration and giving up and breaking all the sticks into a bunch of tiny pieces.

But she thought of Magnolia, and her cousins, and the possibility that Thomas was out there even now trying to save her, and she gave it another try.

Then another.

And another. Until finally it *felt* like something gave inside the knob.

She was shaking again, and nothing seemed to stop it. She worked hard to give the knob a careful test, just to see if it would turn.

It turned completely. She didn't push it open yet, though, and carefully let it go. She blew out a shaky breath, then moved back to the shelves. She grabbed the two heaviest cans she could find. Her shaking made them hard to hold, but if she could use them as weapons, she would.

She went back to the door, sucked in a steadying breath. She tucked one of the cans underneath her armpit, leaving one free to open the door. But before she could even reach out to feel for the knob, a gunshot exploded outside the door.

Far, far too close.

Chapter Twenty-One

The flames were jumping from the car's hood. Dark smoke billowed upward. There was absolutely no movement from the house.

Thomas waited, hidden behind a pole that had maybe once been some kind of security light for the property. It undoubtedly no longer worked, but it was big and bulky enough to hide him from view of the house.

Unfortunately, as time ticked by, he was coming to the conclusion that the distraction hadn't worked.

He should wait, he knew. He was by far the closest to the house—everyone else having to spread out farther to remain hidden. He should reconvene. Replan.

But damn it, the sun was starting to set and he was done with this.

He wasn't waiting any longer. He was moving in. It was an impulsive decision, but not a bad one. Not fully, anyway. And he wasn't so reckless as to not take a minute to text Laurel what he was doing and instruct her to redistribute everyone to support him.

He didn't wait for her response. He knew she wouldn't like it. He just started to move forward. Gun drawn, trying to stay low. He kept the burning car between him and the house as long as he could.

Once he'd reached that point, he sucked in a breath and crept into the open. Anyone inside the house could see him now if they were looking out the windows, but the windows were covered in curtains.

Thomas watched them as he approached, looking for any sign of movement or life—a warning that he'd need to get down or run.

But the house seemed perfectly, utterly, *deathly* still.

He carefully moved up the front steps, trying to avoid rotting wood and places that would creak. It wasn't as quiet as he had hoped, but no one stormed out, and nothing seemed to be going on inside.

His heart sank for a moment. What if no one was inside? What if they'd gotten another car and gone to a second location? What if—

He didn't let his mind finish that what-if. He reached out for the front door and turned the handle. It gave, surprisingly, but when he tried to ease the door open, the door didn't budge. Something was blocking it.

He swore inwardly, then moved back off the porch. But he didn't go back to his hiding place like Laurel would have no doubt preferred. Instead, he began creeping around the side of the house.

There were no windows here, so he wasn't quite as worried about being caught. He paused as he reached the back of the house, being careful to come around the corner without stepping into an ambush.

But the backyard—overgrown and full of trash—seemed to be empty. Wind rustled in the towering grasses. Thomas could make out a back porch and a back door. The porch was covered in wild vines, but the door itself looked cleared, like it had been used recently.

Thomas took a breath, shoved every *emotion* out of his mind, and focused on what needed to be done. Finding out who or what was inside that house.

Using as much cover as possible, he moved around the porch to a place that looked like he could enter. He studied the back door again—it had a small window, but it was covered by a curtain, so Thomas couldn't see inside. As silently as possible, he moved up the warped, splintered stairs of the porch to the door.

He was about to reach out, test the knob, when something flashed in the sunlight right at his foot.

A dime.

It seemed like the world around him went completely silent. And he did what he'd done all those years ago when he'd narrowly avoided a head shot.

Slower, this time, with more awareness, he bent down to pick it up—and almost immediately the glass of the door exploded. A bullet slammed into the post of the porch.

Just behind where his head had once been.

Thomas looked at the door. He couldn't shoot back. He didn't know what was going on inside. Where Vi might be if she was in there. And he could hardly stay where he was, because if the shooter had shot out through the glass, they were only going to keep shooting.

As if to prove his point, another shot went off echoing in the yard around them.

"Come any closer and she's dead," a man's voice called out. "You shoot, she's dead."

"Drop your weapon," Thomas called out, ignoring the ice

that centered in his gut. He could hear everyone else coming closer. "You're surrounded. Drop your weapon and—"

The man's gun went off again, and this time Thomas knew he hadn't been quite so lucky. Pain sliced into his left arm and knocked him back a step or two, but he didn't let it knock him down.

He gritted his teeth, and against everyone yelling at him not to, charged forward.

AFTER THE SECOND SHOT, Vi figured it was now or never. Eric had to be shooting at *something*, and maybe it was dangerous to jump into a situation without being able to see what was going on, but Vi couldn't take it anymore.

She flung the pantry door open, hoping it would cause enough of a surprise that she could do *something*.

And since Eric was essentially *right there*, the barrel of his gun poised in the broken glass of the back door's window, she *could* in fact, do something.

She bashed the heavy can of food as hard as she could against his head—it would have been the back of his head, but he'd turned at the sound of the pantry door opening and it hit him right in the temple.

He crumpled, the gun clattering on top of him and then the can too, when she dropped it. For a second, she just stood there frozen while Eric groaned. It was when he began to move that she scrambled into action.

Gun first, was all she could think. She grabbed it, but so did Eric. He had a hand on the grip, and she had a hand on the barrel, which was terrible positioning. So she jerked it as hard as she could, and nearly toppled backward when it came as easily as it did.

She scurried to turn the gun around, to get her fingers

on the trigger, to point it at *him*. She was shaking, damn it, she was shaking so hard. But she would shoot him if she had to. She *would*.

"You *wouldn't*," Eric seethed. He'd gotten onto all fours. Blood poured out of a gash on his head. But he was alert. He was moving. She hadn't won yet.

She checked the gun to make sure if she pulled the trigger it would shoot. She didn't know much about shotguns, but she thought she had it right.

The back door splintered open at the same time the front door did. For a moment, Vi was *almost* distracted enough to look away, but Eric sort of lunged.

She pulled the trigger without any thought to aim or anything other than stopping that lunge. The gun exploded as his body barreled into her legs and she fell backward, narrowly missing hitting her head on the floor.

She kicked away, holding on to the gun for dear life, scrambling back and away, and it took until she was free of his weight to realize Eric wasn't fighting. He was utterly still. Blood oozed not just out of his head, but out of his shoulder now as well.

Everything went to chaos then. Both front and back doors crashed fully open, and Thomas charged through the back, his gun drawn. He was kneeling next to her in a flash, helping her to her feet.

"Vi. Are you—"

"You're bleeding. Thomas. Oh my God." There were rivulets of blood going down his left arm. She reached out as if to do something about it, but she didn't know what.

But Thomas was looking beyond her. At the body a uniformed sheriff's deputy was crouched over.

"He killed her," Vi managed to whisper. "Choked her. I thought maybe she was still breathing at one point, but..."

Thomas's gaze moved back to her. "It's all right," he soothed. She held on to that gaze, the blue, steady gaze of the man she loved.

Because she'd survived.

"Ambulances are on their way. You're all going to need one," Laurel announced grimly.

"Is he...still alive?" Vi managed to ask, though her gaze never left Thomas.

"For now. Let's focus on getting you out of here. Both of you." Laurel looked at the front door, then the back. Both with lifeless bodies. She grimaced but nodded for the front. "This way."

It wasn't lost on Vi that even while his arm bled and bled and *bled*, he was trying to shield her from seeing Dianne's body again. But she saw it.

Dead. No doubt dead.

But *she* wasn't. Somehow, Vi had survived this. This awful thing. She let Thomas lead her outside, surprised to find it almost pitch-black, with only spotlights from police cars in different areas that allowed her to see what was going on.

She could hear sirens in the distance. Ambulances. Thomas needed one. Hell, she probably needed one, but...

She turned to Thomas, and she wanted to crumple, but she didn't let herself. She did let herself lean though. She leaned her forehead into his chest. "You found me."

He held on to her with his not-shot arm. "I may never let you out of my sight again. Vi, I am so so—"

She pulled back. Fast enough it hurt him and her, and she'd be sorry about it later. But for right now? "No sorrys.

There was no way of guessing Dianne was mixed up with Eric." But she saw the expression on his face. She had a feeling it would take a while to convince him of it.

But she *would*. She *would*. Because this was over.

Somehow, she'd survived. Because she'd believed she would, because she'd found her strength and fought, because she'd believed in him.

And now it was over. Really over. The kind of over that meant they got to live their lives without fear. Without envelopes showing up or having to worry.

If Eric lived, he'd go to jail for Dianne's murder. She'd testify a million times over to make sure of it.

And if he didn't…

Well, then she'd live in peace knowing she'd finally fought for herself.

Chapter Twenty-Two

Thomas was furious.

First, the paramedics had insisted on splitting them up. They'd determined Thomas needed to ride in the ambulance but let Laurel drive Vi to the hospital. Thomas would have told them to go to hell, but Laurel took over and Copeland restrained him.

Okay, not his finest moment. He'd ridden in an ambulance with a very dead Dianne Kay, while Copeland and Jack Hudson had ridden in an ambulance to watch over Eric Carter.

Thomas had been admitted to the hospital, poked and prodded, all of his demands and questions ignored. When he tried to refuse surgery, one of the nurses—whom he'd gone to high school with—told him to shut up.

He supposed it knocked some sense into him. And since Laurel was able to come update him on everything before the surgery, he supposed that helped too.

Well, except for the part where she told him Vi was getting cleared to be discharged.

"She was injured." He could see it all too clearly. The bruises on her face, her neck. And God knew what else that monster had done to her. She might have said no sorrys, but he didn't know how he wasn't supposed to feel responsible for that.

"Yes, and they've checked her out," Laurel said evenly. "She can go home and recover there. With her daughter and lots of help and love and attention from her cousins."

That's not her home anymore. But Thomas didn't know what... She'd said no sorrys, but how could some of this not be his own damn fault?

"Dianne Kay was dead on arrival," Laurel continued while the nurses prepped him for surgery. Apparently the doctor thought the bullet had fractured a bone. "Eric Carter is still in surgery. He might live. He might not. If he does, he'll go away for the rest of his life. He can't weasel his way out of this one, even if the whole state of Virginia vouched for him. Now, I need you to be a good boy and get your surgery. Maybe I'll bring you a present if you don't cry."

He glared at her, but also knew she was just trying to lighten the tension banded inside of him.

"They're not going to let her in to see you before you go, so just... Stop being a jerk and let the medical professionals do their job. When you wake up, you'll be able to see her."

If she wanted to see him. But that at least was up to Vi. He sighed. "Fine," he muttered.

And he did as he was told. So much so that the last thing he really remembered was Laurel telling him to stop being a jerk. When he woke up, he was groggy, not really sure what had happened.

It took a while to really come to, to remember, to hear what the voices in his room were saying.

"Tata!" He managed to get his eyes opened, focused. Vi was standing there, Magnolia on her hip. They both looked clean and bright and perfect.

Thomas tried to say something, but he realized it only came out garbled when Vi frowned and inched closer.

"I'm awake," he finally managed to say firmly. "Just a little groggy." He looked at his arm, all bandaged up. Desk duty for him for a while. *Ugh.*

Then he looked at Vi, and thought, well, maybe he'd just take some medical leave and soak her up.

If she even wants to be there.

"I wasn't sure if I should bring her," Vi said, her voice a little shaky. "I thought the hospital stuff might freak her out, but the hardest part has been keeping her from climbing into bed with you."

"Tata!"

If he wasn't so out of it, he might have cried. He tried to reach his arm out for Magnolia, but it didn't quite work that way yet. "Heya, sweets. You're both a sight for sore eyes."

Vi smiled at that, but her eyes were full of tears. She cleared her throat and looked around, then tugged a chair over to his bedside. She sat, putting Mags in her lap and letting her lean forward and slap at the side of the hospital bed.

"I'm glad you're here."

She reached out, touched his temple. "You saved me."

"You did a lot of saving yourself, Vi."

She nodded, blinking back those tears in her eyes. "I did. I'm proud of myself for that."

"You should be. I am."

She sniffled a little, one tear falling over. "I'm sorry you got hurt. I—"

"I thought we weren't doing sorrys."

She heaved out a sigh. "We're both going to really suck at that."

"So hard."

She laughed, and the sound was a balm for everything. Just everything. She was alive, okay, here. Mags was here. Everything… It would just be all right now. Before his surgery he'd been running on pent-up anger and terror, but now he was just…relieved. Just relieved.

So he watched her as she sat there and let Magnolia play with the hospital bed, and he tried to let that relief really sink in. But it had been so close. And she'd been so brave. And if they hadn't…

She gave a watery laugh. "Stop *looking* at me like that."

"Like what?"

"Like you can't believe I'm alive."

"It's not that, Vi. I just keep thinking, if Franny hadn't called me, I wouldn't have known. For hours more. I was going to be late and…" It was no good. Thinking in what-ifs. He'd told a hundred people that in his line of work before, but it was hard sometimes. Hard to let go of how close a call they'd had. "I was going to be late. I was going to buy a ring."

"A ring?"

"An *engagement* ring."

"For me?"

He closed his eyes. He wanted to laugh but couldn't quite manage it. "Vi."

"Sorry, I just… Thomas…"

"Don't worry. I'm not going to ask you *now*." He was too tired to open his eyes. Too tired to…

"Why not?"

He blinked them open. She was frowning at him now. Blue eyes…petulant.

"Because… Because we've just been through something traumatic."

"Sure, but you were going to ask me before that." She

waved it all away like it didn't matter. And he realized it did and it didn't. It mattered in that it happened, but it didn't *matter* to who they were or what they would be.

"And I would have said yes."

"You would have?"

It was her turn to say only his name in a kind of disapproving tone. "Maybe I wouldn't have been *quite* as sure as I am right now. Maybe there would have been a few doubts about…myself. Not you. Never you. *Myself.* But I don't have them anymore. I saw…" She swallowed against the emotion in her throat. "It's awful, but I watched that woman fall victim to the same thing I did. I saw it, and nothing has ever made me realize how little was my fault than seeing it on someone else." Vi shook her head. "Good thing I've got a therapist, I guess."

He wanted to reach out and touch her but couldn't manage it. So he figured he might as well ask. "Give me your hand, Vi."

She heaved out a sigh, but reached out and took his right hand in hers. She squeezed. Mags babbled.

"Did they tell you what's going on with Dianne and Eric?"

She nodded. "Last I heard, Eric was still alive, but they weren't sure how long he'd last. If he does survive, if he goes to trial, I'm going to testify. Whatever I need to do to put him behind bars, I'm going to."

"Me too, and that's a promise."

She looked down at their joined hands. "Dianne didn't deserve to die."

He wished he had the empathy to agree with her. "She kidnapped you. She might have been his victim, but she made choices that you never made. To hurt other people. You aren't the same."

"Maybe not. But she didn't deserve to die at his hands."

"No, maybe not."

Vi swallowed and shook her head before meeting his gaze again. "I don't want to celebrate the end of people's lives, but I feel… Free. For the first time in a long time, there aren't any clouds hanging over me."

"So, marry me, Vi. Be my wife. I'll adopt Mags. We'll get her under your name where she belongs. We'll be a family."

Vi nodded. "Yes. I'll marry you." She leaned in carefully, keeping Magnolia from grabbing any wires. "Because we *are* a family."

THEY DIDN'T WAIT to get married. What was the point? Neither of them wanted anything fancy. Just their friends, their family and each other.

But Vi *did* buy Magnolia a ridiculously frilly flower girl dress. And they had to wait a few weeks still, to get their parents out to Bent. Her mother couldn't—wouldn't—make it, but Dad and Suze did. Vi was more at peace with that than she'd ever been.

Thomas could get around and do most things for himself, though he pushed harder than he should. To take care of Mags, to help with whatever wedding things.

And still, she appreciated the time. Where he didn't have to work, and they could sort out how this all would *go*. It wasn't as if they agreed on everything, but merging their lives felt more natural than anything she'd ever done.

Because this year had given her perspective she'd desperately needed. To stop and be grateful for every good thing.

And she had so much good.

On the day of the wedding, she got ready in her old bedroom at the Young Ranch. She was wearing a simple white dress, and she didn't need a lot of fussing to get into it, but still, Audra, Rosalie, Franny and her stepmother all packed into the bedroom and helped her get ready, passing Mags around.

"He was such a skinny thing," Suze kept saying, as if she couldn't quite believe that fifteen years later Thomas might have grown up. "I just can't get over it."

Vi smiled every time. Because sometimes she still saw a glimpse of that skinny teenager in the amazing man he'd become. And she loved them both. Always would.

Once she was ready, they headed outside.

Audra and Rosalie had set up a simple archway, some chairs and a runner down the middle of the chairs to create an aisle. For the past few days, Vi had taken Mags out to do a couple trial runs. Her daughter liked playing with the flower petals more than anything, but Vi knew she wouldn't do that at the wedding.

The chairs were full now with her family and his. And *their* friends. Because the world Thomas had built for himself had folded her and Mags into it. Everyone but Magnolia and her father took their seats as Vi got ready to walk down the aisle.

Thomas stood under the pretty floral arch, waiting for her. Wearing a suit. A big grin on his face.

Vi crouched to Magnolia. "Okay, Mags, do you remember what to do?"

"Tata!"

Vi laughed. "Yep. Throw your flowers and walk down to Tata. Slowly."

She let Magnolia go, and just as Vi had suspected, Mags did not walk slowly or throw flower petals as they'd practiced over and over. She just ran for it. Right to Thomas. Who scooped her up into his arms.

He only winced a little.

Then her father walked her down the aisle. "I always liked Thomas," he whispered.

Vi laughed in spite of herself. "No, you didn't."

"Well, I didn't hate him," he grumbled. And he led her right to Thomas under the arch.

"Hi," he said, and she thought about that moment outside the general store all those months ago. When she'd been at her wits' end, a completely different person.

And all she'd really needed was this man in her life again. Now here he was. Hers. Forever.

"Hi," she offered.

Then they turned to the minister, who gave a short introduction and led them through their vows to become man and wife.

It would take some time to get through the red tape, but by the end of the year, they'd all be Harts.

But it didn't really matter. Not names or paperwork. They were each other's, no matter what. A family.

And that was what she told him, promised him in their vows. While he held her little girl. *Their* little girl.

Because *this* was the life she deserved. And she'd fought for it. Always would. For him, for Mags, for herself.

Always.

* * * * *

HUNTED IN THE REEDS

CARLA CASSIDY

Chapter One

"It's okay, Colette. You're safe here. Nobody is going to hurt you again. You can wake up now."

The deep, rich voice penetrated the darkness that surrounded her. Colette Broussard listened to the familiar voice that called to her. This wasn't the first time he'd spoken to her.

He would talk to her, and then there would be silence once again, and then he would come back to talk to her some more. "Colette, honey, I need you to wake up now. Climb out of the darkness and open your eyes."

She wanted to please the voice, but there was still a deep fear inside her. She wasn't sure exactly what she was afraid of, but there was safety in the darkness, and so she clung to it tightly.

Then he was gone again, and there was nothing but silence. The next time he came, once again he assured her that she was safe, that nothing was going to hurt her again, and she needed to wake up. And once again she found herself wanting to please this man who had talked to her so many times before…the person who had been an odd kind of comfort in the perpetual nighttime of her world.

This time, instead of wrapping the darkness around her,

she slowly climbed toward the light and cracked open her eyes. She immediately winced against the illumination in the room.

Her senses all went wild… The scent of disinfectant and the sounds of beeping and buzzing from a variety of machines that surrounded the hospital bed she was in created a cacophony of stimulus that was immediately overwhelming.

Finally, there was a handsome man with dark, curly hair and gray eyes. Still, his features were fuzzy as her eyes tried to adjust to the light.

He grabbed her hand and smiled at her. "Good morning, Colette. It's so good to see you here with me. I'm just going to go get the doctor, okay?" He released her hand and walked out of the room.

She looked around frantically. What was she doing in the hospital? How had she gotten here, and what was wrong with her?

As she tried to remember why she was here, a headache bloomed across her forehead, and she just wanted to close her eyes and escape into the safety of the darkness once again.

However, before she could slip away, a man with gray hair and wearing a doctor's coat entered the room followed by several female nurses. "Hi, Colette," he said with a kind smile. "I'm Dr. Dwight Maison. We've been taking care of you while you've been asleep."

She frowned. "H-how long…" Her voice felt scratchy, and her mouth was exceedingly dry. One of the nurses got her a small cup of water from the sink in the room, and she drank it greedily, the cold liquid sliding down to soothe her dry throat.

She looked at the doctor once again. "How long have I been asleep?"

"We'll talk about all that after I check your vitals," he replied.

As he listened to her heart and the band around her arm pumped up to take her blood pressure, she wondered what had happened to the man with the voice. Who was he? And where had he gone? Had he only been a figment of her imagination?

"Now, how are you feeling?" Dr. Maison asked as he sat in the chair next to her bed.

"I have a bit of a headache, but other than that I'm feeling okay. I'm just not sure why I'm here. Was I in some sort of car accident?" she asked in confusion.

Dr. Maison looked at her in surprise. "Uh...what's the last thing you remember?"

She frowned thoughtfully. "I remember working late into the evening writing an article, and then I decided to make a quick run to the grocery store. I wanted to get some eggs for breakfast the next morning." Her frown deepened. "I remember leaving my shanty, and... I...uh... That's the last thing I remember. So how did I get here?"

"Colette, you were kidnapped and held by the Swamp Soul Stealer."

She stared at him. It was as if he had suddenly started speaking in a foreign language. "Kidnapped," she echoed faintly. "The Swamp Soul Stealer?"

"That's the name the newspapers have given him. He's kidnapped five people besides you, and nobody knows if those other people are dead or alive. Somehow you must have managed to escape him, and you were found at the edge of the swamp. You'd been beaten and starved, and we immediately put you into a medically induced coma so you could heal."

A half-hysterical burst of laughter escaped her. It sounded so outrageous. "Why don't I remember any of that?"

"It's possible your mind is protecting you right now from those memories, and they'll eventually come back to you," the doctor explained.

"So how long had I been kidnapped?"

He hesitated a long moment. "Almost three months," he finally replied.

Once again, she stared at him, not knowing whether to scream or cry. Three months? How was that even possible? "And how long have I been here in the hospital?"

"You've been here with us for almost three months," he replied.

Six months? She'd lost six months of her life, and in that time, she'd been beaten and starved, escaped from some kidnapper and then been put to sleep? Oh, how she longed for the comfort of the darkness right now.

Dr. Maison placed a hand on hers. "I know this is a lot for you to take in, but, Colette, we've got you healthy again, and you have survived it all. You are a very strong and brave woman."

At the moment she didn't feel strong or brave. She was overwhelmed by everything he had told her. Her headache intensified as she struggled to understand it all.

"Was...was I raped?" she asked, almost afraid of the answer.

He smiled at her kindly. "We saw no signs of sexual assault when you were found."

Thank God, she thought in relief. It was crazy that she'd

been beaten and starved, but being sexually assaulted would have upset her the most.

"When can I go home?" Surely, she would feel much better once she was back in her shanty and amid her familiar things.

"First thing in the morning, we'll remove your feeding tube and other things and then I'd like to keep you for another two days or so to make sure you can hold food down and your bodily functions return to normal." He stood. "And now, since it's the middle of the night, we'll just leave you to rest until morning. If you need anything at all, hit the button for a nurse and somebody will come in. It's wonderful to see you awake, Colette."

"Thank you, Dr. Maison," she replied even though she was disappointed that she'd have to stay here for another couple of days. What's another couple of days when she'd already lost six months of her life, she thought half hysterically.

Minutes later she was alone in the room and still grappling with everything she had just learned about herself. No matter how hard she tried to remember anything from the last six months, those memories remained elusive.

Maybe it was better if she never remembered the time she'd been held by a kidnapper.

She wished the man with the voice would come back to assure her everything was going to be okay and that she was safe. Maybe he had been some sort of a guardian angel sent to help ease her from the darkness to the light.

As she closed her eyes, she imagined him talking to her now, soothing and comforting her through the darkness of her life.

CHIEF OF POLICE Etienne Savoie paced the small confines of the hospital waiting room. September's early-morning sunshine flooded through the nearby windows as he waited for Colette's release.

She'd been awake now for three days, but Etienne hadn't seen her since the night she'd first opened her eyes. The doctor had refused to allow her any visitors while she adjusted to being awake and all that came with it.

Dr. Maison had called Etienne earlier that morning to let him know that Colette was being released. He was hoping Etienne would take the woman home since she had no family to pick her up.

Etienne had been champing at the bit to talk to Colette. He was hoping she could tell him about the man who had kidnapped her. The Swamp Soul Stealer had managed to kidnap two women and four men without leaving any clues behind. Hopefully, Colette held all the answers as to the identity of the man.

Etienne had hoped that the other victims were all still alive since Colette had been found after three months of captivity. But she'd been barely clinging to life when she was found, and Etienne worried that a clock was ticking for all the missing.

He stopped his pacing as Dr. Maison came out to greet him.

"Chief," the doctor said with a nod of his head.

"How's our girl? Is she ready to get out of here?" Etienne asked.

"She's definitely ready to leave, but I need to talk to you about something important before you take her home."

"Something important?" Etienne looked at the older man curiously.

"She doesn't remember anything."

Etienne frowned. "What do you mean?"

"She has no memory of her captivity. The last thing she remembers is deciding to go to the grocery store and then waking up here, but she remembers absolutely nothing in between."

Etienne stared at the doctor in surprise and more than a little bit of dismay. "Is this…uh…amnesia normal in these kind of circumstances?"

"I've done some research into it, and yes, it can be quite normal."

"Is it permanent?" For the past three months, Etienne had hoped and prayed she would awaken and have enough information that he could make an arrest. The disappointment that swept through him now was all-consuming.

"Actually, it may not be permanent. I believe right now Colette's mind is protecting her from remembering all the trauma she went through. Once she feels safe and strong enough, it's very possible her memories will start to return."

Etienne felt a little better about the situation. His job would now be to make sure she felt safe and supported. He desperately needed her memories to do his job as chief of police and catch the man who was terrorizing the swamp.

"She should be ready for release any minute now. My nurses gathered up some clothes for her to wear home since she had nothing of her own. I'll just go get her for you." The doctor turned on his heels and disappeared through the double door marked DO NOT ENTER.

Etienne found himself ridiculously nervous to interact with the sleeping beauty he had sat next to and talked to night after night. Of course, she wouldn't know that. But during those nights, as crazy as it sounded, he had felt a strange connection with her.

The door reopened, and Colette walked out. She was clad in a pair of slightly baggy black sweatpants and a blue T-shirt. Her long dark hair was held at the nape of her neck with a large gold barrette. She was still too thin and looked incredibly fragile, but there was no question that she was a beautiful woman.

Dr. Maison walked by her side, and when they reached where Etienne stood, the doctor introduced her to the lawman. "Chief Savoie has offered to take you home and see that you get settled in okay."

Etienne had wondered about the color of her eyes. He hadn't noticed in that moment when she first opened them. They were a beautiful dark chocolate brown with thick long dark lashes.

She gazed at him tentatively. "Thank you, that's very kind of you."

He'd also wondered what her voice would sound like and was oddly pleased that it was low and melodious. "Are you ready to go?" he asked.

She looked up at the doctor and then gazed back at Etienne. "I guess I'm ready."

"You're going to be just fine, Colette," Dr. Maison said with a warm smile. "Remember what I told you. You are a very strong and brave woman."

"Thank you, Dr. Maison. Thank you for everything," she replied and then looked at Etienne expectantly.

"My car is parked right outside the front door," he said and gestured her toward the exit. Together, they walked down the long hallway and out the hospital doors.

He opened the passenger side of his car, and she slid into

the seat. He hadn't driven his patrol car to pick her up but had driven his personal vehicle instead, a dark blue sedan. He also wasn't in uniform but wore a pair of jeans and a navy T-shirt. However, he did wear his shoulder holster and gun, something he always did when he was out and about.

Once she was inside the car, he hurried around to the driver side and got in. He shot her a quick smile as he started the car. "How does it feel to be awake and finally leaving the hospital?"

"To be honest, it's all a little bit overwhelming right now."

"I can certainly understand that," he replied.

"I still can't believe I've lost six months of my life."

"Hopefully it won't take you too long to adjust and go forward from here." He glanced over at her once again.

She stared out the front window, an anxious expression on her pretty features. As if feeling his gaze on her, she turned and looked at him. "Thank you, Chief Savoie, for taking me home. I really appreciate it."

"No problem. I'm assuming I need to go to the big entrance of the swamp."

"Yes, and from there I can walk in to my shanty." Her anxious expression intensified. "Hopefully, it's still standing, and no squatter has taken it over while I've been gone."

"I'll be walking in with you to make sure everything is okay there," he assured her.

"I'd like to tell you that isn't necessary, but I'd really appreciate having you with me."

"Colette, I intend to be with you as much as possible as you transition back into your life. There's nothing more I want to do than support you."

He sensed her gaze on him once again. "Why?" she asked.

"Why? Because I know you have no family to see you

through all this. Also, as chief of police, I feel responsible for everything you've been through," he replied. And there was the small fact that he needed her memories, but he certainly didn't want to tell her that…at least not yet.

For the next few minutes, they rode in silence. As he went down Main Street, he couldn't help but feel a strong sense of pride.

Crystal Cove, Louisiana, was a small town with lots of heart. The buildings downtown were painted pink, yellow and turquoise, giving the town a special visual charm. The people here were warm and friendly. They were, for the most part, hardworking individuals who were always willing to lend a hand to help a neighbor.

Etienne took his job as chief of police very seriously. The fact that there was a man moving with impunity through the swamp and kidnapping people was beyond upsetting. He was still reeling with the information that Colette had no memories right now of her kidnapping. All he could hope for was that given a little time and getting settled back in her own routine, those memories would begin to return.

They reached the parking area where people who lived in the swamp left their cars. He pulled up and parked and they both got out of the car.

The swamp entrance in this area was like a big gaping mouth leading into a dark and mysterious jungle of tangled greenery. Etienne had been in the swamp many times, especially since the kidnappings. He and his officers had searched and hunted the marshland for the monster preying on the people who lived here.

They took several steps forward on a narrow path, and

she suddenly stopped. She drew several deep breaths and then visibly relaxed.

"This I remember," she said softly. "The smell of greenery and flowers and just a faint hint of decaying fish." She offered him a bright smile that unexpectedly warmed him. "It's the fragrance of home."

"Then it must feel good to be back here," he said as they continued walking.

"It feels very good." She led him up one trail and then onto a narrower one. As it began to disappear, the sun still fought to shine through the large leaves of the cypress and tupelo trees overhead. Spanish moss dripped from some of the trees, the lacy patterns glittering when the sun found them.

The sound of fish jumping and the splash of gator tails came from pools of water nearby, and small animals scurried to get out of their way as they continued walking.

They passed several other shanties. He had been to one of them not that long ago when somebody had tried to kill Angel Marchant.

Angel, a strong, beautiful woman who lived in the swamp, had met and fallen for Nathan Merrick. Nathan was a writer/photographer who was working on a book about the flora and fauna in the swamp. Angel had agreed to be his tour guide, and as the two of them worked together, they had fallen in love. However, that had stirred a jealous rage in one of her male friends who believed she belonged to him.

One night, Louis Mignot attacked Nathan, hitting him over the head and rendering him unconscious. Louis then confronted Angel in her shanty. His love for her had turned to a deadly rage, and he attacked her with the intention of killing her. In the end, Angel managed to stab Louis, ending his life.

Etienne had been there to investigate and clean up the crime scene and to assure Angel that she had done the right thing. Thankfully, she and Nathan were happy together and were now planning a wedding.

At least that case had a happy ending, he thought as they passed by Angel's shanty. Colette led him up another narrow path, and then after several more minutes of walking, a shanty came into view.

It was like most of the other ones in the area. Built of wood and on stilts over a large expanse of water, it had several windows and a wraparound porch. A wooden rocking chair sat on the porch by the front door, as if just waiting for her to come home and sit a spell.

"At least it's still standing," she said as they walked across the narrow bridge that led to the front door. Once she got there, she grabbed the doorknob and then turned and frowned at him in dismay. "It's locked, and I don't have the key."

"Is there a back door?" he asked.

She brightened. "Yes, and a lot of times I would forget about locking it."

"Then, let's go check it out." He led her around the porch and to the back door. The knob turned easily. He drew his gun and went in before her, just in case somebody had decided to move into the shanty while she was missing.

He took several steps inside and then stopped and listened. The house held the complete silence of vacancy. He turned back to her. "It's safe to come in," he said as he holstered his gun.

She followed him in, and they went through the small kitchen and on into the living room.

"Does everything look like it's supposed to?"

She looked around and slowly nodded. "Yes, it does."

"Why don't you sit tight here, and I'll just check out the rest of the place?" he said.

She nodded and sank down onto the dark brown sofa with its bright yellow throw pillows. There was an overall brightness to the living room with a matching brown chair and a small desk and accents of yellow all around. It was quite a warm and attractive space.

He stepped into the bedroom where a double bed was covered with a bedspread filled with sunflowers. A nightstand held a battery-operated lamp, and a dresser with a mirror was against one wall.

He checked the closet to make sure nobody was hiding there and then walked across the hall and checked out a small bathroom that only had a sink and a stool. He had learned that most of the shanties had outdoor showers that ran with rain and bottled water. Everything inside ran on complicated systems of water that he knew little about.

With the space entirely checked out, he went back into the living room and sat on the sofa next to her. "No human critters hiding anywhere," he said with a smile.

"Thanks, and looking around, I don't see anything that's missing. I guess I've been very lucky."

"You know what I think? I believe the people here in the swamp have great admiration for you as a survivor, and they're hoping you can help me catch this Swamp Soul Stealer."

"But I can't help you. I don't remember anything to help you," she said, her eyes appearing to darken.

"I'm hoping that will change in time," he replied.

At that moment, a knock sounded on her front door.

Etienne stood as Colette got up from the sofa and answered. It was Ella Gaines who worked at the café. Immediately, the two women hugged.

"Oh, Colette, it's so good to see you alive and well," Ella said as she released her hold on Colette. The two women sank down onto the sofa.

"How did you know I was home?" Colette asked.

"You know how the grapevine around here works. The minute you stepped into the swamp, people started talking," Ella replied.

"Well, I'm happy to see you," Colette said.

"You've gotten far too thin," Ella continued. "I'm going to have to fatten you up with some of my deluxe cornbread and big fried shrimp."

"That sounds good to me," Etienne quipped, making the two women laugh.

Ella sobered and grabbed Colette's hands. "Oh, I've missed my best friend."

"And I've missed you," Colette replied.

There was another knock on the door, and more people arrived to visit. There was Jaxon Patin, who was Colette's closest neighbor. Then there was Layla and Liam Guerin, Hudson Decuir and Levi Morel, all friends and neighbors of Colette.

They pulled in chairs from the kitchen, and Jaxon and Levi sat on the floor, while Etienne stood by the front door and just watched the interactions going on.

"Have you told Chief Savoie who the Swamp Soul Stealer is?" Levi asked. He was a big guy with broad shoulders and thick thighs. Etienne knew he was a gator hunter, as was Jaxon Patin.

"Unfortunately, right now I have no memory of my time in captivity," Colette replied.

"For real? You don't remember anything?" Levi asked.

"Nothing," she said.

"That doesn't matter, we're just happy you're back here safe and sound," Layla said with a reassuring smile.

"Seriously, you don't remember anything at all?" Levi pressed, his dark eyes gazing at Colette intently. "Not a single thing?"

"Levi, knock it off. She already answered you," Ella said with a glare at the man.

"I just wanted to be sure that she has amnesia," Levi replied. "I've never known anyone who had it before."

"Well, now you know somebody," Colette replied with a smile.

It was at that moment Etienne realized an important issue he hadn't considered before now. He'd initially believed that Colette would be able to give him enough information to make an immediate arrest in this case. The Swamp Soul Stealer would be caught and put into jail, and nobody would have to worry about him again.

Unfortunately, it hadn't happened that way. And now Colette would be in even bigger danger from the monster who had kidnapped her.

The Swamp Soul Stealer would eventually hear that they were waiting for her memories to come back to her. He would want to get rid of her before that happened. With this thought in mind, Etienne stepped outside and made a phone call to the station to make some arrangements, and then he returned to the living room.

As he watched her talk and laugh with her friends, he realized she was in imminent danger. He wanted her memories, but his real job now was keeping her alive so she had the time to retrieve them.

Chapter Two

It was late afternoon by the time all her friends left, and Colette was positively exhausted. Ella was the last to leave, and once she was gone, Colette turned and smiled at the handsome chief of police.

"Chief Savoie, thank you so much for all your time today," she said as she sat back down on the sofa.

"Please, make it Etienne," he said and sank down next to her. "You seem to have a nice group of supportive friends."

"They're all great. Most of them I've been friends with since we were young kids," she replied.

Etienne Savoie was a very handsome man with strong, bold features. His dark curly hair begged a woman's fingers to dance through it, and his dark gray eyes held streaks of silver like the wings on a blackbird. He reminded her of somebody, but she couldn't remember who.

He smelled as good as he looked. His cologne was spicy and rich and threatened to pull her in, but the last thing she needed right now was a crush on the chief of police. She had plenty in her own life to figure out without adding issues.

"We have a few more things to talk about before I leave," he said.

"And what's that?" she asked curiously. Right now, what

she really wanted to do was get something to eat and then veg out on the sofa until bedtime. Her first foray back into real life had been positively exhausting.

He gazed at her soberly. "We both know that you have no memories right now to help me make an arrest in the Swamp Soul Stealer case. Eventually, this man is going to hear that we're waiting for your memory to return."

She frowned. "Okay... I'm not sure what you're saying."

He leaned toward her. "I'm saying that I believe you are now in danger from the Swamp Soul Stealer. He's going to want to stop you before you can give me any information that might lead to his arrest."

She stared at him as a new horror crept through her. Of course, he was right. She just hadn't had time to process everything yet. "So what happens now?"

"I've already arranged for armed guards to sit on your porch. You should be safe here, and if you need to go anywhere, call and let me know, and we'll see what we can do. Meanwhile, the sooner you can retrieve your memories, the better. You helping to identify this creep will get him under arrest, and then nobody will be in danger from him again."

The weight of his words, coupled with the fear that raced through her momentarily, left her speechless. She stared at the handsome man before her. Even though she had no specific memories of her time with the Swamp Soul Stealer, when she thought about it, her general reaction was an abject fear that tightened the back of her throat and made it difficult for her to draw a full breath.

Now Chief Savoie was asking her to retrieve those details to find the kidnapper who might be a killer as well.

As she gazed into Etienne's smoke gray eyes, she wanted to pull up those memories and hand them to him. But she couldn't. She simply didn't have them right now to give to him.

"I promise I'll give you all my memories as they come back to me," she replied fervently.

He reached out and took her hand in his, his touch holding an odd familiarity and a wealth of comfort. "Colette, we'll get through all this together," he said reassuringly. He pulled his hand back and stood. "And now I'm sure you're exhausted. You've had a long first day, and I'm also sure you're more than ready to be alone and really get settled in here."

"I am tired," she admitted and rose to her feet as well. Her brain struggled to process everything she'd been told since opening her eyes three days before. There was no question that it all was overwhelming.

They walked to her front door, and Etienne opened it and gestured to a uniformed officer seated in the rocking chair. The officer smiled at her and waved.

"Colette, this is Officer Joel Smith. He'll be sitting on duty outside here for the night."

"Thank you," Colette said to the officer, once again overwhelmed by everything that was happening.

"And I'll check in with you sometime tomorrow," Etienne said. "Now get some rest and enjoy being home."

With that, he left, and she was finally alone in her shanty. She walked from room to room as her brain bubbled with one thought after another.

Apparently, she had been kidnapped and held by somebody for three months. She'd been found half-dead and then had been in a coma for the next three months. As if that wasn't enough, the man who kidnapped her could possibly still be a threat to her life. And the cherry on top of it all was the fact that she was suffering from amnesia. Could her life get more complicated?

Since it was getting dark, she went around the room and lit the battery-operated lamps she had. She was thankful they all still worked. She then collapsed onto the sofa and looked around.

This room had always been her sanctuary. It was both her workspace and her relaxing place. As she looked at the small desk against one wall, she thought about what she'd been doing months ago before she had been kidnapped and her life had been so disrupted.

She had been a fairly popular blogger and had also been writing and selling articles about swamp life to a couple of magazines. She could only assume after her six-month absence she'd lost those jobs and her blogging business as well.

In the next few days, she'd see if she could pick back up where she'd left off. She'd write a few articles and offer them to the magazines she'd sold to before.

She got up from the sofa and went into the kitchen where she found a packet of tuna that hadn't expired and a box of crackers in her food cabinet. She sat at the kitchen table to eat them. She definitely needed to get some groceries. Everything in her cooler had gone bad. Thankfully there hadn't been a lot in there.

Once she was finished with the tuna and crackers, she quickly cleaned the cooler out. But that wasn't the only thing that had caught her attention as she'd walked through the shanty earlier. Every piece of furniture was covered with a fine layer of dust.

Tomorrow would be a cleaning day. Tonight she was just too tired to worry about any of it.

Even though it was relatively early, she decided to call it

a night. She turned out all the lanterns and then went to her bedroom. The bed beckoned to her, and she quickly changed into a clean nightshirt from one of the dresser drawers and then fell into the soft mattress.

Almost immediately her brain filled with all the stress she had going on in her life. It was all so overwhelming, like a bad dream. Only she wouldn't easily awaken from it. It was definitely disconcerting to know there was an armed guard just outside her door. It was especially upsetting to know the guard was there because another man might try to kill her.

Still, it wasn't long before the sounds of frogs croaking and crickets chirping filled the night. Soft bird calls and the white noise of the swamp slowly relaxed her and lulled her to sleep.

SHE AWAKENED THE next morning, surprised that it was after nine. She dressed for the day and then went out to her back porch to start her generator. It had lain dormant for six months. She breathed a sigh of relief when it started right up.

She went back inside, made herself a quick breakfast and then moved to her little desk in the living room. She dusted everything off, turned on her laptop and began perusing files, trying to familiarize herself with what she might have been working on before her kidnapping.

Work was the best way she knew not to dwell on everything else in her life. She'd always been able to completely immerse herself in her writing, and today was no different.

She jerked to awareness as a knock fell on her door. Instantly, a knot of fear formed in the back of her throat. She suddenly remembered there was supposed to be an armed guard outside. She peered out the front window and saw Etienne with several bags in his hands.

A quick look at the clock as she hurried to the door let her know it was just after noon. She had definitely lost track of time while working.

He was clad in a pair of jeans and a light blue polo that displayed his broad shoulders and taut biceps. He looked incredibly handsome, and as she opened the door, his smile warmed her from head to toe.

"Afternoon, Colette," he greeted her.

She opened the door wider to invite him in. "Good afternoon."

"I took the liberty of picking up some things for you at the grocery store. I suspect your cupboards are probably pretty empty."

"They are," she admitted. "Please, bring them in." She led him to the kitchen where he set the bags on the small wooden table.

"It's mostly just staples…bread, milk, eggs, with a few other items. I would prefer you not go to the grocery store right now, so I figured while I'm here you could make me a list and I can bring the things to you this evening. I'll be back here on guard duty. There's a block of ice in this bag. I knew your cooler would need that." He pulled out the ice and placed it in the back of the large cooler that served as her refrigerator.

She began to empty the other bags he'd brought with him. "I really appreciate all this. You need to tell me how much you spent so I can repay you." Thank goodness the jar of cash she kept had been right where it was supposed to be, hidden away in the bottom of her closet. At least she had money on hand to pay him.

"Don't worry about it," he replied easily.

She put a carton of eggs in her cooler and then turned

back to face him. "Oh no, Chief Savoie, while I appreciate your kind offer, I pay my own way."

"Okay, but I told you to make it Etienne."

She grinned at him. "Okay, then I pay my own way, Etienne."

"That's better." He smiled at her once again. Oh, the man had a wonderful smile. It crinkled the corners of his amazing eyes and lit up all his features.

"So, how did it feel to sleep in your own bed last night after being gone from it for so long?"

"It felt wonderful. In fact, I slept later this morning than I ever remember doing before." She put the last of the grocery items away and then gestured for him to follow her back into the living room.

He sat on the sofa and she settled in a chair facing him. "How are you feeling this morning?" he asked.

She knew what he really wanted to know. "I'm sorry, but no memories have come to mind yet."

"I really was just asking about you, not your memories," he chided gently. "You look better rested today than you did when I left you last night."

"Getting some extra sleep definitely helped, and I've had a nice morning. I spent the morning writing, and it felt good to be back in the saddle, so to speak. Before all this happened, I wrote articles about swamp life, and I had a fairly successful blog."

"That's interesting," he said, his gray eyes curious. "Do you sell the articles you write?"

She laughed. "That's the general idea. I used to sell to several magazines, and I had a nice following. Of course, a six-month absence means I'll be starting all over again now."

"That's unfortunate, but hopefully it won't take you too long to get back to where you were."

"And hopefully it won't take me too much time to remember things that can help you in your pursuit of this soul stealer man."

His eyes narrowed slightly. "So far, the man has been like a damned ghost who leaves nothing behind. But now that you mention the whole memory thing, I've been thinking of ways we might possibly jog your memory."

The muscles in her stomach instantly tightened. "What have you come up with?"

He leaned forward. "We believe this man is holding his captives somewhere here in the swamp. My officers and I have searched, but we've been unsuccessful in finding the lair. I was thinking maybe you and I could take some walks through the swamp? Might jog something loose in your memories about the location."

The idea of walking in search of the place where a monster lived, a monster who had held her for three long months and had nearly killed her, caused a new fear to tighten up the back of her throat. "Wh-when would you want to start this?"

He gazed at her for several long moments, obviously hearing the abject dread in her tone. "We'll wait a couple of days until you feel a little stronger."

She felt as if he'd handed her a small reprieve, but more than ever she knew she needed her memories to return to her. The only problem was, she was almost as afraid of those memories as she was of the monster who was after her.

ETIENNE LEFT THE swamp with a grocery list in hand and thoughts of Colette weighing heavy in his mind. She'd looked so much better today. Far more relaxed and obviously comfortable in her own space. Clad in a pair of jeans that had hugged her slender legs and slim hips and a light pink T-shirt that clung to her breasts, she had stirred something unexpected...something raw and hot inside of him.

He needed to keep his relationship with her strictly professional. However, those nights of sitting with her while she'd been in her strange slumber had somehow connected him to her in a nebulous way. He didn't understand it, but he felt it.

He headed straight to the police station, wanting to check in before he headed home for a few hours of sleep. He had guard duty tonight and needed to make sure he'd be alert through the entire night.

He parked in his space behind the police station and went in through the back door. The hallway was empty as he headed to his office. Once at his desk, he quickly checked his emails and notes to make sure nothing demanded his immediate attention.

He'd just finished up when a knock fell on his door. "Enter," he called.

Trey Norton came in. A tall, fit dark-haired man, he was Etienne's right-hand man.

"Hey, Chief," Trey greeted him and took the chair in front of Etienne's desk.

"What's up?" Etienne asked.

"Nothing much. What about with you and our sleeping beauty? Anything exciting and new on that front yet?"

"I wish. So far, she's remembered nothing. I'm going to give her a few days to relax and get comfortable. If nothing changes, I'm going to start trying to push her." He told Trey about his idea of taking Colette for walks in the swamp. "I'm also going to suggest she get some therapy with Dr.

Amber Kingston. From what I've heard, she's a great therapist. Maybe she can help Colette retrieve some of her repressed memories."

"Sounds like a good plan to me. Hopefully it will work," Trey said. "I heard through the grapevine that you were taking the night duty at her place."

"Yeah, and I'm going to be depending on you to hold things down here during the days ahead. I'm planning on coming in for a couple hours each day, but I need to work in some downtime so I can be awake all night for guard duty."

"Got it," Trey replied. "You know you can depend on me."

Etienne grinned at his friend and coworker. "If I couldn't depend on you, then you wouldn't be my assistant chief. Instead, you'd be emptying all the trash cans and cleaning out the jail cell bathrooms."

"I'd much rather be your assistant chief," Trey said with his own grin. "Is there anything specific you need for me to do today?"

Etienne released a tired sigh. "Actually, there is something. I'd like Levi Morel's alibis checked for the nights of the disappearances. He seemed far too interested in what Colette remembered when he was visiting with her yesterday. He lives in the swamp, but I'm not sure where. If you talk to some of Colette's neighbors, I'm sure they can tell you where his shanty is located."

"Levi Morel... Got it. I'll get on it this afternoon," Trey replied.

"He's probably nothing more than an overly curious friend, but still, I'd like him checked out," Etienne said.

"I'll see what I can find out about him."

"Good. I'm going to head home now and get a couple hours of sleep."

"Etienne, I know how heavy these whole Swamp Soul Stealer crimes have weighed on you," Trey said. "We all hope Colette will remember some crucial clues that will get the man under arrest and the people he's kidnapped free."

"I just hope and pray those people are all still alive." Etienne released another deep sigh. "I have to consider the possibility that Colette might never remember anything that will help us."

"All we can do at this point is hope this guy makes a mistake and leaves us some clues to follow," Trey replied.

"Yeah, well, so far that hasn't happened." Etienne raked a hand through his hair in frustration. "Have you heard anything more on the recall effort?" A small knot tightened in his belly.

For the past couple of weeks there had been some rumblings around town about a recall for his position. Some people had become unhappy that this crime hadn't already been solved. They had become disillusioned with Etienne and believed somebody else could handle the job better.

"Etienne, that recall isn't going to go anywhere," Trey replied. "It's just a handful of loudmouths leading the charge. Most of the people here still strongly support you."

"We'll see," Etienne said and stood. "I think I'll go ahead and head home now."

Trey got up from his chair and walked to the office door with Etienne. "Then I guess I'll see you sometime tomorrow."

"Yeah, I should be in around 8:30 a.m. I've got J.T. coming on guard duty at the shanty at eight in the morning."

Together, the two men left the office and went in opposite directions.

Trey was a high school buddy, and Etienne had been

pleased when he'd joined the police department six years before. At that time, Etienne had been twenty-seven years old and had just become the chief of police in the small town.

In the past seven years, Etienne had devoted himself to the job. He'd rarely dated, but lately he did find himself a little lonely. However, it was something he didn't dwell on. Besides, he'd been too busy trying to solve the Swamp Soul Stealer case to focus on much of anything else.

His house was about fifteen minutes from the police station in a nice neighborhood. It was a modest three-bedroom ranch that he'd bought two years ago. An added benefit was that it was only a block away from where his aging parents lived.

As he pulled into the garage, a weighty exhaustion rode on his shoulders. For months, he'd found sleep nearly impossible. The Swamp Soul Stealer case had tormented him, haunting his sleep with nightmares and the cries of victims.

Once Colette had been found, his sleepless nights had been spent with her. He'd watched her cuts and bruises slowly heal and her body put on much-needed weight. Through her transformation, he'd talked to her as he sat with her night after night.

During those times, he spoke to her about anything and nothing. He recounted his days for her and told her his dreams to eventually have a wife and fill his home with the sound of little feet and laughter. He'd also told her that he hadn't found that special someone yet and wasn't sure he ever would. In truth, he'd decided that he was a man destined to live alone with his work as his wife and family.

Once Colette had been pulled out of her medically induced coma, he'd spent each night trying to get her to wake up. He doubted that she'd been aware of him, but the moment she opened her eyes, he'd been filled with a tremendous joy. It came from more than the answers he needed from her to solve a crime. It was the sheer joy that a woman so broken had successfully survived her ordeals.

The minute Etienne was inside his house, he dropped his wallet, keys and utility belt on the end table next to his black recliner. Lately, he spent as much time sleeping in this chair as he did his bed. It often felt like far too much trouble to get into bed with the lack of sleep he got.

And, if he was perfectly honest with himself, he'd admit that it was that edge of loneliness he felt that kept him from the big bed that begged for two bodies.

Even though he knew it probably wasn't necessary, he set an alarm on his watch to wake him for his night duty. It was going to be a long night. He planned on being at Colette's place at seven and would remain there until eight the next morning.

He had taken the long hours of the night shift mostly due to a lack of manpower and the fact that he believed if the man came after her, it would be during the darkness of night. And he wanted to be the one to get the bastard. He wanted that so badly.

He must have fallen asleep for he awakened at five, feeling refreshed and ready for the night to come. He took a quick shower and then dressed in a clean uniform. Strapping on his utility belt and gun, he then grabbed the grocery list Colette had given him earlier in the day and left his house.

His first stop was at Big D's Burgers, a drive-through where he ordered a cheeseburger and quickly ate it in his car. Then he was off to the grocery store.

Maynard's Grocery was located in the middle of Main Street. It did a brisk business as it was the only grocery store in town, and today was no different. The parking lot was nearly full as Etienne pulled in.

Colette's list was fairly short...some meat and fresh vegetables. He was greeted pleasantly by the other shoppers and in no time at all, he was headed for the swamp.

It was 6:45 p.m. when he parked at the swamp's entrance. He grabbed the bags of groceries and strode into the marshland.

He hoped the kidnapper made a move on Colette tonight. Etienne's blood heated at the very thought. He'd told his officers to keep quiet about the guards at her house. Hopefully, the Swamp Soul Stealer would believe Colette was alone and vulnerable in her shanty.

Thankfully, he remembered the way to her place. When he arrived, Joel, who had been on duty during the day, stood from the rocking chair.

"Evening, Chief," Joel greeted him.

"Evening, Joel. Everything quiet?"

"Has been all day," the officer replied. "She did have one visitor. Layla Guerin stopped by and brought Colette some fresh fish and a couple of potatoes. I stopped her at the door and brought the items in to Colette and that was the only person who's been here."

"Thanks, Joel. Now, go on, get out of here and get yourself some dinner," Etienne said.

"Linda will have a nice meal waiting for me," Joel replied. Joel had been dating Linda Michaels for the past year, and two months ago she had moved in with him.

"Well, enjoy it," Etienne said.

"Have a good night, Chief," Joel said. He crossed the bridge and disappeared into the encroaching twilight shadows and the tangled greenery.

Etienne knocked on Colette's door, surprised as a small edge of excitement shot through him. He told himself it was just because he was hoping she had remembered something since he'd last seen her, but the truth of the matter was he looked forward to seeing her again.

Strictly professional, he reminded himself. No matter that she stirred him in a physical way that no other woman had before, he had to keep their relationship professional.

At that moment she opened the door. "Etienne, come in," she said with a smile that instantly warmed him.

"I brought you the groceries you ordered," he said as he followed her into the kitchen. The air smelled of freshly fried fish.

"Great, let me just get them put away." She took the bags from him and set them on the table.

"How was your afternoon?" he asked as she began putting the meat into the cooler. The fresh vegetables and fruit she pushed to one side of the small counter.

"It was pretty quiet. I spent most of the time doing a little housecleaning. Everything was so dusty, and I was just glad to get rid of all of it."

She offered him another one of her lovely smiles. "I'm just getting ready to sit down and eat a little dinner. It isn't anything fancy, just some fried fish and potatoes, but I'd love it if you'd join me."

He shouldn't sit at her table and enjoy a meal with her. It would blur the lines between them. However, he wanted her to be completely comfortable with him. He needed to support her through this journey to regain her memories.

In this particular case, he realized, he had to blur the lines. He needed to get as close as possible to her as a friend and yet ignore the fact that he was incredibly physically drawn to her.

"I'd love to have some dinner with you," he finally replied.

Her responding smile lit him up inside and made him realize just how difficult a task he'd set for himself.

Chapter Three

Colette was ridiculously pleased that he'd agreed to eat with her. He looked incredibly handsome in his official blue uniform, and she couldn't help the way her heart warmed in his presence. "Please sit," she said, gesturing him toward the small table. "It's ready right now."

"It certainly smells good," he replied as he sat.

She set silverware on the table and then set two plates next to the skillet so she could fill them. Thankfully, the fish Layla had brought her that afternoon was a good size. There were several big pieces.

She placed one of the bigger ones on a plate for Etienne and added a bunch of diced browned potatoes. She brought it and a plate for herself to the table.

Even though the fish smelled good, Etienne smelled much better. His attractive, slightly spicy cologne mingled with the faint scent of shaving cream and a fresh-scented soap.

"Can I get you something to drink? I have water, or I could make a pot of coffee," she offered.

"No, I'm good," he said with a smile. "Sit down and relax. I'm ready to dig into this."

She sat in the chair opposite him. "Then let's."

"This is absolutely delicious," he said after taking his first bite.

"Thank you." Her cheeks warmed at his compliment. "The breading on the fish is my mother's recipe."

"Do you enjoy cooking?" he asked.

"I do, although I usually don't go to too much trouble when it's just me. What about you? Do you cook or do you have somebody at home who cooks for you?" It was hopefully a subtle way for her to learn if he had a significant other in his life or not.

"The only person who occasionally cooks for me is my mother. I've got no wife and no girlfriend, but sometimes my mom will take pity on me and bring me some of her home cooking," he replied.

"Oh, that's nice." What was really nice was the fact that he was single. "So you're close to your parents?"

"Very close. I'm their only kid, so it's always been just the three of us. In fact, I now live just a block away from them, and we often visit with each other." He frowned. "At least we did before this whole Swamp Soul Stealer case came along. For the last few months, I haven't had much spare time to visit with anyone."

"I could help with that if I could just remember anything," she said in frustration.

He reached out and lightly stroked the back of her hand. The simple touch sparked something exhilarating and breathless inside her. It only lasted a moment as he pulled his hand back from hers. "Colette, I know you're doing the best that you can," he said.

"To be honest, I'm a little bit afraid of my memories," she confessed.

"Afraid? Why?" He looked at her curiously.

"Because I know they are filled with horrors. Dr. Maison told me about the condition I was found in. So I'm a bit afraid to revisit them."

"Those horrors can't hurt you anymore. You survived everything that happened to you, and that part of your life is now over. It can't hurt you anymore. None of your memories can harm you."

She stared at him for several long moments, slowly digesting his words. Of course, he was right. Whatever horrors lived in her brain couldn't hurt her. She had survived whatever she had been through with the monster who had held her.

"Thank you. You've just made me feel a lot better," she said.

He grinned at her. "Good."

His smiles should be illegal. It was ridiculous the way they made her feel. Unfortunately, his smile quickly fell away. "I'm sorry you don't have your parents with you, especially now while you're going through all of this. I'm sure it would help you if they were here."

A familiar grief stabbed through her even though it had been three years since she'd lost them. "I had a bad feeling the morning they left here to drive to New Orleans for their anniversary," she said. "They had so many fun plans for that weekend. So excited to get away." A touch of anger rose up inside her. "All drunk drivers should be arrested and put into jail for the rest of their lives."

"What happened to the man who hit your parents' car?"

"He was charged with two counts of manslaughter and received a sentence of three years. In the next couple months, he'll be back out on the streets living his best life, but my parents are gone forever."

"He got a ridiculously light sentence," Etienne said.

"His parents are wealthy, and he had a good defense team. But enough about that," she insisted. "We'd better finish eating while it's all still warm."

"I can tell you right now that I definitely intend to clean my plate," he replied.

For a few minutes, they ate in a comfortable silence. She had to remind herself that he was only here because he was on guard duty.

Despite her attraction to him, she'd do well to remember he wasn't here because he was attracted to her or because he was eager to spend time with her on a personal level. He was doing his job and just happened to accept her invitation to a meal.

"I'm curious, would you be interested in getting some therapy?" he asked once they had finished eating.

"I could probably use some, and I'm certainly not averse to the idea."

"We have a good therapist right here in town. Her name is Dr. Amber Kingston, and she does FaceTime appointments."

"I would definitely be interested in that. Tomorrow I'll look her up and see what we can arrange," she replied. After a six-month absence from her life and with a case of amnesia, it certainly wouldn't hurt to get some therapy.

"I was also wondering how good your memory is for the time before you were kidnapped," he replied.

"I think I remember everything up until I decided to make a late evening run for groceries," she replied. "I wanted to get eggs for breakfast the next morning. Instead, I got kidnapped."

"Okay, enough about your memories," he said and stood. "Now tell me how I can help with the dinner cleanup."

"That's easy. You can't help," she said firmly as she got up from the table.

"Well, thank you for the meal," he said. "It was definitely the highlight of my day."

"And thank you for the company. It was the highlight of mine," she replied. They walked together to her front door.

He stopped at the door and turned to look at her. His smoke gray eyes held a wealth of sympathy. "I imagine it's going to be a bit lonely for you since we aren't letting anyone come in or you out until we get this guy behind bars. At least you had one opportunity to visit with your friends when you came home from the hospital before we changed the rules."

"It will be a bit lonely, but I'll survive," she replied. Her work as a writer forced her to be alone a lot of the time, but there was no question that before all this happened, she'd been a social person. Rarely did a day go by that somebody didn't stop in to visit or she went out with her girlfriends.

"As long as you understand that I'm doing all this to keep you safe," he said.

She smiled. "Trust me, I understand."

"On that note, I'll get out of here and let you enjoy the rest of your evening. Thank you again for the unexpected and wonderful meal."

"I'm just glad you enjoyed it," she replied. And then he was gone, swallowed up by the darkness of the night as he left the shanty.

She locked the door behind him and went back into the kitchen to clean up. As she worked, her thoughts were filled with the man who had just gone outside.

It was surprising that he didn't have a wife or a significant other. With his dark, slightly curly hair and his beautiful gray eyes and bold chiseled features, she couldn't imagine a single woman in town who wouldn't want to claim him as her own.

She certainly didn't know him well at all, but there was no question she was physically drawn to him. A single touch from him had ignited a surprising flicker inside her. When he gazed at her, she wanted to fall into the warm gray depths of his eyes. She couldn't remember ever having such a visceral reaction to a man before.

Even though she didn't know much about him, she felt a strange comfort when he was around. It was more than just the fact he was a law officer in charge of her safety, but she couldn't explain it.

But no matter how attracted she was to him, she was just a job to him. She had to remember he wanted nothing more from her than her memories, and she was going to do her very best to give him what he wanted as soon as possible.

Hopefully, the therapy would help her retrieve her lost memories and the bad guy would end up in jail. The only downside was that would be the end of her time with the handsome lawman.

ETIENNE SAT IN the darkness, listening to the sounds of the swamp all around him. Frogs croaked their deep-throated songs, and small nocturnal animals rustled through the brush. He was hoping for a much bigger animal to show up.

There was no question in his mind the Swamp Soul Stealer would come after Colette. Ettienne knew it was just a matter of when.

Everyone in town now knew that Colette didn't have her memories…yet. That information had flown around like wildfire as everyone wanted the monster caught. Even though the crimes had taken place in the swamp and only affected the people who lived there, everyone in Crystal Cove wanted these crimes solved and the perpetrator arrested.

Etienne frowned and touched the butt of his gun as he thought about the man he sought. Four men and three women had been plucked from their lives and apparently taken someplace to be starved and abused. Why? He couldn't even begin to guess at the motivation for such a crime.

It was obvious from the condition that Colette had been found in that the victims were being treated horribly. Again, why? Etienne and his team had checked the backgrounds of all the victims to see if they intersected in any way by somehow angering or having issues with a specific person. There was nothing there, nothing obvious to tie the victims together.

So who was this monster and what was his end goal? Why was he kidnapping these people? Where in the swamp was he hiding these four men and now just two women? Was it somebody who lived in the swamp or somebody who lived in town?

There were certainly far more questions about these crimes than there were answers. He still hoped many of the answers resided in Colette's brain and she'd be able to access them soon, but only time would tell.

Meanwhile, he and his men would continue to investigate anything that came up in an effort to find the Swamp Soul Stealer and his victims. Etienne prayed that all the victims were still alive.

He didn't have to worry about falling asleep. Even if he wasn't on guard duty, it would have just been another sleepless night in his recliner.

As the night deepened, the shanty emitted a soft glow,

letting him know Colette had turned on her lanterns in the living room. About an hour after that, all the lights went out, and he knew she'd gone to bed.

Colette. He was shocked by his intense physical attraction to her. Never before had a woman affected him on such a primal level. Was it all mixed up because of her importance to his case? He didn't know. What he did know was it was something that wouldn't and couldn't be explored. He had to do everything in his power to tamp down his desire whenever he was around her. She had enough to deal with in her life.

A deep guilt swept through him as he thought of her and her memories. He was asking her to recall what he knew would be horrible things. Right now, there was a soft innocence about her, but once she pulled back the veil and remembered her time in captivity, she would probably lose that softness.

He'd lied to her when he told her that her memories couldn't hurt her. He knew they could... They would deeply hurt her. While she had survived her time with a monster, remembering everything that had been done to her by him might break her forever.

He was a lawman who needed her memories to catch the monster, but he was also a man who didn't want her to have to suffer. It was definitely a challenging situation.

The night deepened, and the swamp darkened. From his vantage point, a small break in the trees overhead allowed him to see a slice of the sky. Stars winked their brilliance in the otherwise dark canvas of the night.

It was hard to believe that in all this primal beauty, a monster stalked in the night. Hopefully most of the swamp people now knew the dangers of going out of their homes after dark. What surprised and perplexed him was that it was not just vulnerable women who had been taken, but also strong young men. As crimes went, this one was confusing.

The night slowly passed, and dawn began to paint the area with a golden glow. It was just after 6:30 a.m. when the sound of Colette's generator thrummed in the air, letting him know she was awake.

At a few minutes before seven, her door opened, and she stood just inside the doorway. He stood from the rocking chair and greeted her. She was clad in a long, coral-colored robe and held a cup of coffee out to him. The color of the robe was amazing against her dark beauty.

"Good morning," she said. "I thought you might be ready for coffee. I don't know how you like it, so right now it's just black."

"Just black is exactly the way I like it," he replied, touched by her thoughtfulness. He took the cup from her and couldn't help but notice her scent. She smelled like a fresh exotic flower. It was a fragrance he found very appealing. "Thank you. It's very kind of you."

"It's the least I can do for a man who spent his night outside in a rocking chair guarding me," she replied. "Do you want to come in to drink it?"

"No, thanks, I'll just drink it out here. It won't be long, and I'll be off duty. But thanks again."

She nodded, offered him a smile and then closed the door. Etienne returned to his seat in the rocking chair. The strong dark brew was welcome, and as he sipped it, he watched the dawn finish its brilliant dance across the sky.

He drank all of the coffee and knocked on her door to return the cup. By that time, J.T. Caldwell appeared to take over watch duty.

J.T. was young with a baby face that emphasized his youth. The other officers teased him about being the baby on the squad, but he was a damn good officer who loved what he did.

Etienne greeted him with a smile. "You ready for this? It's going to be a long day."

J.T. held up a canvas bag. "I have a couple of peanut butter and jelly sandwiches, a thermos of hot coffee and a soda in here. I'm ready to take on the day," he replied with a boyish grin.

"Then I'm going to leave you in charge here, and I'll see you this evening," Etienne replied.

"See you then," J.T. replied cheerfully.

Minutes later Etienne was in his car and headed to the police department. He was eager to see if Trey had managed to connect with Levi the day before.

Levi was a big man, accustomed to wrestling with gators. He would have the strength needed to take down a victim and then carry them off to wherever his den was located. Still, the only thing that had raised Etienne's suspicions about the man was the way he questioned Colette about her memories when all the friends had been together at her house.

He was one of few men who had raised any suspicions at all since the beginning of the kidnappings. Etienne knew it wasn't much to go on, but right now he would leave no stone unturned in the hunt for the Swamp Soul Stealer and his victims.

As usual when he entered the police station through the back door, the hallway to his office was empty. Most of the officers on duty would be out on the streets. There was always an officer at the front desk, and Trey should be there as the top officer when Etienne was away.

As he sat at his desk, thoughts of the victims played in his mind. Luka Lurance was a good-looking young man. He was lean and fit and had been one of the first people to just vanish into thin air.

Then there had been Colette, Haley Chenevert and Sophia Fabre, all taken in fairly quick succession. Haley was the youngest of the three at twenty years old, and Colette had been the oldest at twenty-eight.

Finally, there was Willie Trahan, Clayton Beauregard and Jacques Augustin. At first it had been believed that Willie got his nose in some moonshine and stumbled off somewhere in the swamp to sleep it off. He'd been known to do that on occasion. But when he hadn't returned to his shanty two days later, the worst was believed.

Clayton Beauregard had left his young wife and newborn son to make a quick run to the store for formula. When he didn't immediately return, his wife called Etienne. He and a couple of his men had gone to Clayton and Lillie's place and discovered grocery bags not far from their shanty but no sign of Clayton. It was heartbreaking how close Clayton had been to the safety of his home when he was taken.

Jacques Augustin had disappeared in the last two weeks. He was a slender man with a pleasant personality who fished for a living.

Mothers, fathers, wives and friends had all cried on Etienne's shoulders, terrified and grief-stricken by the disappearance of their loved ones. Their tears and fear filled Etienne's heart with a heaviness he thought might never go away.

Dammit, he didn't care about the recall effort that might

oust him from his job. If the people of Crystal Cove had lost their confidence in him, then he needed to go for the good of the town he loved.

But not quite yet. This was a job he had to finish. He wanted to be the lawman to catch the man who had terrorized the people of Crystal Cove and haunted his sleep for the past five months or so.

Somewhere along the line, this had become personal to him. Now, more than anything, he wanted to catch the man who had tortured Colette so badly. He desperately wanted to capture the man who had nearly killed her and put the dark shadows into the depths of her beautiful eyes.

These thoughts snapped away as Trey appeared in his office door. "Just the man I was going to go find," Etienne said and gestured Trey into the chair in front of his desk.

"Long night?" Trey asked.

"Yeah, but I managed. Tell me what's new here," Etienne said.

"Joel and I caught up with Levi Morel late yesterday afternoon," Trey said.

Etienne leaned forward, any tiredness from the long hours of the night before momentarily gone. "And?"

"And he was definitely not happy to talk to us. He said he was deeply offended that we would even think he had anything to do with the kidnappings."

"That doesn't surprise me," Etienne replied. "Of course that's what he would say."

"He had damn little in the way of alibis for the nights of the kidnappings. He couldn't remember what he was doing and assumed he was out in the swamp hunting gators all alone. Or he was in his shanty alone."

"So no real alibis," Etienne said thoughtfully.

"Do you really think he's a viable suspect?"

Etienne thought about the big man who had pressed Colette so hard about her memory on her first day home. "He's certainly big and strong enough to carry bodies around."

"And as a gator hunter, he would know places in the swamp that we wouldn't," Trey added.

"I think he's a potential suspect," Etienne replied. "Why don't you see if we can get Judge Cooke to give us a search warrant for his shanty? Even though we don't have any real evidence against Levi, hopefully the judge will see things our way and grant the warrant."

"I'll get to work on it right away," Trey said.

"Call me when you hear something," Etienne said, his weariness back to weigh heavily on his shoulders. "This might all be a crapshoot, but it's one I want to follow up on. Maybe we'll find something in his shanty that incriminates him."

"It would definitely be good to have an end to this case," Trey said.

"It would be better than good," Etienne replied.

What would be really great was if they could solve these crimes without Colette having to revisit the horror of her memories.

Chapter Four

Colette turned the two pork chops browning in her pan. She'd already made skillet cornbread and had a bowl of coleslaw in the cooler.

It was just before seven…about when Etienne would come on duty to guard her. She was wearing a pair of jeans and a pink sleeveless blouse she knew looked good on her. Her long thick hair was pulled back at the nape of her neck with a pink tie.

She hoped the handsome lawman would come in to eat with her again tonight, but she really had no idea if he would or not. If he didn't, she would just have leftovers tomorrow night.

She told herself she would welcome anyone coming into the shanty for a visit. Really, she just wanted Etienne to come in because she was a bit lonely. Besides, he wasn't coming to her shanty for a friendly visit. He was coming here because he was on guard duty, keeping her safe from a man who wanted to kill her.

But that didn't explain the little dance of pleasure inside her heart as she thought about spending more time with him. There was no question that she was intensely drawn to him, and it had nothing to do with the fact that right now he was her only connection to the outside world and he was protecting her from some unknown monster in the swamp.

She turned down the heat of the electric stovetop beneath the skillet. Then she made sure the table was clean and ready for company.

At a couple minutes before seven, a wave of nervous energy swept through her as she walked to her front door. She unlocked and then opened it.

He sat in the rocker, a handsome blue knight keeping her safe from all harm as the sun was setting. He smiled at her and a wave of warmth filled her chest. "Evening, Colette," he said.

"Good evening, Etienne. I have some dinner ready in here if you'd like to join me."

"I'd love to join you," he said without hesitation. He rose from the rocking chair, and she opened the door wider to allow him in. As he walked past her, she once again smelled his scent. It was one of clean male and spicy cologne.

"Come on in and have a seat. I've got it ready to serve," she said.

He sat at the table, and she felt his gaze on her as she filled their plates with the pork chops, coleslaw, mashed potatoes and the golden-brown cornbread.

"You know you don't have to cook for me every evening," he said as she placed the plate before him. "Although this all looks and smells delicious."

"I really don't mind making a little extra each evening," she said and sat opposite him with her own plate. "Besides, I enjoy your company."

"And I enjoy yours," he replied with the smile that always warmed her in a way she couldn't explain.

"Well, let's eat while it's hot," she suggested. He'd said he enjoyed her company, but was it simply because he needed something from her? Was he just being kind to her because he needed her memories? Or did he truly enjoy her company?

She decided at that moment she wasn't going to overthink things with him. She enjoyed his company and intended to continue to do so until her memories returned or the Swamp Soul Stealer was caught and placed behind bars.

"This is all really good," he said after taking several bites.

"Thanks. My father always liked pork chops, although fried fish was his very favorite," she replied.

"Was he a fisherman?"

"He was." She smiled at thoughts of her dad. "He was a quiet man who loved fishing, my mother and me. He sold his fish to the people in the swamp who couldn't, for whatever reason or another, fish for themselves. There were many in the swamp who depended on my dad for their dinner each night."

"They must miss him then," Etienne replied.

She nodded. "I'm sure they do. So, how was your day?" she asked, wanting to change the topic and not dwell on the heartache that came from the loss of her parents. If she thought about it for too long, she could still cry over the loss of them.

He took a bite of the mashed potatoes and then washed it down with the bottle of water she'd set on the table. "Interesting," he finally answered, his gray eyes thoughtful.

"Interesting how?" she asked curiously.

"I think we finally have a new suspect in the Swamp Soul Stealer case."

She stared at him, her heart jumping with excitement. Was it possible he'd found the perpetrator without having her memories? That would be beyond amazing. "Oh, that's wonderful. Who is it?" she asked eagerly.

"I'm sorry, but right now we're keeping the information close to our chests," he replied and then frowned. "I probably shouldn't have even brought it up."

"But maybe if you told me who it is, it would jog something loose in my head," she said, still excited about the prospect of a new suspect.

He shook his head. "If I did that, then a defense attorney would have a field day and could argue I put things into your head. I'm sorry, Colette. Like I said, I probably shouldn't have said anything about it."

"I understand," she replied, although she was a bit disappointed that he wouldn't tell her the suspect's name. "Still, it's exciting that you have a new suspect. Maybe you can catch the man without me."

"I won't lie, Colette. It would be much easier to make a case if we had your memories to help us," he replied, his eyes the soft gray of a late twilight sky.

"I know... I'm really trying," she replied fervently. "I've been thinking about it almost all the time." It was true. In the quiet hours of the day, she'd tried over and over again to bring forth the memories that were trapped inside her mind.

"Maybe you shouldn't try so hard," he suggested. "Maybe you just need to relax about it, and then something will come to you when you least expect it."

"That's what Dr. Kingston told me today. I called her this morning, and we had a nice talk. We set up a FaceTime every other day for the next two weeks."

"That's great. So you connected with her," he replied.

"Definitely. I felt an instant connection with her, and I

think we're going to work together just fine. Now, let's talk about something else."

He offered her one of his beautiful smiles. "How was the rest of your day?"

Once again, a sweet heat swirled through her. "It was pretty good. I got some more writing done, and I was happy with what I wrote. That always makes it a good day."

"Tell me more about this series you wrote about swamp life."

She laughed. "Oh, surely you don't want me to bore you with all that."

"I wouldn't find it boring at all," he replied. "I'm interested in it."

She was vaguely surprised and pleased that, though they had finished eating, he seemed to be in no hurry to leave the shanty and go outside. Rather he was lingering for more conversation with her.

"I started writing the articles to educate others about the people who live in the swamps. The general consensus has always been that the swamps are filled with drunks and lowlifes and criminals. I wanted to shine a light on the hardworking and good people who live here."

For the next fifteen minutes or so, she talked about the articles she had done in the past. She had written about everything from the people to the lifestyles and the beauty of swamp life. She had also detailed the dangers of living in a place where all kinds of wild animals existed.

"I'm so sorry," she finally said with an embarrassed laugh. "I've been rambling on and on."

"Please don't apologize. I enjoy listening and learning more about you and what you find important," he replied.

"It's obvious you're passionate about what you do, and it's also obvious you love it here."

"I do love it here, but keep in mind I don't know anything else," she replied.

"Would you ever consider living in town?" he asked.

She frowned thoughtfully. "I don't know. I've never really thought about it before. I guess it would depend on a lot of things."

"I was just curious if it would be difficult for people who live here to transition from swamp life to town life," he replied.

"Lots of people have successfully made the transition," she said. "You're a town guy through and through, aren't you?"

"I am, but I have to be because of my job, although I might not have that for too much longer." His eyes darkened and a frown deepened the lines across his forehead.

"Why?" she asked in surprise.

"I've heard that there's a recall petition making the rounds."

"A recall? But, why?"

"I guess there are some people who aren't very happy with the way I've been conducting the investigation into the Swamp Soul Stealer," he replied. "They think this should have been solved a long time ago."

"But you can only do what you can do. When I was in the hospital, I heard that this man was like a ghost, stealing people without leaving any clues behind. How can anyone expect you to solve a case without any leads or clues?"

"I've done everything I can so far to catch this perp," he replied, his eyes appearing to grow darker.

"I'm sure you have," she replied, indignant on his behalf.

"Let the person who started the recall petition solve the crimes. Let's see how far they get catching the monster."

He grinned at her. "I must say, I appreciate your support."

"Well, you definitely have it," she said fervently. "I was a victim of this monster. Of all the people who should be upset about the investigation, it should be me. But for years I heard what a good lawman you are, and I know you've been working hard on this case."

"Thank you, Colette. It's easy to forget that for most of my years as chief of police, people were happy with me and my team and the work we did to keep the peace in Crystal Cove."

"Etienne, you can't let this case define you." She reached out her hand and grasped his, wanting him to feel supported. His fingers curled around hers as if seeking her touch.

"I know," he replied. He squeezed her hand and then pulled away to rake the hand through his black, curly hair with a deep sigh. "I appreciate the meal and the pep talk," he said.

"A pep talk will be available anytime you need one, Etienne. There will also be a meal ready for you every single night for as long as you're on duty here," she replied.

"You know that isn't necessary," he said as he rose from the chair.

"I know, but I do enjoy your company, and I will enjoy cooking for us." She also got up from the table. "So it's settled. Every night dinner is on me."

"That's really nice of you, Colette."

"It's the least I can do for the man who is sitting at my front door through the hours of the night," she replied.

Together, they walked to the front door and just like the night before she was sorry to see him leave to sit in a chair in the dark. She was sure they were long hours for him, and she knew the only reason he was doing it was to protect her.

"Then I guess I'll see you tomorrow evening," he said when he reached the door.

"Etienne, I just want to tell you how much I appreciate what you're doing for me," she said as she placed a hand on his forearm.

He took a step toward her, and for a long moment they stood intimately close to each other. The air suddenly snapped with an electricity that also sparked inside her.

His dark gaze appeared to focus on her lips, and she leaned toward him. Her heart suddenly beat a quickened rhythm. Was he going to kiss her? Oh, it surprised her how much she wanted him to.

"It's my pleasure," he replied and jerked back from her.

She dropped her hand from his arm.

"Good night, Colette."

"'Night Etienne. I'll see you tomorrow." She closed and locked the door behind him. Leaning against the door, she relived the moment that had just happened between them.

She could have sworn she'd seen an impending kiss in his eyes. For a split second, it had shone bright and hot in those gray depths. And it had shocked her how much she wanted him to kiss her.

She shoved away from the door to start clearing the kitchen.

She hated the fact that Etienne seemed to be entertaining doubts about himself when it came to his job. She'd told him the truth when she said that before her ordeal, she had heard nothing but good things about the man who kept the law in Crystal Cove.

In all the years he'd held his job, she'd never had any

interaction with him and hadn't even seen him except at a distance. Still, when he arrived at the hospital to take her home, there'd been an odd familiarity about him...as if they'd known each other for a long time.

Maybe her whole ordeal had made her more than a little crazy.

Even though she knew she was in danger, she felt no fear. With an officer guarding her through the day and Etienne on duty through the nights, she felt completely safe and protected.

Now, if she could just get her memories back, she'd be able to give them to Etienne so he could solve the crime. Knowing how he was feeling about himself made her want to retrieve them even more, though she was sure that would mean her time with him would end.

HE WATCHED CHIEF of Police Etienne Savoie go into the shanty, and his stomach twisted and churned tight with rage. He crouched low in the thick brush as he stared at the shanty where she was right now.

He'd thought the bitch was on death's doorstep when he took her back into the swamp to bury her. He hadn't intended to kill her, but he guessed he'd gone too far with her and she'd been too weak to survive. He was certain death was about to claim her, and he'd figured the best place to dispose of a body was deep in the swamp.

That night he had placed her on the ground next to him and began to dig a shallow hole to put her body in. All of a sudden, she sprang to her feet and took off running. It was so unexpected it took him a couple seconds to respond.

He'd chased after her, but the night and the swamp were so dark, he quickly lost track of her. He'd hoped she would collapse and die someplace in the tangled vines and thick brush. He was positively shocked when she was found the next morning.

He'd been scared as hell that she would be able to identify him. Thank God she'd been in such bad shape she was immediately placed in a medically induced coma. He prayed over and over again that she would never come out of it, that she would die in the hospital before ever awakening.

Then when she did, he learned she had amnesia. She couldn't remember him or what he had done to her. The amnesia was the only thing that was saving him...so far.

But she was still a danger to him. If her memories returned, she'd probably be able to identify him as the man who held her captive for three months, the man who had beaten and starved her.

There was no question about it, he had to kill her soon. She had to die before she started to regain any of her memories. It was obvious the cops knew she was in danger, as there was an officer outside of her door 24/7. But that wasn't going to stop him.

Somehow he'd figure out a way to get to her, and sooner rather than later.

"We got our search warrant for Morel's shanty," Trey said in greeting the next morning. "It just came in a few minutes ago from Judge Cooke."

Any tiredness from the night duty sloughed off Etienne's shoulders as a new adrenaline punched through him. "I'm surprised he bit since we had no real evidence to tie Morel to the kidnappings."

"I think the judge is as eager as we are to find the guilty party," Trey replied.

"Then let's get some men together and head out," Etienne said.

In the end it was Etienne, Trey, Joel Smith and Thomas Grier who loaded up in two cars and headed to the swamp to conduct a search of Levi Morel's shanty.

"It would be great if this pans out, and we find something from the victims inside Levi's place," Etienne said as he turned onto the street that would take them to the swamp's entrance.

"It would be better than great," Trey agreed.

"But it's possible this is just a wild-goose chase. It's also possible since he has the people in his control, he's not a souvenir taker." Etienne tightened his hands on the steering wheel.

"Still, it's something we need to check out. You told me that Levi really pressed Colette about her memory. Why would he care about it that much?"

"He definitely seemed to," Etienne replied. He looked in his rearview mirror where the other patrol car followed closely behind his. The four of them should easily be able to execute the search warrant.

As he drove, he couldn't help but think of the night before and his time with Colette. He'd enjoyed the meal and their conversation, but what surprised him was the fact that he'd nearly kissed her. He had wanted to take her lush lips with his and taste the fire he saw burning in her eyes. Thank God he had stopped himself before a kiss happened. He had a feeling if he started kissing Colette, he'd never want to stop.

He shoved thoughts of that moment away as he pulled into the parking area right before the swamp's entrance. Joel pulled his patrol car next to his, and together the four of them got out of the cars.

Adrenaline rushed through Etienne, quickening his heartbeat and flooding through his veins. Was it possible that this could be it? Could Levi be the one he sought? "We'll let Trey lead us in since he knows where Levi's shanty is located."

Trey nodded.

Etienne continued, "Be ready for anything. If this is our man, then he could be dangerous. Remember we need him alive to lead us to his captives. Besides, he might not be our man. Now, let's go."

Trey headed into the junglelike growth with the others following close behind him. Their path took them past Colette's shanty. Etienne saw Officer Michael Tempe seated in the rocking chair outside of her door, looking alert. He raised a hand and waved at them as they passed by.

The air was rich with the scents of greenery, mysterious florals and the ever-present underlying faint smell of decay. Little animals scurried from the trails in an effort to escape the human presence invading their space.

Not far from Colette's, they took a narrower path, and after a short walk, a small shanty appeared. Trey stopped walking and turned to the others. "That's Levi's place," he said quietly.

It was 9:30 a.m. Hopefully the gator hunter was home after his hunt or whatever it was he did during the night. Etienne moved in front of Trey and approached the front door. "Levi Morel," he called out as he knocked on the door.

They waited several moments for a response, and then Etienne knocked again, this time harder and louder. "Levi, it's the police. Open your door."

There was the sound of rustling inside, and the door flew open. It was obvious the big man had been in bed. His shaggy black hair was mussed, and he was wearing a pair of loose blue shorts and a stained gray T-shirt.

"What the hell is going on here?" he asked, his dark eyes blazing with irritation. "What the hell do you all want?"

"We're here to conduct a search of the premises," Etienne replied. He pulled the search warrant out of his pocket and handed it to the man.

Levi tossed it aside with a snort. "What gives you the right to come into my shanty and search?" He held the door tightly closed behind him with his big hand.

"That piece of paper you just threw aside gives us the right," Etienne replied. "Look, Levi, we don't want any trouble here. Just let us come in and do our job."

"So what are you looking for? Some kind of evidence that I'm the Swamp Soul Stealer?" Levi snorted again. "You all are crazy if you think I'm the one kidnapping people and holding them somewhere."

"Then let us come in to conduct our search," Etienne replied evenly. Interesting that the man had jumped to the conclusion that they were here about the kidnappings. "It won't take us long, and then we'll be gone and you can go about the rest of your day."

It was obvious Levi didn't want them inside his private domain. But no matter how much the man stalled and protested, Etienne was more determined than ever to get this done.

"Come on, Levi. I'd like to do this the easy way, but if you insist, we can do it the hard way. One way or another, it's getting done," Etienne said firmly.

Levi hesitated another long moment and then flung his door wide open and stepped outside. "Knock yourselves out. You stupid fools are completely wasting your time here."

Etienne motioned for Thomas to remain outside with Levi, and then he, Trey and Joel went inside. The first thing that struck Etienne was the smell. It was a combination of dirty laundry, gator and moonshine.

It was a small one-room shanty with a cot covered in ratty blankets pushed against one wall, a chest of drawers against another and the usual potbellied stove in a corner. There was also a three-shelf bookcase holding an overflowing variety of items. Dirty clothes formed a large pile at the foot of the bed. It was obvious Levi wasn't much into cleanliness.

"Trey, you check around the bed and go through the dirty clothes. Joel, look in and around the stove and then check out the drawers. I'm going to tackle this bookcase. Look for hidden compartments in the wood. Keep in mind if this is our guy, hopefully he's kept some souvenirs from the victims here. That's what we're looking for."

With that, the men all got to work. Etienne began to check the items on the bookcase. The top shelf held an open brown bottle. One sniff let him know that it was moonshine probably made by Jackson Renee Dupree, an old man who had a still somewhere in the swamp.

For the most part, the shelves held a lot of fishing items. Big hooks and spinners, broken reels and jars of stink bait filled up the space. What wasn't there was anything to tie Levi to the kidnappings.

"Nothing here," Joel said.

"Same here," Trey added in obvious frustration. "I went through the clothes one piece at a time, and it's obvious they all belong to Levi."

"Let's all look around the room and check the woodwork and the floor for any hidden compartments, then we'll go back outside and search the area around the shanty." Etienne released a deep sigh. The adrenaline that had initially pumped through him slowly began to depart.

Forty-five minutes later, they were finished with the search.

"I told you there was nothing here, because I'm not the man you're searching for," Levi said with obvious irritation. "You really got a problem with the case if you think I'm a good suspect. Now, get off my property and leave me alone." He returned to the shanty and slammed the front door shut.

Etienne and his men quietly made their way back to their vehicles. Exhaustion from his night duty and the disappointment from an unsuccessful search sat heavily on his shoulders.

"We knew it was a long shot," Trey said once they were in the car and headed back to the station.

"Yeah, I'd just hoped for a different outcome," Etienne said. "It's very possible our perp hasn't kept any souvenirs."

"That's absolutely possible. As long as he has the victims, he doesn't need the souvenirs. Unless another suspect pops up, I guess it's all up to Colette now."

Etienne frowned. He'd really hoped to do this without her. He'd hoped she would never have to remember her time in captivity when she'd been starved and beaten by some monster.

But now, it was more important than ever that she remember. What he feared was that in remembering, she'd be so traumatized she would never be the same again.

Chapter Five

For the past three nights, Etienne had shared dinner with Colette. The time with her had deepened their friendship and had also increased his physical draw to her.

She had told him over dinner that she'd had another session with Dr. Kingston, but no memories had returned to her yet.

He now sat in the rocking chair on the porch as the moon climbed higher in the sky. Insects buzzed and clicked, and frogs croaked their nightly songs.

There had been no breaks in the Swamp Soul Stealer case, but the dinners with Colette had definitely been enjoyable. They'd shared stories about their childhoods and had laughed together. He'd shared some incidents about various arrests he'd made, although he hadn't told her any names. She, in turn, had told him about funny times among the people in the swamp.

He found her not only beautiful and bright but also witty with a great sense of humor. His physical attraction to her was a constant battle he had with himself. He was desperate to maintain a close friendship with her but knew to explore a physical relationship with her was just plain wrong.

He didn't know how long he'd been sitting there with

thoughts of Colette when he heard it…a slight rustling that came from the brush at the foot and to the right of Colette's short bridge. He grabbed the butt of his gun as a burst of adrenaline rushed through him.

The rustling got louder. Something…or somebody was definitely in the brush. He slowly rose to his feet, his heart beating a wild rhythm.

Would the Swamp Soul Stealer make so much noise? Did he want some kind of a showdown? If that was the case, then Etienne was ready for it. Dammit, he wanted this all over and done. He wanted Colette to be safe again and going about her life without the fear of some monster being after her. He also wanted the entire town of Crystal Cove to breathe a sigh of relief knowing the bad guy was behind bars and his victims had been saved.

He crept across the bridge, guided only by the faint moonlight overhead. He pulled his gun and held it steady in his hand as he moved closer to the rustling noise.

He kept his gaze divided between the moving brush and Colette's front door. It was only as he drew closer to the thick overgrowth that he heard a different sound. It was a series of snorts and grunts that immediately made him relax.

Beyond the brush was a small clearing, and in the clearing was a sounder of wild boar. The five big hogs rooted in the ground with their long snouts, overturning the soil and destroying the ground.

These wild beasts were a scourge in the swamp and could be quite dangerous when confronted. With his gun still in hand, he broke through the brush and began to shoo them away. They squealed and snorted and thankfully didn't approach him, but ran off into the darkness.

Disappointed that it hadn't been an animal in the form

of a man, he holstered his gun and walked back across the bridge to the rocking chair. As he eased back down, he thought of that moment when his attention had been divided between the moving brush and the porch.

He'd been lucky that it had been a bunch of wild boar and not somebody providing a distraction so another person could get through the front door and inside the shanty.

Was it possible the Swamp Soul Stealer was really two men working together? There had been no evidence pointing to that, but then again there had simply been no evidence at all.

In his heart of hearts, Etienne didn't believe it was two men working together. He and all his men believed these kidnappings were the work of one sick man. He could only hope that at some point the man would make a mistake and Etienne would be able to arrest him.

The rest of the night passed uneventfully, with thoughts of the monster in the swamp and Colette to keep him company. Early dawn was just streaking across the sky when the thrum of Colette's generator filled the air.

Twenty minutes later, the front door opened, and she stood there with a cup of coffee in her hand. Once again, she had on the coral-colored robe that looked so beautiful with her skin tone, black hair and brown eyes. "Good morning," she said and held out the cup to him.

He took it from her and grinned. "You're spoiling me, Colette."

She laughed, the sound musical and pleasant. "I enjoy spoiling you. Besides it's just a cup of coffee."

"Still, it is much appreciated," he replied and then sobered. "Colette, I'd like for us to take a walk through the swamp this afternoon. Would you be up for it?"

Any mirth that had been on her lovely features fell away. Her eyes appeared to darken, and her lower lip trembled slightly.

"Colette, I promise you'll be safe with me," he said softly in an effort to cut through the fear that radiated from her.

She slowly nodded. "Okay, I'm up for it. What time do you want to do this?"

"I was thinking maybe right after noon. That will give me a chance to check in at the office, and then I'll come back out here." He hated like hell to do this to her, but he was hoping a walk in the swamp might cause something to jog loose in that beautiful head of hers.

"Okay, then I'll be ready," she replied. "I'll just see you then." She stepped back inside and closed the door behind her.

He frowned and took a sip of the hot brew. He hated that he'd upset her. But something had to be done to try to retrieve her memories. He now believed it was the only way to catch the man he sought. Unfortunately, he had to sacrifice the one for the many.

Once his relief came, he left the swamp and headed into the office. For the next hour, he read over arrest reports for the last week, needing to keep up with what else was happening in his town.

A young man had been arrested for shoplifting at the convenience store. Five speeding tickets had been handed out, and Brett Mayfield had been taken into jail after another bar brawl at the Voodoo Lounge.

It wasn't the first time the big handyman had been arrested after a bar fight. Whenever Brett got drunk, he became belligerent and picked fights with other drunk people. Even when sober, Brett was a big mouth with a temper. Etienne had heard through the grapevine that Brett and a couple of his friends were behind the recall effort against him.

Once he'd read the arrest reports, he spent the rest of his time going over and over the notes from the investigation into the Swamp Soul Stealer. Somehow, someway, he kept believing they were missing something.

Finally, it was time for him to return to Colette's place. Despite his exhaustion, an edge of excitement lit up inside him.

Would this work? Was it possible just walking around the swamp would make her remember things...things that would identify the monster? He hoped this succeeded even though he dreaded her having to suffer any pain from the memories that might return to her.

If there was any other way to get an arrest, he would have done it. But the truth of the matter was that right now Colette was his last hope. The kidnapper could strike again at any time, and another person would just disappear from the swamp. Etienne wanted to get the man behind bars before that happened again.

He also knew as long as the Swamp Soul Stealer was out there, Colette was in danger. Etienne was vaguely surprised the man hadn't made a move on Colette yet.

He parked before the swamp entrance and went in. It didn't take him long to reach her place where Michael Tempe was once again on duty.

The officer sat up straighter in the rocking chair as Etienne approached him. "Hey, Chief," he said in surprise. "I didn't expect to see you at this time of the day."

"I'm here to take Colette for a walk. Even though she'll be gone from the shanty for a little while, I want you to sit tight here."

"Of course," Michael replied. "Unless you tell me otherwise, I'm on duty until you relieve me this evening."

"Good man," Etienne replied and then knocked on Colette's door. The door opened, and as usual, she looked beautiful. Her jeans fit her slender legs, and the red blouse she wore emphasized her light olive complexion and the rich chocolate of her long-lashed eyes. Her hair was a waterfall of rich darkness that fell down her back.

A wave of intense desire punched him in the gut as she offered him a tentative smile. "I'm ready," she said with a slight lift of her chin.

"Then let's take a little walk together," he replied.

She stepped out of the shanty, and he followed her down the bridge. When she reached the bottom, she paused and turned to him. "Which way are we going?"

"Why don't we start with what you remember from the night you decided to run to the grocery store for eggs?" he replied.

"From here, I walked toward the entrance of the swamp to get to my car," she said. Her features were tense with obvious stress.

He hated to see her this way. She had told him in one of their dinner conversations that her neighbors had not only taken care of her shanty while she'd been gone, but they'd also taken care of her car by starting it up every day so the battery wouldn't go dead.

"Then let's walk that way," he suggested.

She nodded, and together they began to walk slowly along the paths she'd taken the night she was kidnapped.

He watched her carefully. If he saw any indication that this was too much for her, then he would call the whole thing off. He also kept a close eye on their surroundings, wanting to make certain she was safe and there was nobody around to pose a danger to her.

It was a beautiful day. Bright sunshine broke through the trees and sparkled on the lacy Spanish moss they passed. Birds called from the tops of the trees, and it was hard to believe there was any evil here.

They hadn't gone too far when she suddenly stopped and slapped at the back of her neck. "It was here... I—I never heard him coming. Something stabbed into the back of my neck, and...and I went down. I... I can't talk... Can't scream. And then everything went black." She stared at him with wide eyes. "I remember, Etienne. I remember that moment when he drugged me."

He reached out and grabbed her hands. They trembled in his. "Who is it, Colette? Did you see his face?" he asked urgently.

She hesitated a moment and then slowly shook her head. "No. I'm sorry. I don't think I saw him then. He came from behind me, and I fell unconscious before I got a chance to see him."

"Still, this is good, Colette. You just gave me valuable information." They had suspected the victims were drugged, but it had just been a supposition up until now. Apparently, whatever drug he used was very fast-acting. This explained how he had claimed his victims.

"Maybe I'll remember more if we keep walking," she said, her eyes shining brightly with her success.

The desire to kiss her suddenly shot through him with a fierce intensity. He wanted to take her in his arms and press her body tight against his as he took her mouth with all the fire that was inside him.

Instead, he squeezed her hands and then released them. "Shall we walk some more?"

"Absolutely," she replied. She smiled, her eyes still glistening beautifully. "That was fairly easy."

"Yes, but we both know some of your memories aren't going to be so easy to retrieve," he reminded her. The memory she had just gotten had been fairly benign, but he knew how difficult and painful others would be for her.

Her smile slowly faded. "I know, but right now I'm feeling particularly strong and ready to remember."

He hoped so. He hoped this was just the beginning, and a rush of memories would return to her. And he wanted to be right next to her, supporting her as she delved into the horrid memories of her time in captivity.

COLETTE STOOD IN front of her two-burner stovetop and added a can of jarred Italian sauce to the browned hamburger in her skillet. In another pot, she had spaghetti noodles boiling.

As she cooked, she fought off a wave of discouragement. She had walked through the swamp with Etienne for about an hour and a half, but no more memories had returned to her.

Oh, she'd wanted to remember…for him…for Etienne. She'd wanted to gift him with the information that would put the kidnapper behind bars and free the other victims. She'd wanted to gift him in order to see his beautiful gray eyes light up and a smile of success curve his lips.

More than that, she wanted him to take her into his arms. She wanted his strong arms to surround her and his mouth to take hers in a kiss that dizzied her senses. The more time she spent with him, the more her desire for him grew.

As they walked through the swamp, he had been particularly attentive to her, asking her often if she was okay and obviously gauging her emotional health. She knew if she had shown too much stress, he would have immediately called the whole thing off and taken her back to her shanty.

There were times when she thought she saw desire in the depths of his eyes, but did he desire Colette the woman or Colette the person who had the potential to solve his case and save him from a recall? At this point she didn't know the answer.

With a deep sigh, she drained the spaghetti noodles and added it to the meat mixture. It was almost seven, and she was expecting Etienne to come in and eat with her as usual. Besides the spaghetti, she'd made skillet-browned garlic bread and intended to serve corn as well.

She was beginning to feel like a captive in her own home. The days were long without any social interaction at all. Was it any wonder she looked forward to these dinners with Etienne? It was the only conversation she had each day.

She didn't even have a phone to talk on. She had no idea where her purse had gone to when she'd been kidnapped. She had no driver's license and no identification. She hadn't had time to replace any of it before she went into protective custody.

At precisely seven, she went to the front door and opened it. As always, Etienne sat in the rocking chair, and he rose at her appearance.

"Good evening, Colette," he said with the smile that always lit her up inside.

"Evening, Etienne. Come on in, dinner is ready."

"Sounds good." He swept past her and she relocked her

door, then followed him into the kitchen. He sat in his usual place at the table, and she began filling their plates.

"How was the rest of your day?" he asked.

"Quiet. What about yours? Did you get some sleep?"

"Yeah, I slept. This all looks good," he said as she placed his plate in front of him.

"It's nothing special," she replied, sitting across from him with her plate. "In fact, I need to give you another grocery list, and I need another block of ice for the cooler."

"You can give me a list tonight, and I'll bring the supplies tomorrow. Will that work?"

"Yes, that will work." She released a sigh.

He gazed at her for a long moment. "That was a very deep sigh. Are you upset about something?"

"No...not upset exactly." She picked up her fork, then set it back down. "I'm just starting to feel a bit like a prisoner here. While I love having you to talk to and eat with, I'm missing some social interaction during the long days. I'm really missing seeing something other than the four walls of my shanty."

He took a bite of the spaghetti, his gaze lingering on her. He swallowed and wiped his mouth with the paper towel she'd provided as a napkin. "Maybe tomorrow we can have lunch at the café and then go to the grocery store," he said.

"Really? Do you think it would be safe?" Her heart lifted at the thought of getting out of the shanty for an afternoon.

He frowned, obviously considering it. "I really can't imagine this guy would make a move on you out in public, so I think we can do this safely."

"Oh, I'd love to get out of these four walls for just a little bit of time," she admitted.

"Then we'll plan on lunch and the grocery store," he replied.

She gave him a huge smile. "Thank you, Etienne, and I promise after tomorrow I'll go back to being a happy captive in this shanty."

He returned her smile. "I want you to be happy no matter where you are."

"For the most part I am happy," she said. Although she'd be much happier if Etienne would take her in his arms and hold her. She would be much happier if the lawman would take her lips with his and kiss her until she forgot everything that was going on in her life. The only time that happened was when she was writing, but she couldn't work all the time.

"When I'm working in here, it's easy to forget that somebody is after me and an armed guard sits on my porch day and night," she said, voicing her thoughts aloud. "To be honest, I'm surprised the Swamp Soul Stealer hasn't made a move to get to me yet."

"I'm a little surprised by that too. Still, we can't let our guard down," he said soberly. "I still believe you're at great risk from this man. You and I both know he'll be afraid of your memories and will want to silence you before they can return."

She released another deep sigh. "I know, but now let's talk about more pleasant things."

"Okay," he readily agreed. "So what's your favorite thing to order at the café?"

For the next hour as they ate, their conversation remained light and easy. They talked about the food at the café and then chatted about some of the stores in town.

When he talked about Crystal Cove, there was a real love of community that shone from his eyes and made him more handsome than ever. It was evident that he loved this little town. It would be a real sin if he was recalled and lost his job.

Once they finished eating, they lingered at the table, talking and laughing as they spoke about some of the more colorful boutiques in town.

"Have you been into Spiritual Haven?" she asked.

"Yeah, I went in to check it out when it first opened," he replied. "A bunch of nonsense if you ask me."

She laughed. "So you don't think crystals, herbs and astrology can change your life?"

"I don't, but apparently there are some people here in town who do. I've heard the store is fairly successful. What about you? Do you believe in crystal magic?"

"Not really," she replied. "But some of the crystals are quite pretty."

"Then there's the Voodoo Queens shop, have you been in it?" he asked.

She grinned. "I have. That store stands for much of what I try to dispel about people who live in the swamps. Spells and voodoo dolls aren't who we are, yet I've heard she sells a lot of her dolls." She released a small burst of laughter. "Heck, for all I know somebody has a voodoo doll out there with my name on it."

"I don't believe that," he scoffed and leaned back in the chair. "Tell me about the romances you've had in your life. Have you ever been in love?"

She blinked at the sudden change in topic. "When I was twenty-two, I dated a man who lives here in the swamp. We were together for about six months. I liked him and enjoyed spending time with him, but the relationship never really developed into anything deeper like real love. He was my only serious relationship, so the short answer is no, I've never been in love before," she replied. "What about you?"

"Kind of the same with me. When I was much younger, I dated a woman for about three months. Everybody said how perfect we were for each other, and I enjoyed her company. One day I realized I did love her, but I wasn't in love with her. I knew then that she wasn't the right one for me and that I was wasting her time, and so I broke up with her."

"How did she take it?" Colette asked curiously.

"Surprisingly well. In fact, within a month she was engaged to another man." He released a dry laugh. "I had assumed she'd cry into her pillow over me for at least a month, but I think she was almost as relieved as I was when I broke it off with her. What about your guy? How did he take it when you broke up with him?"

"He took it okay. Thankfully we managed to remain good friends," she replied.

"That's nice." He scooted back from the table, obviously ready to head to his post outside.

"I think that's the way it should always be," she said. "When two people part ways, there should be no reason for any acrimony between them."

"It would be nice if it always worked out that way," he agreed. "As usual, thanks for dinner," he added as the two of them got up from the table and then walked toward the front door.

"It's always the highlight of my day," she replied. As she walked closely next to him, his cologne seemed to wrap around her. The talk about romance once again stirred up her crazy desire for Etienne.

He paused at the door and turned back to face her as a

fire danced in the very depths of his silver-gray eyes. She knew that fire... It heated the very center of her being.

For a moment, they were frozen in place, their gazes locked together, his body heat wafting toward her.

She leaned forward, mere inches from him. "Kiss me, Etienne." The words left her lips on a whisper of desire... of want.

His eyes flared even hotter, and he pulled her into his arms. His mouth captured hers in a kiss that immediately dizzied her senses as she wrapped her arms around his neck.

He pulled her closer, deepening the kiss. Their tongues swirled together in a heated dance, and she was lost in all things Etienne.

His body was so strong, so solid against her own, and she moved her hands across his broad back. She'd thought about being held in his arms for so long, and it was every bit as wonderful as she imagined.

He finally broke the kiss and stepped back from her. His eyes simmered with a wealth of emotions she couldn't even begin to discern. "I'm sorry, Colette. That should have never happened." His voice was deeper than usual.

"Why not? I wanted you to kiss me, Etienne," she replied softly. "In fact, I've been wanting it for some time now."

He frowned. "Well, it was a mistake, and it just isn't a good idea. Trust me, it won't happen again. Now, I'll pick you up around eleven thirty for lunch tomorrow. I'll just say good night." He turned and went out the door.

She closed it behind him and walked back into the kitchen. Her lips were still warm with the imprint of his, and her heart still beat an uneven rhythm of desire.

It wasn't a mistake. The kiss had been inevitable. There was no question there had been a haze of sexual tension that swirled around the two of them since the moment he had brought her home from the hospital. It was a sexual tension that had grown bigger and hotter every day they spent together.

He'd said it was a mistake, but she'd tasted the desire in his kiss.

One thing was for certain, she was definitely falling for Etienne. Now not only did she have to worry about a monster trying to kill her…she also had to worry about getting her heart broken by the very man who was supposed to protect her.

Chapter Six

At 11:30 a.m. the next day, Etienne approached Colette's shanty. He'd had all night to think of the kiss he'd shared with her, and he still couldn't get it out of his head.

Her lips had been so soft and so inviting, and as her body had pressed against his, he'd become almost fully aroused. That had snapped him to his senses, and he'd ended the kiss.

She was a potential witness in a crime, a woman whose life was in his hands. She was vulnerable right now, and the last thing he wanted to do was take advantage of the situation or of her.

Still, even this morning as he thought about the brief but very hot kiss, he couldn't help wanting to repeat it. She was definitely a sweet temptation, but it was important that he be stronger than his desire for her.

His thoughts had also been filled with their outing today. He'd worked it from all angles, and he believed he could take her out and keep her safe. Surely the perp wouldn't be stupid enough to try to get to her in public where there would be witnesses everywhere. While taking her out of the shanty wasn't something he wanted to do every day, he'd give her today. He'd loved seeing her eyes light up with excitement at the possibility of the outing. He'd loved seeing her so happy.

As her shanty came into view, he couldn't help the small edge of anticipation that sliced through him. There was no question that he enjoyed spending time with her. He looked forward to the dinners they shared each evening.

Hopefully this outing would go off without a hitch. He understood her cabin fever, and he believed going to the café and the grocery store would be safe. As long as they were out in public, it should be okay.

He headed across the bridge and grinned at Thomas Grier, who sat on duty. "Hey, Thomas, I'm taking our girl out for a little while. Why don't you knock off here, go get some lunch and come back in about two hours?"

Thomas stood and stretched. "Sounds good to me. I'll see you in a little while."

Etienne watched as the man went down the bridge and disappeared into the green thicket. Etienne turned and knocked on the door.

She answered immediately, and he couldn't help the lick of desire that tightened his stomach at the sight of her. She wore a light pink flowered dress that clung to her breasts and fell to just below her knees, showcasing her shapely bare legs. The pink of the dress complemented her cascade of dark hair and the glittering depths of her big brown eyes. She looked utterly beautiful and sexy. She offered him a huge smile that only increased his intense attraction to her.

"Ready to go?" he asked.

She released a musical burst of laughter. "I've been ready for the last hour."

"The only thing you need to remember is to stay close to me and do whatever I tell you to do."

"That won't be a problem," she replied as she grabbed his arm with a teasing smile.

She had the intoxicating scent of exotic fresh flowers, and once again a small flame lit inside him. As they walked away from the shanty, he kept her close to his side as his gaze shot left and right, seeking any potential trouble.

They reached his car, and he was grateful to get a little distance from her as she climbed into the passenger seat and he slid behind the wheel.

"I have to admit, it feels nice to be out of the shanty for a little while," she said as he headed toward town.

"Did you go out a lot before this all happened?" he asked.

"Ella and I would go out at least once a week for shopping or lunch or to get ice cream at Bella's Ice Cream," she replied. "But it isn't just about going out, it's also about nobody being able to come in to visit with me. Layla and Liam Guerin would often pop in for a visit, as did Jaxon and Levi."

"I'm sorry you're missing your friends," he replied sympathetically. "In fact, I'm sorry you're missing your normal life."

"It's okay. Eventually, I'll get my normal life back, and in the meantime, I really appreciate you taking me out today. I promise afterward I'll go back to being a good little prisoner in my own home."

He flashed her a quick glance. "I hate that you have to be a prisoner. I really hate that you have to go through all this, Colette."

She smiled. "It is what it is, right? I'd much rather be a prisoner in my own home than dead. I'm just thankful for getting out for a little while today."

"All you need to remember is if I tell you to do something, no matter how crazy it sounds, just do it without question," he said as he turned into the café's parking lot. "This should go without incident. As long as we're out in public, I can't imagine anyone coming after you."

He pulled into an empty space and parked. "Sit tight, and I'll come around to your door," he said.

Minutes later, the two of them entered the café. The scents of fried fish, hamburger and onions and different simmering vegetables mingled with the yeasty fragrance of freshly baked bread and the sweet smell of cakes and pies.

Crystal Cove Café was owned by Antoinette LeBlanc, a woman from the swamp. She had bought the café years ago and now lived in a room in the back of the business. It was decorated for home comfort with antique cooking tools hanging from the walls and a large copper fork and spoon that took up nearly one full wall.

It was always busy, but thankfully Etienne found an empty booth toward the back. He guided Colette toward it, and as they passed most of the other diners, several called out a pleasant greeting to her.

Etienne motioned her into the booth seat facing the back wall while he sat facing the diners where he could see who might approach them.

Colette's friend Ella headed toward them, an order pad in her hand and a wide smile curving her lips. "Colette, it's so good to see you out. I've missed you."

"I've missed you, too," Colette replied with a wide smile. "When this is all over, we'll make plans to go to Bella's and get ice cream."

"I'll be ready whenever you are. How are things going? Have any of your memories returned yet?" Ella asked.

The smile instantly fell from Colette's lips. "Unfortunately, no... Nothing yet."

"Well, it will all work out fine," Ella said with an encouraging smile. "Now, what can I get for you two to eat?"

Colette ordered the shrimp platter, and Etienne got a big burger with onion rings. While they waited for their food to be delivered, they talked about the work she'd gotten done over the last couple of days.

"I finally got my nerve up, and this morning I submitted two articles to the magazines I used to sell to," she replied.

"That's great, Colette. Congratulations on that," he replied. "So how long before you know if they'll buy them?"

"It could be days or weeks or even months. But it felt good to actually submit something after all this time."

Her eyes sparkled brightly as she spoke about her work. They were beautiful long-lashed eyes Etienne could easily fall into. His head filled with the memory of the kiss they had shared, and he tried to push it out of his head.

He tensed as he saw Brett Mayfield and his friend Adam Soreson approaching their booth. He'd heard through the grapevine that both men were pushing hard for the recall.

"Hi, Chief… Colette," Brett greeted them.

"How are you doing, Colette?" Adam asked. He was a big man with wide shoulders. Rumor had it he was one of the best gator hunters around.

"I'm doing just fine," she replied.

"What about you, Chief? You getting any closer to finding the Swamp Soul Stealer?" Brett asked.

"We're working hard to identify him," Etienne said.

"You still got that amnesia stuff?" Adam asked Colette.

"Unfortunately, yes," she replied.

"But that doesn't mean my team isn't working hard to solve these cases," Etienne said. "In fact, we already have several suspects in mind." It was a little white lie, but he couldn't help himself.

"Colette, if you could just remember some stuff, maybe the chief could make an arrest," Brett said. "Everybody in town is waiting anxiously for that to happen."

"I'm trying my very best," she replied, obviously stressed by the conversation.

"If there's nothing else, gentlemen," Etienne said in an obvious dismissal of the two.

Thankfully at that moment Ella appeared with their food, and the two men returned to their seats. However, they weren't the only ones who stopped by their booth.

Angel Marchant and Nathan Merrick said hello to Colette and wished her well as did Shelby Santori, another woman from the swamp. For the most part, the people who stopped by their booth were friendly and offered their support to Colette.

However, besides Brett and Adam, there were a few other men who were less than friendly as they questioned Colette about her missing memories. Etienne took note of everyone who stopped by to talk to her.

Finally, the trail of people stopped, and they were able to eat their meal in relative peace. "I didn't realize I'd be so popular," Colette said between bites.

"You're the woman of the hour," Etienne replied with a grin. The last thing he wanted was for her time away from her shanty to be stressful or unpleasant. "It's the first time people have seen you out and about since your kidnapping so many months ago."

"It was nice to meet Angel's Nathan," she said.

"Do you know Angel well?"

"Not really. We're friendly when we run into each other,

but we've never really socialized. Dr. Maison told me what happened to her when I was in the hospital and he was catching me up on recent events." She picked up one of the fried shrimp from her plate and popped it into her mouth... That mouth that taunted and teased him with the desire to cover it with his own.

Damn, what was wrong with him? Never before had a woman affected him in this way. The bad thing was he suspected that if he kissed her again, she would welcome it. If he kissed her again, then he would never want to stop.

"This has been nice," she said once they were finished eating.

"Do you want some dessert?" he asked.

"No, thank you. I'm so full of shrimp I can't eat anything else. But if you want some, go ahead."

He smiled. "I'm so full of burger I can't eat anything else." He gestured to Ella for their check.

"How about we go Dutch on lunch?" she suggested.

"I invited you out. I pay, and I don't want any argument about it," he replied firmly. He paid the tab, and they left for the grocery store.

When they arrived, the store's small lot was filled with cars and trucks. He finally found an empty space near the back and close to the dumpster.

"I don't need too many things," she said.

"Get whatever you need." He shut off the engine, got out and then went around to the passenger door to let her out. Before opening the door, he looked all around the lot, but there was nothing there to give him pause.

"It looks like everyone is shopping today," she said as they walked to the front door.

He kept her close to his side as his gaze continued to shoot around the area.

They entered the store, and she grabbed one of the shopping carts. "What sounds good for dinner tonight?" she asked as they started walking down the produce aisle.

"Whatever you want to cook," he replied. He watched as she put a head of lettuce, a couple of green peppers and an eggplant into the cart.

Several people stopped to say hello to Colette while others simply stared at her with open interest. She remained composed, offering friendly smiles to everyone. Once again, Etienne couldn't help but admire her inner strength.

He continued to stay close to her, looking for any danger that might come their way. But he saw nobody suspicious.

She moved fairly quicky through the aisles, adding items to her cart as Etienne walked beside her. They got to the meat section where she picked up hamburger and pork chops, round steak and other items he knew she would make for his dinner.

Finally, she was finished, and they headed to the cashier where he insisted on paying the tab.

"You didn't have to do that," she chided as they left the store.

"It's only fair I pay for the groceries since you cook for me every night," he replied firmly.

"Still, it wasn't necessary," she replied.

They left the building and headed for the car. She pushed the cart just ahead of him, and before he could tell her to slow down and walk with him, a sharp crack sounded.

A gunshot.

Colette instantly hit the ground. Oh God, had she been shot?

Etienne grabbed his gun, hunkering down close to the

pavement. His heart beat wildly as he looked around, seeking the gunman. Another shot went off, and Etienne identified where the shooter must be. Between two parked cars.

A young couple left the store just then and started to walk into the parking lot.

"Stay back," Etienne yelled at them. "Active shooter!" The last thing he wanted was for any innocent shoppers to get hurt. In fact, he was afraid to return fire, concerned about hitting somebody he didn't want to.

His main concern at the moment was Colette. She was on her back and hadn't moved at all since the first shot.

He grabbed his radio from his utility belt and called for help, then he began crawling toward Colette. His heart beat a dull, sickening rhythm. Was she dead? Had the first bullet struck her? Oh God, that couldn't be. He was supposed to protect her. Why hadn't he sensed the danger lurking in the parking lot? Why hadn't he been more careful?

He finally reached her. He'd been foolish to allow her to leave the shanty.

"Colette?" he whispered to her, his heart already uneven with grief.

Her eyes were closed, and he feared the worst.

"I'm okay," she replied breathlessly and opened her eyes. "He didn't hit me."

A deep relief whooshed through him. He immediately covered her body with his. "We need to stay down until help arrives," he said.

"Okay," she replied and closed her eyes once again.

Etienne remained tense with his gun drawn and pointed in the direction of the shooter. He could feel the frightened tremors that shook Colette's body.

Despite his focus on trying to keep them safe, he couldn't

help but notice the softness and warmth of her body beneath his. He was all too aware of the press of her breasts against his chest and her breath warming the hollow of his throat.

Several times he shouted to stop shoppers from coming into the parking lot. Seconds turned into minutes as he remained covering Colette's body, anticipating another gunshot.

"Chief!" Officers Michael Tempe and J.T. Caldwell finally appeared, guns drawn. Slowly, they approached the area where the gunshots had come from.

Etienne rose to his feet, certain the shooter was gone by now. He grabbed Colette's hand and pulled her up, then hurried her to his car where she slid into the passenger seat.

Michael and J.T. met him at his car, where Officer Joel Smith also joined them. Etienne quickly explained what happened, and Michael went back to the area where the shooter had been to search for evidence. J.T. and Joel loaded the groceries that were still in the cart into the trunk of the car.

All Etienne wanted to do now was get Colette back to her shanty as quickly as possible.

It had been so foolish for him to take her out today. He'd made the decision on an emotional level in an effort to make her happy. He should have kept emotions out of it and made her stay put in the shanty where he knew she was safe.

There would be no more outings. They had gotten lucky today, and she hadn't been physically harmed. They might not be so lucky the next time. Therefore there would be no more next time.

He'd believed she was in danger from the Swamp Soul Stealer, and today merely confirmed that fact. Obviously, the man was desperate to make sure she died before she could retrieve her memories.

He drove away from the grocery store, livid that his bullets had missed her. It had been the perfect opportunity to take her out. He couldn't believe his luck when he saw her out of her shanty and at the grocery store. It was a moment of vulnerability he'd hoped to take advantage of, and he'd missed the damn mark.

He slammed his fist into his truck's dashboard. Dammit, he had to kill her before she remembered where she'd been and who had held her.

If people found out what he'd done and why, they would never understand it all, even though he thought it made perfect sense. His head filled with a vision of his mother, lying in bed as she cried day after day over his father's long-standing affair.

His father had spent years having an affair with a swamp bitch named Sonya, and he had watched as his mother, Cara, became a shadow of herself. She had refused to divorce his father, but instead lived in a world of grief and humiliation over her husband's long affair.

"Those people from the swamp have work ethics better than you, boy," his father would say to him. "They're stronger and better than you and your snot-nosed friends."

The words whirled around and around in his head. All he'd ever wanted was his father's love and support, but his father was enchanted with the damn swamp people.

So, his captives were experiments. He was testing them to see just how strong they were. And the truth of the matter was he hated all of them, but he especially hated the beautiful Colette who looked so much like Sonya had when his father's affair first started. It felt good when he beat her. If he could, he'd blow up the entire swamp and all the people in it.

But for now, he just needed one woman dead. He punched

his dashboard once again as he thought about his failed attempt moments before.

One way or another, he was going to get to her. And sooner rather than later. Her memories could return at any moment, and then he would be screwed.

He'd blown it today, but there was no way he'd miss the next time. She was a dead woman walking, and in a very short period of time she would just be a dead woman.

COLETTE SAT IN the car and fought against the frightened shivers that still raced up and down her spine. She had heard the first bullet whiz by within inches of her head. It had been sheer terror that dropped her to the pavement.

Some of the terror had now dissipated, but she still couldn't believe that somebody had tried to shoot her... that somebody had truly tried to kill her.

It wasn't any random somebody. It was the Swamp Soul Stealer. God, he'd been in the parking lot with them. Etienne wanted her memories, and the Swamp Soul Stealer wanted her dead before she could give them to him.

She looked out the window where two more officers had joined the others. Etienne was speaking to them all, obviously giving them instructions.

An ambulance pulled up, and Etienne insisted she be checked out by the EMTs. Thankfully, her only injuries were a bruised knee and a skinned elbow, something that must have happened in her fall to the pavement. Etienne insisted he was all right and didn't need to be seen.

It wasn't long after that when he got into the car and turned to her with somber eyes. "Are you doing okay?"

Tears misted her vision, and she quickly swiped at them. She hesitated a moment and then nodded. "I'm okay. I'll tell you one thing…it's going to be a very long time before I'll want to leave my shanty again." Her voice was shaky, and more tears filled her eyes.

"I'm sorry, Colette. I'm so damn sorry about all this. I should have never taken you out and about knowing you were in danger," he said regretfully.

"Please don't apologize, Etienne. I encouraged you to let me go out. I wanted to go out. At least the bullets missed me."

He started the car and pulled out of the parking area, his gaze divided between the front window and his rearview mirror. He reached his hand over and clasped hers. "Thank God you're okay. When I saw you hit the ground, I thought… I thought…" His voice trailed off, and his hand squeezed hers tightly.

She returned the squeeze and once again fought off tears that filled her eyes. He pulled his hand back, and she blinked several times in an effort to rid herself of her tears. "At least we're both okay," she said.

"Thank God for that," he replied.

"Things could have gone much worse," she added.

Neither of them spoke anymore as he continued to drive toward the swamp. Colette still fought off tears of residual fear, but by the time he parked in front of the swamp's entrance, she had managed to get herself under control. Etienne got the groceries from the trunk, and together they headed for her shanty.

Officer Grier rose from the rocking chair as they reached her place. "It's good to see you two okay," he said, a worried frown etching his forehead. "I heard some radio chatter that had me very concerned for you."

"Yeah, somebody took a couple of shots at us in the grocery store parking lot. Thankfully, the bullets didn't hit us, so here we are," Etienne explained. "I'll see you later when I come on duty." He opened the door and ushered Colette inside.

She followed him into the kitchen where he set the grocery bags on the table.

"Are you sure you're okay?" he asked, his beautiful gray eyes concerned as he gazed at her.

"I'm fine. I'm just glad to be back here," she confessed. She felt safe in her shanty. However, as she gazed at the handsome lawman, she realized he looked utterly exhausted. "Etienne, I know you sleep during the afternoons so you'll be awake for your overnight duty here. It's gotten late in the afternoon, and if you want, you can just crash here in my bedroom for a nap rather than driving all the way back to your house," she offered.

He frowned and looked at his watch. "I might just take you up on that."

"I'll make sure it's quiet," she added. Even though she felt safe now, she would feel even more safe if he was here. Besides, if he drove home, it would take even longer for him to get some sleep. "My bedroom is ready whenever you are."

"Are you sure you don't mind?" he asked.

"I don't mind at all," she replied.

He stood and she took him by the hand and led him into her bedroom. She would have preferred to be leading him into her bedroom for something other than him napping, but there was no question that he appeared exhausted.

"Thanks for letting me crash here," he said as he removed his utility belt and gun and placed them on the nightstand.

"It's no problem," she replied easily. "I'm just going to

grab a change of clothes. Crawling around on parking lot pavement isn't great for dresses."

She opened a dresser drawer and grabbed a pair of jeans and then went to her closet and pulled a red blouse from a hanger. "I hope you get some good sleep," she said and then pulled the door closed behind her.

She went into the kitchen where she quickly changed out of her dirty dress and into the jeans and blouse. Once she had put away the groceries, she sank down onto the sofa and released a deep sigh.

It had been a harrowing afternoon. When the first bullet whizzed by her, she'd fallen to the pavement in hopes it would make it more difficult for the shooter to hit her. She had been absolutely terrified, not only for herself, but for Etienne as well. The bullets could have killed him just like they could have killed her. She had never, ever been so frightened in her life.

Thank God they had both survived the attack. She was comforted by the fact he was now sleeping peacefully in her bed.

She got up and went to the back porch to start her generator. She would write for the rest of the afternoon. It would be soothing and would hopefully take the bad taste from the unexpected attack out of her mouth. She had another appointment with Dr. Kingston the next day, and the therapist would probably be able to help her process everything that had happened.

She tried to write, but instead found herself distracted by thoughts of Etienne. She could imagine herself in the bed with him, cuddled up by his side after a bout of lovemaking. The very idea filled her with a heat of desire.

Did he feel the same fire of desire for her? There were

moments when she believed he did, when she thought she saw a naked hunger for her shining in the depths of his eyes.

She worked until 5:30 p.m., then closed her laptop and went into the kitchen to see what she was going to make for dinner. She settled on smothered steak and mashed potatoes. She had just begun to gather the ingredients when Etienne came in.

His hair was slightly mussed, and he looked less tired than when he'd gone into the bedroom.

"Did you get some sleep?" she asked and gestured him toward the table.

He lowered himself into a chair and smiled. "Actually, I slept better than I have in months. The sounds of the swamp are very soothing."

"Yes, they are," she agreed and sat in the chair next to his. "How does smothered steak sound for dinner?"

"Sounds good." He paused for a long moment, his gaze locked with hers. "You are an absolutely amazing woman, Colette."

She looked at him in surprise as the warmth of a blush filled her cheeks. "Thank you, but I don't know what's so amazing about me."

"For one thing, you nearly took a bullet earlier today, and now here you are calmly talking about what's for dinner as if nothing at all happened," he replied.

"Oh, trust me, I was terrified this afternoon, but thankfully it's over, and life goes on," she said.

His eyes were filled with admiration. "Most women would have crumbled and been afraid for at least the rest of the day. You are an amazingly strong woman, Colette."

"I wasn't so strong when I was in that cage next to Luka." The memory sprang to her mind unbidden, and her gaze shifted to the wall behind Etienne as it continued to unfold. "Everyone was in a small cage. Occasionally he'd come down to feed us a little or to take us out to beat us." The words tumbled out of her. "He wore a ski mask, but he was a big man who enjoyed hurting us…and especially me." A shiver raced through her and the back of her throat momentarily closed up.

The memory broke, and she focused back on Etienne. "That's all. I still can't tell you who he is," she said in frustration.

He reached out and grasped her hand. "That's okay," he replied. "Maybe now more things will start to come back to you. You said he came down to feed you. So that implies you were underground. Do you remember how it smelled?"

She frowned and closed her eyes as she concentrated. "Dank and earthy."

"Like a cave of some kind or a basement," he asked.

She hesitated and then opened her eyes. "I'm sorry, I don't know. It could be either."

"That's okay," he repeated and squeezed her hand. His eyes were lit with a new excitement.

"But I didn't remember anything to help you catch this guy," she said in dismay.

"You remembered Luka and that you were held underground someplace. Next time you might remember even more," he replied. "Hopefully your memories are going to start returning to you now." He squeezed her hand once again and then released it.

"I hope so," she said. "Now, how about I go ahead and make dinner, and we can eat a little earlier than usual?"

"That works for me. I might as well hang around here rather than go home before my official guard duty begins."

While she began to cook their meal, he remained seated in the kitchen and the two of them small-talked while she worked. It felt right...having him here in the kitchen with her while she cooked for him, especially since the small snippet of memory had shaken her up.

She loved Etienne's company. She loved the sound of his voice. The truth was she was definitely falling in love with him. However, she didn't expect him to love her back. Oh, he might desire her, but ultimately, she was somebody he had to protect until she remembered enough to get the Swamp Soul Stealer arrested. Once that was done, Etienne would be gone from her life.

Even knowing that, she intended to enjoy each and every moment spent together. And if they fell into bed, she would gladly make love with him even knowing they didn't have a future.

Chapter Seven

The smothered steak was delicious, and their conversation remained pleasant and easy. Etienne was amazed by how quickly she'd bounced back after the afternoon's terrible events.

He definitely admired her strength, not just today, but for all she'd been through, and still she remained standing strong. Despite all that she was facing, she had a cheerfulness and a brightness about her that was incredibly appealing.

He was excited by the fact that memories had begun to return to her. While he didn't have what he needed from her yet, he had hope that in the very near future she would remember something that would lead to an arrest. And God, he hoped it happened sooner rather than later.

He'd told her the truth when he said he had slept better here than ever. The mattress had been soft and seemed to envelop him. The bed had smelled of her soft, floral scent, and he'd fallen asleep almost immediately. He now felt fully rested and ready for the night ahead.

Let him come tonight, he thought as he ate dinner. Let the bastard come for her tonight so Etienne could finally get him under arrest and in jail.

When he remembered her prone on the parking lot pavement, all his stomach muscles tightened, and he felt slightly sick. He would have never forgiven himself if she had been shot. Thank God she had been okay.

As usual, she looked beautiful tonight. The jeans fit her well, and the red blouse enhanced the darkness of her hair and eyes. He wanted to tangle his hands in her rich, dark cascade of hair. He wanted to kiss her again, this time until they were both breathless and mindless. But he tried to push these thoughts away, knowing they were dangerous.

The steak and mashed potatoes tasted great, but he was definitely hungry for something else. He was having more trouble than usual tonight getting his desire for her under control.

"That was delicious," he began when a knock pulled them both up from the table. "I'll answer it," he said. He drew his gun and opened the door. He immediately relaxed as he saw Thomas Grier.

"Whoa, Chief. Don't shoot me. I just wanted you to know that I'm taking off."

"Okay, I've got it from here," Etienne said as he realized it was seven o'clock and time for Thomas to go off duty.

The two men said their goodbyes, and Etienne closed and locked the door. He knew he should just go on to his post outside, but he was reluctant to end the evening with Colette. Instead, he returned to the kitchen where he offered to help clean up dinner. As usual, she insisted he sit and talk to her while she took care of the dishes.

He told her more funny stories about being the law in Crystal Cove. He loved to make her laugh. Her laughter was full-bodied and contagious, and he loved hearing it.

"Have I told you about Harry, the pet pig?" he asked.

"No," she replied. Her dark eyes were filled with mirth as she finished washing the last of the dishes. "Why don't we go sit in the living room and you can tell me all about Harry the pet pig?" she suggested.

They sat on the sofa together, close enough that he could smell her attractive scent and feel the warmth of her body heat.

"Harry was a miniature pig that belonged to an older woman who treated him like a baby. She dressed Harry in clothes and pampered him like crazy," he said. "But Harry didn't want to be her baby, and the pig was constantly escaping from her home."

"Then what would happen?" she asked.

"Then we would get dozens of calls from the hysterical owner to find Harry. So I would put all my deputies to work finding the pig. And Harry knew all kinds of places to hide. The owner would whine and cry and force her neighbors to join in the hunts until it seemed like the whole town was looking for Harry."

"You're making this up," she accused, her eyes glittering with humor.

He laughed. "I swear it's true. For months, Harry had my deputies and half the town running around to find him. Each time we'd find him and return him until the fateful day when we couldn't find him. We looked high and low for Harry, but he wasn't anywhere to be found."

"You never found him?" she asked.

"No, we didn't. But a week later one of Harry's owner's neighbors had a big barbecue for the neighborhood. He served hamburgers and hot dogs and had a large pot of pulled pork."

"Oh no." She winced and then laughed once again. "You think it was Harry?"

"I do. That was the end of the pig, and I think everyone in town who had dealt with Harry and his owner were extremely happy."

"What about Harry's owner? What happened to her?"

"She moved to Black Bayou," he said, mentioning a small town nearby. "And last I heard she got another pet pig."

"At least you and your deputies don't have to worry about searching for a missing pig anymore," she replied with a grin.

His stomach muscles bunched as fresh desire roared through him.

She got up to turn on the lights against the encroaching darkness of the night. She moved with a natural grace from one lamp to another until a cozy glow filled the room. Returning to the sofa, she sat closer to him than before.

"I should probably get outside," he said.

"Oh, don't go yet," she said, her dark eyes pleading with him. "It's still early, and I'm really enjoying talking to you."

"I suppose I can sit for a few more minutes," he replied.

What he really needed to do was gain some distance from her. Her beautiful, long-lashed eyes beguiled him, and her scent dizzied his senses. Her nearness was a definite temptation, and for some reason tonight he felt particularly weak where she was concerned.

"I've told you my story about Harry the pig," he blurted. "Now it's your turn. Got any swamp stories to make me laugh?"

"Now you've put me on the spot," she replied with another small laugh. "Okay, there was a time a bunch of us got together for a little party. Jackson Dupree provided some of his moonshine..." Her eyes widened, and she clapped her hand over her mouth. "I shouldn't have said that."

Etienne released a small dry laugh. "I know Jackson has a still somewhere in the swamp. We've found it a couple of times and torn it down, but he always manages to get another one up and running before my officers can even leave the old one."

She laughed. "He takes great pride in keeping you all guessing on where his latest still is. Anyway, on this particular night, he brought a bunch of his latest brew for all of us to enjoy, and enjoy we did. Well, I didn't drink any of it because I don't drink, but everyone else wound up pretty smashed."

As she continued to tell him about the antics of the people at the party, all he could focus on was the lusciousness of her full lips. His head filled with the memory of the kiss they had shared, and there was nothing more he wanted to do now than repeat it.

She finished her tale, and suddenly their gazes were locked. The tip of her tongue danced out to moisten her upper lip. She leaned forward in obvious open invitation, and he couldn't help himself.

He placed his hand on the back of her head, pulled her closer and took her lips with his. Her lips were pillowy soft and so incredibly hot, and her mouth opened up to him. He deepened the kiss, sweeping his tongue over hers.

She leaned even closer and wrapped her arms around his neck. Her breasts pressed against his chest, and all he could think about was how much he wanted her. He felt as if he'd wanted her for months...for years.

The kiss continued until they were both breathless, and

he was half-mindless. Her eyes were lit with flames that threatened to consume him.

"Etienne, make love to me." Her voice was slightly husky as she gazed at him. "Come into the bedroom and please make love with me."

"I... We..." He tried to find the words to get things back under control, but control was the last thing he was feeling.

"You know you want to, and I want you to," she continued. "Please, Etienne...give me this one night with you." She grabbed his hand and stood, her dark eyes simmering pools of desire.

He should stop this. He should get up and head directly outside where he belonged.

But that wasn't what he wanted to do. He wanted to take her up on her bold invitation, and when he stood, instead of going straight outside, he allowed her to lead him into the bedroom. Even knowing it was the wrong thing to do, he was absolutely powerless against his desire for Colette.

COLETTE'S HEART THUNDERED in her chest as she led Etienne into her bedroom. Never had she wanted a man as much as she wanted him in this moment. Never had she been so daring with a man as to ask for what she wanted.

His kiss had stirred her to a level she didn't remember ever feeling before. She was on fire with her desire for the lawman...for Etienne. As soon as they stepped into the bedroom, he wrapped her in his arms for another searing kiss.

His hands moved up and down her back, and she was so close to him she could feel his arousal. It only increased her desire for him.

Breaking off the kiss, she moved to the nightstand and turned on a light that gave a soft glow to the room. She watched as he took off his utility belt and placed it on the nightstand.

Stepping closer to him, she unfastened the buttons on his shirt one by one. He stood perfectly still until she was done. Then he shrugged the shirt off his shoulders, and it dropped to the floor behind him.

She released a deep breath as she saw the magnificence of his bare chest. His washboard abs led up to a firmly muscled chest and shoulders that nearly took her breath away. He was so sculpted and beautiful.

He moved closer to her and worked the buttons on her blouse, his touch firing heat through her from head to toe. She let her blouse fall off her shoulders, leaving her in her jeans and a pale pink bra.

He reached for her again and pulled her against his chest as his lips found hers. His naked skin felt wonderful against hers, and her blood heated even more as his fingers worked behind her to unfasten her bra. It fell away, making their skin-to-skin contact even more intimate.

"Colette," he whispered into her ear. "I've never wanted a woman like I want you."

"I feel the same way about you," she replied breathlessly.

He rained kisses across her jawline and then slowly down her neck. She leaned her head back to give him full access to her throat. Each of his nipping kisses fed the fire inside her, a roaring inferno burning eager and hot.

They broke apart, and she removed her jeans while he took off his blue slacks. Him in his black boxers and her only in a wispy pair of light pink panties, they slid beneath the sheets and their lips found each other's once again.

His tongue danced with hers as his hands stroked up her body to cup her breasts.

She moaned with pleasure as his fingers captured one of her nipples and toyed with it until it was peaked with her desire. Then his mouth left hers and slid down to lick and kiss first one nipple, then the other. Electric currents shot from her breasts to the very center of her.

One of his hands slid from her breast and down her stomach. She caught her breath as he reached the waistband of her panties.

At the same time, she stroked across his chest and down his stomach. His skin was warm and felt so good, and he smelled of his wonderful cologne and clean male. He moaned as she caressed farther down until she was at his boxers. She wanted them off. She wanted his complete nakedness next to hers.

She pushed them off him, and in turn he slid her panties down her legs. They came together for another scorching kiss as they writhed against each other. Her naked skin positively loved his.

Once again, he stroked down her body... Slowly, until his fingers reached her most intimate place. She gasped with pleasure as tension began to build inside her. Faster and faster his fingers danced against her moist heat, and the tension inside her reached a peak. She cried out his name as her climax shuddered through her.

Not even waiting to come down from her own pleasure, she took his erection in her hand. Soft, velvety skin covered a hardness that pulsed with an energy that excited her. Despite her climax, she wanted more from him. She slowly moved her hand up and down the hard shaft, and he moaned in obvious pleasure.

He allowed her to caress him for only a couple of moments before he pushed her hand away and rolled her on her back. He knelt between her thighs, and his eyes glittered with a deep hunger as he hovered above her.

"Yes," she whispered urgently, and he slowly entered her.

Another moan escaped her as he filled her completely. He paused for a long moment, his gaze holding hers in a connection that took her breath away with the intimacy of what they were doing.

Slow at first, he moved against her in long, deep strokes. She moved her hips upward to meet him thrust for thrust.

She was lost in him, and as he quickened his strokes, a new rising tension filled her. She clung to his shoulders as he moved faster and faster, taking her to new heights of pleasure.

Then she was there again with another climax exploding inside her. As her body shuddered against his, he found his own release.

Afterward, he leaned down and kissed her with a tenderness that spoke to her very soul. He collapsed just to the side of her, both of them speechless as they each tried to catch their breath. After a couple minutes, he propped himself up on one elbow and gazed down at her.

She could tell by his expression he was about to denounce what they had just shared.

"Don't," she said and reached up to place two of her fingers against his mouth. "Don't you dare tell me that this was all a big mistake."

His lips moved into a grin, and she dropped her hand back to the bed. "Was it that obvious that's what I was going to do?"

"It was obvious enough," she replied. "And it wasn't a mistake. Etienne, if you're honest with yourself, you'll admit that you've been carrying around a lot of desire for me. And

I have felt a lot of desire for you. Tonight, we decided to act on that. We're two consenting adults with no significant others, so how can what we just shared be wrong?"

"Well, when you put it that way... I just don't want us to forget what we're here for." He reached out and gently brushed a strand of her hair off the side of her face.

"Etienne, if you're worried about me expecting something from you, then don't. I'm very much aware of what the ultimate goal is."

"As long as we're both on the same page."

"We are," she replied, even though her heart hurt more than a little bit. It was apparent that he didn't feel the same way as she did about their new intimacy. "But I've got to say, I found your lovemaking beyond wonderful, Etienne."

"Same," he replied, his eyes glowing soft in the lamp's light.

She sensed him ready to get up, and she didn't want him to go. She reached up and cupped the side of his face where she could feel the slight stubble of whiskers. "Sleep with me tonight, Etienne. Stay here in my bed for the night. You'll still be on guard duty whether you're outside or in here with me."

He hesitated a long moment and then nodded. "Okay, I'll sleep here tonight."

She smiled as a wave of happiness danced through her. She dropped her hand from his face. "If you want, you can use the bathroom first."

He rolled away from her and got out of the bed. He grabbed his boxers from the floor and left the room.

She released a deep sigh. Their conversation had definitely been disappointing. There had been a romantic, fanciful part of her that hoped he would confess he was falling in love with her. Instead, the conversation was a reminder that once she regained her memories and the swamp monster was in jail, Etienne would be gone from her life.

Even knowing this, she couldn't stop herself from wanting him. She couldn't help that she enjoyed their conversations and how she looked forward to seeing him each day.

She definitely couldn't help the fact that she had fallen in love with him…and she definitely couldn't help that he didn't love her back.

Even knowing that, she had no intention of guarding her heart. She'd lost six long months of her life, and now she wanted to live it to the fullest. She'd love Etienne until he was gone, and then she'd pick up the pieces of her broken heart.

When he was finished in the bathroom, she grabbed one of her nightshirts and took her turn getting ready for bed. Within minutes, she was back in bed with him, the lamp on the nightstand turned off.

He pulled her into his arms and spooned her with his arm around her waist. She snuggled into him, loving the feel of his solid body against hers. His breaths were a warm whisper against her ear, and she'd never felt so safe and protected.

"Good night, Colette," he said softly.

"Night, Etienne," she replied.

She knew the moment he fell asleep. His breaths became deep and rhythmic. He began to snore softly, the sound not bothering her at all. Rather it added to the swamp symphony with the bullfrogs croaking and insects clicking and whirring with their nighttime songs.

This felt so right, like this was where they belonged. Yet he'd told her that wasn't the case. Ultimately, she was simply a piece of his puzzle concerning the Swamp Soul Stealer case. He might physically want her, but he didn't love her.

With a deep sigh, she relaxed her body and waited for sleep to overtake her. It was only in her dreams that Etienne the lawman protected her and Etienne the man loved her.

Chapter Eight

Etienne awoke around dawn with Colette still asleep. He was spooned around her warm body as he had been all night, and for a few minutes he simply lay there. Her floral scent surrounded him, and her body heat radiated outward to warm him. It took only minutes of simply enjoying her being in his arms, and then his mind began to race.

Had it been wrong of him to make love to Colette last night? Absolutely. He was in a position of power in their relationship, and as chief of police he should have known better.

Had it been utterly amazing to make love with her? Again, absolutely. She had been giving and so passionate, and her passion had pulled forth a desire in him he'd never felt before. Even now, just being in his arms, she stirred him all over again.

Hell, he hadn't even used birth control. He seriously doubted that she was on pills. He had an old condom in his wallet, but at no time had he thought about putting it on. Things had exploded so quickly between them that protection hadn't even entered his mind. All he could hope was that she hadn't gotten pregnant. That was the very last thing they both needed right now.

It was time for him to get up and get away from her before he repeated his mistake and made love with her all over again. Gently, he pulled his arm from around her, rolled over and slid out of bed.

He moved as quietly as possible, grabbing his utility belt and gun from the nightstand and his uniform from the floor. He crept into the living room, quickly got dressed and went outside to sit in the rocking chair on the porch.

This was where he should have been last night, instead of enjoying the comfort of her bed. This was where he should have been instead of making love with Colette.

Still, what was done was done, and they had to move forward from here. He just didn't want Colette to believe that he was offering her any kind of a relationship when this was all over.

Despite the loneliness he sometimes suffered, he had known for some time that he was destined to live alone. He was married to his job, and there was no room or time for anyone else in his life.

There was no question that he had feelings for Colette... Strong feelings. He loved her laughter and admired her strength. He loved their deep conversations and had an overwhelming desire for her.

However, he didn't know how much of his feelings for her sprang from the fact that she was his star witness. If he didn't need her memories, would he feel the same way about her?

It was evident that she had feelings for him too. But would she feel the same way about him if he wasn't protecting her from a serial kidnapper who wanted her dead? Would she still entertain feelings for him if he wasn't the only person in her life right now?

There were simply too many variables at play to think about any kind of a relationship with her.

Dawn's light painted the swamp with a golden glow, and morning birds called from their perches high in the trees. He was surprised that the Swamp Soul Stealer hadn't made a move on her last night. The rocking chair had been empty all night long, and it probably looked like there wasn't a guard. But the man hadn't shown up.

It was about a half hour later that the generator sounded. Soon after that, the door opened, and Colette smiled at him.

"Good morning," she said, offering him a cup of coffee.

"Thanks," he replied as he took it from her. "And good morning to you."

"How did you sleep?" she asked. She looked beautiful with her long hair slightly tousled and still clad in a light pink nightshirt. It was obvious she had just rolled out of bed and had gone directly to the coffee maker.

"I slept wonderfully well," he replied. It was the truth. With her so warm in his arms, he had fallen asleep almost immediately and slept through the entire night. "What about you?"

"I also slept wonderfully," she replied with a warm smile. "Well, I guess I'll see you later." With that, she went back inside.

At about ten till eight, J.T. arrived to relieve Etienne. "How you doing, Chief?" the young officer asked.

"I'm doing okay. I see you came prepared for your day of duty." Etienne pointed to the refrigerated bag J.T. carried.

J.T. grinned. "A couple of sandwiches, a couple of sodas, and I'm set for the day."

"Then I'll see you at seven this evening," Etienne replied.

Minutes later, he was in his car and headed to the police station. Later in the day he'd need to go home and take a shower, then try to catch a nap so he could be awake all night. And tonight, he'd be spending his guard duty outside on the rocking chair where he belonged.

He pulled into his parking space behind the station and went in the back door.

Trey met him in the hallway, a frown cutting deep across his forehead.

"What's up?" Etienne asked.

"We've got another one," Trey replied.

Etienne's stomach dropped to the ground. "Who?"

"Kate Dirant's mother just called to report that Kate never made it home last night from a friend's," Trey said.

"Gather everyone, and let's head out there," Etienne replied. He hoped this was just some sort of misunderstanding between mother and daughter. He'd been called out to the Dirant home several times over the past few years when Bettima had called him about young teen Kate running away from home. Kate was now seventeen years old and, according to her mother, just as headstrong as she'd ever been. He hoped this was just another family tiff and not another missing person.

It took twenty minutes before Etienne and Trey were in Etienne's car and heading back to the swamp. Following them were two more patrol cars with four more officers.

"Maybe this time we'll get some clues," Trey said with an optimism Etienne didn't feel.

"That would be nice," Etienne replied. All his muscles were tensed with fiery adrenaline. Along with the adrenaline there was also a deep anger.

Dammit, if Kate had been taken, then who was this person? Why was he doing this? All the questions that had plagued Etienne for the past five and a half months swirled around in his head once again. What the hell was the motive? And where was he keeping his victims?

This one definitely felt personal. It was as if the creep was letting Etienne know that ultimately, he held all the power. Etienne might have Colette, but that didn't stop the perp from taking others at will.

Damn but Etienne wanted this man so badly.

They arrived at the swamp's entrance, and all the officers got out of their cars.

"I know where the Dirant shanty is, so just follow me," Etienne said.

His heart pounded with anxiety as he walked into the swamp to investigate yet another disappearance. God, but he hoped this was just an instance of Kate driving her mother crazy and nothing more ominous. Damn the bastard if he'd taken another one.

Etienne could only hope that this time the swamp monster had gotten sloppy and left something of himself behind.

The men followed him in a silent parade of blue until they reached the Dirant place. Bettima answered on the first knock, her dark eyes filled with tears. "Chief Savoie, she never came home. Kate never came home last night, and I just know she's been taken by the monster. Oh Lord, she's gone, and she's in the grips of the Swamp Soul Stealer."

"Whoa, slow down, and let's take this one step at a time. Where was she supposed to be?" Etienne asked gently.

"At about six last night she went to visit with her friend, Barbie Frasier. Barbie lives just down the way a bit." Bettima wiped away the tears that coursed down her cheeks. "I told her if she was going to go, she should stay the night there. I didn't want her walking home in the dark. I didn't learn until this morning that she left Barbie's about ten last night to come home. But she never got here."

Etienne put his hand on Bettima's plump shoulder. "We're going to look for her now. Can you take me to Barbie's place?"

Bettima nodded, her eyes still brimming with tears. Out on her porch, she pointed to a shanty in the distance. "That's Barbie's place," she said. "It's close, so Kate probably thought she could make it home okay. Oh, that girl, why didn't she listen to me and just stay the night there?"

As they walked toward the Frasier shanty, Etienne and the officers looked for anything along the path that might be evidence.

They hadn't gone too far when just off the path, Trey found a pink bejeweled cell phone.

"That's Kate's," Bettima said with a deep moan. "Chief Savoie, she would have never just left it here. It was one of her most prized possessions. Oh, she's been taken. She's now one of the vanished."

As the woman began to loudly weep, Etienne motioned to one of his officers. "Bettima, Officer Tempe will take you back to your place, and I'll meet you there in a little while."

Once the two were gone, Etienne turned to his men. "Right around here is where Kate must have been taken. She must have had the cell phone in her hand when she was attacked. So, let's spread out and see if we can find some kind of evidence around here."

For the next two hours, the men searched the area, but they found nothing that might help identify the killer. In truth they found nothing at all. Once again it was like the man was a ghost who took what he wanted and left nothing behind.

They searched all the way to Barbie's place and back to where the phone had been found at least a dozen times. Finally, Etienne called the search off. He instructed two of the officers to conduct interviews with anyone who lived around the area and the rest to go back to the station and resume their normal activities.

He and Trey headed back to Bettima's place to tell the woman the bad news. There was no question in Etienne's mind that the young woman was a victim of the Swamp Soul Stealer.

A half hour later, Etienne and Trey were in Etienne's patrol car and headed back to the station. Etienne had another mother's tears heavy in his heart, staining his very soul.

"Dammit, I wish we would have found something...anything," he finally said in frustration.

"Yeah, me too," Trey replied. "But I don't understand why people in the swamp continue to go out alone after dark knowing they're at risk to be taken?"

"I guess it's human nature to believe it might happen to somebody else, but not to them."

"I figured this creep would be too busy trying to figure out how to get to Colette to be taking any more people," Trey said.

"I'd hoped he wouldn't take anyone else. We definitely can't seem to catch a break in this case." Etienne tightened his grip on the steering wheel, his anger once again rising. "We've gotten nothing from the crime scenes. The guy shoots at us in a parking lot, and we got nothing from that, not even bullet casings. I swear, I want this man so badly I can taste it."

"We all want him, Etienne. We're all doing the best we can to support you," Trey replied.

Etienne shot his right-hand man a quick glance. "I know, and I appreciate the support I get not only from you, but also from all the men and women on the force."

It was true, he had never questioned the support he got from the people who worked for him. He knew they all had his back, and he was grateful for that.

Back at the station. Etienne went directly into his office to check on other pending issues while he waited for the officers he had left behind in the swamp to check in. As with all the other cases, nobody had seen or heard anything when Kate had been kidnapped. Finally, he headed home, his heart heavy with the day's events.

He showered and pulled on a clean uniform, then fell back in his recliner to catch a quick nap before guard duty that night.

However, sleep remained elusive as the events of the day battled with thoughts of Colette in his mind. He hated the fact that another young woman had disappeared. He needed Colette's memories now more than ever.

What he didn't need was another night like last night. He had to be strong enough to fight the desire that plagued him for Colette. Tonight, he would definitely spend guard duty in the chair outside and not in her bed.

He wound up sleeping for about an hour, and at 6:30 p.m., he left his house to head back to the swamp. His heart was still heavy with the disappearance of Kate. He could only pray that she was still alive, along with the other victims.

He knew this would only feed the recall effort against him. However, he couldn't be bothered by that right now. He knew the mayor was still supporting him, and in any case, more than anything, he wanted—needed—to be the one to catch this perp. He could only pray that all the victims were still alive.

He pulled into the parking area and left his car. As he walked through the brush and ducked under the Spanish moss hanging from the trees, his thoughts were a jumbled mess.

His anticipation of seeing Colette again mixed with the tragic event of Kate's disappearance.

He hoped like hell the perp came for Colette tonight. While he'd like to shoot the bastard through his black heart, Etienne needed to keep the man alive so he could tell Etienne where all his victims were being held.

As Colette's shanty came into view, Etienne's heart stopped. J.T. was slumped in the rocking chair, and Colette's front door stood wide-open.

He raced across the short bridge to J.T. The officer was alive, but had a nasty head wound. J.T. appeared to just be regaining consciousness, so Etienne ran into the shanty in a panic.

"Colette," he cried out.

There was no response.

"Colette," he yelled even louder.

She was not in the shanty. His heart dropped, and his knees weakened as the reality of the situation slammed into him. Oh God, the Swamp Soul Stealer had already been here, and he had taken Colette.

COLETTE HAD BEEN in the kitchen finishing up cooking the evening meal when she heard heavy pounding at her front door. She stood in the living room, frozen as her heart beat the rhythm of sudden fear.

The door bowed inward with each heavy blow. With the fourth blow, the lock broke, and the door flew open.

The man of her nightmares stood on the threshold. He was wearing a ski mask, and he wielded a big knife. "I'm going to cut you into little pieces, bitch," he growled in a low, gravelly voice.

With a scream, Colette turned and ran. Without thought, functioning only on fear, she went through the kitchen and ran toward her back door. She threw the door open and rushed outside.

Once out on her deck, she quickly realized she'd run herself into a dead end. Running either way around the deck would only take her back to the front where he could easily catch up with her.

She eyed the murky water below. His rage-filled roar was just behind her. Knowing her very life was on the line, she went over the railing and jumped into the water below.

She gasped as she surfaced, then quickly began to swim toward shore. There were hungry gators and snakes in the water, and there was no way she wanted to be in it a minute longer than she had to be.

As she crawled back up onto land, she looked back toward the shanty. Her attacker was gone. But where? Where was he at this moment?

Terror rose up in her throat. Tears nearly blinded her. What happened to the officer on guard duty? Oh God, had the masked man killed baby-faced J.T.? She didn't want to be responsible for anyone's death.

She had just gotten to her feet when the crashing of the brush behind her let her know the man was still coming after her. She ran—blindly, wildly—through the swamp, her heart threatening to beat right out of her chest. She ran, her progress hampered by the swamp she loved. Spanish moss obscured her vision, and tree roots tried to trip her up.

Despite her best efforts, the man was gaining on her. The darkness of night had begun to fall as she left the narrow path and plunged into tangled limbs and thick brush. Here the darkness was more profound, and as she jumped into a thicket of bushes, she crouched down to hide. She clapped a hand over her mouth to staunch her frantic, terrified cries.

She drew in a deep breath as she heard him coming closer and closer to where she hid. She held completely still, knowing a single twitch or an inadvertent shudder might give away her location.

He came so close to where she hid that she could hear his ragged breathing, imagined she could smell the acrid scent of his sweat. Oh God…so close he came, and then he veered off on another path.

She released a deep sigh of relief, but remained in place, her heart still racing with frantic beats.

And then she heard it… Etienne's voice calling her name.

It came from her shanty and filled her with a new rush of adrenaline. She slowly rose to her feet, the need to be with Etienne searing through her soul. There was safety with him. All she had to do was get back to him and the shanty.

She moved as silently as possible back toward her home. She listened for signs that the attacker heard her… Could he be following her with the intention to kill her before she reached safety?

Tears of fear chased each other down her cheeks as she crept through the tangled vegetation. She stifled a scream as an animal rustled the brush next to her. Where was her attacker now? Was he on a trail walking away from her, or was he silently sneaking up behind her? Finally, her shanty was in sight, and she broke into a full run, her breath escaping her in frantic sobs.

Etienne stood next to J.T., who was seated in the rocking chair with blood running down his face.

"Etienne," she cried as she raced across the bridge.

"Colette!" He drew his gun and opened an arm for her. She finally reached him, and his arm closed around her as he pulled her against his side.

Safe... She was finally safe. The heat from his body warmed the icy chills that filled her. His scent surrounded her like a veil of protection, and her tears were now ones of intense relief.

"I thought you were gone," he said, his voice deeper than usual. "I thought he had taken you again." He squeezed and then released her, his gun still in hand. "Are you okay?"

"I am now." She wrapped her arms around herself and looked with concern at J.T. "Is he all right?"

J.T. offered her a faint smile. "I am now."

"I'm just waiting for some officers to join us here and for the ambulance to arrive to get J.T. to the hospital," Etienne explained.

"I don't need to go to the hospital," J.T. scoffed.

"J.T., you took a hard blow to the head. It was hard enough to render you unconscious and bloody. You're definitely going to the hospital," Etienne said firmly.

"Chief, he came out of nowhere. I didn't see or hear him until he was on top of me. I don't know what he hit me with, but the blow instantly knocked me out." J.T. released a ragged sigh. "I'm so sorry, Colette. I let you down, and I'm only grateful that you're okay despite my failed guard duty."

"Oh, J.T., please don't apologize. I'm so sorry that you got hurt," Colette replied.

By that time, several other officers had arrived on scene, along with a paramedic who led J.T. off the porch and away from the shanty.

Once he was gone, Etienne gestured Colette and the other three officers into the shanty. He checked the bedroom, the closet and bathroom to make sure the perp hadn't somehow circled back and was hiding somewhere in the place. Once the space was secured, Colette went into the bedroom and changed out of her wet clothes, towel-drying her hair as best as possible.

Back in the living room, she let Etienne lead her to the sofa. He sat next to her while Officers Michael Tempe, Trey Norton and Thomas Grier stood by the front door, ready for whatever he needed from them.

"Now, tell me exactly what happened?" Etienne asked, his eyes the color of cold steel.

"I was in the kitchen when I heard a loud banging on the door." She told him about the door springing open and seeing the man wearing a ski mask and wielding a large knife. She recounted jumping into the water and swimming to shore where the man found her again.

Tears once again fell down her cheeks. "I... I was so sure h-he was going to find me. H-he told me he was going to slice me up, and I knew if he found me, I'd die a horrible death."

"You heard his voice?" Etienne leaned toward her, obviously excited by this news. "What did he say to you?"

"He told me he was going to cut me up into little pieces." She shivered with the horrible memory of that moment.

"Would you be able to identify his voice if you heard it again?"

She hesitated a long moment and then slowly shook her

head negatively. "I... I don't know. I don't think so. It was more of a growl. I don't think it was his normal voice."

"Okay." Etienne stood from the sofa. "Let's search to the back door and then outside to see if we can pick up the area where she came out of the water. Thomas, you stay here with Colette."

Minutes later, she was alone with Thomas. She'd known him before her kidnapping, and she used the time with him to catch up on his life and to try to forget what she'd just been through.

"Susie and I got married a month ago," Thomas said.

Colette knew Thomas had been dating Susie Lansbury for a couple of years. "Oh, that's wonderful. Everyone could see that the two of you belonged together. Are you deliriously happy?"

Thomas laughed. "I am happy. We're already planning our family."

"I'm so happy for you, Thomas." She released a deep sigh. "That's what I want for myself...true love and a houseful of babies."

And she knew who she wanted that with, but she had a feeling she was wrestling with the wrong gator. All she knew right now was that she was grateful to be alive after the close call she'd just suffered.

She and Thomas continued to chitchat as they waited for the other officers to come back. Residual fear still danced through her veins, and all the while questions whirled in the back of her head.

Would she still be safe here with a guard sitting outside her door? Her front door definitely needed to be fixed before she'd even consider staying here. But even then, would she feel safe?

The Swamp Soul Stealer had nearly gotten to her tonight. What would keep him from doing the same thing on another night? He could sneak up on another guard too. Then he would come inside and…

Surely Etienne would figure out a plan to make sure she wasn't vulnerable here again. She trusted him. After all, she was his star witness once enough of her memories returned to give him an arrest.

It was about an hour later when Etienne and his men came back to the shanty. Their expressions were grim.

"Nothing," Etienne said in disgust. "Once again, this creep has left us with absolutely nothing to go on." He sat next to her and raked a hand through his hair in obvious frustration. He stared at the broken door for several long moments, his eyes still a deep steel gray…hard and focused.

"You can't stay here," he said to her. "It's obviously no longer safe."

"So, where am I going?" she asked curiously.

"Pack some bags," he said tersely. "You're coming home with me."

Chapter Nine

Colette's head reeled as she packed some clothes and toiletries to go to Etienne's house. The entire evening felt like a bad dream. The attack had definitely been something out of her very worst nightmare.

As she thought about the man with the knife, icy chills shot through her body. There was no question that had he caught her, she'd be dead. He would have killed her in a most painful way. He'd almost been successful at getting to her tonight.

Surely, she'd be safe at Etienne's house. He wouldn't be taking her there if he didn't believe that.

She finished packing her things and carried her bag into the living room where Etienne was pacing the floor.

He stopped in his tracks at the sight of her. "Ready?"

"Ready," she replied.

He walked over and took the bag from her. "Go ahead and pack up your laptop too. I'm sure you'll want that while you're at my place."

She quickly packed it up in its padded case, then turned back to Etienne expectantly.

"I'm leaving Thomas here to stand guard until we can get the door fixed," he said.

"I can call Brett Mayfield in the morning. I'll arrange with him to come out and fix it as soon as possible," she replied.

"At least that hotheaded loudmouth is good for something," Etienne growled as the two of them headed for the door.

Outside, Thomas sat in the rocking chair. "Don't worry, Colette," he said. "I'll make sure nobody goes in the house while it's unlocked."

"Thank you, Thomas. I really appreciate it."

"And I'll continue to keep a guard on the place until the door is fixed and the shanty can be locked up," Etienne added.

Minutes later, they were in Etienne's car and headed toward town. He was quiet on the ride and gave off a tense, angry energy. Was he angry because he was taking her to his home? Was he mad that she would now be his full-time burden? When he'd taken her home from the hospital, he certainly hadn't signed up to become a full-time babysitter.

If she had anyplace else to go, she would go there. But she refused to stay with any of her friends and bring this danger to their doorstep. A motel room certainly wouldn't offer any sort of great protection.

Damn her own mind for keeping her memories locked up so tightly. If only she could remember what had happened to her in the three months she'd been with the monster, then Etienne might be able to arrest the man and save the others. If she could just remember, then this would all be over.

Just when despair started to take hold of her, he reached over and covered her hand with his. "You doing okay?" he asked with a softness that soothed the ragged edges of her current thoughts. He pulled his hand away and placed it back on the steering wheel.

"I'm okay," she said. She hesitated a moment and then continued, "But you seem angry. Are you upset that you have to take me home with you?"

"Not at all," he replied immediately. "But I am angry. I'm mad that this creep attacked my officer and then went after you. I was so scared, Colette." He paused for a moment. "When I went into the shanty and you weren't there, I was certain you'd been killed or taken once again." His voice was deep and filled with myriad emotions.

Maybe he did care about her a little bit. Maybe he cared about her more than just as a piece to his crime puzzle. Perhaps he cared about her simply as a woman.

She sat up straighter in the seat as he pulled into the driveway of an attractive ranch house. In the darkness of the night, it was impossible for her to tell what color it was. With the push of a button on his visor, the garage door opened, and he pulled inside. He grabbed her bag from the back seat, and she reached for her laptop. As the garage door closed, he guided her into the house.

They entered an airy kitchen with a nice black table and four chairs. Turning on lights, he led her through an attractive living room with a black sofa and a matching recliner. A big television was mounted on one wall. A glass-topped coffee table matched the end tables. It all appeared rather cold and sterile, with no photos on the walls and nothing to indicate that Etienne lived here. The house could have belonged to anyone.

From the living room, she followed him down the hallway and into the first room on the right. There, a queen-size bed was covered with a dark blue spread, and matching curtains hung in the single window. A double dresser lined one wall, and nightstands with attractive silver lamps flanked the bed.

"I hope you'll be comfortable here," he said as he placed her bag at the foot of the bed. She set her laptop there as well.

"This is lovely. I'll be just fine here," she replied.

"There are several empty drawers in the dresser, and the bathroom is across the hall. You should find everything you need in the cabinets beneath the sink. Now, since it's so late, we'll just call it a night, and I'll see you in the morning."

"Etienne…thank you for all of this," she said.

He smiled, the smile that always melted something deep inside her very soul. "No problem. I'll just say good night now, and if you need anything at all, I'll be in the living room."

It wasn't until he closed the door behind him that she wondered why he would be in the living room and not in his bedroom. The thought only lasted a moment as she opened her bag and pulled out a nightgown. She would unpack and really settle in tomorrow.

She grabbed her gown, along with her toothbrush and toothpaste, and went across the hall to the bathroom. She found a washcloth under the sink and proceeded to wash her face, brush her teeth and change into the nightgown.

Back in the bedroom, she pulled the curtains more tightly closed over the window. Only then did she fold down the bedspread to expose inviting light blue sheets. Finally, she crawled into the bed and turned off the lamp.

The room was plunged into total darkness. She'd never been afraid of the dark before, but tonight it definitely bothered her.

Where once she had found the dark comforting, she now

found it cloying and claustrophobic. This was where the monster lived...in the shadows of the night. This was where the monster played his games of taking people away from their loved ones and into his lair.

The dark had once been a safe place for her, but now she knew it could be a very dangerous place.

As these thoughts whirled around and around in her brain, she reached out and turned on the bedside lamp once again. The soft glow would keep the monsters away.

She finally closed her eyes and fell into a nightmare where she was being chased through the swamp. She tripped over roots and tangled with tree limbs that tried to hold her captive. Spanish moss wrapped around her, further impeding her frantic escape from whatever was chasing her.

She was desperate, her breaths releasing in deep pants as tears blurred her vision. She had to get away before he caught her. She had to... Thick fingers touched the small of her back, and she screamed.

She jerked upright in the bed, her gaze shooting around the room. Light lit around the edges of the curtains, letting her know it was after dawn.

She released a shuddering sigh and then screamed again as the bedroom door flew open and Etienne entered with his gun drawn.

He took one look around and then holstered his gun. "You okay?" he asked.

She nodded, embarrassed that she must have screamed out loud with her nightmare. "I'm sorry. It...it was a bad dream."

"As long as you're okay, that's all that matters," he replied.

What she wished in that moment was that he would embrace her, maybe stroke her hair or her cheek and tell her he was sorry she'd had a nightmare.

He was already dressed in his blue uniform, and he smelled of minty soap and shaving cream.

"What time is it?" she asked.

"A little after eight. Whenever you're ready, I'll get breakfast going."

"Oh, Etienne, you don't have to cook for me," she protested.

He offered her a small grin. "Are you planning on never eating while you're here?"

"Hmm, let me rethink this," she replied with her own grin.

He laughed. "Whenever you're ready, the coffee is made. I'll be in the kitchen." With that, he left the room.

She got out of bed and grabbed a pair of jeans and a light purple T-shirt from her bag. She got dressed, washed her face and brushed her teeth and hair. By the time she left the bathroom, the nightmare had begun to recede from her thoughts.

After all, was it any wonder she'd had nightmares after the night she had endured?

The smell of fresh-brewed coffee led her to the kitchen where she found Etienne seated at the table and drinking a cup. He jumped up to his feet at the sight of her.

"Here…sit," he said as he pulled out one of the chairs at the table.

She sat while he went to a cabinet, pulled down a cup and poured her coffee. "This feels backward," she said. "Normally, it's me offering you a cup of coffee in the morning."

He set the cup before her and smiled. "Different circumstances call for different actions." He sat back down in the chair opposite her. "Except for your nightmare, how did you sleep?"

She wrapped her fingers around her cup, seeking its warmth as memories of her bad dream rushed through her head again. "I honestly couldn't tell you. Even though I know it's not true, it seemed like I fell into the nightmare immediately."

"Do you want to talk about it?" he asked with a gentleness that washed over her.

"There isn't a lot to tell. I was just running away from something or someone chasing me through the swamp."

"With what you went through last night in real life, it's no wonder you had a nightmare like that." He took a sip of his coffee, then stood. "On the menu this morning is bacon and eggs any way you like them."

"That sounds good to me, and I like my eggs however you want to make them," she replied. "Actually, if you'll show me where things are, I'd be glad to cook."

"This morning you're getting a visitor's welcome, and I'll cook for you," he replied. He pulled a skillet out of one of the lower cabinets and got a pound of bacon from the refrigerator.

"Okay, but I'm offering my cooking skills to you whenever you want them," she said.

"How about I cook our breakfasts, and you can take care of the evening meals?"

"That sounds like a good deal to me," she agreed. She watched as he laid the bacon strips into the skillet. Within minutes, the meat was sizzling, filling the air with its aromatic scent. "So, we now know who is cooking what meal, but what are we doing in between those times?" she asked curiously.

"Unfortunately, you're going to be going to the station

with me during the days. Needless to say, you'll be completely safe there. We'll set you up in one of the interview rooms, and you can work there. I know it's not ideal, but it's where we're at right now."

"And it will be just fine," she assured him. "Etienne, the last thing I want is to be an unnecessary burden. Stick me wherever you need to, and I'll be just fine."

He smiled at her. "I appreciate that." He turned back to the skillet and began removing the crispy bacon. "Now, how do you want your eggs?"

"Really, Etienne, I don't care. Whatever is easiest for you," she replied.

"Okay then, scrambled it is."

As he made toast and cooked the eggs, they small-talked about favorite breakfast foods. There was something quite intimate about sitting in the kitchen laughing and talking with a man making the morning meal.

His uniform really fit him well, emphasizing his broad shoulders and slim waist and hips. Just looking at him brought up memories of their lovemaking, something she would love to repeat.

However, it was clear that wouldn't happen, and sadly, she would have to live with that.

It didn't take long before he had breakfast on the table. As they ate, he explained what their schedule would be during the days…noting that it could change at any given moment. "No matter what I'm doing, you'll remain in the interview room where we've set you up," he explained. "I'm sure this creep won't even try to come for you in the police station."

"I agree," she replied. "Surely he wouldn't be that stupid."

"One thing is certain, this man isn't stupid," Etienne replied.

They finished eating, and she helped with the cleanup.

He pulled a couple pork chops from his freezer and set them on the counter to thaw. She went back to her bedroom and grabbed her computer case, and they were ready to go.

They left the house through the garage, just as they had entered the night before. As she slid into the passenger seat, he opened the garage door with a touch of a button on his visor.

They both were silent for the rest of the ride to the police station. Once there, he hurried her to the back door, and they walked down a long hallway to a relatively small room. A table for six took up most of the space.

"You can get settled in here," he said.

She put her computer case on the table and smiled. "I'll be just fine here," she replied. "Now, you go do your police work and don't worry about me."

"Then unless something comes up, I'll see you around noon for lunch." With that, he left the room and closed the door behind him.

She took her computer out of the case, plugged it into a nearby wall socket and got set up to work. At least with all this uninterrupted time, she should get a lot of writing done.

Unfortunately, with all the uninterrupted time, she also had plenty of time to think. And her thoughts always went to Etienne.

She couldn't believe how easily he'd won her heart. Was it simply a matter of circumstances? Would she have fallen in love with any man who was protecting her from a potential killer? A man who was her sole connection to the outside world?

No, she didn't think so. She had fallen in love with Etienne the man and not Etienne the lawman. Her love for him sprang from the long conversations and the laughter they shared. It had grown from the intense physical attraction they had for each other and a million other things.

But no matter how much she loved him, she couldn't make him love her back. His love remained as elusive as the memories locked so tightly in her mind.

ETIENNE SAT IN his office, his thoughts on the woman he had left in the interview room. She could have been so difficult. She could have complained about being stuck in a small room with no television, no sofa, nothing but a table and her laptop for company.

However, one thing he'd learned about Colette was she was definitely not a complainer. Instead, she easily rolled with the punches and remained pleasant under almost all circumstances.

There was no question that he admired her. She was the strongest woman he'd ever met. There was also no question that he wanted her. He'd never felt such wild, sexual attraction for a woman before.

But that didn't mean he was in love with her. He refused to even consider that he might be.

He also doubted that her feelings for him were real. They were in an unusual situation, filled with forced proximity and danger. It was only natural that emotions would run high between them. But those emotions definitely couldn't be trusted.

With a deep sigh, he pulled out the large file he had on the Swamp Soul Stealer kidnappings. It held all the circumstances of the disappearances, all the interviews that had been conducted and any other information pertinent to the investigation. It now contained the interview and information about Kate's kidnapping as well.

He began to read through the file in hopes of spotting something that had been missed. He had read it all a hundred times before, but he kept thinking he was missing something. As he read, he took notes, fully immersing himself in everything having to do with the crimes.

It took him well over an hour to read through everything, but when he was finished, he had another suspect in mind. Pierre Gusman was another one of the gator hunters in the area. He was physically capable of carrying a body through the swamp.

Etienne hadn't paid much attention to the man when he showed up at the scene when Colette had been taken. It wasn't until right now, reading through the file, that he realized Pierre had shown up at all of the crime scenes.

When the police arrived to investigate a disappearance, it always drew a small crowd of onlookers. But Pierre had been there every single time, and there was no reason for him to be. The crimes had occurred all over the swamp.

Etienne knew from his study of criminals that often the guilty party would insinuate himself somehow into the investigation. While Pierre had remained a silent observer, the fact that he was at each scene definitely drew Etienne's attention now.

He pulled out his phone and called Trey. "Come to my office."

"Be right there."

Moments later, Trey sat down in the chair in front of Etienne's desk. "What's up?"

"I've just been going through the file and something caught my attention," Etienne began.

"Oh yeah?" Trey leaned forward.

"As usual, it might mean nothing, or it might mean everything. Have you or any of the men had any run-ins with Pierre Gusman?"

Trey frowned. "No, not that I'm aware of. I've seen him around town, and all I know about him is that he's a quiet man and somewhat of a loner. Why?"

"Did you realize each time we've gone out to investigate a disappearance, he's been around in the group of people we always draw?" Etienne asked.

Trey frowned. "No, I didn't realize that. He's been at every single one of the crime scenes?"

Etienne nodded. "According to the notes where we chronicle who's present at each scene."

Trey's frown deepened. "That's odd. Was anyone else present at all the scenes?"

"No, just Gusman."

"So, is he the Swamp Soul Stealer and checking up on our investigation at each scene? Or is he just an odd man interested in police work and what's going on in the swamp?"

"This is definitely something I'd like to follow up on. Why don't you and Joel go have a conversation with the man and see what kind of a vibe you get from him? Check his alibis for the nights of the disappearances and see if you think he's a viable suspect."

"Got it," Trey said, "I'll grab Joel, and we'll leave as soon as possible. I'll get back to you with what we find out."

Etienne would have liked to be the one going to speak to Pierre, but he felt an odd obligation to stick around the building with Colette here. Besides, he trusted Trey. If there was any information to get, Trey and Joel would get it. It was probably a crapshoot anyway.

Etienne went back to reading the file. He finally stopped

when his stomach rumbled with hunger, and he realized it was 12:30 p.m.

He got up and stretched, then headed down the hallway to the interview room. "Did you think I was going to starve you to death?" he asked as he entered.

Colette looked up from her keyboard and laughed. "I figured sooner or later you'd come and take pity on me."

"We have a couple of options for lunch. I can get one of the guys to get us burgers from Big D's, or we can order something from the café, and they'll deliver it here."

"I love Big D's cheeseburgers, so that would be fine with me," she replied.

"Okay, then burgers it is. French fries or onion rings?"

"French fries," she said.

"And what would you like to drink?"

"A regular soda is fine."

He nodded. "Got it. I'll come back when the food arrives."

He left the room that now smelled of her soft floral scent. He asked Michael to run to Big D's for them, then he sat back down at his desk.

Twenty minutes later, Michael was back with the food, and Etienne brought it to Colette in the interview room. "I've got your cheeseburger and fries right here," he said as he took the food out of the paper bag.

"And what did you get?" she asked. She took a straw from him and punched it into the plastic top of her soda.

"A double burger with onion rings and an iced tea to drink," he replied.

They unwrapped their sandwiches and began to eat. They talked about their favorite menu items at Big D's, and the conversation remained light.

It was always like that with her. Their conversations always flowed so effortlessly. Even when they disagreed about something, it still remained easy between them.

"Are you bored to death in here?" he asked.

She popped a french fry into her mouth and chased it down with a quick drink of soda. "No, not at all," she replied. "I finished one article, got it ready for submission and started on a new one. I was just about to take a break and jump on the internet for a little while. As long as I have my computer, I won't get bored. How has your morning been?"

"Fairly quiet. Do you know Pierre Gusman?" he asked and then bit into his burger.

She looked at him in surprise. "Yes, I know Pierre, although not well. Why?"

"His name just came up as I was reading through the kidnapping file. I find it odd that every time we've gone out to investigate one of the disappearances, he's been around the scene."

"He's an odd fellow. He lives in a small shanty near mine, but he keeps to himself. He's not exactly unfriendly, but he doesn't go out of his way to be friendly with anyone either," she said.

This information only made Etienne more interested in the man. Pierre was somebody who would know the swamp like the back of his hand. He would know places to hide and keep people captive.

But he might just be an odd, innocent man, Etienne reminded himself.

They finished their lunch, and Etienne left her once again. It was about two o'clock when Trey and Joel returned. They immediately came into Etienne's office to share what they'd learned from Gusman.

"He does seem to be an odd duck," Trey said. "His alibis for the kidnappings were all the same. He was in the swamp gator-hunting alone. That was also his alibi for the night Kate went missing."

"He said he was at each scene when we were investigating because he was interested in what was going on in the swamp," Joel said. "He wanted to know if we'd found any clues that would catch the man responsible for the disappearances."

Etienne released a deep sigh. "So, the man might be guilty, or he might not be guilty."

"That's about the size of it," Trey replied. "I will tell you that something about the man gave me the creeps."

"Me too," Joel said.

"Any reason for that?" Etienne asked curiously.

"Nothing I can put my finger on, he just gave me the creeps," Trey said.

"Same," Joel added.

"Tomorrow, maybe I'll take one of the other men and have another conversation with him," Etienne said thoughtfully.

"That's probably a good idea. Maybe if we put a little pressure on him, he'll crack if he's guilty," Trey said.

"We should be so lucky," Etienne replied wryly.

At five o'clock, he went to pick up Colette from the interview room. She packed up her computer, then they left to head to his place. At least with Colette in the police station during the days and staying with him at night, he could return to his normal work routine.

Once they were home, she got busy cooking dinner. He sat at the kitchen table while she worked, telling himself it made sense that he be on hand to help her find things in the kitchen. Along with the pork chops, she was making honey-sweetened carrots and mashed potatoes. He was definitely going to have to get groceries. What with Colette cooking him meals when he was on guard duty at her shanty and him rarely being home at dinnertime at all, his cupboards and refrigerator were pretty bare.

"It's a real treat to have an oven and four burners," she said.

"And just think, you don't have to go outside to take a shower."

The minute the words left his mouth, he was tortured by a vision of her naked body beneath a steamy spray of water. He was in the vision with her, slowly sliding a bar of soap across her shoulders and down her back and across her full breasts.

He shook his head and consciously forced the vision out of his brain. What the hell was he doing to himself? And why was he thinking such inappropriate thoughts about her? All he needed to do was keep her safe and nothing more. It shouldn't be this difficult.

Her voice pulled him from his thoughts. "This is going to take another thirty minutes or so before it's ready."

"That's fine," he replied. He'd like to leave the kitchen for some much-needed distance from her, but he also didn't want to leave her alone in case any trouble appeared.

He had good security around the house with alarms on all the doors and windows. As the chief of police, he'd wanted good security in case some disgruntled criminal came after him. But security systems could be breeched, so he intended to stay ready for anything.

She set the table and then took the chair opposite his. "Before this case sucked up all your time, what did you do to pass the evenings?"

"When the weather was nice, I would walk down to visit with my parents, or I'd just watch television until bedtime."

"I'll bet your favorite shows are the crime dramas," she said.

He laughed. "You'd be wrong. Usually, I watched sitcoms and game shows. The last thing I want to do after a long day of worrying about crime is watch it on television."

"That makes sense," she replied. "So tonight, you can educate me on game shows and sitcoms since I've never watched either."

He nodded. "Sounds like a plan."

What he'd really like to educate her on was how to retrieve memories that could possibly put the Swamp Soul Stealer in jail. And the sooner, the better.

Because he knew this arrangement of Colette staying here with him was going to be a test of his willpower. It was a test he feared he might fail.

Chapter Ten

For the next five days they fell into an easy routine. Colette spent her days in the small room at the police station. Each day, Etienne ate lunch with her, and around five o'clock, they would come home. She would cook dinner and in the evenings they watched television.

She was grateful that J.T. was back at work after having suffered a concussion. While at the police station, she had also met Officer Annie DeRossit, the only woman on the force. Brett Mayfield had replaced her front door, so her shanty could be locked up and no longer needed a guard on duty there. Colette continued her therapy with Dr. Kingston, but she still hadn't remembered anything more.

It was around 6:30 p.m. when a knock fell on the door. They had just cleaned up the kitchen after dinner. Etienne immediately grabbed his gun and went to check the door.

He looked considerably more relaxed when he returned, ushering in an older couple. He introduced her to Diana and Lester Savoie, his mother and father.

"I hope we aren't interrupting your evening, but Mama wanted to check in with her baby boy," Lester said with a fond look at Diana.

"You aren't interrupting anything at all," Colette said, smiling warmly.

They were an attractive couple. It was easy to see where Etienne got his curly hair as Lester had salt-and-pepper curls. His mother had chin-length dark hair and gray eyes that matched her son's.

When they were all seated in the living room, Diana offered Colette a smile. "I've been wanting to meet you for a while, Colette. I'm so sorry for everything you've been through. What incredible strength you must have."

Colette returned her smile. "Thank you. And thanks to your son, I'm still here. Still standing."

Lester grinned with obvious affection at his son. "He's a good one."

"Have you heard about the recall effort?" Etienne asked.

"Ack…a bunch of foolishness by a bunch of fools," Diana scoffed.

"I definitely agree," Colette said. "I can certainly attest to how hard Etienne has been working to solve these cases."

"We know how hard he's been working," Lester replied and looked at Etienne. "Are you sleeping any better?"

"Maybe a little bit better," Etienne replied.

"I'm sure he isn't getting enough sleep," Colette replied with a long look at the lawman. She now knew he spent his nights in his recliner chair in the living room. Not a place to get good, restful sleep.

"But I am eating well," Etienne said. "Colette cooks dinner every night, and she's a very good cook."

"Well, that's good," Diana replied. "A mother always wants to know her children are well-fed."

"I'm definitely enjoying the benefits of a kitchen with

all the modern bells and whistles," Colette said with a small laugh.

"Do you miss your home in the swamp?" Diana asked.

"Not too much. I'm enjoying your son's company, and that makes it easier to be away from my shanty," Colette replied.

In fact, she'd been surprised by how little she had missed her home. This felt like home...right here with Etienne. Still, eventually she knew she would return to her shanty, probably sporting a very big broken heart.

For the next few minutes, she listened to Etienne and his parents visit. They talked about relatives who didn't live in Crystal Cove and the latest project Lester was working on. Apparently, the man had a wood-carving hobby he was quite good at. He was currently carving a unicorn out of a fallen tree limb.

"It's coming along beautifully," Diana said. "But you know your father... Once he starts on one of his projects, he forgets he has a wife who might need a little attention too."

"Oh, now, Mama, that isn't true. I always have time and attention for you," Lester replied with a wink at his wife.

It was around eight o'clock when they left. "Your parents are absolutely delightful," Colette said as Etienne closed the front door after telling his parents goodbye. "It's obvious they love you very much."

"Yeah, I'm kind of fond of them too," he replied with a grin.

"They also seem to be pretty crazy about each other. How long have they been married?" she asked.

"It will be forty-one years this November," he replied.

"That's amazing. So you've had a really good example to follow when it comes to marriage."

"True, but that doesn't mean marriage is something I want for myself." His gaze didn't quite meet hers.

"Why not, Etienne?" she asked curiously.

He finally looked at her. "I thought I wanted it at one time, but over the past couple of years, I've realized I'm probably better off alone."

"Why would you come to that conclusion?" she pressed, wanting to understand him. If he didn't want a relationship with her, then why shut himself off from any relationship in the future?

"I'm married to this job. There's really no time for anything else in my life," he replied.

"Etienne, once this case is over, you'll be back to regular working hours, and you'll have time for a special woman in your life," she said. Oh, how she wished she could be that special woman for him, but obviously she wasn't.

"Why do you care whether I get married or not?"

A blush warmed her cheeks. "Because I care about you, Etienne, and I just know you would be a great husband to some woman. I'd like you to find a special woman who would love and support you and could be your soft place to fall." Couldn't he see that woman was her? Oh, why couldn't he love her like she loved him? It felt so unfair. After all she had been through, why couldn't fate or whatever grant her this particular wish?

"I appreciate your sentiment," he replied. "And I wish the same for you. I hope you find a special man who will love and support you and be your soft place to fall. And now, it's getting late, so I suggest we head to bed."

She had a feeling it was the topic of conversation that

made him ready to call it a night. Half an hour later, Colette slipped beneath the sheets, but she kept the lamp on the bedside table on. She hadn't had any more nightmares and had actually slept peacefully each night. But she kept the light on every single night...to keep the monsters away.

She awakened early the next morning refreshed after another good night's sleep. The scent of coffee let her know that Etienne was already up and around.

She gathered clean clothes and went across the hall where she started the water for a shower. As she stood beneath the warm spray, she admitted that she had been fully seduced by the conveniences a place in town offered.

Cooking meals with the luxury of an oven, a microwave and four burners was terrific. But the real luxury was being able to step into a shower that had hot water and a healthy spray, something she definitely didn't have in her relatively primitive shower on her back porch.

Dressing quickly in a pair of jeans and a maroon long-sleeved blouse, she pulled her wet hair into a low ponytail, ready to face the day.

"French toast," Etienne said in greeting when she walked into the kitchen.

"Sounds yummy." She grabbed a cup from a cabinet. She poured herself some coffee and then sat at the table.

"You sleep well?" he asked as he turned back to the skillet.

"Like a baby," she replied. "What about you?"

"I slept off and on."

"What time did you get up?" she asked.

"Early enough," he replied vaguely. "I already ordered some groceries, and they arrived a few minutes ago."

So, as usual, he hadn't gotten a good night's sleep. She

had no idea how late he stayed up at night, and he was always up before her in the morning. The man was running on an empty tank. The fact that he functioned so well during the day spoke of his inner strength.

He was being eaten alive by the Swamp Soul Stealer case. That must be what kept him from sleeping. As always, guilt filled her heart—she could help him if she just could remember.

"I'm hoping for the morning when I ask you how you slept and you tell me you slept like a baby," she said.

"Ha, I'm hoping for that day too. I've always had a little trouble sleeping, but since these disappearances, it's gotten much worse." He dropped two of the egg-and-milk-covered slices of bread into the pan.

Dammit, if only she could remember something...anything that might help solve the crime. So far, she'd pretty much been deadweight for him, unable to offer anything that might move the case forward.

It wasn't long before the French toast was ready, and they sat down to eat. "I love maple syrup," she said as she poured a liberal dose over her French toast.

"I see that," he replied in amusement. "You just drowned a perfectly good breakfast."

"I didn't drown it," she protested with a laugh. "I just enhanced my breakfast."

"If you're lucky, I'll make you waffles tomorrow morning and you can have a plateful of syrup again."

"That sounds delightful," she said with another laugh.

Once they were finished eating, she helped clean up the kitchen, and they left for the police station.

She stared out the passenger window as he drove, her thoughts as scattered as the leaves knocked down from the trees by the gusty wind blowing outside. While she knew it was necessary for her to be ensconced in the little room in the police station, there was a part of her that wondered how long this arrangement would last.

She knew this was the best way to keep her safe, but spending all day in the room was becoming quite monotonous. How long before this whole ordeal would be over? How long before Etienne became sick of her presence in his home?

Right now, they seemed to still be in a sort of honeymoon phase. She thought he enjoyed spending his evenings with her. Their conversations remained pleasant, and they often laughed together. But eventually she feared the honeymoon would be over. Not for her, but for him. He'd tire of her presence, and then what would happen?

Damn, if only she could just remember something.

She released a deep sigh as he pulled into his parking space at the back of the police station.

He shut off the engine and turned to look at her. "That was a pretty heavy sigh. Is everything all right?" His eyes held a wealth of concern.

"Everything is fine," she assured him.

"Are you sure?"

"I'm positive." She offered him her brightest smile. There was no way she was going to share with him her troubling thoughts, especially since he couldn't say or do anything to solve her worries.

"Okay, hang tight, and I'll be around to get you out." He opened her door and gestured for her to step into the safety of one of his arms.

As always, his close proximity caused her heart to flutter. He smelled of shaving cream, his spicy cologne and a male scent that was his alone. If she was blindfolded and five men stood before her, she was certain she could pick out Etienne by his scent alone.

The minute they stepped into the building, his arm dropped from around her. They walked down the hallway, and she turned into her room and set her computer case on the table.

"Would you like for me to grab you a bottle of water or a cup of coffee?" he asked.

"No, thanks, I'm fine. I'll just see you around noon." She opened her laptop as he murmured a goodbye and left the room.

She set up her computer, plugged it into a nearby outlet and sank down in the chair. There was one thing for certain, with all the uninterrupted time, she was getting a lot of writing done. Not only had she submitted several articles, but she had also restarted her blog. It would take months for her to build up the readers she had once had, but at least she was working on it again.

She turned her computer on and waited for it to load. While she was waiting, a vision slowly unfolded in her mind. She closed her eyes to bring it into clearer focus.

She was chained to a wall in a cage...a concrete wall. She and the others were in a basement. Not some cave or anyplace in the swamp. A basement! That was all the vision showed her, but it was enough.

She jumped up out of her chair, ran to the door and tore it open. She wasn't sure where Etienne was right now, but she had to find him as soon as possible. Somewhere in Crystal Cove there was a basement filled with the missing.

J.T. suddenly came into view at the opposite end of the long hallway.

"Officer Caldwell," she called out to him.

"Hey, Colette." In five long strides, he was before her with a concerned look. "Is everything all right? Do you need something?"

"I need to find Etienne as quickly as possible," she replied urgently.

"I think he's in his office. Come on, I'll take you there."

She fell into step next to the tall, lean, youthful officer, her excitement burning inside her. They didn't go far before he stopped at a closed door and knocked.

Etienne's voice drifted from inside, bidding them enter.

J.T. stepped aside and gestured for her to go in.

"Thanks," she told him and opened the door.

Etienne sat behind a large desk, but at the sight of her, he rose in surprise. "Colette, is everything okay?"

"It was a basement, Etienne," she said with excitement. "We were all being held in a basement with concrete walls."

"Are you sure?" His eyes lit up.

"I'm positive. We weren't being held in the swamp at all. It was definitely a regular basement. The memory just came to me. This will help, won't it?"

"Oh, honey, this definitely helps," he replied. "All of our searches have been in the swamp. But it sounds like we need to change all that now." He walked around his desk and pulled her into his arms. "This is great, Colette," he murmured into her ear.

She thought he was about to release her when his lips claimed hers in an unexpected kiss. She leaned closer to him, reveling in the fire his mouth created against hers.

The kiss lasted only a moment, and then he stepped back from her. "You've just given us a whole new direction to take the investigation. Now, honey, you go back to your room, and I'll get to work."

"I hope you find it. I hope you find the right basement, Etienne," she said fervently and then turned and left his office.

As she walked back down the hall to the interview room, her lips still burned with the imprint of his. As much as she had enjoyed the kiss, it also made her sad.

It broke her heart a little bit, knowing that he hadn't kissed her because he loved her. He had kissed her because she had brought him a memory. It merely confirmed that the memories were what he was after...and nothing more.

ETIENNE IMMEDIATELY CALLED TREY, Michael and Joel into his office. He didn't want to think about his motive for kissing Colette. It had been completely spontaneous. Merely due to his excitement and the fact that she had just looked so damn kissable.

Right now, his focus was on the information she'd brought him. Basements were not all that common in Crystal Cove. The water level excluded most houses from having them, but there were some homes on higher ground that did.

"All this time we were sure the victims were being held someplace in the swamp," Joel said.

"They disappeared in the swamp. It was a good bet that they were being held there too," Trey said.

"Apparently, we were all wrong," Etienne replied. "Michael, I'd like you to go check with the city's assessment office and get the addresses for all the homes and businesses that have basements in town. Once we have those addresses, we'll contact Judge Cooke about search warrants for each place."

He felt a new energy roar inside his veins, an energy that snapped in the air. He saw the fire of renewed vigor in the eyes and posture of his officers. They all were hungry for a win. Hopefully this would be the ultimate win. Perhaps by the end of the day they'd have the perpetrator behind bars and the victims all saved.

Michael left to get the addresses. While they waited for his return, Etienne pulled out a large map of the city and placed it on his desk. Together he, Trey and Joel studied the map.

"It's obvious the places under sea level will not have basements," Etienne said.

"So, that pretty much takes out this whole area," Trey said, running his finger over a particular neighborhood.

"But on this side of town, the houses are high enough on land to potentially have basements," Joel said and indicated another area on the map.

"Thank God we got this new tip or memory or whatever from Colette," Trey said.

"Otherwise, we'd still be spinning our wheels out in the swamp," Etienne replied.

It took almost forty-five minutes for Michael to return. The search had yielded six addresses of homes that had basements. Etienne immediately contacted Judge Cooke to get the search warrants he needed. Thankfully, the judge was a friend to the prosecution, and after learning about Colette's new memory, he immediately granted the search warrants.

"Here's what we're going to do. We'll go together to each address. I want each of you to be prepared for anything. As we go into each basement, we don't know what we might be facing," Etienne said. "Keep in mind that it's possible our missing people will be there. We have to go in with great care so none of them get hurt in the process. Trey, you ride with me. Michael and Joel, you follow."

Etienne quickly popped into the interview room to tell Colette he was leaving. He also spoke to J.T. and Annie and told them to keep an eye on her.

Electricity jolted through his veins as he and Trey got into his vehicle.

"This takes our two potential suspects off our list," Trey said once they were on their way to the first house.

"I seriously doubt that Levi Morel or Pierre Gusman would have access to a basement here in town," Etienne replied. He hit the center of his steering wheel. "Damn, I can't believe how wrong we've been about this case from the very beginning and how much time we've wasted searching in the swamp."

"We followed logic," Trey said in protest. "Etienne, it was only logical that a person from the swamp was kidnapping those people and hiding them someplace. And it was only logical that he'd be hiding them in the swamp, where he was most comfortable."

"So, what he must be doing is knocking his victims out in the swamp and then loading them into a vehicle to bring them to a basement in town. Too bad we don't have security cameras in the parking area outside the swamp."

"Yeah, that would have been helpful."

They were headed to 825 N.E. Cypress Drive…the home of Tommy Radcliffe. Thankfully, it was Sunday, so most of the homeowners should be in their houses. "And just because Tommy is the prosecuting attorney doesn't mean he gets an automatic pass."

"Who knows what's in the mind of the perp? He could

be a well-respected man around town during the day, yet at night he could have demons that for some reason or another have him doing these crimes," Trey replied.

"I'd still love to know the motive for these disappearances," Etienne replied. "Why is he taking these people and holding them? For what purpose? What's his end game?"

"Who knows? Maybe his dog or cat or his pet canary is talking to him and telling him to kidnap all these people," Trey said wryly.

Etienne released a small laugh. "I don't think our perp is that insane. Once we catch him, let's hope he doesn't use his talking canary as a defense."

"I would think it'd be difficult for him to use an insanity defense. He obviously knows right from wrong and has gone to great lengths to hide these crimes from law enforcement," Trey replied.

They fell quiet as Etienne pulled into Tommy Radcliffe's driveway. The house was an old but well-kept two-story painted a light gray with black trim.

The other patrol car pulled in behind Etienne, and all four men got out of their vehicles.

"Remember, be ready for anything," Etienne told the others, and he led them up the stairs to the front door.

He knocked and waited for a response. After a few moments passed, he knocked again, this time a little harder.

The door flew open, and Tommy looked at all of them in surprise. "Chief...what's going on here?" he asked with obvious confusion. Despite it being Sunday, the slightly portly man was clad in black dress slacks and a crisp white shirt.

"Tommy, we have a search warrant to check out your basement," Etienne said and pulled the warrant out of his pocket.

"My basement? Why? Wait…you think I have something to do with the kidnappings?" Tommy said with a touch of outrage. "Are you out of your mind? I'm the prosecuting attorney in this town. I'm a respectable man, not a criminal."

"It's nothing personal, Tommy. We have information that the kidnapped are being held in a basement, so we're checking all the basements in town, no matter who they belong to," Etienne explained.

Tommy took the warrant from Etienne and then opened his door wide enough to let them all in. "The door to the basement is in the kitchen. Knock yourselves out." He walked over to the sofa and sat, now appearing calm and unbothered.

Etienne and his men went through the living room and into the kitchen where a door obviously led to the basement. Etienne opened it and listened. Hearing nothing, he started down the stairs, followed closely by Trey and the other men.

Etienne hadn't expected to find anything here, and he didn't. The basement walls were covered with wood paneling, and a sofa and chair faced a television.

From Tommy's house they headed to Dr. Dwight Maison's home, another place where Etienne expected nothing and found nothing. By that time, it was noon, and he called the office to make sure somebody got Colette lunch.

The men grabbed burgers at Big D's, then headed to 9509 N.E. Tupelo Lane. The owner of the home was Jason Maynard, known around town as a computer guru. Etienne didn't know the man well, but Jason had a reputation of being extremely bright and a loner.

Once again, adrenaline raced through Etienne as he knocked on the door.

Jason answered almost immediately. "Just don't touch

anything down there," he said as he led them to the basement door.

Downstairs there were tables with computers in various stages of disrepair. "I fix them for people," Jason explained. "That's my business…repairing computers and cell phones, among other things."

They were halfway through the list of addresses, but hopefully the one they sought was still within reach. Next up was the home of Wesley Simone, now occupied by his widow, Millie.

Wesley had been a successful businessman who, unfortunately, had begun to dabble in illegal drugs. He was murdered by a dope dealer he owed money to. Initially, Heather LaCrae, the woman found covered in blood next to Wesley's dead body, had been charged with the crime. Her defense attorney, Nick Monroe, had worked hard to prove her innocence. In the end, she was exonerated of all the charges against her. While working on the case, Heather and Nick had fallen in love, and now were a happy couple planning a wedding.

Love had certainly been in the air in Crystal Cove for the past couple months. First Angel Marchant had found her forever person, and then Heather had found hers. Cupid had been around the small town, but he'd certainly not been around Etienne, nor did Etienne want him around.

The Simone home was another large, old two-story, and Millie answered the door on the second knock. Since her husband's murder, Millie had lost weight and wore a sadness that was heartbreaking. She had professed to know nothing about her husband's drug deals and had been as stunned as everyone else when the truth about Wesley had come out.

There was no way Etienne believed Millie would have

anything to do with the disappearances from the swamp, but Wesley and Millie had three big, strapping sons who would have access to the basement.

However, again it was a bust. The basement held nothing but old furniture covered with sheets and random boxes.

Two more addresses. Etienne tightened his hands on the steering wheel as they drove to the next to last house on the list.

"It has to be one of these last two," Trey said.

"Let's hope so," Etienne replied. The excitement he had started with had diminished a bit with each basement cleared. "If this doesn't pan out, then I really don't know where we go from here."

"Maybe Colette will remember more," Trey said.

"Her memories are starting to come back, but they are returning very slowly," Etienne replied.

"She remembered a basement, so we're going to find it in the next hour or so," Trey said optimistically.

It was just after four now. There was no way he'd be back at the station by five. Once again, he called one of his officers and arranged for Colette to order some dinner from the café. By the time he finished up the day, it would be too late for her to cook dinner at home.

Minutes later, they pulled up into the driveway of Lincoln Mayfield's home. Lincoln was father to the hotheaded, loudmouthed Brett, who lived here with his father and mother.

The home was one of the largest in Crystal Creek, a two-story painted forest green with white trim. Etienne knocked on the door, and after a moment it was opened by Lincoln. He was a tall, good-looking older man with graying hair and piercing blue eyes.

"This is utterly preposterous," he said when Etienne explained why they were there. "Why on earth do I have to let you into my home?"

"Lincoln, I have a search warrant," Etienne said.

"And why do I have to honor your search warrant?" He pinned Etienne with an arrogant glare.

"If you don't allow us to conduct this search, then I'll have to arrest you," Etienne replied as he held the man's gaze. Why would Lincoln kick up such a fuss?

He held Etienne's gaze for another minute, then opened the door wider. "I'll tell you right now, I don't know the condition of the basement. I don't know what goes on down there. That's Brett's space, and I don't ever go down there."

"Where is Brett now?" Etienne asked.

"He's someplace north of town working on a project," Lincoln replied.

The only information the basement yielded was the fact that Brett lived like a pig. Dirty clothes were strewn around the room along with old fast-food wrappers and rusty construction tools.

Etienne's stomach tightened as they drove to the last location. *This has to be it*, he thought. This absolutely has to be the place. The house was owned by Arnold Swan, a single businessman that Etienne didn't know other than seeing him around town.

It's got to be here, he thought again as he knocked on the door. It was now after five o'clock, and it felt as if the day had gone on forever.

As he waited for his knock to be answered, despite the long hours of the day, he once again felt energized and ready to make an arrest. He exchanged a look with Trey, who appeared just as ready. All his men seemed on high alert, believing this last basement was the one holding their victims... This was the basement where Colette had been held and beaten.

Arnold opened the door. He was a tall man with broad shoulders.

"Mr. Swan...we have a search warrant for your basement," Etienne said.

"For what? What are you specifically searching for?" Arnold's eyes suddenly widened and then narrowed. "Oh wait, I guess this means I'm the Swamp Soul Stealer." He laughed. It was a nasty sound that instantly raised Etienne's hackles.

"We're just interested in looking in your basement," Etienne replied evenly.

"I hear there's a recall effort going on against you. Some people around here want to kick your butt right out of office," Arnold said.

"I hear the same thing, but it hasn't happened yet. I'm still the chief of police, and I'm still working this case. Now, if you would just guide us to your basement, I would appreciate it," Etienne replied evenly. Arnold was definitely a piece of work, but Etienne kept his temper in check.

After going back and forth for several more minutes, Arnold finally opened his door and led them to the kitchen where there was a door.

"I hope I got all those victims hid real good in the basement," Arnold said sarcastically.

"Mr. Swan, this is nothing to joke about," Trey said. Etienne heard the barely suppressed anger in his friend's voice.

The minute he opened the basement door, Etienne knew there was nothing there. His heart sank as he saw the sofa and love seat, along with a television mounted on the wall. It was an ordinary rec room, not a lair holding abused, kidnapped people.

"I wanted to punch that guy in his face," Trey said as they drove back to the station.

"Yeah, he's definitely an unpleasant man," Etienne replied. "It's no wonder he isn't married. He's somebody only a mother could love."

Etienne was positively sick with defeat. All the energy that had driven him all day long was gone now, crushed by the failure of the searches. He'd been so sure the perp would be behind bars by now. Instead, they were out of basements and back to square one, and he had never felt so ill.

It was almost 6:30 p.m. when he got back to the office.

Colette already had her computer packed up, and she greeted him with a tentative smile.

He shook his head, and her smile fell away. "Let's get out of here," he said dispiritedly.

She immediately got up and followed him down the hall. Once outside, he held her close against his side until she was safely in the car. He didn't feel like talking on the way home, and thankfully she seemed to read his mood and was silent herself. They got back home and went into the living room where he sank down on the sofa.

"Have you eaten?" she asked, breaking the silence at last.

"No, but I'm not hungry," he replied. "What about you? Did you eat?"

"I did." She walked over and stopped before him. She reached for his hand and pulled him up to stand in front of her. Then she leaned into him and wrapped her arms around his neck. She stared into his eyes for a long moment, then nestled her head into the hollow of his throat.

He wanted to push her away. He knew he needed to push her away, but there was sweet comfort in her arms…in the warmth and softness of her body. So, even knowing it was wrong, he pulled her closer to him and allowed her to be a soft place for him to fall.

Chapter Eleven

Colette knew Etienne was devastated by the day's lack of results. She hoped holding him in her arms would take away some of the sting of defeat.

He held her tight against him and she responded in kind. All she wanted to do was comfort him and take away the deep shadows of failure that darkened his gaze. They held each other for several long minutes and then he raised his head and looked deep in her eyes. Then he kissed her.

The kiss was filled with a wild hunger and more than the hint of a desperate need.

In this moment she wanted to give him whatever he needed, so when he grabbed her hand and led her down the hallway and into his bedroom, she went willingly…eagerly.

He kissed her once again, and then they were undressing in a frenzy. Clothes flew off, and he yanked down the bedspread, gray eyes smoldering, and stretched her across the bed.

There was little foreplay before he took her, but she didn't need any. Instead, there was a ravenous hunger and a fierce need that radiated from him. He pumped into her quickly, and she grabbed his buttocks to encourage him. Fast and frantic, he moved in and out of her.

She was suddenly overcome with a fierce climax that left her weak and gasping his name. He found his own release soon after, groaning and then collapsing breathlessly next to her on the bed.

After several long minutes, he released a deep sigh. "I'm so sorry, Colette. I… I just used you," he said.

"I know. It's okay," she replied softly.

He rolled over on his side and propped himself up on one elbow. He reached out and gently shoved a strand of her hair away from her eyes.

"Why did you allow me to do that?" he asked, his eyes dark and enigmatic. "Why would you let any man use you that way?"

"Etienne, you aren't any man, and I wanted you to use me. Trust me, if I had felt differently, then we wouldn't be here right now. I care about you, and I knew you were in a really bad place. You don't have to apologize to me, Etienne. I wanted to be with you. I wanted to comfort you in any way I could."

He held her gaze for another long moment and then rolled away from her and sat up. "Why don't we get dressed and go back to the living room?" He picked up his clothing from the floor and disappeared into an en suite bathroom.

She got her clothing and padded down the hallway to the bathroom she always used. Once she was dressed, she went out to the living room where he was already seated in his recliner.

She settled on the sofa and looked at him. "I don't believe my memory was a false one. I still think we were being held in a basement."

"I don't believe your memory was false either. However, we checked out six basements today, all that were listed in the assessor's office," he replied. He looked completely exhausted, lines of stress etching across his forehead and other lines deepening at the outer corners of his eyes. "And we found nothing…absolutely nothing."

"Is it possible the assessor is behind in their recordkeeping? That maybe some new construction hasn't been listed there yet?" she asked.

He released a deep sigh and ran a hand through his hair. "At this point, I guess anything is possible. We'll see what we can figure out in the morning. Somehow, somewhere, we're missing something."

"Maybe I'll remember something more that will be more help in pinpointing the location," she replied, angry with herself that her memories were coming to her so slowly.

He cast her a tired smile. "I know you're doing the best you can, Colette."

"But it's not good enough," she replied in disgust and then stood. "Now, how about I make you a sandwich? You don't even have to get out of your chair. I'll bring it in here for you to eat, and, Etienne, you do need to eat something."

"I guess I could eat a sandwich," he replied, weariness evident in his voice.

"I'll be right back." She went into the kitchen where she made him a thick ham-and-cheese sandwich, added a handful of potato chips to the plate and grabbed a soda from the refrigerator. She went back into the living room and handed him the plate and soda.

"Thanks," he said. "What did you have for dinner?"

"The meat loaf special from the café," she replied.

"How was it?" He took a bite of the sandwich.

"It was good. It came with mashed potatoes, corn and

applesauce," she replied. "You should be eating something like that instead of a sandwich."

"This sandwich is fine for tonight." For the next few minutes, they both were silent as he ate. The only sound in the room was him crunching on potato chips.

She still felt defeat radiating from him. It had to have been so frustrating to get to the last basement on their list and realize there was nothing there.

There had to still be a basement somewhere out there that was a den of evil with victims who had been beaten and starved. That basement must have somehow slipped through the cracks today. Tomorrow was another day. Hopefully Etienne and his men would find it.

"Thanks," Etienne said again when he'd finished eating. "I thought I wasn't hungry, but that tasted really good."

"Do you want another one?"

"No, thanks. I'm good." He set the plate on the end table next to him and stared off to the space over her left shoulder.

"Etienne, you're going to get him," she said softly.

He focused his gaze back on her. "I hope so. I need to find him soon because I worry about the victims who are being held." He frowned. "If he's beating them as badly as you were beaten, then one day longer in captivity is too damn long."

"He seemed to take a special pleasure in beating me," she replied thoughtfully.

"Is that a memory of yours?" he asked curiously.

"Maybe a bit of one. I just remember wondering why he seemed hell-bent on beating me more than the others... Not that I wished it on the others."

"I'm just so damn sorry you had to go through it." His

gaze lingered on her. "You were so broken when you were found. We weren't sure you were even going to make it."

"It's amazing how the will to survive can keep a person alive," she replied.

"Have you written about your experiences with all this?" he asked curiously.

"No, not yet. I won't write about it until the Swamp Soul Stealer is in jail and all the vanished have been found again," she replied. "Now, even though it's relatively early, why don't we get ready for bed? And if you want me to, I'll give you a nice, relaxing back rub to send you off to sleep."

He looked at her in surprise. "Now, that's an offer too good to refuse." He got out of his chair and headed to his bedroom.

She took his plate back into the kitchen and placed it in the dishwasher, then went to her room and changed into a soft light pink nightshirt.

He was already in his bed and was facedown with his bare back exposed. She got onto the bed next to him and began running a hand down his warm, beautiful skin. Up and down, she caressed his back and slowly felt the tight knots of tension melt away beneath her ministrations. She loved just touching his skin. Despite the long day, she still smelled a whisper of his cologne.

After several minutes, he rolled over and looked at her. "Thank you, that felt amazing." He gazed at her for several long moments. "Stay in here with me for the night?"

As an answer, she simply slid beneath the sheets next to him. He reached out and turned off the lamp on the nightstand. Immediately, he pulled her against him as he spooned around her back.

She snuggled in against him, and he tightened his arm

around her waist. "Colette," he whispered. "When you find your special person, you're going to make him a terrific wife."

"Thanks," she replied and fought against a sudden burn of tears. She'd already found her special person. She was in his arms right this very minute.

But apparently, she wasn't his special person. When this case was solved, it was going to take her a very long time to get over the heartbreak of loving Etienne Savoie.

HE WAS PARKED just down the street from the lawman's home. He'd been watching them each evening when they returned from the police station. He wasn't fool enough to try to get at her while she was there, surrounded by cops.

He had decided he no longer wanted to kill her. What he really wanted was for her to be back in her little cell where he could beat her whenever he wanted.

The bitch reminded him so much of the swamp whore who had been his father's lover for years. While Colette had been in his captivity, he'd beaten her like he'd wanted to beat the woman who destroyed his family and broke his mother.

He wanted that again. He wanted her back so he could beat her all over again. That would be so much better than killing her and ending it with her. Even now, just thinking about having her back in captivity shot a wild wave of sweet anticipation through him.

Yes, he'd been watching and learning their habits and he now thought he knew a way to get to her. But he wanted to think about it some more and make sure it was possible.

One night very soon, he'd make his move. Hopefully

when it was all over, Colette would again be in his basement and he would be in control of her.

Once again, a sweet rush of pleasure roared through him as he thought of beating the beauty right out of her.

ETIENNE SAT AT his desk with Trey and Joel by his side as they studied the map of the city. Earlier in the day, Joel had gone back to the assessor's office where the clerk admitted that the records hadn't been updated for several years.

What Etienne and his men were looking at now were areas in the city and the surrounding outskirts that would have the appropriate land height to have a basement.

"This area here might have basements," Joel said and pointed to an area on the north side of town. "I know there's a couple of relatively new homes there."

"Let's get addresses for those," Etienne said.

"And here's another area that we might need to put on our search list," Trey said and pointed to the map. "There are a few new homes there as well."

"Again, let's put together a list of addresses as soon as possible so we can get them to Judge Cooke for more search warrants," Etienne said.

Minutes later Joel left to look at city records and get the addresses of places they needed to search.

"You doing okay?" Trey asked Etienne with concern when it was just the two of them in the office.

"Yeah, I'm doing all right," Etienne replied. "I'll admit last night I wasn't doing so great, but I'm feeling much better today." His phone beeped, and he looked at the text, then looked up at Trey. "The mayor is on his way in to talk to me."

"Then I'll get out of here," Trey replied. "Don't let him get to you."

Etienne released a dry laugh. "I doubt he's coming in to tell me how great I am."

"Just keep your head up," Trey said and then he left the office.

A few moments later, after a sharp knock on the door, Allen Larrick walked in.

Etienne immediately rose and held out his hand. "Mayor Larrick," he said in greeting, and the two men shook hands.

Allen was a short, squat man who was very popular in the small town. He was a glad-handing, baby-kissing kind of man who had always been very supportive of Etienne and the police department.

He now sat across from Etienne and wore a small frown on his plump face. "Etienne, I've pretty much stayed out of your business on this whole Swamp Soul Stealer case."

"And I've appreciated that," Etienne replied.

"I know you and your officers are doing everything possible to catch this creep. How is the investigation going?"

"Hopefully we're getting closer to catching him. Colette remembered that she had been held in a basement, so we spent all day yesterday checking out basements around town. Unfortunately, those searches didn't yield the results we wanted. Today we're planning on checking out more basements in hopes of finding this madman's lair."

"That sounds quite promising," Allen replied.

"We're getting closer, Allen. I feel like we're definitely getting closer to finding this creep," Etienne said firmly.

"Now that's what I like to hear," Allen replied with one of his trademark wide smiles. "I just felt like it was my duty to come and check in with you."

"Thank you for not putting additional pressure on me. Trust me, I feel the heavy pressure of people wanting this man caught and the victims all to be saved."

"You're a good man, Etienne. I have all the faith in the world in you."

"Thanks. Nobody wants this guy in jail more than me. If there was any way to catch him before now, I would have done so. However, this has been a tough one with no clues to follow and no leads to guide us in the investigation."

"I think everyone in town knows this has been a tough one," Allen replied sympathetically.

"But I also know there are some people who are unhappy with me. I've heard about the recall effort."

Allen waved his pudgy hand. "Don't worry about it, Etienne. It's all just a bunch of nonsense by a disgruntled few." He rose, and Etienne did as well. "The people of Crystal Cove are still firmly behind you, and we're good, Etienne. I just thought it was time I did a little check-in."

"I appreciate it," Etienne replied. The two men shook hands again, and Allen left the office.

Etienne leaned back in his chair and breathed a sigh of relief. His conversation with the mayor could have been much more difficult. Thank God, Allen continued to be a support rather than a hindrance.

With the office quiet for the moment, Etienne's thoughts went to Colette. She seemed to have known exactly what he'd needed the night before. He felt terrible for the way he had taken her...so hard and fast. But he'd needed the mindlessness of sex to alleviate the tremendous pressure of failure inside him.

He didn't want to think about how nice it had been to sleep with her in his arms. Her body had been so warm, and her scent had swirled around in his head. For the first time in a very long time, he had slept...really slept in his bed.

He knew the reason for his good sleep was her. She had tended to every need he'd had last night. The sandwich had fed his belly, and the sex and the back rub had fed his very soul.

Damn, his feelings toward her were a tangled mess. He knew she believed herself in love with him, but her feelings toward him were probably a tangled mess too. They'd been in close proximity for too long. She saw him as her protector, and he wanted her memories to return.

Once this was all over, their connection would probably end. She would no longer need him to protect her, and he would no longer need her memories.

He would miss her.

The thought surprised him, but it was true. He would miss their conversations in the evenings. He would definitely miss her full-bodied laughter. She had filled his house with a liveliness and an energy it had been missing since he'd bought the place.

A knock on his door sounded, and he called out a welcome. Trey came back in, a hesitant expression on his features. "How did it go with Larrick?"

"Good," Etienne replied.

"Ah, that's great," Trey said as his expression cleared. "I was afraid he was here to chew you out."

"No matter how much anyone chews me out, that won't get us any results," Etienne replied. "But he really just stopped in to check the progress of the investigation."

"Did you tell him about the basement tip?"

"I did," Etienne replied. "I told him I thought we were

getting very close to finding this creep and freeing the captives. Let's hope that's true and the victims are all still alive."

"And let's hope Joel comes back with the addresses of the places we need to check out," Trey replied.

"Yeah, and we get through them all quickly," Etienne said.

"And with success by the end of the day," Trey said optimistically.

Joel returned almost an hour later with the addresses of ten homes. They didn't know if these places had basements or not, but they would know within hours.

The addresses were faxed to Judge Cooke with the request for search warrants for each of them. Thankfully, the judge responded quickly. Once they received the warrants, it was Etienne, Joel, Trey and Michael who took off in two patrol cars to check the first address on the list.

The day was another bust, and at five o'clock Etienne collected Colette to go home.

"No luck?" she asked once they were in the car.

"None. We only found two more basements, and needless to say, neither of them was the place we wanted," he replied. The defeat today was less heavy than the day before. Maybe because at this point, he'd come to expect defeat.

"It looks like it's going to storm," she said.

The evening had turned preternaturally dark with black, angry clouds filling the sky and swallowing up any hint of the sun. "Yeah, the forecast was for some rain and thunderstorms this evening," he replied.

"It's spooky for it to be so dark at this time of day," she replied.

"Spooky? Are you scared of storms?" he asked with a

glance at her. She looked so pretty in jeans and a hot pink blouse with her hair loose down her back.

"Maybe just a little bit even though I know it's silly," she replied. "Are you hungry?" she asked in an obvious effort to change the topic of conversation.

"I could eat," he replied. "What's on the menu?"

"Chicken cutlets with scalloped potatoes and corn."

"Sounds good to me," he replied. It was important to him that tonight they stay on an even keel with no deep emotions making unwise decisions for him.

"They were jail-like cells...where he kept us," she said suddenly. "The basement was full of these wooden little cells with some of us chained to the wall and others free inside their tiny cages."

He glanced at her in surprise. "Another memory?"

She looked surprised herself. "Just a little snippet. It popped into my head just now. But why don't I see his face in the memories that are returning?"

"I don't know. Maybe the vision of him would still be too traumatic for you, so your brain is still protecting you," he replied.

"Well, I wish it would stop it." She sighed heavily. "I just wish my memories would come back all at once."

"Every little bit you get is helpful," he replied encouragingly. "Don't beat up on yourself, Colette."

"I just want to help so badly."

"And you are. Without your memory, we'd still be spinning our wheels out in the swamp." He turned up his street, his headlights illuminating the road. When he turned into his driveway, he punched the button on his visor to raise the garage door.

"It's nice to be home before the rain," she said.

"There is that," he agreed. He pulled into the garage and pushed the button again to close the garage door. As the two of them got out of the car, there was a sudden flash of movement, and the garage door opened up once again.

For a brief moment Etienne's brain couldn't process what was going on, then reality slammed into him.

Dammit, the creep had gotten in. Etienne fumbled for his gun as he yelled at Colette to get inside the house and lock the door. Before he could do anything else, a shot rang out. A piercing pain stabbed through his upper arm and momentarily stole his breath away.

At the same time the man—dressed all in black and with a ski mask hiding his features—grabbed hold of Colette's arm and yanked her out of the garage. She screamed, and the sound of her terror ripped through Etienne's very soul.

Still gasping with pain, he ran after them, but by the time he got out of the garage he didn't see them anywhere. Nor did he hear any more of Colette's cries for help. It was as if the dark night had swallowed them up whole.

Etienne got on his phone and called in all his officers, then he found a clean cloth in his tool chest and wrapped it firmly around the injury in his upper arm.

The wound was painful and bleeding quite a bit. He knew he probably needed to go to the hospital to get it tended to, but that was the last place he was going while Colette was missing.

Damn, it had all happened so fast. He'd been so taken by surprise and so ill-prepared for the attack. He couldn't believe she was again in the custody of the Swamp Soul Stealer. Oh God, was she already dead? Had the man already killed her, and that was why her cries had stopped so abruptly?

Etienne was supposed to have protected her, and he'd failed. Dammit, he had failed. His heart crashed against his ribs in a frantic rhythm. He stood outside to wait for his men to arrive and fought back the thick emotion that attempted to crawl up the back of his throat.

Would they be able to find her? Or was it already too late, and they would simply find her body?

HE'D DONE IT. He yanked the ski mask off his head and tossed it on top of the drugged woman slumped in the passenger seat next to him.

The thrill of success rushed through him. The whole thing had gone exactly as he planned. The minute the garage door went up, he'd rushed inside and placed a small box in front of the sensor so that the door wouldn't close. And now she was his once again.

He glanced over at her and tightened his hands around the steering wheel. She looked so much like Sonya, the woman who'd had the yearslong affair with his father.

The affair had only ended when Sonya was killed in a car accident. But by that time the damage had already been done. Years of love and devotion that should have belonged to his mother had been stolen away by the swamp whore who had infatuated his father.

How many nights had he heard his mother weeping alone in her room while his father was out gallivanting with his swamp bitch? How many days had his mother been unable to get out of bed because of the utter grief that consumed her?

He didn't know why she had stayed with his father. She should have left him when the affair first began. But she hadn't. Love and devotion had kept her with him even though he didn't deserve it, didn't deserve her.

He wanted to punch Colette in her beautiful face. "Self-control," he said aloud. He needed to display some self-control right now. It wasn't the right time for beating her. She was drugged and out of it. He wanted her fully conscious when he hit her. But the drug would only keep her unconscious for a short period of time, and then he would not only beat her, but he needed to figure out a way to punish her for escaping him in the first place.

Thank God she hadn't remembered anything that would lead to him. Otherwise, he would already be under arrest. Thank God he'd gotten to her before all of her memories had returned.

What he needed to do right now was get back to the basement as quickly as possible. It wouldn't take long before cops would be roaming the streets and checking vehicles. He needed to get home before he got caught up in the manhunt he knew was about to happen.

He laughed out loud. He was so freaking proud of himself. He had managed to kidnap a woman right under the nose of the chief of police.

He wished he had a friend he could crow to, somebody who would see his absolute genius and appreciate it. While he had lots of good friends, he knew better than to talk about this part of his life with anyone.

All he wanted to do now was get Colette back in her little cage where he could take her out and play with her at will.

"Let the games begin," he said and then laughed with the sweet anticipation of what was to come.

Chapter Twelve

"You need to go to the hospital," Trey said to Etienne. The two men stood in front of Etienne's house while other officers combed the area looking for anything that might help them find Colette. Others were driving the streets in search of the perp and his captive.

"I'll go to the hospital once Colette is found safe and sound," Etienne replied firmly.

"That's got to be painful as hell," Trey said, gesturing to Etienne's gunshot wound.

At that moment a steak of lightning lit the sky, followed by a clap of thunder.

"It's not too bad," Etienne replied. "It's just a graze." The pain in his upper arm didn't even begin to compete with the utter pain in his heart. Colette was gone, in the grasp of the monster who had nearly beaten her to death the last time he had her. To make matters worse, a storm was upon them. Colette was afraid of storms. Somehow that made everything worse.

"Let's head into the office," Etienne said. "It will make it easier for me to keep track of the search." He took hold of Trey's arm. "We've got to find her, man," he said fervently. "She's in serious danger."

"We'll find her, Etienne," Trey replied just as fervently. "I swear we're going to find her."

Etienne dropped his hand from Trey's arm and released a deep, shaky sigh. "Okay, let's get to the office."

A few minutes later Etienne was in his car and headed toward the police station. As he drove, he looked hard at any car on the street.

The Swamp Soul Stealer had to have drugged her and then carried her to a waiting vehicle. That would explain her sudden silence and their immediate disappearance.

Why hadn't Etienne realized that moment of vulnerability when the garage door was closing? Why hadn't he seen that as a potential danger? It hadn't even entered his mind that the moment the garage door went up, somebody could get in. But he hadn't seen it, and now he was paying the consequences.

No, she was paying the consequences. That thought shattered his heart into a million pieces.

He reached the police station, and he and Trey went straight to his office where he pulled out the city map. From here, he should be able to coordinate a full city-wide search. He wanted his officers checking out cars and knocking on doors. He wanted this little town to be torn apart in the search for Colette.

While he'd been waiting for his men to arrive at his house, he'd interviewed all his neighbors to see if they had witnessed anything. Unfortunately, none of them had.

Another boom of thunder shook the building. Where was she now? Was she back in her cage in a basement, or would they find her dead body tossed on the side of the road someplace? Etienne squeezed his eyes tightly closed as another rush of emotion threatened to consume him.

He needed to keep his emotions in check right now. Colette didn't need a weepy, emotional man searching for her. She'd want him to be strong and focused.

As his officers checked in with him, he formed a grid search with some of the men starting at the south end of town and others at the north end. They were instructed to knock on every door and check every building. He had other officers checking cars for the missing woman.

The minutes ticked by, and as time passed, Etienne's hope for finding her began to wane. One by one his men checked in with nothing to report.

Searing pain still burned in his arm, but it was nothing compared to the agony that roared through his heart. By midnight, the storm had passed overhead, and Etienne came to the painful conclusion that the searches had yielded nothing.

He sat at his desk with Trey in the chair facing him. "She said they were all held in a basement," he said, trying to think through his heartbreak.

"But we've checked all the basements," Trey replied.

"Somehow, someway, we've missed one," Etienne said in abject frustration.

"I agree, but damned if I know where it is," Trey replied. "What else did she tell you? Did she have more memories about the place where she was held?"

Etienne frowned thoughtfully. "She said the basement had little cells in it where the people were held. However, she was often chained to the wall in her little cell." The idea of her being back in that place of nightmares positively killed him.

"Cells? Like little jail cells?" Trey asked.

Etienne nodded. "Only she said the cells were constructed of wood."

"Wood?" Trey frowned. "So the guy has to know his way around building things."

Etienne's mind whirled. The Swamp Soul Stealer had to be a big man to carry the victims from the swamp to his vehicle. He was handy at building things.

A name suddenly popped into his brain.

"Brett Mayfield," he said and stared at Trey. Was it possible the loudmouthed handyman was behind all this?

Trey's frown deepened. "But he lives with his mother and father, and we checked the basement there."

Etienne got up from his chair, a burst of adrenaline exploding inside him. "I think we need to have a long chat with Brett."

By the time Etienne got a couple more officers with him, it was almost one o'clock in the morning. But time had no meaning to him as long as Colette was gone.

Trey rode with him, and Joel and Michael followed in their own car. Etienne was grateful that all his officers were still working, no matter how many hours they had already put into the day. They had all come out to help find Colette.

As he headed to Lincoln Mayfield's home, Etienne's heart beat a million miles a minute. Was it possible this was it? Was it possible Brett was the Swamp Soul Stealer? Etienne had no idea where Brett would be keeping the captives. He reminded himself it was equally possible Brett wasn't the kidnapper.

But one thing was certain, if he'd hurt Colette, Etienne would have no problem putting a bullet in the center of the man's evil soul. And hopefully when they found Colette, they would find all the others being held captive.

He clenched the steering wheel tightly as he drove through the night. When they reached the large house, the four of them got out of their cars and approached the front door.

Etienne knocked. They waited for several moments, and then he knocked again more loudly. Finally, he heard movement inside, and the door flew open.

"Chief Savoie, do you have any idea what time it is?" Lincoln asked indignantly.

"I know it's late, and I apologize for that," Etienne replied.

"What's so damned important it couldn't wait until morning?" Lincoln asked. He pulled a blue-checkered robe closely around him.

"We need to talk to Brett," Etienne said.

Lincoln frowned. "What has the poor excuse for a son done now? Another bar fight? I swear that boy doesn't know how to keep his mouth shut. I told him I was done bailing him out of jail and paying his fines."

"We need to talk to him about another matter. Could you go get him for us?"

"He's not here."

Etienne frowned. "Do you know where he is?"

"If he's not in a bar somewhere, then he's probably out on his property," Lincoln replied.

"His property?" Etienne's heart beat a little bit faster. "And where is that?"

"On the north side of town, on Oak Drive. He's building a house for himself out there, and I can't wait to get him out of my basement."

Almost before the words were out of Lincoln's mouth,

Etienne and Trey were running for the car. "New construction... That's how we missed it," Trey said eagerly.

"It's possible we're just on another wild-goose chase," Etienne said. "We don't even know if this house he's building has a basement."

"Admit it, this all feels right," Trey said, excitement filling his voice.

"It does feel right, but I'm almost afraid to get my hopes up. We've been disappointed in the past," Etienne replied. He was so afraid to hope. And he was so afraid that they might be too late for her.

He glanced in the rearview mirror, assured by the presence of Michael and Joel behind him. He was grateful for the extra man power. He had no idea what they might be walking into. If Brett was their man, then he could be quite dangerous. The last thing Etienne wanted was any kind of a hostage situation with the kidnapped victims.

He drove as fast as he could given the wet conditions of the streets. Lincoln hadn't given them an exact address, but Oak Drive was a short road with few homes on it. They should have no trouble finding a new house under construction.

Unfortunately, there wasn't a single ray of moonlight to aid them in the inky darkness of the night. When Etienne reached Oak Drive, he slowed to a snail's pace.

"You look on the right side of the street, and I'll look on the left," Etienne said.

"Bingo," Trey said when they hadn't gone far. Etienne braked and looked to the right.

The ranch-style house was framed in, and a bright light shone out the missing front door. None of the windows were in yet. There were only gaping holes where they would eventually be.

Etienne pulled to the curb and killed his headlights. In his rearview mirror, he saw Joel pull up right behind him and turn off his lights as well.

Etienne's chest tightened, and his mouth went completely dry. This had to be it. The monster's lair, where four men and four women including Colette were being held inside. At least he hoped Colette was here and not dead.

"We need to go in as quietly as possible, especially since we have no idea where Brett might be in the place," he said. "We need to get him in custody as quickly as we can…before he can use his captives as hostages."

"Agreed," Trey replied tersely.

"You and I will go in the front, and I'll have Joel and Michael circle around to the back."

The four men descended on the house. Etienne held his gun steadily before him. He would prefer not to have to kill the man, but if he was the Swamp Soul Stealer, then Etienne definitely wanted him in custody.

He entered through the empty front door into a room that would probably be the kitchen. He had just crossed the threshold when a door along another wall opened, and Brett appeared.

His eyes widened at the sight of Etienne. Then he turned and ran for a window, vaulting through the empty hole.

"Don't shoot!" Etienne cried out as he raced after him.

Thankfully, Joel and Michael held their fire, joining the chase for Brett. Etienne wanted him. This was a fantasy he'd dreamed about for the past five and a half months. This man had tormented his sleep and beleaguered his days.

"Halt!" he yelled at the man running ahead of him.

Despite the sharp pain in his upper arm, in spite of his desire to find Colette as quickly as possible, he raced after Brett, keeping the big man in view. He ignored the stitch in his side, the pain in his arm and simply ran, driven by the need to bring the man down.

Closer and closer, until he could hear Brett's loud gasps for air. Etienne holstered his gun, and when he was close enough, he jumped on Brett's back and took him down to the ground.

"Brett, it's over!" he yelled breathlessly, attempting to control the struggling man.

"Get the hell off me!" Brett exclaimed. "Why are you people on my property?"

Joel, Trey and Michael had reached them, and they pulled him to his feet.

"What the hell is going on here?" Brett asked as Trey handcuffed him.

"We're just here to check out your basement," Etienne replied.

"You have no right to do that. Do you have a search warrant?" Brett asked belligerently.

"Don't need one. You hear that, men? I just heard the cry of somebody in great distress," Etienne replied. "We need to check it out."

"You're a damn liar," Brett said, his brown eyes blazing with anger.

"Go on, Etienne. We've got him," Joel said.

"We'll put him in the back of our car," Michael added.

Etienne didn't have to be told twice. With his heart swelled up in his chest, he turned and ran back to the house, aware of Trey following close behind. He dashed into the kitchen and yanked open what had to be the basement door.

He knew immediately he had found the captives. Moans and groans came up the stairs. It was the sound of pain and human despair.

Etienne raced down the stairs and straight into a nightmare. "Get some ambulances out here," he called to Trey.

Just as Colette had described, there were small wooden cells where each captive was held.

A set of keys hung on the wall, and he grabbed them. He turned to the captives' cages, frantically seeking the one he most wanted to see. God, where was she? Was she even here? His heart banged unevenly in his chest.

"Etienne!" Her cry rose above the others and led him to the last cell.

Tears misted his eyes. Thank God…thank God, she was alive. He fumbled with the keys, trying desperately to find the one that would open the door. She was weeping, but thankfully she appeared to be in good shape.

He finally got the door open, and he pulled her out and into his arms. She clung to him, and despite the pain in his arm, he held her tightly against him.

It was finally over. The Swamp Soul Stealer was in custody at last, and the captives had been saved. Colette continued to weep, and Etienne tossed the keys to Trey.

"Open them all up, Trey. Let's get these people out of here," he said.

By this time, most of the other captives were crying with the relief at finally being saved.

"I've got ambulances coming, and I told J.T. to contact Black Bayou and have them send us some ambulances as well," Trey said.

"Good, we're going to need them." Etienne finally released Colette. The others needed him now.

As Trey unlocked the cells, Etienne checked the condition of each captive. Most of them were painfully thin, and the women appeared to be in worse shape than the men.

Finally, everyone was free from the cages that had held them. Etienne led the captives up the stairs and out of the house where they all got their first breath of fresh air.

"I thought we'd never get out of there," Luka Lurance exclaimed.

Sophia Fabre grabbed hold of Etienne's hand and cried. "Thank you…thank you," she said tearfully over and over again as she squeezed his hand tightly.

"I'm never going to take my mother for granted again," Kate Dirant said as tears coursed down her cheeks.

It didn't take too long for the first ambulance to arrive. The first person loaded in and taken away was Haley Chenevert, who appeared to have a broken arm among other bruises. After that, more ambulances arrived, and the captives were loaded up one at a time and taken to the hospital.

Colette went on one of the last ambulances. She didn't want to go, but Etienne insisted. He wanted her checked out by a doctor.

The vanished had finally been found, and they would get the medical help they needed. He prayed that they all would recover. The nightmare was truly over.

As the last ambulance pulled away, Etienne stood in the darkness of the night, and a deep relief washed over him. For the first time in months, he felt as if he could breathe.

"Now it's your turn to go to the hospital," Trey said firmly as he joined Etienne on Brett's front yard.

"We still need to process the crime scene," Etienne replied. Photos needed to be taken, and reports needed to be written.

"Etienne, we can take care of all that without you. You need to go and get that arm looked at," Trey replied firmly. "You've put if off for too long already."

The pain in his arm was still fairly intense. "Okay, I'll go now. Are you sure you guys have it here?"

"Positive, and we'll also process your garage as a crime scene... Now go."

Minutes later Etienne was in his car and headed to the hospital. His arm hadn't stopped hurting all day, and he'd had to change the bandage on it several times due to bleeding.

The last thing he wanted to do was take a doctor away from treating the people who had been pulled out of that hellhole of a basement. But he admitted he did need some medical help.

The emergency waiting room was filled with family members of the captives. They greeted him happily, joyously, and thanked him profusely for getting their loved ones back to safety.

Etienne was immediately taken to a small examining room where he sat and waited for a doctor to come in. As he waited, his head filled with thoughts of Colette.

She was free now. The danger had passed, and she was free to live her life without fear. Thankfully, she had remembered just enough to help them get Brett under arrest. Hopefully now she would never have to remember the rest of the horrific time she had spent in her initial captivity with him. Etienne now hoped those terrible memories would remain locked in her mind forever.

The door to the room opened and Dr. Maison came in. "What a night."

"How are the captives doing?" Etienne asked.

"Most of them were starved and dehydrated. All of them had been beaten, but thankfully with a little tender loving care, they're all going to be okay."

"Thank God," Etienne said in relief.

"I see a makeshift bandage on your arm. What's going on?" Dr. Maison asked.

"I got shot earlier," Etienne replied.

The doctor raised an eyebrow in surprise. "Let's take a look at it." He gently unwrapped the bandage and frowned. "That's a nasty wound. You'll need to take off your shirt, so I can look at it more closely."

An hour later, Etienne walked out of the hospital, his wound cleaned out and rebandaged. He was armed with two prescriptions, one for antibiotics and one for pain. He'd fill them eventually.

He called Trey, who said that the crime scene processing was going fine and there was no reason for Etienne to return.

"We'll process your garage sometime later today, but in the meantime why don't you go home and get some rest?" Trey replied. "Seriously, Etienne, we don't need you here. Get some sleep, and I'll catch up with you later in the day."

There was one thing Etienne wanted more than sleep. He wanted answers. With this thought in mind, he headed back to the police station.

In the hallway, he bumped into Jimmy Riley, one of his officers. He told Jimmy what he wanted and then went to the interview room where Colette had spent so much time. He sank down in a chair at the head of the large table and waited.

Within minutes, Jimmy and Billy Sylvia, another one of his officers, led Brett into the room.

Brett was handcuffed, and Etienne motioned for Jimmy to take the cuffs off. The two officers then took up positions on either side of the prisoner as he sat opposite Etienne.

"The victims have all been released and are getting medical attention," Etienne said.

Brett's eyes darkened as a smirk crossed his face. "Who cares? They were nothing but swamp trash."

"Why, Brett?" Etienne leaned forward. "Help me understand why you took these people, held them and then beat and starved them."

"You'd never understand," Brett replied as a hint of anger replaced the smirk on his face.

"Try me," Etienne replied.

Brett's nostrils flared as he looked down at the table and then back up to Etienne. "This is all my father's fault. From the time I was young, he told me how wonderful the people from the swamp were. He pounded it into my head that the men and women there were stronger and smarter than I'd ever be."

Brett's anger grew. His face turned red, and his voice deepened. The words began to tumble from him furiously. "My old man loved the swamp people so much, he had an affair with a swamp whore. It destroyed my mother. Most days she didn't even get out of bed. I'd hear her crying, and I hated my father."

"I'm sorry to hear that, but what does that have to do with you taking and keeping all the victims?" Etienne asked.

"It was an experiment. I wanted to find out just how strong the swamp people really were. So I started hunting them. When I caught one, I'd drug them and take them to my basement. I beat and starved them to see how much they could take."

Brett's eyes sparked with what appeared to be pleasure. "I especially liked beating Colette. She looked so much like my father's swamp whore."

Etienne had to tamp down the rage that roared up inside him. He wanted to jump across the table and strangle the man with his bare hands for all that he had done to Colette. Instead, he rose from his chair. He had his answers, and he didn't want to look at Brett's face a minute longer.

"Cuff him and take him back to his cell," he said to the two officers.

Minutes later, Brett was gone, and suddenly sleep sounded like a good idea. Etienne had been running on empty for some time.

When he was in the emergency room, he'd asked Dr. Maison about Colette's condition. The doctor had told him she was fine. In fact, she'd already been released and had left the hospital.

Now, more than anything, Etienne wanted to go home and sleep with Colette in his arms. He wanted to hold her soft, warm body in his arms and smell the dizzying scent of her as he drifted off to sleep.

A deep relief filled him. The investigation was over, and the bad guy was finally behind bars.

Brett had been right about one thing—Etienne would never understand his motive for what he'd done. All he knew was Brett was a deeply troubled man.

With the case solved and all the captives taken care of, Etienne just wanted Colette and dreamless sleep.

He pulled up in his driveway—but not into the garage, which was now a crime scene—and got out of the car. He walked quickly to the front door, eager to see Colette.

Unlocking the door, he went inside. "Colette?" he called

out, surprised when there was no immediate reply. He went into the kitchen, but she wasn't there.

Maybe she had already gone to bed. Lord knew she'd been through plenty today. He walked down the hallway. The door to her room was open, and he peeked inside. Not only was she not there, but her bag and her clothing were gone as well.

She was really gone. Apparently, she had gone back to her shanty.

His heart dropped. She had left him without even saying goodbye. She didn't need him anymore to protect her, and her absence now spoke volumes.

The love she'd felt for him had been all about her needing him to keep her safe. Nothing more. It was what he had expected to happen, but he hadn't expected the stabbing pain in his heart.

He walked across the hallway and looked into the bathroom she had used. She'd left a small cosmetic bag behind. He'd take it to her tomorrow, and they could say their official goodbyes to each other.

His heart was heavy as he headed back to the living room. Maybe he had cared for her more than he'd wanted to admit. The house felt so empty now without her presence.

Instead of going back to his bedroom, he sank into his recliner. He had no interest in being in his bed without her there with him.

At least tomorrow he would see her once again. It would probably be the last time. That thought made his heart hurt way more than his gunshot wound.

Chapter Thirteen

Colette sat in the rocking chair in front of her shanty and watched as dawn broke overhead, painting the swamp in soft shades of gold. Morning birds began to sing from the treetops, their songs happy and bright.

However, the cheerful bird songs couldn't begin to penetrate the deep sadness that gripped Colette. She thought she'd cried all the tears she had in her, but then a new bout would overtake her, and she'd cry all over again.

She was beyond happy that the Swamp Soul Stealer had been caught. The captives had all been released and were going to be fine. But that happiness was tempered by the fact that her time with Etienne was over.

Even though she had known it was coming, despite telling herself she'd just come home and nurse her broken heart, she hadn't expected this level of heartbreak and pain.

He no longer needed her. He didn't need the memories that had flown back into her head the moment Brett had locked her in her cell once again.

She'd remembered everything then... The pain of being starved, the dizziness of dehydration, the agony of being beaten nearly every single day. It had all come rushing back to her... Everything.

However, her tears weren't because of the return of those memories. Rather, they were for the loss of Etienne. He'd been clear all along that he hadn't loved her. Oh, he'd wanted her, but he hadn't loved her.

So, just as she'd anticipated, she was home now with a broken heart.

Her love for the lawman hadn't changed. She hadn't loved him because he was protecting her. She'd fallen in love with him through their deep talks and shared laughter. She loved him for his sense of duty and his love for the town. There were a million reasons why she was in love with Etienne, but none of them mattered now.

She finally got up from the rocking chair and went through the shanty to the back deck where she started the generator.

Thank goodness, despite the late hour, Ella had been able to pick her up from Etienne's and bring her home. Colette hadn't wanted to say goodbye to Etienne. She knew she'd break down and make a complete fool of herself. It had been so much better just to leave without seeing him again.

She ate breakfast and then sat down to her computer at her desk. She wanted to lose herself in her work, so no other thoughts of Etienne would intrude into her mind.

But her mind refused to cooperate, and thoughts of the man she loved did intrude. She sat there for two hours before she gave up and turned her generator off.

By that time, it was around ten o'clock. She lay down on the sofa and closed her eyes.

She'd been so terrified when Brett grabbed her in the garage. No matter how hard she tried to get free from him, she couldn't. He hadn't run far with her before he had drugged her, and she'd fallen unconscious.

Waking up in that cell had been horrifying. It was there that her memories fully returned, slamming into her with a horrendous force. And as she had thought about suffering at the hands of Brett once again, terror had filled her.

She didn't know how long she'd been stretched out on the sofa when a knock came at the door. It was probably one of her friends. Ella had told her they were all eager to see her again.

Colette went to the door and opened it, and there he stood.

Etienne was wearing a pair of jeans and a blue polo shirt, and he looked amazingly handsome. She couldn't help the flutter of her heart at the unexpected sight of him.

"Etienne," she said.

He smiled. "Hi, Colette...do you mind if I come in for a moment?"

"Uh...okay." She stepped aside to allow him entry. She gestured him toward the sofa where they both sat.

"You forgot this last night when you packed up," he said and handed her the small cosmetic bag she'd apparently forgotten in his bathroom. So, that was why he was here. He just wanted to return her bag.

Suddenly she saw the bandage on his upper arm. "Oh, Etienne, what happened to you?"

"When we were in the garage and Brett came after you, he fired a shot and managed to hit me," he replied.

She stared at him. He'd been shot? Tears filled her eyes. He'd been shot while protecting her. Her eyes teared up, blurring her vision, and then the tears fell faster and faster down her cheeks.

"Hey, don't cry," he said. He leaned forward and wiped the tears from her cheeks. "I'm okay. The doctor even told me I was going to live," he said with a grin.

"Don't even joke about it, Etienne." She swiped at the last of her tears. "You must have been in so much pain."

He dropped his hands from her face, and his beautiful smoke gray eyes held her gaze. "Why did you leave last night?" he asked.

She leaned back from him. "I knew I was safe from the Swamp Soul Stealer... That it was over. And I knew you didn't need my memories... That you didn't need me anymore." The words came from her haltingly.

He raked a hand through his hair and released a deep sigh. His gaze was soft as it lingered on her. "I've spent all of my time with you fighting the feelings I had for you. I tried to convince myself that I didn't care about you because I was afraid once this was all over, you'd realize your feelings for me were false."

"Oh, Etienne, my feelings definitely aren't false. Don't you know? I am deeply in love with you." The words tumbled from her mouth, words she'd wanted to tell him for a long time. "I've been in love with you for some time."

"Colette, I don't need your memories, but I do need you." Oh, the gray of his eyes was so soft, so inviting. "Don't you know? I'm deeply in love with you too."

She stared at him. "For real?" she asked tremulously.

He laughed. "For real." He stood and reached for her hand, pulling her up off the sofa and into his arms. "When I got home last night and you weren't there, I was devastated. I realized then I couldn't fight my feelings for you anymore. I love you, Colette and I can't imagine my life without you in it. Thank God you're safe now. Nobody will ever hurt you again."

You're safe now. Nobody will hurt you. The soft male voice telling her she was safe and it was okay for her to open her eyes. She stared at him for a long moment as the memory suddenly leaped into her brain. The soft male voice talking to her...the soft male voice that had soothed and comforted her in the darkness.

"It was you," she whispered in stunned surprise.

He frowned. "It was me what?" he asked curiously.

"It was you who came to me in my sleep. You were there with me in the darkness of my mind."

"I sat next to you in the hospital night after night," he admitted.

She looked at him incredulously. "You talked to me. You soothed me, and I loved hearing your voice. Oh, Etienne, you were my guardian angel while I was sleeping."

He brushed his thumb gently down her cheek. "I think I fell a little bit in love with you as night after night I watched you sleep and heal. Colette, come home with me and be my wife."

Her breath caught in her throat. "I would love to be your wife, Etienne," she said as an enormous joy bloomed in her heart.

He kissed her then, a tender kiss that spoke of desire and love and a happily-ever-after with the lawman of her dreams.

Epilogue

It had been two weeks since the arrest of the Swamp Soul Stealer, and the town had breathed a deep sigh of relief. Finally, all of the vanished had left the hospital and were back where they belonged. Back with their loved ones.

Etienne sat at his desk and checked his watch. It was almost five o'clock, almost time for him to leave and head home. Home. The house had never felt so warm, so embracing as it did now with Colette in it.

Thank goodness the crime in Crystal Cove had returned to such things as speeding and shoplifting. Nothing serious had come across his desk, and he hoped it stayed that way forever.

Without the Swamp Soul Stealer taking up all the hours of the day, Etienne now had the time to walk the streets and speak with people.

Apparently, the recall efforts had died with Brett's incarceration. Etienne knew the people in Crystal Cove were behind him and supporting him and that made him want to work harder than ever for them.

A knock fell on his door. "Come in," he called out.

Trey came in and sat in the chair across from Etienne's desk. "I figured I'd catch up with you before you headed home."

"Is there something going on that needs my attention?" Etienne asked with dread.

"Absolutely nothing," Trey replied with a grin.

"Damn, you had me worried there for a minute," Etienne replied.

"Isn't it nice that things have been so quiet lately?" Trey said.

"Yeah, it's nice, and let's hope things stay quiet," Etienne replied. "I'm getting ready to leave and go home."

"You know, I've never seen you as happy as you've been since you have Colette in your life."

"I've never been as happy as I am now," Etienne admitted. "She has brought me such happiness, and I can't wait to marry her."

"Are you two making wedding plans?" Trey asked curiously.

"Absolutely. We just want a simple ceremony in front of a judge. She's asked Ella Gaines to be her maid of honor, and I would like it if you would be my best man."

"Oh, wow. I'd be honored," Trey said with a surprised smile.

"Great. I'll let you know the date when we've decided on one. Trust me, it's going to be very soon, and on that note, it's time for me to go home to my bride-to-be." Etienne got up from his desk, and Trey stood as well.

"Then I'll just see you in the morning," Trey said as the two men stepped out into the hallway.

"See you then," Etienne replied.

Minutes later, Etienne was in his car and headed home. A sweet anticipation filled him as he thought of the woman waiting for him there.

Some people might say they were in the honeymoon of

their relationship, but that wasn't true. Etienne's love for her was deep and abiding. He recognized now that he had loved her for a long time. Fear had kept him from seeing his love for her. He'd been afraid to embrace that love, afraid that she would realize she wasn't in love with him.

He wasn't afraid anymore, and he'd never been so happy. He pulled into the driveway and opened the garage, which had finally been cleared for Etienne to use once again. He parked inside and stepped from the garage into the kitchen.

Colette turned from the stove and smiled. "Hi, Chief Savoie."

As always, she looked pretty in a pair of jeans and a brown blouse that perfectly matched her chocolate-colored eyes. Her luxurious hair was loose down her back.

"Hello, Ms. Broussard. Something smells delicious in here," he said and took her in his arms.

She smiled up at him. "That would be chicken cacciatore. How was your day?"

"Fairly boring."

"And that's the way we like them, right?" she said, her eyes sparkling brightly.

"How was your day?" he asked.

"I sold an article."

"Colette, that's great," he exclaimed, knowing how much it meant to her.

"You know what's really great? Sharing my news with the man I love. And I do love you, Etienne."

His heart warmed at her words...words he would never tire of hearing from her. First, she'd been a sleeping beauty he wanted to awaken. Then she'd been a woman who needed his protection. Now she was the woman he loved more than anything or anyone in the world.

"I love you too," he replied and then took her lips with his in a kiss that held all the love, all the desire he felt for her. He knew they shared a love that would see them through life for many years to come.

* * * * *

COMING SOON!

We really hope you enjoyed reading this book.
If you're looking for more romance
be sure to head to the shops when
new books are available on

Thursday 28th August

To see which titles are coming soon, please visit
millsandboon.co.uk/nextmonth

MILLS & BOON

FOUR BRAND NEW BOOKS FROM
MILLS & BOON MODERN

The same great stories you love, a stylish new look!

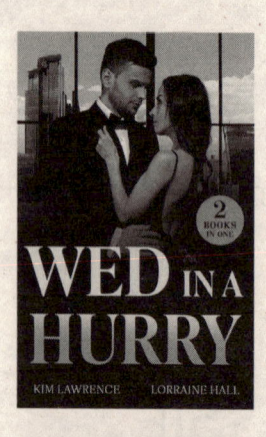

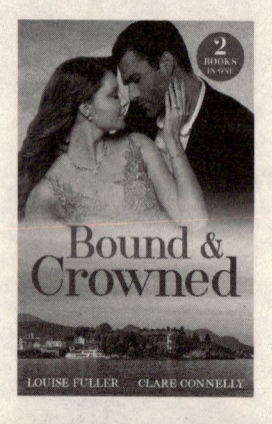

WED IN A HURRY
KIM LAWRENCE — LORRAINE HALL

Bound & Crowned
LOUISE FULLER — CLARE CONNELLY

Love to HATE HIM
JULIA JAMES — MILLIE ADAMS

RECLAIM ME
CATHY WILLIAMS — DANI COLLINS

OUT NOW

Eight Modern stories published every month, find them all at:

millsandboon.co.uk

afterglow BOOKS

Afterglow Books is a trend-led, trope-filled list of books with diverse, authentic and relatable characters, a wide array of voices and representations, plus real world trials and tribulations. Featuring all the tropes you could possibly want (think small-town settings, fake relationships, grumpy vs sunshine, enemies to lovers) and all with a generous dose of spice in every story.

@millsandboonuk
@millsandboonuk
afterglowbooks.co.uk
#AfterglowBooks

For all the latest book news, exclusive content and giveaways scan the QR code below to sign up to the Afterglow newsletter:

SCAN ME

LET'S TALK
Romance

For exclusive extracts, competitions and special offers, find us online:

- **f** MillsandBoon
- **X** @MillsandBoon
- **◎** @MillsandBoonUK
- **♪** @MillsandBoonUK

Get in touch on 01413 063 232

For all the latest titles coming soon, visit
millsandboon.co.uk/nextmonth